T0023490

Other Books by Stacy Green

Killing Jane

Stacy Green

USA Today Bestselling Author

Killing Jane

Cover Credit: Michael J. Canales
www.MJCImageworks.com

Edited by Liana Gardner

ISBN: 978-1-944109-28-8

VESUVIAN BOOKS

Published by Vesuvian Books
www.vesuvianbooks.com

Printed in the United States of America

10 9 8 7 6 5 4 3 2 1

*For Rob and Grace, for your love, support, and patience,
and to Mom and Dad for always believing in me.*

CHAPTER ONE

I am compelled to do this horrible thing. It is as if I am pulled by some larger force, a demon that will not rest. He whispers despicable things into my aggrieved mind. My heart knows I should not act, but my brain does not listen. I am no more than a slave to the blood I will yet spill tonight.

—JTR
31 August 1888

I drink in the words for the hundredth time. They make me feel out of breath, my lungs on fire like I'd just finished a morning run. Breathing harder, I bask in the sensation.

Jane Blackwood wrote those words over a century ago when she roamed the dark London streets and terrorized the poor, stupid residents. The authorities—all men, of course—dismissed the chief inspector's idea that a woman, perhaps a midwife, committed the gruesome crimes. A fragile, innocent woman lurking in the London streets alone? Impossible.

Male chauvinists.

But I wish I could thank them. Jane escaped with her letters, and now they're mine.

I tiptoe through the attic. I don't want to screw up the big surprise.

Shoving my fist against my mouth, I imagine Bonnie's shocked face. She'll never see it coming. Not me—and not my beautiful knife.

A noise drifts up from downstairs: the bedroom door opening and closing, followed by Bonnie's girly voice.

I slash the knife through the air, watching the steel glint in the afternoon sun.

Time for her punishment.

CHAPTER TWO

Erin Prince needed to grow a pair. And she would, as soon as she yanked her nerves out of her throat. This murder would be different—her first case as a lead homicide investigator. According to the sergeant, it wasn't the usual drug dealer gunned down in the street, but a young woman "torn all to hell."

Due to construction along the way, it had taken over an hour to make the thirty-minute drive from her parents' house in McLean. Her fingers dug into the stitching on the steering wheel as she took a deep breath. She needed a minute of peace before heading into the fray.

Guilt slid into the pit of her stomach as she pictured her brother, Brad, sitting on the end of Abby's bed, reading her a story as she drifted off to sleep. Storytime—the best part of the day, when all your cares could be pushed aside to enter a new world. She hated to miss those moments as much as she hated not being there to tuck Abby in.

The blazing lights in the row house made it look like an anemic jack-o'-lantern, its creep factor eclipsed only by the strange evening sky. Night had fallen more than an hour ago, but swollen clouds shrouded the harvest moon her nine-year-old daughter had waited all day to see. The resulting weird reddish hue made the sky look fantastically photogenic.

Erin checked her reflection in the rearview mirror. She'd actually done her makeup for the evening, choosing a lovely violet eye shadow to bring out her eyes and accentuate her dress. Her summer tan had faded, the foundation making her skin look almost porcelain save for the deep wrinkles between her eyes. The expensive lipstick Mother had given her for her last birthday still looked freshly applied.

She spoke to her reflection, searching for the right tone of voice for the occasion: brisk, businesslike, and controlled. "You clean up nice despite being on the downhill slide to forty and never getting enough sleep. But the boy's club is going to love seeing you walk in all dolled up and living up to their stupid nickname."

Princess. Hardly original. But tonight, she fit the bill.

She sneered at the mirror. "Too bad you look like a wannabe beauty queen when you've got a homicide to handle."

A crowd surrounded the perimeter and called out questions to the officers holding them back. A uniform who couldn't have been out of the academy more than a few months hid near a cruiser, his skin pale as a vampire's.

No more time to waste. Erin stepped out of the car, heels scraping against the concrete. Smoke plumes from the nearby factory filled the air, their miasma blanketing the sewer fumes.

Fall wind sliced down the street and over Erin's bare legs. She tightened the belt of her dress coat. Tomorrow morning, she'd throw a change of clothes and a pair of tennis shoes in the trunk.

A teenage kid, showing off for his buddies, ran full tilt toward the crime scene perimeter. Erin bit back a laugh. It was his bad luck to have picked the wrong cop to run past.

Officer J. Acosta had the kid face down on the grass and arms cuffed behind him before he even knew he'd been stopped. She might look like she'd dressed up as a police officer for Halloween, but Erin would rather have Jay on her team than any of the other new recruits.

As Jay pulled the kid off the ground, Erin locked eyes with her for a moment, and they gave each other a nod of respect. Jay worked hard and volunteered for everything … anything to get ahead. But don't ever make the mistake of calling her by her first name. Even some of the top brass had been given an icy stare along with the reminder that she could be referred to as Officer Acosta or Jay—the use of Julie was a privilege few shared.

Someone on the fringe of the crowd pointed to Erin. The news of her approach spread like wildfire through the mob and drowned out the click of her heels against the sidewalk.

Erin's cheeks flamed. She yanked the badge from beneath her coat and strode past the medico-legal death investigator's van.

The scent of backyard barbecue saturated the night air and mingled with the stench of body odor. A college-aged man held tongs greased with dark red sauce. He absentmindedly licked the end while some sauce ran down the handle and onto his fair skin.

She reached the yellow perimeter tape. The muted chatter beyond the line stopped. No turning back, not with everyone watching. She'd be damned if she'd give them a reason to spread any gossip.

A tall Black man with graying hair and a slight limp made his way over to her. Detective Sergeant Vincent Clark needed to suck it up and succumb to knee surgery, but he refused to take the time away from the squad.

"'Bout time, Prince." He spoke in a hushed tone but sounded

worried and rushed. "We've got a new shooting in Anacostia, and half the squad is working the Ted Moore murder."

Moore was the CEO of Endeavor Entertainment, a multimillion-dollar cable network. That sort of high-profile case could make a homicide investigator's career. Yesterday she had cursed her luck at not getting the chance to work the Moore case. But today, not getting the case might be a blessing in disguise. At least there would be plenty else for the media to focus on while she found her legs as the lead homicide investigator.

She ducked under the yellow tape.

Clark glanced at her attire, and his gray eyebrows raised at the sight of her high heels. "This is a new look for you."

"Dinner with my parents." She jammed her hands into the pockets of her Burberry. "Jeans and a hoodie are not *acceptable attire.*" Erin mimicked her mother's withering tones on the last two words. She'd heard them too many times to count.

They walked halfway to the house before Clark stopped—far enough from the crowd not to be overheard and far enough from the house to be left alone unless it was urgent. Bad mojo rippled from the row house, and every official coming out looked a little green around the gills.

Erin scanned the crowd pressing against the crime scene tape. "Who's questioning the locals? This is a busy area. Surely, someone saw something."

Countless sets of eyes stared at the scene, demanding answers and a few juicy stories to share at work the next day.

Clark jerked his head toward the official vehicles clogging the street. "Two patrol units responded to the initial call. Most of the block was at a house party down the street. Officers went inside, saw the body, and immediately called for a full investigative unit and the medical guys."

"And you arrived then?"

Clark always liked to arrive early and do a walk-through to get the feel of the place. Then he let his people run the case.

Clark stroked his chin, his dark eyes filled with worry. "The patrol officers had the scene secure when I arrived. We set up a command post." He pointed to the end of the cracked sidewalk where a lone officer stood with a clipboard and a pen. "We've set up a twelve-block perimeter, and I've got units looking, but this guy is long gone. Victim's going into rigor. The uniforms are still talking to people, but you and the new guy need to follow up ASAP. He's already inside."

KILLING JANE

Already? Damn that lengthy drive from McClean. She wanted to start on equal ground with the new guy, not tag along like a trained puppy. He had worked some high-profile cases, so he had the edge anyway. Pain darted to her temples from clenching her jaw. Now wasn't the time for a stress headache or a plunge into self-doubt.

He might have more time on the job, but she knew the fine art of navigating the convoluted mesh of D.C. crime and the always-attached political ramifications. "His background's impressive."

"He's not interested in talking about it or showboating. He's just doing his job." Clark stared directly into her eyes. "Do yours, and you'll be fine."

Erin nodded.

"Prick who did this probably knew about the party, too. The victim's name is Bonnie Archer."

"Who found her?" Erin craned her neck to see whether anyone had been taken to one of the patrol cars.

"A boyfriend. Or, as he put it, 'a friend who hangs out.'"

Erin got the gist. "He tell you anything about her?"

"She's a recovering drug addict getting her GED and works as a waitress part-time. I ran her through the system. She's got a couple of misdemeanors for drugs. He says she's been clean for months."

"Where is he?"

"We had a unit take him to the Old School. He's holding up, but we wanted to get him out of here."

The Criminal Investigation Division and other specialized metro divisions worked out of a converted school on M Street. Still, the nickname ruined the charm of the old building by bringing to mind the smell of sweaty gym socks.

"Any sign he's our bad guy?"

"He's shook up," Clark said. "Asked for a victim's advocate, which means jack." He gazed over her head at the growing crowd. "Listen, I'm going to keep a lid on as many details as I can, but the friggin' media has a way of finding out shit. They've got eyes in every nook in the department—and have their lips pressed against a few assholes, I think."

Erin closed her eyes briefly as she inhaled. "Any sign of sexual assault?"

"Big time. Your background in sex crimes will be a huge help, here."

Her nails bit into the palms of her hands as she clenched her fists, and bile burned the back of her throat. She talked women into testifying against their attackers, but she hadn't reported her own. *What a bloody*

5

hypocrite.

Clark reached into his pocket and then cursed. "Forgot I quit smoking last month."

His eyes bore into Erin's, their gravity igniting an icy wave of apprehension.

"You caught a bad one, Prince. We've got to catch this guy quickly because when the details get out, people will panic."

What the hell was she about to walk into? Nothing rattled Vincent Clark. Erin struggled to keep her expression neutral.

Before she could ask any more questions, headlights reflected against the house. Clark cursed under his breath at the sight of the Channel 4 news van. A salon-styled redhead slithered out and made a beeline for Clark.

"Speak of the miserable devils. I'll handle her. You go on inside."

As she approached, Erin signaled to Murray, the point officer charged with keeping the wrong people out of the crime scene. The strong lights bleached the color from the scene, and Murray looked almost ghost-like. When she reached the red tape perimeter, she blinked. The pallor on his face had nothing to do with the crime scene lights. His hand trembled, and he clenched his pen in a death grip.

She clutched the slick red tape of the interior perimeter. "You okay, Murray?"

He ran his hand over his cropped gray hair. "I've been doing this job for twenty-five years. What I saw in there …" His jaw tightened. "Prepare yourself."

Erin's stomach soured. "Thanks for the warning." She glanced around once more, half searching for an excuse to put off going inside. Then she ducked under the red tape and made her way down the crumbling sidewalk.

The patrol car's red and blue lights flashed off the building's peeling yellow paint, creating a dizzying disco ball effect.

Bonnie Archer's home seemed well cared for despite the sorry-looking trio of front steps and bowed porch. The small patch of grass in front of the duplex was neatly maintained, the ancient windows clean, and a pot of mums decorated the ugly stoop.

Bars rested over the lower window, and the deadbolt on the door offered some protection. Had Bonnie let her killer inside?

A lanky man, dressed professionally in a blue button-down dress shirt and black slacks, stepped out of the house. He leaned against the house, his chest heaving as though he might vomit. With short brown hair cut precisely to code, he had to be her new partner. He had the plain face of an everyman, easily forgettable save for a ridiculous mustache. Strands of silver threaded the hair at his temples, but he was so unremarkable he could have been thirty or fifty.

"Are you Todd Brooks?"

He nodded.

She stretched out her hand. "Erin Prince. I'm happy to be working with you." Not the entire truth, but having a partner had its merits.

"The pleasure is mine," Brooks said. "Although I wish our first meeting wasn't under these circumstances." An undercurrent of nerves laced his soft tenor. "This is the worst thing I've ever seen."

Hopefully, he didn't notice the sweat beads sprouting on her forehead. Brooks's impressive file flashed through her head. Two different serial killer cases, each more gruesome than anything she'd experienced.

"Worse than the Trevor case?"

Brooks's jaw flexed. "I didn't actually work that case, but I'm familiar with the crime scene photos. And yes. Far worse." He took another deep breath, still leaning against the weathered clapboards. "Uniforms are questioning the crowd and knocking on doors."

Brooks glanced over her head—an easy feat considering he had several inches on her five-foot-five-inch frame. "They likely won't get much. There was a party—"

Erin cut him off. "I heard."

Brooks slowly raised his eyebrows.

The tops of Erin's ears burned. "Sorry. Didn't mean to snap."

The longer she waited to view the crime scene, the harder it would be. Everyone else's reactions, including Brooks's, had her on edge. "I don't know how you did it back in Philadelphia, but normally we'd have a few more detectives here. The Ted Moore case and a gang shooting have us stretched thin. We'll have to follow up with most of these people ourselves." Good grief, why did she have to start babbling about manpower? A fresh wave of embarrassment flushed her cheeks.

"Of course. We'll want to get initial impressions from everyone. Cases like this ..." He shook his head. "I hope it's not a problem that I didn't wait to view the scene."

She mentally cursed the construction. "Nah, it took me longer than anticipated to get here. You couldn't wait forever." She secretly wished he would have, though. Her first case as lead, and she felt handicapped at the start—everyone else knew more about it than she did. She cleared her throat. "I suppose we should get to it. Sergeant Clark is dealing with the press."

She reached into a box sitting next to the pot of mums and retrieved a set of booties and a pair of gloves. The blue footwear slipped awkwardly onto her heels, the stilettos threatening to tear the fabric. Erin yanked the heels off, tucked them under her arm, and pulled the booties onto her bare feet. "I usually dress with more common sense, but I had dinner with my parents tonight." *Really, Erin? Justifying your attire?*

Between the shoes and her sweating hands, she couldn't get the damned gloves on.

Brooks watched her without comment, and the back of Erin's neck heated. Was he judging her already? The Philadelphia police had a reputation for harboring a grudge against anything perceived as threatening the male status quo. Did he resent her being a woman? Indignation flashed through her, and she glared at him.

He smiled and held up his large hands. "Always clammy. I hate the gloves, too."

Irritation turned to shame as her brother's childhood taunts singsonged in her head. *You know what they say about assumptions. They make an ass out of you, not me.* She stuffed her insecurities down and placed her shoes a few feet away from the door, folding her coat over them.

Brooks disappeared through the narrow doorway.

A flash of vertigo forced Erin to lean against the doorframe. The house seemed to clench, blowing the foul stench of death in Erin's face. Her muscles tensed, pain shooting down her legs. The fear in Murray's eyes haunted her. *Get it together, Prince.*

"You coming?" Brooks waited a few feet away, watching her.

Erin gathered her composure and marched forward, the paper booties feeling strange against her bare feet. Immediately, the stench of dried blood and death bloomed in her nose and clung to her tongue like a moldy pasta sauce. Additional odors followed: the lingering hint of Chinese takeout, a musky perfume, the faintest tinge of bleach. The tiny entryway had less room than a sardine can.

Erin breathed through her nose and found her voice. "Victim is Bonnie Archer, age twenty-six, right?"

"Right." Brooks's eyes focused somewhere over Erin's head. "The guy who's not a boyfriend discovered her close to two hours ago. Rigor hasn't fully set in, so the death investigator estimates she's been dead about six hours. Maybe less."

A steep staircase hugged the wall to her right, a living room area to her left. The old floor beneath her paper-clad feet seemed uneven, different parts having settled over the years. She touched the shared wall, then brushed the gritty plaster from her fingertips.

"What about the house next door?"

"The responding officer reported that no one answered," Todd said. "A neighbor two houses down said the woman works nights."

"Perfect," Erin said. "We'll have to get that confirmed, but it's sounding like my luck."

"Mine too," Todd said. "Add that to the big party, and I get the feeling we're screwed before we get started."

Erin almost smiled, but the cloying scent of blood, sweat, and bodily fluids threatened to dredge up her dinner. She moved into the living area, bracing for the horrible thing Clark and Murray warned her about. The living room and the combined kitchen and dining area held nothing of interest. Someone had turned on the halogen lamp in the corner, the bulb casting a yellow tone over the home's worn furnishings.

Bonnie Archer appeared to be a tidy person; the crooked coffee table and cheap shelving were devoid of dust. Not a lot of personal touches scattered about, but she liked her tawdry romance novels. Her paperbacks appeared well-read, the spines heavily creased. One of the crime scene guys had already started collecting trace evidence. Maybe they'd get lucky with some hair or fiber matches.

"Prince?" A familiar female voice called from the narrow hallway.

Erin turned to see a tall woman wearing protective gear heading toward them. Built like a runway model with striking, exotic eyes, Marie Valari had been one of the first civilians to enter the Forensic Science Division at Metro P.D. Shortly after starting with the force, Erin watched the normally patient Marie skewer someone who made the mistake of assuming her excess of beauty meant a lack of brains.

Marie pulled off her mask, breathing as if she'd been sprinting. "Jesus Christ, Erin. I had to walk away for a minute." Her olive skin had turned the color of flaxen, melting wax. "Dan Mitchell's upstairs doing his thing. You should go ahead. Just brace yourself." Marie's voice trembled.

Those words yet again. Tension lodged in Erin's shoulders, and her fingers numbed. She struggled to maintain some sort of control over the anxiety threatening to cripple her. She had prepared for this moment, studying crime photos and reading the literature on how good cops coped. This wasn't her first dead body, yet the chill emanating up her spine made her cold and electrified all at once. Erin glanced at the

STACY GREEN

crooked mirror hanging on the pockmarked wall. Her skin resembled gray ash, and her strained expression made her look like a Botox victim. What if she couldn't handle the horrific thing that rattled everyone else? "Tell me our killer left us something we can use to find him. Name and address, preferably." Bad humor made working on a crime scene bearable, but her attempt at a joke came out crooked and pathetic. Marie's gaze jerked to meet Erin's. "That's exactly what he did."

CHAPTER THREE

E rin kept her hand against the wall for balance. The narrow wooden steps groaned as though they might collapse at any moment. The trio's footsteps clunked against the wood, each individual's pace different yet still dragging in a slow march toward the inevitable.

"This place is awfully big for a single girl working a part-time job and going to school. How could Bonnie afford to live alone?"

The District—especially an emerging area like Columbia Heights—was expensive. Families struggled to afford a condo, let alone a house. Most single people, especially those without a full-time job, needed a second or even a third source of income.

"Well, I'm new in town, but this area's not exactly high-end," Brooks said. "How much does rent cost?"

"High-end doesn't matter," Erin said. "I'd bet a place like this is at least $1800 a month."

Brooks whistled. "That's a lot, especially if she's just working part-time. Maybe her parents are helping out."

"That's why I live in Arlington and have a renter." She could always dig into her trust fund for a place closer to work, but she didn't want to live off her trust when she worked so hard to escape the family notoriety.

Upstairs, the smell of death intensified, trapped in the confines of the hallway. A yellow evidence placard sat to the side next to several large droplets of blood.

"So our killer missed something in his cleanup," she said. "If we're lucky, he cut himself, and he'll be in the system."

"That's not his blood." Marie looked at the ceiling as something dripped onto the floor.

"Holy shit." A metallic taste coated her mouth. How much blood did a person need to lose for it to seep through the floorboards?

"Exactly." Marie led them past the second-floor bedrooms. "We haven't found much downstairs or on this floor. Everything's up here." She took a deep breath and then disappeared up the attic stairs.

Anxiety burrowed into every synapse of Erin's brain. *Why did it have to be in the damned attic?*

The space narrowed further as though the house squished in on

11

itself the higher they ascended.

Brooks's shoulders brushed the walls as he climbed the steps, which were barely deep enough for the balls of his feet. He glanced down at her. "You coming?"

Her armpits heated. Her fall dress seemed as heavy as a soldier's equipment pack. The man who'd raped her lived in an attic apartment. A year later and attics still terrified her.

Had Brooks noticed the dampness on her forehead or how her thick, wavy hair had gone limp from the sweat on her scalp? She wanted to cut and run, but Erin wasn't about to be victimized a second time.

The smell blistered her nostrils. Blood, urine, feces, already-decaying flesh.

She climbed the dark stairs, the pressure in her head building by the second.

Evil.

An act borne of pure cruelty had occurred in the attic and left behind negative energy that wound its way into every cell in Erin's body. The strange cone of light peering through the railing surrounding the attic's landing only heightened the sense of malice.

It didn't come from the crime scene lights—their blue glow illuminated everything else, a garish gloom fit for a horror movie. She reached the top, dizzy with morbid anticipation. Everything came into hyper-focus.

A studio light typically used for photography had been knocked over, one of its muslin panels ripped. Its stream cast much of the attic in harsh shadows. The low-hanging beams seemed to float above them. Ghostly piles of discarded junk lurked in the corners.

Then the body.

Bile thickened in Erin's throat. The ghastly image imprinted on her consciousness. Some naïve part of her insisted it was a mannequin used for target practice.

Bonnie Archer lay in the middle of the attic, surrounded by a river of blood cascading into the shadowy corner. Arms and legs stretched out in an X-pattern, her youthful, soft skin appeared waxen and almost lavender under the harsh glare. Blood loss had turned her hands and feet blue.

Erin cataloged each visible injury. Deep gouges on her skin had been cut meticulously. Slashes on her snow-white arms and legs. The hilt from a kitchen cleaver protruded from her lower body.

She turned away, sucking in air and praying for composure. How could one human being inflict so much pain on another? Erin's chest ached with the need to breathe deeply, but the combination of all things death and the musty stench of the attic wouldn't allow it.

"We wanted you to see her like this before we moved her." Dan Mitchell, lead medico-legal death investigator for the Office of the Chief Medical Examiner, looked mournfully at Erin.

His skeptical eyes and sagging cheeks reminded her of Droopy, the cartoon dog, and his perpetual need to shave didn't help the situation.

"All the necessary pictures have been taken, so as soon as you're done, we'd like to move the arm before rigor makes it impossible."

Erin focused on the mangled corpse. Bonnie Archer had most certainly felt pain. Her suffering was etched into her face—the only part of her that remained relatively untouched. She'd died screaming, her mouth stretched open and somehow frozen in place. Wide, terror-filled eyes, the color of blue sky, stared lifelessly at the ceiling. Her bloody left arm reached toward the steps; her slender, blue fingers curled and dug into the wood. A phone sat less than an inch away. The bright Klieg lights beside the body added a final macabre touch worthy of the most gruesome horror films.

"How many times was she stabbed?" Erin's voice sounded as though she spoke through a tube. She needed to pull herself together. A female homicide investigator was still a rare gem in the District, and Erin would be damned if she broke down. Not after the way she'd busted her ass to get the position.

And her duty was to the woman lying prone on the attic floor. Bonnie Archer deserved justice.

Mitchell beckoned Erin to come closer. "Stabbed isn't the right word. Ripped is more like it." His gloved finger made a circling motion. "Come around to her right. The worst of the blood ran out of her left side from her carotid artery. Femoral, too. But the throat came first."

Brooks stepped aside. "I've already been up close. Go ahead."

She didn't want a closer look. Four feet away seemed like more than enough. So much blood, with only paper booties to protect her feet. Erin imagined the blood soaking through and getting into some cut on her toe she didn't know she had. Why had she worn heels tonight?

Mitchell looked at her expectantly, and she skirted around to stand over Bonnie.

The gashes to her throat had nearly decapitated her. With most of the young woman's blood drained out of her body, the knife wounds gleamed purple-white, the edges of the skin serrated like a bad cut of meat. The coppery stench of dried blood made her still-full stomach turn. God help her if she tossed up her mother's catered prime rib. Erin swallowed back her disgust and leaned closer for a better look.

Instead of the killer simply cutting her throat from side to side, he'd jabbed the knife straight into her throat, turning her larynx into shredded meat. Blood stained Bonnie's neck and shoulders—a cordlike, sinewy section of artery barely visible.

Mitchell spoke again. "He slashed her over and over again until he cut the carotid. I don't think he was in a hurry to kill her."

Erin squinted at the ruined flesh and tried not to think that this girl had once been a human being. "Can you tell whether the knife entered from the front or behind?"

Mitchell pointed to the small strings of remaining skin. "Look at the wound pattern. The M.E. will confirm, but I say front. Given her position and the blood spatter on the downed portrait light, I'm guessing the killer used his right hand."

Erin followed his gaze. She hadn't noticed the haphazard dark-red splotches on the thin muslin. The weird cone of brightness emitted by the photography light seemed to flow into nowhere, swallowed up by the dark corners of the attic. Erin snapped her arms around her chest and hoped no one noticed her trembling fingers.

Mitchell shined his light left and up onto the low beams, and more red streaks glowed in the dim light. "Pretty clear those are arterial spurt."

Fresh sickness swirled in Erin's stomach. "I hope he did that first, and she died quickly."

"I don't think so." Mitchell eased to his knees, his gloved hands hovering over Bonnie's bloody, naked body as though he was praying. "He cut her from the pelvis to breastbone."

The gashes on Bonnie's thin stomach ran deep. Encrusted with drying blood, they resembled the red velvet cake Erin'd had for dessert.

"The first stab was to the stomach, right above her pelvis. She's a small girl, and the wound is fairly deep, although not life-threatening, but severe enough to incapacitate. There's bruising on her cheek and above her eyebrows. He hit her early on before she bled out." He pointed to Bonnie's open legs. "Those bruises on her knees are new. Definitely perimortem. And you can see lividity on the backs of her heels. We'll see more when we turn her over, but she bled out so much, it won't be as significant as it could have been."

Lividity meant the blood pooled to the lowest part of the body. She narrowed her eyes, surveying Bonnie, trying to get a clearer picture, but Mitchell's words didn't quite make sense. Bruises of all colors dotted the upper part of her thighs, not covered with blood. Another bruise decorated her thin upper arm.

"She lands on her back, and he starts in? The fighting came before? What about the bruises on her thighs and arm?"

"Those are yellowing around the edges," Mitchell said. "Look at her fingers, the bottom of her feet. Defense wounds and scrapes. She fought, but once she fell on her back, that was it."

"So." Brooks's soft voice made Erin jump.

She'd nearly forgotten about him.

"He surprises her up here, or he brings her up here. He hits her, and she fights back. She's stunned, likely in intense pain. He jabs the knife into her gut." He shifted his head to the side, lips pursed, his mustache nearly blocking his nostrils. "She falls to her knees?"

"And then is slammed to the floor." Mitchell cradled the back of Bonnie's head. "Big bump back here, nearly dead center. My guess is after she fell to her knees, he shoved her to the floor." He grimaced.

"And then he takes her clothes off?" Erin was completely out of her element.

"Possibly. Or they were getting ready to have sex. She's disrobed, doing half the job for him. She definitely expected the man who found her. Look at her makeup."

Smoky eyes, smeared red lipstick. Bright, straight teeth stained with blood from biting her tongue.

"And we checked the non-boyfriend for blood and trace?"

"I did it myself," Marie spoke again. "No blood on him. Some hairs, but that's normal. We've all got strays."

"But he came to see her. So was the door unlocked, or does he have a key?"

"Unlocked," Brooks supplied, edging closer. "So he told Sergeant Clark. He went through every room. He wouldn't have gone into the attic, but he saw the blood leaking through the ceiling." He looked at Erin, his eyebrows slashed into a tight line. "And we've just gone over the first cuts. Right, Dan?"

Mitchell took over again. "It took several tries to get deep enough to slice to her breastbone. The knife he used wasn't strong enough to do more than nick it."

"Pre- or post-mortem?" Erin prayed for the latter, but Dan's sad eyes told her it wasn't the case.

"Definitely pre." Mitchell gently touched the gashes. "He cut through flesh and muscle, making her bleed profusely. If the arterial spurt happened before this cutting, the heart would have stopped, and there would be little to no bleeding from these wounds."

"He cut deep enough to make her bleed," Brooks said. "But not enough to get through the major organs."

"Correct," Mitchell said. "My guess is that was intentional."

"To make sure she felt it." The blood and gore Erin could handle, but the idea of any human being suffering something like this, feeling every minute of it …

"Until she passed out from the pain, yes." Mitchell nodded. "Like I said, severing her carotid is what killed her." He shifted to her lower extremities. "I think he hit the femoral artery next, and probably very quickly. Thus the sea of red." He cleared his throat, hand poised over the knife sticking out of Bonnie. "It looks like he thrust this in several times. Perimortem, judging by the bloody tissue."

Everything outside seemed frozen in place while Erin's emotions ricocheted and dipped like a roller coaster. She knelt, Brooks hovering near her shoulder, the scent of his mint gum providing a welcome perfume to the smell of drying blood and decaying flesh. She tried not to think about the rancid odor of Bonnie's bowels.

Her pelvis was no more than a milky white slab of flesh, repeatedly sliced into.

"It's a cleaver, right?" Erin's legs threatened to give out on her. She was unable to take the proximity any longer.

Mitchell nodded. "Likely the murder weapon."

A heady silence descended in the crowded attic between those living and the poor girl whose blood cascaded at their feet.

Brooks finally broke it. "Absolute rage. And he came here intending to kill her."

"How do you figure?" Erin asked.

"Look at the area around her." Brooks made a sweeping motion with his long right arm. "Notice what's missing?"

Dan Mitchell clucked in agreement.

Erin searched frantically, knowing the answer probably dangled in front of her. She only saw blood turning the wood into a muddy river.

"No tracks leading from the body," Brooks said softly. "The killer had to have been covered in blood."

Erin's face flushed. "He had to take his clothes off and go down at least one floor to clean up."

"He likely used the upstairs bathroom," Marie said. "It reeks of bleach. So far, no blood anywhere but right here. Not even on the steps." She shuddered. "Except for the leak."

Brooks stuffed his hands into the pockets of his pressed slacks. "He probably brought a trash bag or took one of Bonnie's. Stripped, put his clothes in, and then cleaned."

Erin rubbed her temples. "But there's no sign of breaking and entering. Either she knew him well enough to let him in, or he appeared completely non-threatening."

"More than likely the former," Todd said. "Rage like this is usually personal."

Erin couldn't stop looking at Bonnie. She had to compartmentalize, focus on the job at hand, and stop thinking of the body as a tortured woman. This poor girl, with so much left to live for ... was she given the gift of unconsciousness before the worst of the cutting started, or did Bonnie endure until the near-end?

Erin cleared the clog of emotions in her throat. "There will be too much damage to tell whether he used anything but the knife. Maybe we'll get lucky, and the M.E. will find some bodily fluid."

"There's more." Mitchell's usually confident voice wavered.

Erin's throat dried up at the change. She tried to force spit into her mouth, but she only succeeded in making her throat burn.

Mitchell made eye contact with Marie, who stood on the opposite side in the dark corner Erin hadn't paid any attention to.

Marie turned on another light, illuminating the twin box bed in the corner. A rope was tied around one of the headboard's rails, and the flimsy mattress hung off the right side.

Panic swarmed Erin as she clung to rationality. The attic wasn't the same. It wasn't a living space. He wasn't there, beckoning Erin to sit with him on the loveseat. Yet, for a minute, she catapulted to that moment a year ago, her date on top of her, threatening her, while she froze in shock and fear.

No. She wouldn't allow the memory to return and unnerve her in front of everyone. If she could work with rape victims, she could handle this.

"What the hell is this?" The scratchy voice belonged to her. Erin pointed to the metal objects scattered on the floor along with the studio light. Miniature pliers held together by a thin chain—nipple clamps. "Were those used on her during the assault?"

"It's possible," Mitchell said. "We haven't found any corresponding marks, but the M.E. might find some once the blood's all washed off."

Sweat ran down her back, and Erin fought to hide her fear. A silver set of handcuffs lay near Bonnie, along with a couple of rolls of twine, a razor-thin black whip, and a dildo so thick Erin internally flinched.

"When was the last time anyone spoke to her?" Erin asked.

"The guy who found her," Brooks said. "Will Merritt. He talked to her earlier in the day. Said she was fine."

"So why is all this stuff up here? I get that the killer brings stuff to torture her with, but he didn't exactly haul the bed with him."

Marie pointed to the other corner of the attic. "The studio light can be used for film or photography." She walked past Bonnie, her eyes flickering from the dead woman to the pile of junk in the opposite corner. "The camera's been taken, but the tripod is still here. We've searched through everything and can't find it or the computer Bonnie used to upload online."

Marie held up an oblong black box. "This is a common wireless video transmitter and receiver. Picked up in any store that sells video equipment or online. You can use a digital camera to record and send video to a computer or whatever the transmitter is hooked up to. My guess is she filmed amateur porn, and someone didn't like it."

"He must be on the recording," Erin stated. "Maybe the guy didn't know about the recording and lost his shit. Or he finds out she's recorded him and put him on the internet. That's enough to make someone snap this bad."

"There are two major hosting services allowing users to post their own videos," Brooks said. "They're both in the Netherlands. Although, the chances of finding any of Bonnie's videos are about as slim as finding Atlantis. Thousands are uploaded per day."

"She could also do a pay-per-view site of her own," Erin supplied. "Either way, the domains and the financial information will bounce overseas unless God grants us a miracle." *Which He won't.*

She ran into the issue time and time again when trying to track down child pornography. The creeps ran hundreds of sites off servers in little foreign countries with no use—or reason to cooperate.

Marie kneeled next to the bed, carefully sweeping the messy bedding aside. "Especially if he's keeping his interest in BDSM a secret. That's what all this looks like to me."

"It's certainly possible someone would want this kept a secret—especially if he's a family man."

"What about the name and address?" Erin remembered Marie's

earlier cryptic answer. "You said he left them."

"That's the annoying part. Brooks, I didn't get a chance to show this to you before." Marie angled her light toward the center of the attic, illuminating the beam directly over Bonnie's head.

Erin craned her neck to read. *Whore* had been scratched into the beam. Beneath that, *1888, Buck's Row* gouged in long, pointed, blood-stained letters.

"The killer had more than one knife, then." Erin's dry throat longed for water. "The cleaver didn't make those marks."

"1888 brings up hundreds of addresses, so I searched by street name," Marie said. "There's no Buck's Row in the District or any of the surrounding suburbs. No street name, no suburb, no neighborhood slang names. Nothing." A lock of hair fell into her eyes. "I've got our forensic examiners searching, but I don't think they'll be able to find anything either."

Brooks cleared his throat. "I don't think you're looking for a street."

His flat tone sent a strange chill over Erin. He stood a few feet from the rest of the group, staring at the carving. His drawn, pale expression appeared far more tortured than it had been minutes ago.

"Then what am I looking for?" Marie placed her hands on her hips. "A business name? Because I searched those terms, too."

"Buck's Row was a street in an area of London in 1888." Fear ghosted in Brooks's eyes. "In Whitechapel. The city changed the name because of the unwanted attention after the murder of the first prostitute."

The floor suddenly turned liquid as Erin slowly looked down at Bonnie's eviscerated body. Her dry lips cracked as she forced them to move. "1888. Jack the Ripper."

"No way." Marie swallowed hard.

Her wide eyes mirrored the heady panic boiling through Erin.

"He murdered prostitutes in the streets. This can't be a Jack the Ripper copycat," Marie protested.

"Weren't all the victims' intestines taken out? Bonnie's are still intact." Erin never understood the infatuation with Jack the Ripper. She didn't consider him any worse than the sickos running around today. The police just didn't have the technology to catch him back then. "And he didn't leave anything sticking out of their bodies." The distinctions mattered. Because Erin simply wasn't ready for a case like this.

"Jack the Ripper cut out some of the victims' entire abdominal cavities," Brooks said. "As well as their breasts. And he removed more than one uterus. Based on the deep cuts, this killer could have been trying to take out her organs. He either didn't have the fortitude or the right knife to get it done. Which means his planning wasn't as thorough as it could have been. That might work in our favor."

Brooks looked at Erin. "But you're right. There are a lot of discrepancies. Bonnie's throat was slashed vertically. As though the killer stood in front of her and hacked away at random. The first canonical victim's neck had a big circle cut into it. The Ripper cut through the tissue, clean to the vertebrae." He shrugged at Erin's stare. "I'm a history buff."

"All right, then." Her voice sounded far more confident than she felt. "Copycats obsess over minute details." What if some freak really did want to become a modern-day Jack the Ripper, and Bonnie's murder was just the beginning? "All we've got here is a date and some mutilation. Probably trying to distract us from the real evidence." Her certainty grew as she spoke. "The Ripper innuendo is nothing but a smokescreen. Not to mention gaining media attention. If the reporters outside hear about this, they'll freak out the entire city."

"I agree," Brooks said. "At least for now." He took a long look around, his gaze lingering on the carved words.

Erin didn't like how his mouth tightened, the cords in his neck straining. She had to keep talking, or she would start thinking about the implications of the name and date. "So, going with the theory Bonnie knew her killer, are we dealing with a stalker? Someone she thought she could reason with?"

"Whoever did this is beyond reason."

Mitchell's eyes were so mournful Erin wanted to cry.

"I'd like to start getting her ready for transport, if you don't mind."

Erin and Brooks descended the two flights of stairs. Every step away from the attic eased the tension in Erin's lungs. In the cramped entryway, they related the gory details of the attic to Sergeant Clark. He listened without reaction, his eyes on the stairs as though he expected the terrible energy in the house to materialize.

"Shit." He pulled on his coat and yanked up the zipper. "So our boy's got a Ripper fetish he wants us to know about."

"I don't think he's a real copycat," Brooks said. "But the inspiration is bad enough."

20

Clark glared out the open door. The crowd had swelled, but no additional press had shown up so far. Ted Moore's murder still held court.

"You two need to talk to the boyfriend. He's down at the CID waiting for you. Tomorrow morning, I'll get our forensic examiners online and see if they can find any of Bonnie's videos."

Erin followed Clark's gaze. He focused on the redhead with the microphone in her hand.

"If we can get information from her bank and find some deposits from one of the big uploading sites, we'll have somewhere to start. But don't get your hopes up. Even if we find them, we don't have enough resources to review the content." Clark turned his back to the door, pitching his voice low. "Keep the Ripper message tight. Word gets out, Moore's murder will be old news and we'll be up to our eyeballs in media. That reporter from Channel 4 is bad enough."

Brooks slouched in the low-ceilinged entry. "If you don't mind, I have a suggestion. What about asking NCMEC for help?" He pronounced the name as *nick-meck*, a nickname only privy to those within the organization and the agencies they intimately worked with. "They specialize in finding people, and they have techs who are skilled in searching the dark web."

"Nick-meck searches for missing kids." Sergeant Clark's tone listed toward impatience. "They aren't going to be interested in this."

"My girlfriend is a case manager there," Brooks said. "She'd help us, I'm sure."

Erin ran through the case managers at NCMEC. She'd worked with all of them, and she couldn't see Todd Brooks as boyfriend to any. Then again, looks didn't mean anything. Policework 101.

Clark shook his head. "Everything stays in-house. I don't want anything other than the basics about this case getting out to the media. The Ripper angle is a reporter's wet dream. You guys head to the CID." He stepped onto the porch and started for the steps. "See if you can get anything from the boyfriend."

CHAPTER FOUR

The CID's M Street location meant relatively easy access to the interstate as well as a view of the Capitol Building. Erin drove on autopilot, gripping the steering wheel so tightly, her knuckles whitened. Moments from the Columbia Heights attic popped into her mind unbidden. She shook her head and forced the images back, but not quickly enough. Her stomach roiled with each new image.

Sooner than expected, she arrived at the CID and pulled to a stop. Her heart kicked into hyperdrive, and her whole body trembled. A suffocating feeling overwhelmed her, so she pressed the button to open the window. Sweat broke out over the bridge of her nose despite the cold air cooling her skin. She breathed deeply and fought for control.

The crime scene had triggered a panic attack, and she was pulled back into her worst nightmare.

Her date had been a casual acquaintance of a colleague. He was handsome, fun to be with, and made her laugh. On their third date, he'd invited her to his apartment for a drink. Then her ordeal began—his overpowering cologne as he pressed against her, the pain as he forced himself on her, the shame of being a victim.

When he had finished, he'd rolled over and smoked a cigarette. How had this happened to her? Why hadn't she defended herself?

Afterward, she told Brad—her brother, best friend, confidant. As twins, they had always shared everything with each other.

Brad pleaded with her to report the rape, but she'd chickened out. How could she hope to maintain any level of credibility in a world still dominated by men? She was a sex crimes investigator and one of a few female investigators in the Violent Crimes Bureau. Reporting a rape would make her colleagues see her as a victim, not an equal. A failure.

The cost of keeping silent ate away at her. She'd jumped at the chance to test for the promotion to homicide. Erin hoped that getting away from all the reminders of her experience would allow her to put the past behind her.

The theory had worked until tonight.

A horn honked somewhere on M Street, snapping her out of the past. She turned off the engine, pulled a pack of tissues from her bag, dabbed at the sweat, and made sure her stupid mascara hadn't run.

Shooting a gun was easy, quick, and decisive. To cut someone up the way Bonnie had been, to make her suffer so horribly ... Erin couldn't understand the type of monster capable of such a thing.

He needed to be locked up before he killed again. A nagging voice in the back of her mind told her she wasn't good enough to catch him. She massaged her temples and drowned out the voice. She refused to let her insecurities stop her from catching this guy. She'd find a way.

The killer *wouldn't* be allowed to walk the streets. As a female rookie homicide investigator, Erin still had to prove herself. *And I will.*

But then self-doubt undermined her resolve. How could she expect to find Bonnie's killer when she crumbled inside at the thought of the crime scene? She didn't have the experience, the right instincts, or the ability. The well-worn soundtrack of her life, narrated by her parents, ran unchecked, telling Erin she wasn't good enough. The recriminations came naturally.

"*It's all in your head.*" The words Brad always said when she went into a tailspin calmed her.

Certain her new partner had beaten her back to the CID just like he'd beaten her to the crime scene, Erin opened the car door. Brooks's reputation preceded him and worked to his advantage. He'd walked into the crime scene as a brand new team member and had been accepted without question. Her first case as lead investigator—a burst of pride flowed through her. He'd better not interview the boyfriend, Will Merritt, without her.

Cold fall wind rustled through the well-lit parking lot as Erin headed into the Criminal Investigations Division offices. The late hour muted the usual sounds of the busy city, making the wind seem louder and somehow more ominous. Traffic and chaos comforted her. They were a sign of life and protection. Less chance of the boogeyman jumping out of the shadows—or Jack the Ripper.

She shivered. This wasn't a copycat killer, but a cruel bastard begging for attention. She wouldn't give him the satisfaction of letting his message shake her objective.

"Will Merritt," she muttered as she swiped her identification card. "Please give us something to find this madman."

While the eye-catching exterior of the old school had remained unchanged, the inside was a different story. When she'd first joined the CID, Erin hoped to be regaled with stories of finding old yearbooks with steamy, silly messages from friends who probably lost touch the moment they accepted their diplomas. Or maybe a ghost story or two, some desperate kid who hanged himself in the bathroom instead of failing his senior year. But the juiciest story ended up being the school's decade-long vacancy before the city purchased it.

Erin first worked upstairs, stuck in the far corner of the sexual assault unit. Her promotion to homicide investigator meant she had the privilege of sauntering into the first-floor unit. Thanks to her miserable heels, instead of sauntering, she limped across the finish line with as much grace as a used-up racehorse.

Old coffee stunk up the squad room. Brooks rocked on the heels of his large, loafer-clad feet near one of the desks.

Nick Fowler, one of the senior homicide investigators on the squad, gave a nod of welcome. "Hey, Princess."

Erin rolled her eyes at the nickname. She tolerated his teasing because Fowler was one of the few old-school cops who were cool with women as equals.

He grinned. "I was just talkin' to your new partner. Sounds like you caught a crazy case."

"That's putting it lightly. The girl's ripped to shreds."

Fowler opened a bag of chocolates and popped a handful into his mouth. "Just cut up to brutalize her, or more specific?" He chewed loudly, his chapped lips smacking together.

Erin had almost ripped Fowler's smacking lips right off him the nights they'd partnered during her training.

Erin steeled herself. "He jammed the murder weapon up her crotch as a final send-off." Brutal, but it helped her keep an emotional distance. "What's that tell you?"

Fowler turned the shade of pond scum. "Jesus H. Christ."

"Dan Mitchell thinks he tried to take out some of her organs and wasn't able to get the job done."

"Call me if you need any help." Fowler offered Brooks the bag and then held it out to Erin.

The mere thought of chocolate turned her stomach. She shook her head. "We'll do everything we can to catch this bastard." She leaned against the desk. "How's the Ted Moore case coming?" She had been jealous to miss out on working the high-profile case, but Fowler deserved it. He was a good cop: no-nonsense and dogged.

KILLING JANE

"It's looking like gang retribution for the documentary," Fowler said. "Moore had six months of death threats starting the night the thing aired."

Brooks looked between them, mild interest in his eyes. "Fill me in?"

"Big-time cable producer," Fowler said. "Endeavor Network. Moore spent a year investigating the gangs of D.C. and then aired a tell-all documentary. Secretary found him the other day with his throat cut and his severed dick in his mouth." Fowler grinned with all the glee of the Cheshire cat. "Our gangs are moving up the brutality scale."

"People do terrible things to one another," Brooks said. "It's an awful world to live in."

"Welcome to Washington, D.C. Metropolitan, Brooks. At least you won't be bored. But after working a high-profile serial killer case, you'd probably welcome a little boredom." Fowler made a show of chewing and smiling, but the savvy cop wanted to twist up the new guy.

Erin enjoyed a brief whiff of satisfaction at someone doing the appropriate hazing.

Brooks's grim smile didn't extend to his eyes. His blazer hung from the chair in the corner, and his yellow dress shirt made his pale skin look slightly sallow. "Nope, I definitely won't be bored."

A chill tore through Erin as images of Bonnie played in the carousel of her mind, and a secret part of her envied Todd Brooks for the experience. The knowledge he must have gained from being anywhere near the high-profile case gave him a unique perspective. Not to mention her superiors' giddy excitement when Brooks requested a transfer.

Fowler grunted and took another handful of candy. "God's honest truth. This city's got enough depravity." Concern overrode his usual cocky grin. "You sure you're ready for this one? It's going to be different than a drug dealer. Every time you think you've hit on the answer, you'll peel back another layer of crazy. That kind of shit wears on a person."

She pursed her lips and tried to look unaffected. Fowler never trod lightly when they rode together, and she respected him for it. "I can handle it."

"I have faith in you," he said. "Cases like these can worm into your head and mess you up. Don't let that happen. Not until you're at least five years on the job." He laughed at his own joke and then glanced up at Brooks, his tone sobering. "You know what I mean, though, right?"

Brooks nodded. "I think she'll be fine. Ready to talk to Will Merritt?"

Her confidence surged. "Absolutely."

CHAPTER FIVE

Erin's stupid heels clicked against the tile, reminding her of the way her sister always sounded when she arrived at their parents'. The clacking of Lisa's expensive, miserable-looking shoes always set Erin's teeth on edge—signaling Lisa would soon be insulting her. She should have worn flats tonight, but Lisa came to dinner, too. As usual, Erin fell victim to the urge to live up to her half-sister's expectations.

"Who's your girlfriend?"

Brooks laughed. "That's a bold question."

Erin turned to face him. "You mentioned she works at NCMEC. I used to be in sex crimes, and I've had several cases with them. I might know her."

"Ellen Davis."

Erin managed to keep her mouth closed. Ellen Davis was a knockout with auburn hair, green eyes, and the kind of curvy figure men loved. Brooks wasn't bad looking but still average. The randomness of attraction amazed her. "I worked a case with her. She's very good. Is that what brought you from Philadelphia?"

"I didn't want to work for Metro, initially," Brooks said. "After the past couple of years, I wanted something less intense. I kept waiting for something else to open up. But it looked like my only shot at moving out here, so I took it."

"What a ringing endorsement for us." They approached the interview room at the end of the hall.

"Sorry," Brooks said. "I didn't mean it like it sounded. Last year … the Trevor case—"

Erin cut him off. "Ellen Davis was involved. I remember reading about it."

Brooks's head jerked up and down. "The media reported mostly bunk, but we didn't want Ellen's name in the press. She planned to take the job at NCMEC and didn't want her ties to the Trevor case to affect her new position. So I got stuck with the credit for things she did. Keep that between us, all right? I don't care about myself, but I don't want Ellen to have to go through another media storm."

"No problem. I appreciate you trusting me." Erin stopped at the

KILLING JANE

door of Interview Room A, the standard room used for witnesses and families and the only one not resembling the inside of a tomb.

Brooks skimmed his right hand over his mousey hair. "So the boyfriend—or whatever he is—is inside with the victim's advocate. Responding officers saw no sign of blood on him, including his shoes. But we'll have to ask him to swab his hands for blood residue. After what he saw, he's going to love that."

"Assuming he isn't our killer." During her first weeks in homicide, Fowler pressed upon her that Occam's razor applied to most violent crimes: the most obvious answer was usually the right one, and more often than not, the assailant was someone the victim trusted.

Casual friend Will Merritt certainly fit the list. "He could have killed Bonnie, left to get rid of his clothes, and then came back to call in the scene. Although putting himself anywhere near her is pretty stupid."

"Thankfully, most criminals are stupid," Brooks said. "Let's hope our killer fits that bill instead of the alternative. We go in as his friends. Let him think we're just crossing him off the list so we can get to the real killer."

"Do you want to question him first?" Watching Brooks question the witness might give Erin the chance to learn from his mistakes.

"Why don't you take the lead? Sometimes men will open up to a female cop more quickly."

At least Brooks wasn't coming in like the star player trying to save the season. Erin knocked, her excitement mounting. This would be the first time she took the lead in a homicide interview.

The victim's advocate answered the door. Heavy wrinkles around her eyes and a pug-like nose matched the air of authority that immediately sparked Erin's memories of every politician's wife who vied for her mother's attention. Big or small, women like this usually ran the show. Working as a victim's advocate had to be akin to picking up dog shit for a living, so Erin put her childhood chip aside.

The advocate glanced behind her. "He's ready to get out of here, as you can imagine." The woman raised her eyebrow and ducked her head, as if to warn Erin that her witness was being a pain in the ass.

"Thanks for the heads-up."

The advocate stepped aside to allow Erin and Brooks to enter.

Unlike the other interrogation rooms, an attempt had been made to make this one slightly more comforting: padded chairs with only a few bits of oozing stuffing, blinds covering the windows, and a plant crying for moisture in the corner. A water cooler along with a table of cups and

27

extra tissue boxes hid in the opposite corner.

The man sitting at the interview table jumped to his feet.

Erin quickly assessed him. He had trendy, over-styled blond hair and wore perfectly distressed jeans, a shiny pair of Hermès shoes, and a designer casual jacket. Not exactly the standard apparel worn in Columbia Heights. His cologne—a cloying scent that sent Erin's olfactory glands running for cover—dominated the room. His fading summer tan barely gave his stricken face any color.

"Bonnie." His eyes flashed from Erin to Brooks. "Who did that to her?"

"That's what we're trying to find out." Erin kept her tone neutral. "What's your name?"

"Will Merritt." He took Erin's offered hand in a clammy grip and shook it once, decisively. "I knew Bonnie."

Erin motioned for Merritt to sit down. She took her time sitting down across from him, acutely aware of Merritt's nerves and Brooks's imposing figure leaning against the door. "You were her boyfriend?"

"Ah, no." Merritt's face flushed. "We hung out."

"Casual," Erin said. "No strings, right?"

Merritt nodded with the exuberance of a happy puppy. "Right."

"And that's why you came over tonight?"

"Bonnie called earlier today, asked me to come over." Merritt's hands rested on the table. He kept his nails clean and manicured. His fingers still shook. "This morning. Then she called back after lunch. Said to come as early as possible because she needed to talk to someone. I got there late. Traffic." The chair whined as Merritt rocked back and forth. "Maybe if I'd been there earlier …"

"That wouldn't have made a difference," Erin said. "She died a few hours before you arrived. Do you have any idea what she wanted to talk about?"

"No," Merritt said. "It surprised me because Bonnie didn't like to talk about feelings and things."

"She was upset?" Brooks asked.

"I don't remember. I was at the Capitol, so I let it go to voicemail." His chest puffed at the mention of the Capitol, his chin lifting a little higher. "I didn't pay attention to how she sounded, and I deleted it. I shouldn't have deleted it."

"Why were you at the Capitol?" Erin hoped this guy didn't turn out to be a protester. The last thing she needed was a bleeding heart with an agenda.

"My job," Merritt said. "I work for Baker-Allen as a lobbyist."

Her teeth clacked together. Her muscles turned to stone, and she willed herself to relax. "The defense contractor."

"We do more than that," Merritt said. "We provide several different consulting services to numerous clients. We also offer cutting-edge aerospace engineering." The standard company line.

"Your major client being the United States government. You specialize in military technology and equipment. Missile defense, biometrics, cybersecurity. The list goes on." Erin needed to tread carefully, pick her battles. But she had grown up surrounded by people like Will Merritt. People who approached life by way of socioeconomic class, who preached the value of their hard, white-collar work while usually riding the tailored coattails of family privilege.

Merritt deserved the chance to prove her wrong.

"So you work for Baker-Allen. You're probably a frequent flyer on Capitol Hill. Right?"

Merritt nodded, chest puffing again. His eyes flickered to Brooks as if he wasn't sure why both cops weren't asking questions.

Erin regained his attention. "And Bonnie lived in Columbia Heights, getting her GED and back on her feet, as you said. Back on her feet from what?"

"Drugs." Merritt lost some of his swollen pride. "I told the officer that, earlier." Sadness swept over him. "She had a rough life and worked her ass off to get clean."

A fresh pang of empathy hit Erin—for Bonnie, not for this pretty boy. "So is that the reason for the casual relationship? Bonnie wasn't up to your standards?"

Splotches broke out on Merritt's cheekbones, making him look like a teenaged girl with too much rouge. "No! We were at different places in our lives, and Bonnie—man, she had emotional issues." He tapped his chest. "I wasn't looking for someone who needed me to support them in any way. I just wanted to have some fun."

"Bonnie knew this?" Brooks spoke for the first time, voice soft. A casual observer.

"Absolutely," Will said. "She told me she felt the same way. She didn't have time for a real relationship."

Erin watched his body language for some sign of deceit. He kept his arms open on the table and had no trouble keeping eye contact, though he still slouched. But some people came out of the womb as skilled liars.

"How did the two of you meet? I can't see her in the Baker-Allen lobby, hanging out around the fountain." She caught her mistake too late, and any hope Merritt would miss it rapidly evaporated.

He cocked his head, narrowing his dark brown eyes. "I thought you looked familiar. You're Calvin Prince's youngest daughter. The cop. You look like your dad."

She refused to give him the upper hand. "Obviously."

Merritt looked at Brooks. "Is this a conflict of interest or something? Since I work for her family?"

To his credit, Brooks didn't hesitate. "Not unless you killed someone at Baker-Allen."

Merritt's eyes popped. "Uh. No."

"Then we're good," Brooks said.

Dead air filled the room. The sticky kind that coats people's skin and makes them crave a shower.

"So, Bonnie." Erin tried to get back on track. "Where did you two meet?"

Merritt shifted in the chair, hands going to his lap. "She waited tables at a restaurant near Capitol Hill. Daniel's."

Erin's father had taken her to lunch at the American steakhouse a few times during college when he still hoped she'd join the family business, and he loved to wine and dine senators there.

"You're sure she worked at Daniel's?" Erin pressed. "Washington's big boys make a lot of deals at those tables. The owners are careful about who they hire. Bonnie's got a couple of priors, misdemeanors. I find it hard to believe the owner would risk his business for wait staff."

"That's where we met." Merritt folded his arms on the table, his gaze listing to the right of Erin's.

Why had Merritt lied about where he met Bonnie? She raised an eyebrow. The light sheen of sweat on his forehead suggested he knew one phone call would confirm his lie, but he'd backed himself into a corner and wasn't ready to give up.

"When was the last time you saw her?" Erin asked. "Prior to today?"

"A couple of weeks ago."

"Had you spoken in the interim?"

"No," Merritt said. "Work kept me busy. She had school and her own job."

Erin wanted to be nice to this guy. She had no reason to think he was anything other than the poor soul who found Bonnie, but everything about him pissed her off. His nice clothes, the smug pride over Baker-Allen, his running his mouth about her family. She'd hoped for at least a few days before Brooks found out the real reason behind her nickname. Not to mention, Merritt hadn't met Bonnie at Daniel's. One lie usually meant more lies, and Erin didn't have time for lies.

"Do you know Bonnie's neighborhood well?" Brooks pushed off the wall and wandered to the opposite side of the room. He touched one of the dying plant leaves, still watching Merritt.

Merritt nodded. "I've been there a few times."

Erin wanted to ask whether it bothered him that the girl he slept with lived alone in a questionable area, but she already knew the answer—Will had never considered it. Men—and women—like him spent their days putting their own needs first.

"I assume you've been in every part of the house." The murder scene flashed in her head, and she couldn't keep a harsh tone out of her voice. "We'll need to get your prints to compare against those found at the scene."

Will's eyes bulged. "Am I a suspect?"

The victim's advocate had remained the background, only there in case Merritt asked for her, but now pressed her palm against the table. "Of course not. They're just going through the standard routine."

Will cross his arms. "Is it necessary?"

Erin played nice. "We need to rule out as many known prints as possible if we're going to identify the killer's. An innocent person usually volunteers, so they don't impede the investigation." She let the implication hang.

The advocate's glare burned into Erin's skin, but she didn't acknowledge it. One of the first rules of police work was to consider everyone a suspect until proven otherwise. Especially the casual sex partner who found the body.

"Right, right," Will said. "Whatever you need."

"Good. Because we need to swab your hands for any blood residue."

"Are you kidding me?" His voice pitched high. "I didn't do this."

"We know," Brooks said.

He came across as the good guy, using a soft voice. Empathetic. Apparently, her role in their partnership was to be the bitch. Wonderful. "What exactly did you touch in the attic?"

"I didn't go any farther than the top step. I didn't need to." Will shuddered against the memory.

"Can you tell us about Bonnie's friends?"

Merritt glanced at Erin, his ears the color of ripe tomatoes. "We usually hung out at her place. We weren't serious at all," he insisted. "I met her parents. But Bonnie kind of sprung them on me."

"I bet you loved that," Erin said. "So maybe Bonnie wasn't as cool with your embarrassment about her as you thought."

Merritt's fist thudded against the table. "She didn't embarrass me. We had an understanding."

Erin wanted to believe the sadness in his eyes and the desperation in his voice, but something held her back. "So, did you guys ever meet at your apartment? Which is in some über hip area like Logan Circle, right?"

Merritt flinched. "The DeSoto. And no. She didn't want to come over."

Brooks messed with his phone. "The reception in here sucks. Where exactly is The DeSoto? Sorry," he said to Merritt. "New guy in town."

"Posh." Erin filled Brooks in. "The DeSoto's on P Street, right in the heart of swank hipster city. There's a Whole Foods across the street, a Starbucks damned near next door, and a fitness center around the corner. What more could a young professional ask for?"

"It's a historic neighborhood near DuPont Circle," Merritt said.

"Northwest of Capitol Hill," Erin clarified. "Yet another gentrified area filling up with young, affluent people driving out the old-time residents. Right?"

"You should talk," Merritt said. "You come from one of the wealthiest families in the District."

Erin dropped against the chair, folding her arms. "Back to Bonnie. She didn't want to come visit you at The DeSoto? My bet is you didn't want the neighbors to see you slumming."

"Investigator Prince." The advocate's harsh voice only made the tension thicker. "Will isn't on trial."

Erin turned an icy gaze on her. "I'm conducting an interview. My job is to serve Bonnie Archer. Not worry about anyone's feelings. And you're not his attorney." She snapped her head back to the man across the table. Let the woman go to Sergeant Clark.

Brooks watched in his unnerving silence.

Merritt's face turned several shades of red, making the roots of his hair appear almost white. "Hooking up with Bonnie was not slumming." His jaw muscles flexed. His eyes looked wet. "Why are you doing this? I'm the one who found Bonnie." His voice rattled, his head whipping from side to side as if to fend off the evil. "He stuck that thing inside of her! She was dead by then, right? Please tell me she didn't suffer." Will Merritt covered his face to hide his tears.

The advocate patted his shoulder.

"Were you aware Bonnie used the attic to film amateur porn?"

Merritt flinched, once again looking away. "She didn't."

"Surely you saw the bed in the corner. The rope. The toys." Erin's voice sounded sharper than she intended, but his dishonesty, highlighted by the sweat beading over his forehead, fueled her irritation. "Did you make the films with her?"

Merritt's cheeks flushed bright red. He turned his head, but still didn't meet Erin's eyes.

Erin glanced back at Brooks.

His impassive face finally flinched, revealing ... disappointment. Maybe she should not have allowed her personal experiences to cloud her line of questioning, but she'd taken the openings Merritt had given her. No way would she leave this room without some information they could use.

"Look, Will. I grew up with guys like you. I know the drill. We're not supposed to mix with certain people, especially if we have political aspirations. Which you do, am I right?"

Merritt wiped his face and shrugged.

"So, a relationship with Bonnie is not good for your career or social trajectory," Erin said. "But you like her, so you keep it secret. Maybe you like her adventurous side, so you agree to make the videos. No judgment there. But then she tricks you into meeting her parents, and you realize she is way more into you than you wanted. You're going to break it off, but Bonnie threatens to use the sex videos against you. You had to take care of her." A weak motive, but Erin needed the guy to tell the truth. He might be able to lead them to their killer.

Merritt jerked up straight, looking desperately at Brooks.

The advocate squawked, but Erin shushed her with the same look she gave her sister when she'd heard enough.

"No! The parents surprised me, especially since they got so excited. Bonnie just wanted to get them off her back. She had to take bi-weekly drug tests to prove she was clean. She wanted to prove to them that she had her life together. She worked really hard at school. Once she explained everything, we were cool again. And we didn't make any movies." Merritt's shock turned to anger. "You said I wasn't a suspect."

"I'm just giving you my working theory."

"You're wrong. Bonnie's dead, and I found her. You think I want to have that image in my head?"

"Will, do you need to stop?" the advocate asked. "We can do this tomorrow."

"No, we can't." Erin kept her eyes locked on Merritt's sweating face. "We need to get as much information as possible."

Brooks sat between her and Merritt, leaning toward the nervous man. "You cared about Bonnie."

"As a friend, sure." Merritt relaxed some, shifting in the chair until he faced Brooks. Closing himself off to Erin and talking to his buddy Brooks. "She …" Merritt's voice caught. "Bonnie deserved better than this."

Brooks's face remained impassive as he made a note in his crumpled notebook. He leaned toward Merritt, half blocking Erin with his wide shoulders.

She gripped her pen until her fingers ached, keeping her mouth shut.

"And Bonnie never talked about anyone else she might have been seeing, since you two were casual?"

"No. She wasn't the type to have a boyfriend on the side."

Brooks nodded, looking as if contemplating some great life secret.

Erin's patience snapped. "Where were you this evening before you discovered Bonnie and called 911?"

The advocate sighed, but the defeat rang in her voice.

Hopefully, she'd stay quiet unless Merritt asked for her.

"At the office," Merritt said. "Working on a project I'm taking to the senate next week."

Good for him. Little puppy trying to play with the old dogs. "I suppose Baker-Allen's state-of-the-art security system can confirm that?"

"I'm sure," Merritt snapped back. "As well as the front desk receptionist. I told her goodbye when I left."

Did he really think she didn't know Baker-Allen had multiple exits? Depending on his security access, he could have gone down to the parking garage and left at any time without the guards seeing him. He should be on film if he'd told the truth.

"We'll confirm your information, no problem." Buddy Brooks had returned, his hand on Merritt's arm. "Did Bonnie tell you about any problems she had with anyone? Maybe someone hanging around who scared her?"

Merritt's hands went to his head, his fingertips digging into his scalp. His legs bounced up and down. "I told your boss earlier that I don't know of anyone hanging around. But we never got too deep into personal things. You should talk to her cousin, Sarah. They were close."

Brooks made another quick note. "You wouldn't happen to have her number?"

Merritt shook his head. "Do you have Bonnie's phone? I'm sure it's in her contacts."

"It's an iPhone," Erin said. "With a lock code. So it'll take some time for our tech guys to break into it. Unless you can give us the code?"

"Bonnie never shared that sort of thing." A shadow crossed his tired face, and he reached for a tissue but didn't use it. Instead, he tore off sections and wadded them into balls.

"Did you buy her the phone?" Erin pressed. She couldn't quite believe Merritt had no idea how Bonnie made her money. "Did she ever ask for help with the rent?"

"No." Merritt's mouth curved into a tight smile. "Bonnie was determined to make it on her own."

"See, that's bugging me." Erin tapped her pen against her lip. "A single girl taking classes and working part-time renting a big house in Columbia Heights. The money doesn't add up—even if she sold amateur porn online. Is there anything you're not telling us? Because I think you're lying." She didn't intend for the words to pop out, but they shot across the table like daggers.

Merritt gnawed his lower lip, the apples of his cheeks pink. "I'm telling you everything. How can you think I'd hide anything after what I saw?"

"It's my job to ask hard questions," she said. "And my gut tells me you're hiding something."

Merritt sneered. "No wonder your sister won't allow you to work for the family business. You're pretty damn dense."

Erin's temper flared, and she shot to her feet.

A heavy hand pressed her shoulder, easing her back into her chair.

She bit the end of her tongue until it burned. Then Erin leaned across the table, purposely invading his space. "Tell me what really happened. Bonnie blackmailed you over the videos. You snapped."

"I didn't kill her." Will Merritt stood, shoving his chair back. "I don't have to sit here and listen to this."

The advocate rose and stood next to him, tugging her blouse down. The look on her face told Erin she'd be having words with someone about her.

"You're absolutely right," Brooks said. "My partner's only doing her job. Please sit down, talk to me. I just have a few more questions."

Brooks hadn't exactly thrown her under the bus, but he'd definitely shoved her out the door. She kept silent as Brooks asked more routine questions, getting nothing from Will Merritt. Baker-Allen would make them get a subpoena for the security tapes.

Will took Brooks's card—a generic Metro P.D. card with Brooks's cell scribbled on the back. He hadn't been around long enough to get business cards, and he still made her feel like an ass.

The advocate wrapped a motherly arm around Merritt and led him out of the interview room, grabbing a handful of tissues as she left.

Erin stalked out of the room, her shoes tapping an uneven beat on the old tile. She couldn't figure out exactly what had pissed her off. Had Brooks naturally been playing off her bad cop?

"You can't do that again." Brooks caught up with her and crossed his long arms. Patches of fine, dark hair covered the top of his hands. They matched his mustache.

She slowed, trying to gather some composure. "Do what?"

"Get combative with a guy before we have anything to use against him. You alienated a potentially great witness."

"He's lying," Erin said. "I'll bet you anything he either willingly gave her money, or she blackmailed him, which would account for her being able to live in a house that size while single. What else is he keeping from us?"

"He may not have known about the porn," Brooks said. "If he went upstairs and found her, chances are her body is all he saw. We've got no physical evidence he did anything more. He agreed to the residue and fingerprinting. His alibi can be easily verified." He held up his hands, placating and gentle, as he'd been with Merritt. "You're not wrong about his lying. He knows a lot more than he's telling us, but we've got to earn his trust."

"I grew up surrounded by people like him. He's the kind of guy a girl from my social class is supposed to settle down with. I can tell you exactly how far they'll take their assumed privilege."

Erin had rebelled against the norm, much to the humiliation of her older half-sister. Their father humored Erin's choices, assuming she would eventually fall into line. When the right sort of man turned out to be a kleptomaniac with a juvenile record, her father hit the roof. Erin didn't listen. Her marriage ended in flames, but she ended up with custody of her daughter, Abby. That made all the misery worth it.

She exhaled a raw breath. "But you're right. I need to stay objective."

"It's an acquired skill," Brooks said. "I'm sure the fact he works for your family worries you."

"It doesn't worry me," she said. "Only solidifies his type."

Brooks smiled, his eyes wary. "People are never who they seem."

"My point."

"Making assumptions based on our own experiences is a dangerous thing to do in our line of work."

If she kept arguing, Erin would start spewing a bunch of unprofessional, hostile crap, and she didn't want to get into a major spat on their first night as partners, especially when they had a murder to solve. "So, you know who I am. Do we have to go through the song and dance about how I earned my job, which has nothing to do with my family?"

Brooks shook his head. "I couldn't care less. Just do your job and have my back."

Erin's phone rang with Sergeant Clark's number. Her shoulders sagged as she put him on speaker.

"Get back to the crime scene immediately. Marie found something else."

The urgency in his voice sent a tremor down Erin's spine.

Some of the chaos had died down at Bonnie Archer's house. Most of the neighbors had retreated into their homes, although Erin caught a few peering out of their windows. The press had scattered. Their morbid curiosity ended when the detectives and the dead body left the house.

The house smelled far worse. Death imprints into the woodwork, leaving a specific smell behind. The various chemicals used by the technicians didn't help matters. A wicked energy still pervaded the air, pressing against Erin as she climbed the stairs to hell on earth.

The bloodstain on the attic floor resembled a baked river. Good luck to the landlord on getting the blood completely out of the wood. Marie stood near the dormer window, on the phone. She held up her index finger, and Erin nodded.

She and Brooks stepped into the space, carefully avoiding the crusted area. Between the narrowness of the row house and the low-hanging beams, the area was a minefield for a man his size.

Brooks scowled. "This place makes me feel like I'm losing my mind."

"Me too," Erin said. "I don't like confined spaces, but I guess that's partially my fault."

"Why?"

Erin had no idea why she felt compelled to share anything with him, but that's what partners did. Somehow, through all the jokes and smack talk, you learned to trust each other. "My parents had a dinner party when my brother Brad and I were about six. Too young to attend, but our older half-sister did. She got to sit next to Nancy Reagan."

Brooks grinned. "Nancy Reagan? Cool. Is she as tiny in person as she looks on TV?"

Erin's muscles relaxed. "Yes. I was so jealous of Lisa because Nancy was an actress." And because Nancy seemed so delicate and poised and soft-spoken—all the things Erin wasn't. "I didn't care about her being the First Lady. Anyway, my brother—we're fraternal twins, if I didn't tell you—and I locked ourselves in the broom closet. We freaked out and got caught. My dad and the president laughed. My mother wasn't impressed."

Erin didn't remember her mother's punishment, but Nancy Reagan's bemused expression tattooed itself onto Erin's memory.

"See, that's a cool story." Brooks stepped onto the attic's threshold.

"Most people think I must have grown up like royalty," Erin said. "The perfect, sheltered life."

"There's no such thing, especially when you're growing up," Brooks said. "It's all varying degrees of shit." His tone deepened on the last word.

Before Erin could respond, he jumped back to the present task. "What exactly are we looking for up here?"

"I'm not sure."

Marie's crew had removed the drapes covering the dormer window, but the reflection of the crime scene lights off the old glass only made the blood appear more garish. All the bedding had been taken into evidence, along with the sex paraphernalia.

Erin tried to ignore the sensation of the space closing in on her. "We've got to cast our online net wider. I wish the department had facial recognition software."

"Ellen has access to it," Brooks said. "She might be able to find Bonnie online much faster than us."

Clark would have their necks. Not exactly the way Erin wanted to start as lead on her first major homicide investigation. "We'd just have a person on a video. We need a location, a way to trace her."

"She can do that, too." Brooks looked down at the floor. "Don't take this the wrong way. I realize I'm the new guy in town, but I've been a cop for more than fifteen years. Unless we get something viable quickly, a girl like Bonnie Archer will slip into the cold case files."

"Won't happen," Erin said. "But I'm not going against Sergeant Clark. It's his show."

Marie finished her call. "So, after you guys left, we found this over by the bed, wadded up and tossed in the corner." Marie held up a plastic evidence bag containing a wrinkled piece of college-lined notebook paper with neat handwriting.

Erin read the words out loud.

I am compelled to do this horrible thing. It is as if I am pulled by some larger force, a demon that will not rest. He whispers despicable things into my aggrieved mind. My heart knows I should not act, but my brain does not listen. I am no more than a slave to the blood I will yet spill tonight.

—JTR
31 August 1888

Erin squinted at the handwriting. The black ink looked generic, and the crisp paper showed no sign of yellowing from age. "This looks like a diary entry. Is this something found during the Ripper investigation?"

Brooks shook his head. "It's definitely not one of the letters he allegedly wrote."

"Since this guy seems to be picking and choosing from Jack's bag of cruelty, it makes sense he'd categorize Bonnie selling porn as a form of prostitution, but what's he playing at? Did he intend for us to find this? He didn't exactly leave it in plain sight like the message on the rafters." Erin glanced up at the beam where the bloody carving seemed to glow in the lousy lighting.

"We photographed it where we found it," Marie said. "But looks like he threw it away and forgot about it."

"I think it's all a game," Brooks said. "He's leaving these breadcrumbs to keep us off balance."

"Even if Will Merritt didn't know about the videos," Erin said, "I'd say finding out his girlfriend's playing prostitute on film would be humiliating and a good motive."

"Why the Ripper reference, then?"

"There's more written on the back."

Something in Marie's tone made Erin's pulse stutter and sent butterflies through her system. Erin turned the paper over, and all of the blood in her body drained to her toes.

More words. This time, emphatically scrawled. Written over and over in an embellished flourish.

Abberline was right.
—Jane

CHAPTER SIX

Brooks carefully took the paper and stared at it. "Inspector Abberline was the lead investigator on the Jack the Ripper murders. He considered the possibility the Ripper could be a woman, possibly a midwife. He believed that might explain the Ripper's ability to escape the crime scenes covered in blood, but Abberline never had enough evidence to prove it."

Erin's lips numbed as she spoke. "What if our killer's a woman, too?"

His gaze flashed to meet hers. "Because of this? If the killer actually wrote the note, then the logical assumption is we're dealing with a Ripper fan who buys into Abberline's theory."

"Then why sign the name Jane?"

"He may not have meant for us to find this," Brooks said. "It's probably his notes and ramblings. Especially since Jill is the name used in the Ripper lore. Or ..." He shook the evidence bag. "It's not a stretch to think our killer is deliberately leaving these crumbs to muddy the case. This is like crack, to a reporter, and keeping a lid on a high-profile murder investigation takes an act of God."

Jane the Ripper. The idea refused to leave Erin alone. "You do realize a lot of women are into true crime stories, right? Why couldn't our killer be one of those?"

Brooks's face had gone blank.

"She left us the note to make sure we knew. She practices the message she wanted to leave. Tosses it aside and forgets it. Or the paper falls out of her pocket while she's fighting with Bonnie."

Heat bloomed at the back of Erin's neck and then crept to her ears and cheeks. Self-doubt chiseled away at her confidence. Jumping to wild conclusions in a case like this usually meant disaster. "It's way too out there. Forget I said anything."

"No," Brooks said. "It's not out there. We keep the idea as a possibility and keep investigating. If this killer is a woman, the evidence will lead us there."

CHAPTER SEVEN

The demon speaks to me again. He basks in the furor stirred up by the slaying of the first woman and demands another. My stomach recoils at the thought of tearing another's flesh, yet my mouth salivates at the prospect. What have I become?

—JTR
8 September 1888

This entry is my favorite. Jane is beginning to understand her own needs. Nine days after the first murder, no one in London knew who roamed the streets or the beautiful things yet to come. Poor Jane is still afraid to accept the demon, but with time, she learns.

Everything good comes in time.
The truth will be preserved.
My identity will be protected.
The world will be right again.

Mina's big, scared eyes always made Charlie feel like he'd been sucked underwater. The little girl had been through so much unfairness in her short life. And yeah, maybe life wasn't fair, but little kids weren't supposed to know that. Kids Mina's age should still believe in Santa Claus and the Easter Bunny and their parents. She shouldn't be clinging to a confused teenager for protection.

But Charlie had made a promise. He kept his promises.

He shoved his blond hair out of his face. It needed to be cut, but the others liked it long, and he didn't want to spend the money. Charlie believed in choosing his battles, so he kept his mouth shut and dealt with the hair.

"Charlie," Mina whispered to him from her hiding spot. "Do you think the cops know about us?"

"No." He wasn't certain of anything, but he couldn't tell Mina. She already hung on by a frayed thread.

"But what about Bonnie?"

Charlie couldn't feel sorry for Bonnie—she didn't have the guts to do the right thing. He checked his bag to make sure the laptop and digital camera were still inside. "Stop worrying and help me find a place to hide these."

"But, Charlie—"

"I'm not talking about it anymore." He hated losing his patience with the little girl. "Don't I always keep you safe? Don't I hide you from all the bad things?"

"Yes."

"Then you have to trust me, Mina. It's the only way we don't end up like Bonnie."

Mina sniffled. "Poor Bonnie."

"Yeah," Charlie said. "But she should have said something when she figured out the truth."

"You know what's going to happen."

"Hush." Charlie's hissed words cut through the quiet night. He searched in the darkness, hoping he and Mina hadn't been discovered. "You need to forget what we saw, or we'll end up like Bonnie. Is that what you want?"

"No, Charlie."

He settled back against the wall. "All right, then. Let's get rid of this stuff and get out of here."

CHAPTER EIGHT

rin met Brooks in front of the Archers' two-story, brick colonial in Forest Hills. Pine trees framed the quintessential family home, providing a nice natural privacy fence. Like every neighborhood except for the wealthy, the houses in Forest Hills sat too close together, every inch of available real estate used up. Growing up, Erin felt sorry for the "regular families," as her sister called them, who didn't have the luxury of sweeping, landscaped yards and large acreages. But those kids had something Erin didn't: a neighborhood to roam and friends across the street and down the block. She deliberately chose exactly that sort of neighborhood for her daughter to grow up in.

"Nice place." Brooks got out of a small Toyota Prius and quietly shut the door. He'd donned a black windbreaker as nondescript as him. "Is this an expensive area?"

"Every place in D.C. is expensive compared to the rest of the country," Erin said. "This is average middle class." She hoped she didn't sound as snobby as it felt. She'd grown up in a house at least twice the size of the Archers', and her parents still held court in the mini-palace. "There are quite a few international embassies in the Forest Hills area, so it's a bit unique. Lots of cultural mix but still affordable, for the most part." She spoke in low tones. It was after midnight, and every house on the street was dark.

Brooks leaned against the fender of her car. "So, your nickname is Princess? Seems kind of obvious. You'd think the squad would come up with something better."

"I'm fine with the nickname, as long they back me up. So far, so good."

"From the way Merritt talked, your father must be a significant political figure. He's a defense contractor?"

"Consulting is the magic word," Erin said. "Baker-Allen provides that on all levels, but it's only a bonus to the defense contracts. My father plays politics to get what he wants. So did my grandfather. I'm sure there's a myriad of things they've been involved in that I don't want to know about."

Brooks nodded. "And you never had any interest in their world?"

"No." Erin started down the quaint cobblestone path. Each stone was individually laid, well-worn from years of use. Dread settled into her shoulders.

They stepped onto the Archers' porch. A wooden swing hung at the far end, and two planters of yellow mums decorated the entrance. Her legs became wooden and heavy. "How many of these notifications have you done?"

"More than I want to admit." Brooks cocked his head. "You?"

"A few." Truthfully, only one. "I haven't quite perfected the technique."

"I don't think anyone ever does. If you want me to tell them, I can handle it."

His placid expression made Erin wonder how he'd perfected the art of compartmentalizing. "Let's just do it together and be as compassionate as we can."

Brooks nodded. "I like the way you think."

Her stomach rolled with fresh nerves. The other death notification she'd made was to the mother of a gangbanger, and while the mother had collapsed in silent tears, the woman wasn't shocked. She'd tried to get her son out of the life for years. But the Archers had witnessed their daughter descend into drugs and then pull herself back out. They must have had high hopes for her future. They certainly weren't expecting a visit like this in the middle of the night.

Erin took a deep breath and rang the doorbell.

An upstairs light flashed on. She breathed through her mouth, focusing on her breath.

The porch light came on. Erin knocked and held up her badge to the tiny peephole. "D.C. Police. We need to speak with Neil and Carmen Archer."

Slowly, the door opened, and a middle-aged man with rumpled pajamas and a balding head peered out. Suspicion filled his small eyes. "What's this about?"

Erin hoped the pity didn't show too strongly on her face.

"Neil?" A sleepy-sounding woman called from somewhere inside the house. "Why are the police here? Is it about Bonnie?"

Erin's heart dropped into her stomach. "I'm afraid so." She refused to break; these people needed her to be strong.

Neil Archer's sleepy face paled. "Is she in trouble? What's happened?"

"Mr. Archer." Brooks's smooth voice soothed Erin's nerves. "May

45

we come in and speak to you and your wife?"

"Oh my God." Carmen Archer appeared beside her husband. Her dark hair, mussed from sleep, had silver strands at the temples. The wrinkles between her eyes deepened. "Bonnie's dead, isn't she? That's the only reason you would be here at this time of night."

Putting the truth off another second felt cruel. "I'm so sorry," Erin said. "But Bonnie was murdered in her home tonight."

Carmen Archer clamped her hands over her mouth, her wedding ring glinting in the porch light. Wordlessly, she shook her head back and forth.

"You can't be right," Neil choked out. The smooth skin on his head flushed. His shaking hand rattled the doorknob. "Bonnie's doing good. She's smart. She wouldn't let someone in who would hurt her."

"Her friend, Will Merritt, found her," Brooks said. "It's Bonnie, and I'm so sorry."

Neil sagged against the doorframe as though his knees had turned liquid.

His wife closed her eyes, and tears smeared the remnants of her mascara. Finally, she took a deep breath. "Who killed her?"

"We're doing everything we can to answer that question," Erin said. "I know this is a horrible time, but can we come in and ask a few questions?"

Carmen nodded, taking her husband's arm and guiding him out of the doorway. Erin and Brooks followed. The door closed with a click, the finality of the sound making Erin jump.

A tabby cat sitting on the arm of the couch stared at Erin with judgmental yellow eyes. "First, is there anyone we can call for you?"

Carmen shook her head, slightly rocking. She had the look of a woman who'd accepted the truth, yet couldn't quite fathom the monumental change in her world. Erin couldn't blame her. A life without her daughter—a life where her daughter had been savagely taken from her—seemed unimaginable.

"Where is Bonnie?" Carmen faltered, then clenched her fist so tight her knuckles turned white. "We'll need to get her to the funeral home and make arrangements."

Erin's heart lurched at the woman's need for control, no matter how small, in the situation.

"She's with the medical examiner." Brooks seemed the picture of compassion and calm. "Her autopsy is tomorrow, and we'll know more then. The medical examiner will call you about releasing the body. It might be a few days."

"What happened to her?" Neil's raw voice sounded like his throat had been torn open. "Was she raped?"

"We don't know yet," Erin said. "Someone stabbed her." She swallowed, trying to gather her nerve. She didn't want to give them the horrific details. What good could it possibly do? But if the cops delivered this sort of news to her, Erin would demand every detail. "I'm going to be honest because I don't want you to hear this from the media. It was brutal."

Erin clamped her jaws tight as she watched the rest of the color drain from Carmen's face. Let the M.E. decide whether or not to give the specifics.

"Did she suffer?" Neil's broken voice cracked.

"The medical examiner will be able to tell you more," Brooks said, managing to defer the question without sounding dispassionate. "We're aware of her past, but can you tell us about her current life? Was she afraid of anyone? Worried about anything?"

"She took classes," Neil said. "She wanted to be a teacher, but needed to get her GED first. She was doing great." He kept staring at them as though this should have been enough to keep some madman from murdering his child.

"Where did she attend classes?" Brooks asked.

"The Adult Learning Center in Edgewood," Carmen said. "She also worked part-time in the evenings as a server at a high-end restaurant in DuPont Circle. Daniel's. We've never had the chance to go. I don't like to drive into the area, but Bonnie said the place was black tie, with great tips." Carmen reached for a tissue.

Erin kept silent. She'd have the information on Bonnie's employment at Daniel's in the morning, but she guessed Bonnie and Merritt had mutually agreed on the lie.

Erin made her voice as gentle as possible. "I hate to ask, but we have to address Bonnie's drug use. Is there a possibility she had started using again and upset a dealer? What drugs did she use in the past?"

Carmen Archer emphatically shook her head, her soft black hair dancing around her face. "Prescription pills. She had a talent for getting doctors to write her prescriptions, and then when that failed, she went to the streets. But there isn't a chance she was using again. Bonnie had bi-weekly drug tests. That's the only way we agreed to help her get on her feet."

A hint of guilt crept into her voice, and her pleading eyes made Erin

STACY GREEN

feel worse by the minute.

"We knew her living here with us wouldn't help. She has our support, but she needed—she wanted—to be on her own. And if she couldn't get clean without a babysitter, then she wouldn't stay clean." Carmen's voice broke. "That's why she lived by herself."

"I think it's very brave of you to help her." Erin reached for the woman's hand, desperate to offer some comfort. "And to stipulate the drug testing. Your support must have worked."

Carmen's cold fingers squeezed back. "It did. She also had to share her class information with us. We weren't going to help if she wasn't attending."

"Where was the drug testing done?" Brooks asked.

"At one of the Howard University Hospital clinics. Bonnie gave them permission to report to us."

"We'll need the contact information," Erin said. "And for you to let them know we have permission to access her records."

Carmen rubbed her cheeks, further smearing her mascara. "Of course. I'll call first thing in the morning."

"Can I ask if you helped her financially in any way?" Brooks said. "This is an expensive area for a single person to live on their own."

A hint of defense crept into Neil's posture. He folded his arms. "Occasional spending money, the first month's rent on the house. Her laptop for school. But she made great tips at Daniel's. She hasn't needed any help for several months."

"It's a high-end place," Carmen echoed the earlier conversation. "Good clientele."

Working part-time wouldn't cover everything. How could her parents not know this? Or had they played ignorant to make life easier? Bonnie's drug tests came back negative, and she went to school. Perhaps Carmen and Neil considered that more than enough.

Erin tried to frame her next question carefully, without giving too much away, but Brooks beat her to it.

"So Bonnie only took GED courses? Nothing recreational like film or photography?"

Carmen nodded. "The Adult Literacy Center has a college prep program, as well. She planned on going through it so she could apply to schools. Once she passed the GED." Her small body seemed to shrink into the cushions as she realized someone had snuffed out her daughter's dreams.

"What about her friends?" Erin asked.

48

"She didn't have a lot of friends," Carmen said. "Her old friends still did drugs, so she walked away. She left all of that behind."

"What about her cousin, Sarah? Will Merritt said they were close. How do we get in touch with her?"

Carmen flinched as if Erin had smacked her. Confusion overtook her grief. "That's not possible."

Neil Archer's face turned stormy. "Bonnie and Sarah haven't spoken since they were little. I don't know why he said that."

"Will found her?" Carmen still held Erin's hand. "He's a nice man. I'm glad he found her and not some stranger. She cared for him."

Erin glanced at Brooks. "How serious were they?"

"Bonnie focused on school, but he treated her really well, and she liked being with him," Carmen said. "I could tell when he came over to meet us. Did he tell you?"

"He did." Erin delicately picked at the scab they'd apparently pulled off. "But he seemed to be under the impression Bonnie and Sarah were close."

"My brother and I had a falling out years ago." Neil Archer's voice sounded like gravel. The grief on his face transformed into simmering anger. "We don't speak to them. We certainly don't hold it against Sarah, but after the argument, the girls didn't spend time together. It's been years since they saw each other."

"I'm just trying to piece together as much of Bonnie's life as possible."

If Bonnie had reconnected with her cousin, she hadn't told her parents. She was in her mid-twenties and probably far wiser than her years. She didn't have to tell them everything about her life. Judging from the hostility seeping through Neil, she wouldn't have told him about her cousin.

"Can you tell me about the falling out?"

He glared at Erin, big hands flexing. "It's a personal matter that happened years ago. There's no need to discuss it. I assure you it had nothing to do with what happened to my daughter."

Erin decided not to push the issue—for now.

"What about the drug use?" Brooks changed the subject. "How long did she use before getting clean?"

"She's been in and out of rehab since she was fifteen," Carmen said. "She was date raped, and she just couldn't handle the trauma."

Erin's insides turned cold. Her breath shortened, and the room took on a red hue.

Brooks glanced at her, a question in his eyes.

She ducked her head. *There's no time for this, and it's all in the past.*

Brooks turned back to the Archers. "Is there a possibility someone from her old life turned up, and she tried to help them?"

"I wouldn't be surprised," Neil Archer said. "Bonnie is—was—the kindest girl. She had so much compassion. She hated seeing anyone in pain, and she wanted to help people. That's why she wanted to be a teacher. She wanted to teach at-risk children. She's a helper." His voice broke again. He covered his face and unsuccessfully tried to mask his sobs.

Carmen released Erin's hand and wrapped her arms around her husband.

Erin bowed her head, and she and Brooks let them cry together. The grief became an entity, taking over the house with the strength of the meanest demon. She fought off tears of her own. She needed to see her daughter.

"Can you give us names?" Brooks handed Carmen his notebook when she finally caught her breath and pulled away from her husband. "Write down anyone you can think of that Bonnie used to know and anyone she's mentioned associating with recently. Any new friends at school."

Carmen's knuckles turned white from gripping the pen.

Erin still believed the crime was about rage, passion, and something else she had yet to figure out. She looked over Brooks's shoulder when Carmen handed back the notebook. Three names, none of them Jane.

"You're sure this is all of them? Bonnie never mentioned a friend named Jane?" She felt Brooks's eyes on her.

"After she finished rehab, Bonnie completely started over," Carmen said. "She kept her circle of people very tight and never told me much about the people in her past life. Those are the only names I know."

Brooks tucked the notebook into his pocket. "This is great, thank you."

Erin stood, unable to sit any longer. The couple's grief made her legs twitch. She wanted to hold Abby, smell her sweet scent. Crawl into bed with her and never let go.

"Did Bonnie have any interest in history, specifically true crime?"

"No," Carmen said. "Why?"

Erin hated to say the words. The couple already knew their daughter's murder had been brutal, but mentioning Jack felt worse than showing them a crime scene photo.

"Bonnie never talked about studying Jack the Ripper, maybe for a school project?" Brooks asked.

Carmen Archer's face twisted into an expression barely resembling a human. "Oh my God. Was she cut up like that?"

"It's just a question." Brooks's mournful voice only made Carmen cry harder.

Neil's face went slack, and he stared at the far wall, not focused on anything.

Their pain made Erin feel helpless. Nothing she had to say would make Neil and Carmen feel any better.

She set her business card on the end table. "Please call me if you think of anything else."

Carmen continued to sob, so Erin directed her question at Neil. "Mr. Archer, did Bonnie have anything valuable other than her television and purse? Did she have jewelry, an expensive camera, or anything someone could pawn?"

His glazed eyes shifted back to them. "Her laptop. It was a cheap eleven-inch, but vital to her. That's about it."

Erin would never forget his stricken face.

"Can you tell us the brand?" Brooks asked.

"Dell. But she had a Wonder Woman sticker over the logo." He covered his face with his hands, shoulders shaking.

"Thank you," Erin said. "We'll let ourselves out."

"Wait." Carmen Archer staggered to her feet like a drunk needing to find a bed. She went to the long table in the hall and dug around in a drawer. "Bonnie makes fun of me for still getting my pictures printed. I like the feel of the pictures." She swayed a little and then handed the picture to Erin. "I want you to know what she looked like in life. This was taken a couple of weeks ago."

"Thank you." The picture fractured Erin's heart. Bonnie had been a beautiful, vibrant girl. Her cornflower eyes danced, her smile genuine. "We'll be in touch."

CHAPTER NINE

Erin shivered, the coldness unrelated to the crisp fall air. "Jesus, that was heartbreaking."

"Yeah." Brooks fell into step next to her. "I know we're doing our job, but I always feel like a bastard when I talk to the family."

The sound of Carmen Archer's guttural crying reverberated in Erin's head. She doubted the memory would ever fade. She pulled out her personal cell phone to check whether her brother, Brad, had texted while it had been on silent. More than anything, she wished she could talk to Abby just to hear her voice, but she'd have been in bed hours ago.

Brooks's phone pinged. "The tech guys were able to retrieve Bonnie's contacts."

"That was quick. Is Sarah on the list?" Erin brought up the phone app and punched in the numbers as Brooks read them off.

The call went straight to voicemail. "Hi, Sarah. This is Investigator Erin Prince, and I need you to call me as soon as you pick up this message, regarding a matter of some urgency." She left her contact details, clicked off the phone, and put it away.

"Figures she wouldn't answer at this hour." Erin massaged her temples, trying to keep a headache at bay. "By the way, thanks for being the one to mention the Ripper."

Brooks leaned against the bumper of Erin's car, his expression contemplative. "So you've gone from thinking this killer may be a woman to believing her name is actually Jane?"

Erin wished she had an explanation for the acidic worry leeching into her nervous system. "I don't know what I think."

Brooks held up a slender finger. "Our killer likes Jack the Ripper. He's either not interested or incapable of copycatting Jack's crimes, but he carved the message into the rafter to pay homage to his inspiration."

"And then he got sloppy and left part of his research notes," Erin finished. "I'm reading too much into the name."

"Bonnie's killer planned her murder." Brooks's low voice matched the worry churning through Erin. "I have a hard time believing he was sloppy enough to accidentally leave that paper. He expected us to find it. The question is whether he's telling us who he—or she—truly is, or whether we're being led in circles."

Erin's head throbbed, the sensation fraying her nerves. "I can't get Jane out of my mind."

"Don't." Brooks pushed away from the car and stretched. "Keep her as a possibility, because whoever did this has a taste for blood."

His unspoken words hung between them. If she and Brooks couldn't find the killer, another woman would end up as a victim. Another murder meant another message.

Brooks started walking toward his car but abruptly stopped. "What do you know about the BDSM scene around here?"

Erin couldn't resist. "You and Ellen looking to join?"

He gave a wry smile. "Not quite."

"Honestly, not a lot," she said. "That's one of the few groups you don't see a lot of in sex crimes. Ironic, I guess."

"It's a culture where pushing boundaries is acceptable as long as both partners are willing. Probably a lot healthier attitude toward life and sex than the general population has, if you think about it."

He made a good point. "There are a few clubs, mostly nightclub types. My brother's not into BDSM, but he's an expert on the D.C. underground," Erin said, unlocking her car. "I'll see whether he has any idea where to start. We'll probably have to show Bonnie's picture around, which may or may not get us anywhere. I'll keep trying Sarah Archer. I hate to deliver bad news over the phone, but we might have to."

She yawned. "I'm calling uncle for tonight. You know where the medical examiner's office is?"

Brooks nodded. "I'll meet you there in the morning. Maybe we'll get lucky and wake up to hear Bonnie's laptop has been found with our killer's picture front and center."

"Keep dreaming."

CHAPTER TEN

E rin quietly slipped through the back door of the Arlington house she shared with her brother and her daughter. They both slept like the dead—a gene Erin hadn't inherited. She normally tossed and turned, her noisy brain never ready to stop telling her a story.

East of the hub of the District and less than a ten-minute walk from historic Arlington National Cemetery and the Pentagon, Erin's modest home sat on a quarter-acre corner lot in the Aurora Highlands area. Built in the early 1900s, the little gray house resembled a carriage house, its location perfect for a young child. The Highlands felt more secluded than many of the other neighborhoods Erin and Brad looked into, almost like a little town hiding in a metropolitan city. Their sister and parents didn't understand their desire to live within their own financial means rather than sucking off the trust funds. Erin had given up trying to explain the desire to be self-sufficient a long time ago. Living like a commoner—as her sister so eloquently called everyone who wasn't from a wealthy, politically-connected family—made Erin happier than she'd ever been.

She moved silently through the cozy house. The heavenly aroma of Brad's homemade pasta sauce lingered. Erin breathed deeply and then whispered a curse when her stomach growled. She tiptoed up the stairs, careful to avoid the squeaky spots. Abby had the little bedroom to the far left. Anyone who broke into the house would have to encounter her and Brad before getting to her daughter.

As usual, Abby's covers rested in a ball around her long legs. A multitude of stuffed animals took up half the bed, the book she must have fallen asleep reading spread out over her small chest. Four American Girl dolls lay on the floor in various stages of undress, all watching Erin with their lifeless eyes. She shuddered and then walked toward the bed, longing to put her arms around her daughter.

Abby sighed in her sleep, rolling over and knocking the book onto the floor.

Tears welled in Erin's eyes. She loved this little miracle more than she could say. What if something happened to her? What if, someday, Erin became the broken parent clinging to a police officer after they told her Abby was dead?

She rubbed the tears away in a desperate effort to banish the idea, leaning down to gently kiss her daughter's temple, breathing in the scent of the vanilla cookie bath soap she loved. Erin picked up the book, set it on the nightstand, and then quietly crept back downstairs to poach some of the leftover pasta.

There'd better be leftovers.

She sat at the kitchen table with pasta, her laptop, and her phone. Department-issued phones meant investigators could use them to take crime scene pictures, but the quality sucked. Dissecting the photos would likely have to wait until tomorrow when Maria emailed copies of the photos the coroner's office had taken.

Erin bit into a spicy tomato, shamelessly moaning at its goodness. She tried to focus on the meal, but her thoughts raced ahead to the morning and to Bonnie Archer's autopsy.

Erin had only attended one other postmortem. The victim had died of a single gunshot wound to the chest, so the procedure was straightforward. She had little hope of the medical examiner finding anything useful in the mess of Bonnie's remains.

The floor above her head creaked, followed by the sound of steady footsteps. Erin listened as her brother descended the home's steep staircase and made his way into the kitchen.

Naturally, he turned on the light and blinded her.

"Why are you sitting here in the dark?"

Erin shielded her eyes. "Because it's three a.m."

Brad ran his fingers through his already wild blond hair. He was the older twin by nine minutes, and the physical similarities ended there. Erin had brown, curly hair she kept shoulder-length, and she walked a fine line between voluptuous and needing to lose a little weight. She might hit five-five with the right pair of shoes. With his blue eyes and toned figure, her twin brother resembled a Ken doll. The boys always liked him better than Erin.

"You look like shit." Brad snagged a penne noodle from her bowl. "How bad was it?"

"Really bad." Her throat suddenly closed. The evil energy from the attic suddenly pulsed through Erin as though some tiny bit had latched onto her during the crime scene investigation. "Brutal."

"Please tell me you have a suspect."

"We have some leads but, so far, nothing concrete." She pushed the remaining pasta away, now nauseated. "This guy cut her up while she was alive." She couldn't bring herself to tell him the gory details.

"Holy hell." He sat down next to her.

Erin leaned against Brad's shoulder. "Whoever did this is a special kind of monster. This girl suffered, and he stood around and watched, which means he'll do it again. Brooks and I need to find him before that happens."

"Brooks?"

"My new partner." Erin sat up straight and opened her laptop. She considered a web search for Brooks and the Trevor case, but she didn't have the mental energy and didn't need her inexperience to shine brighter next to the guy. She quickly logged into Facebook and searched for Bonnie Archer. No profile. Will Merritt's was set to private, same as Sarah Archer's.

Her brother perked up. "What's he like? Is he single?"

"He's fine so far, but hard to read. He's definitely competent." She shook her head. "He's taken and straight. And I thought you were seeing someone."

Brad picked at his manicured nails. "He's still not ready to own his sexuality, and I don't know whether I have the time or patience. The guy's thirty-five, and this is the age of gay rights. Own it and forget about it."

"It wasn't so long ago you were afraid to tell Mom and Dad," she reminded him. "So watch out, because you sound like a hypocrite."

"Totally different," Brad said. "Dad saw me as a problem to his political connections and his business. Scott's parents are divorced, and he's bi-racial. It's not like they haven't had their share of prejudice. He's just not ready, and I can't change that. It's got to be his decision."

Erin's joints popped as she retrieved the picture of Bonnie from her bag. Prescription drugs didn't affect the teeth and skin like meth or heroine. Her bright smile came from whitening products. Not a cheap grooming habit.

"Is that her?" Brad asked. "So pretty."

"Yeah." She prodded him in the ribs. "As for your guy, have some sympathy."

"I do," Brad said. "Don't act like I've got it easy. Dad still doesn't love the idea, and if it weren't for you, we probably wouldn't even be talking."

"Maybe." Erin couldn't believe their father would be so cold. When Brad came out as a young adult, Calvin Prince had been shocked and then worried about how his mostly conservative clients would take the news. Eventually, Erin and her mother convinced him to accept Brad for who he was. Erin liked to think her father would have come around on his own.

Of course, their older half-sister patronized Brad, making a show of supporting him while talking out of the other side of her mouth about how it affected her social and political standing. Her two-faced attitude had been the cause of one of the first of many blowouts among the siblings. Calvin stood up for Lisa, allowing his guilt to override his common sense. She was a selfish narcissist whose main interest in the family revolved around money. But Calvin would never see the truth.

"We notified her parents." Erin closed the laptop, exhausted. "I thought getting out of sex crimes would be better, but after tonight, I'm not sure. Their pain was unlike anything I've ever experienced."

He wrapped his arm around her. "You had to get out. Dealing with rape victims ate you up inside."

Because she was a hypocrite. Laughable, since she'd just accused her brother of the same thing. The daughter of Calvin Prince as a rape victim? The local media would have jumped on the story and would've kept it alive for as long as possible. Her father's reputation and power extended around the world, and he counted the last three presidents as personal friends. She didn't want to relive the experience over and over in the public eye, let alone what it would do to her career and how she was treated by her colleagues.

Brad stood and yawned. "The best thing you can do right now is sleep. You can't kick ass without rest."

She rolled her eyes, but he was right. "How did Abby do? Did she pass out quickly?"

"Oh yeah." He locked the back door. "Grandma and Grandpa's gigantic mansion always wears the poor kid out."

Erin followed him down the hall. "Thanks so much for taking care of her. I'd be screwed without you."

"You need to get screwed. How long has it been?" Brad took the stairs two at a time.

"Oh my God, shut up." She shoved her brother across the second-floor landing, dropping her voice to a hiss. "I can take her to school in the morning, but can you pick her up? I have no idea how my day is going to go."

"Sure," Brad said. He worked from home as a web designer. "Keep us posted about dinner. If you're not home, we're going out for pizza."

"Speaking of sex, do you know anyone into BDSM?"

Brad stopped shuffling and stared at her. "Wow. I said you needed to get laid, not spanked."

She rolled her eyes. "We think our victim made amateur BDSM videos and sold them online. Whoever killed her might be connected to the culture. So, answer the question."

He yawned again. "The whole scene is very private, even with the new BDSM craze. I'd start with The Black Rose. It's the biggest club. Beyond that, I don't know. I'm not that kinky."

Erin sank into a deep sleep as soon as she closed her eyes. Bonnie's desecrated body floated through her dreams, illuminated by the gaudy glare of the cheap studio light. Sudden bursts of red splashed against the back of Erin's eyelids as though someone had thrown a bucket of blood into her dreams. Somewhere in the background, a woman screamed. Not a scream of pain, but animalistic and frenzied.

Jane the Ripper.

The dream changed. A cloaked female figure chased Erin, and the wild screaming grew louder. Erin clawed to the surface of her dreams, but fatigue kept her eyes pinched shut—until her cell phone rattled on the nightstand.

Erin flailed in the dusky darkness of her bedroom. A pink slice of dawn glimmered behind her curtains. Red digital numbers showed she hadn't slept two hours.

"Erin Prince." Although she'd never touched a cigarette, she sounded like a veteran smoker.

"Is this the Princess?" A little girl's voice, soft and frightened.

Fuzzy-headed, Erin sat up. "Who is this?"

"Is this the Princess?" Demanding, now, a petulant kid determined to get her way.

"This is Investigator Erin Prince. Who's this? How did you get this number?" She tried to keep her nerves at bay and focus on the scared child. "What's your name, sweetheart? Do you need help?"

Fast, frightened breathing. "Buck's Row was just the first one."

Ice formed in Erin's veins, turning her entire body frigid. "What's your name?"

The screen flashed, signaling the call had ended.

Pain wracked Erin's chest as though a hammer had hit her. Dozens of scenarios raced through her mind, none of them good. But the child's voice overrode them all. She checked the caller ID—blocked number. A blocked number whose owner had Erin's unlisted cell number. A bad feeling settled in the pit of her stomach.

Erin scrolled through her contacts and hit the green circle. Todd Brooks answered as groggily as she expected and listened in silence as Erin told him about the call.

"You're sure this was a child and not someone playing a joke?" He yawned, and a woman's husky voice rumbled in the background.

"Absolutely. I've got a nine-year-old daughter. I know a scared little girl when I hear one. And how did she know about Buck's Row unless she's with the killer? If she—" Erin could barely stomach the next thought. "She had to have witnessed the murder or, at least, the aftermath."

"Call your service provider and see if they can trace it, and make sure your doors are locked." Brooks ended the call.

Erin paced to the window. The sun rose, red-gold in the clear blue sky, making the frost on the brown grass and rooftops sparkle. Was Bonnie's killer watching the sunrise, too?

How long before another woman—or child—was found slaughtered?

CHAPTER ELEVEN

T racking the call proved impossible. Erin confirmed with her service provider that the call came from a pre-paid phone with its GPS turned off. She quickly showered, dressed, and then tried to force down a bowl of cereal.

Brooks called back, this time more alert. "Ellen said the news mentioned your name, but their initial coverage didn't go into detail. I think someone used their kid to play a sick joke. I'm more concerned with how this person got your personal cell number. Do you give that out to work colleagues?"

"Only you and Clark. I always use my department cell for work, and I've made sure to keep my personal information as buried as possible. Every time my father makes the news, the press tries to find me. I don't have time for them."

"And your brother wouldn't give the number out, right?"

"Absolutely not." Brad had gone off the rails when she told him about the call this morning, going so far as to suggest she get a new phone number immediately. Erin refused. If the child called again, she might be able to help or trace the call.

"Buck's Row," Erin reminded Brooks as she washed out her bowl. "Only someone associated with the scene would know that, and if we had a leak, the press would have run with it."

"Unless they wanted to screw with you," Brooks said. "One of the crime scene people could have talked, maybe told a friend who turned it into a practical joke."

"That little girl wasn't joking. She was terrified, Brooks. She knows what happened, and she's trying to tell me another woman will die." Erin's pulse accelerated. If someone tracked down her number, they might find out where she lived, putting Brad and Abby at risk. She had to figure out a way to protect her daughter without scaring the hell out of her.

While Abby thundered around upstairs getting ready, Erin watched the Channel 4 morning news. The perky reporter's previously taped story ran front and center. Footage showed Clark, Erin, and Brooks talking on the steps, the crowd swelling and tittering, while Bonnie's body was carried out in a black bag and placed into the medical van.

So far, the worst of the details remained out of the public eye, but with descriptions like "mutilation" and "a sea of blood," Erin had little doubt someone had fed the reporter information. She gave it twenty-four hours before the bloodthirsty vultures reported everything, right down to the cleaver and Jack's message.

Abby skipped down the stairs with her backpack thumping on each step behind her. At the sound, Erin grinned. Abby packed half her life into her backpack each morning.

"Go eat your breakfast, sweetie."

Abby chattered with Brad in the background while Erin focused on the last few seconds of the news bite.

Erin switched off the TV and pulled up several websites. She needed to know more about the Ripper's killing spree. Five known victims over the course of two and a half months, although there'd been a large gap between the fourth and fifth kills. Bonnie's murderer hadn't been nearly as vicious as the canonical five, as the Ripper experts called them, but definite similarities existed. Hysteria hampered the case from the start, along with the lack of the technological advances cops today took for granted. A main suspect list over thirty, with hundreds more speculated on, over the years.

She jumped when Brad touched her shoulder.

"Do you need me to take Abby to school?"

She patted her chest. "No, I'll take her as soon as my heart is no longer trying to claw its way out of my body."

Brad smirked. "You didn't hear me call your name. Twice."

"I've got to get this guy, Brad. I can't get the … caller's fear out of my head." Erin nearly said *little girl*, but she didn't want Abby to know anything about a girl being in danger.

"Mom, come on. I'm gonna be late."

Erin grabbed her keys and hurried out the door with Abby. On the drive to school, she couldn't keep her thoughts off the case.

Jack or Jane? Some of the sites she had looked at had a section labeled *Jill the Ripper*. A woman suspect surprised Erin. None of the females investigated panned out, however, and most experts believed Jack likely dressed as a woman to avoid attention.

Were the signed passages their killer's way of causing confusion? A modern-day Jack trying to be a Jane and putting his own flavor on the legend?

The Ripper's second known murder had occurred nine days after the first. Erin prayed she had time to find the murderer before another woman—or worse, a child—was killed.

"Earth to Mom!" Abby's voice pulled her thoughts back to the present and the school carpool line. "Are you going to be home for dinner tonight?"

"Probably not. I just started a bad case." Guilt crept over Erin. When she worked in sex crimes, her schedule was more reliable.

"The woman who was murdered in Columbia Heights?"

Erin nodded. Racing around doing her morning routine, chattering like a banshee, Abby missed nothing. "But I'll try to get home before you go to bed. I'm sorry."

Abby smiled, revealing the missing right molar she'd been so proud to lose last week. "I get it. Uncle Brad lets me watch bad TV with him anyway."

Erin planted a kiss on her daughter's cheek before she could escape the car, breathing her in one last time for the day. She never got enough of Abby's scent. When Abby was a baby, Erin held her for hours to inhale the sweet goodness coming from her delicate head.

"Mom!" Abby looked out the window to see whether any of her friends had noticed. Her blue eyes shone with embarrassment. "You're not supposed to do that here."

"Why not? You're still a little girl."

Abby shouldered her backpack and flung the car door open. "I'm almost double digits."

Erin bit back a laugh at her serious expression. "Uncle Brad's picking you up from school. You don't leave with anyone but him. Right?"

"Right. See you!" Abby slammed the door and raced to catch up with two of her friends.

Erin navigated the treacherous traffic, holding the steering wheel tight. The medical examiner locked the doors to the autopsy suite during the procedure. Bonnie's started in thirty minutes.

Erin hit the gas.

CHAPTER TWELVE

The surgical mask made Erin's face hot, but she appreciated the thin layer between her nose and the chemical scent in the autopsy suite. Bonnie Archer's body had been refrigerated before the worst decomposition began. Still, Erin rubbed Mentholatum beneath her nose to help tame the stench that would be released when the assistant unzipped the bag to start her initial examination.

Deputy Medical Examiner Judy Temple noted Bonnie Archer's height and weight, snapping photographs and dictating her findings. "The X-rays showed a broken wrist, probably from trying to break her fall. She also had a broken nose, most likely from the assailant's efforts to subdue her."

The woman's monotone voice made Erin want to run out of the room. Everything was cold and sterile, including the last person who would take care of Bonnie Archer. Her practical side accepted that detachment was necessary for the job, but Erin could hardly bear to listen.

In death, with the blood and torn flesh washed away, Bonnie looked more alien than human. Her once-porcelain skin had taken on the gray pallor of dead flesh. With her carefully applied makeup removed, her face appeared even more childlike. Her luxurious eyelashes reminded Erin of Abby's.

She fought the urge to reach out and take Bonnie's hand.

"Did Sarah Archer return your calls?" Brooks kept his voice low so as not to interrupt the autopsy.

Erin shook her head. "I called twice more this morning and said I needed to discuss her cousin."

Brooks stood tall and motionless, eyes focused on the medical examiner. "If Will Merritt's telling the truth, why hasn't Sarah called? She should be one of the first in line demanding we find out who killed her cousin."

"She's probably not calling back because she and Bonnie aren't supposed to be speaking, but I should hear from her today. Clark released Bonnie's name this morning." If not, she'd have to hunt Sarah down.

Dr. Temple removed the paper sheet, and Erin gasped. In the harsh light of the suite, Bonnie's nude body revealed the true scope of her suffering. Bruises ran all the way down her knees and shins. Her right wrist bent at a painful angle. A tattoo of angel wings on her hip had a superficial slash through it. The cleaver had been removed and bagged as evidence.

Erin drew a shuddering breath to combat the swell of dizziness. "Maybe Merritt's lying."

"The bruises on her knees appear to be fresh, but perimortem." Temple glared over her recorder, pursing her thin lips.

Brooks rubbed his temple. "You don't sound convinced."

Erin kept her eyes on Bonnie's face, partially out of respect and partly because she couldn't seem to draw her gaze away. She lowered her voice to a rasping whisper. "It's a dumb thing to lie about, and it makes sense for Bonnie to keep her reconciliation with her cousin from her parents. Whatever happened between the two families, Neil's clearly still pissed off."

"I thought so too, which brings us back to my original question. Why isn't Sarah Archer calling you back?"

Erin didn't have the answer and didn't like the worry percolating in her head. Did Sarah have something to hide?

"Dan Mitchell believed the first stab was to her stomach," Brooks said to the medical examiner as she brushed past him. "Did she fall after that?"

Temple's gray eyes met his. A renowned medical examiner and a veteran of the 9/11 death investigations, Temple resembled a bulldog in both demeanor and appearance. Fleshy and stout, she had wobbly cheeks and a burgeoning extra chin. She also took no shit off anyone in her autopsy suite.

"Since you're new to us, I'll give you one pass, Investigator Brooks. I don't make guesses. There's no definitive way to say, short of the entire thing being recorded. Mitchell's theory is sound, especially since lividity makes it clear she didn't get off her back once her killer got her into that position. Anything beyond that is speculation."

Brooks didn't seem fazed by the derisive tone. He nodded and waited for Temple to proceed.

Erin swayed as she watched the doctor inject the needle into Bonnie's right eye. Vitreous fluid was essential to chemical testing in an autopsy, but Erin hated anything to do with eyes.

She refused to do Bonnie the injustice of looking away. She and

Brooks stayed silent while the medical examiner and her assistant continued to work.

"A series of bruises on her thighs and upper arms appear to be in various states of healing," Temple said, examining the yellowing blemishes Erin noticed last night.

"How old do you think those are?" Erin asked.

Temple sighed. "Everyone heals at different rates. The bruises on the arms are fading purple, while the upper thighs are clearly yellow, suggesting Bonnie received them at different times. My rough guess is between a few days and a couple of weeks—but that's a guess."

Erin murmured her appreciation and then turned to her partner. "One set of old bruises I could chalk up to an accident or being clumsy, but two? We need to chat with Will Merritt about those."

"He doesn't seem like the abusive type," Brooks said. "Of course, those guys are usually the meanest. By the way, I checked in with the Archers this morning." Brooks turned to Erin, his soft voice barely audible behind the paper mask. "They didn't have any more thoughts on who might be responsible."

He paused, then shook his head. "If they think she worked at Daniel's, I've got a feeling there's a lot about Bonnie's life her parents didn't know—including the fact Sarah had come back into it. Have you confirmed with Daniel's already?"

"Not yet, but I will." Restaurant owner and extreme cynic John Daniel ran in the same circles as her father. He didn't believe in any sort of second chance—unless it earned him something major in return.

Erin refocused her attention on the autopsy. "Dr. Temple, how long before we get tox results?"

"A couple of weeks."

"Any chance you could rush them?" Erin didn't shrink from Temple's sharp look. "We need to rule out this being drug-related."

Temple grunted.

Erin couldn't hope for anything more.

The next few minutes passed in silence as Temple and the assistant made the Y-incision and pulled Bonnie's chest apart. Erin gritted her teeth as the doctor's incision tore open Bonnie's already ruptured abdomen.

"The killer nicked her spleen," Temple said. "She would have slowly bled out if he hadn't cut her carotid. His work in the abdominal area was fast and sloppy, and her organs are all still intact. He may not have had the stamina to finish the job, but there's been no serious effort made to remove them."

"Was she still alive when he made those cuts?" Brooks asked the question they already knew the answer to.

"As I said," Temple's voice sharpened, "she would have bled out from the nicked spleen. But the coloration of the organs demonstrates blood flow. So yes, she was very much alive. I can't tell you if she was conscious, so don't ask."

"Have you narrowed down the time of death yet?" Erin asked.

Temple continued to work as she answered, her eyes narrowed until her eyebrows touched. "Mitchell's original timeline is correct. I'd say she died at least six hours before Mitchell moved her."

Another round of silence, the only noise coming from Temple and her assistant.

"Did you ask your brother about the BDSM scene?" Brooks's whisper didn't faze Temple or her assistant.

"He said to start with The Black Rose. It's the biggest club. But we're facing the same thing with online stuff: too many people to go through."

Brooks murmured his agreement. "We should split up and try to hit as many as we can."

"The cleaver sliced through her cervix," Temple said. "Her uterus is still here. Prince, did you say her boyfriend found her body?"

Erin's pulse accelerated at the interruption. Temple never spoke directly to the police during the autopsy unless she had something important.

"Yes," Erin said. "Why?"

"Because she was pregnant."

CHAPTER THIRTEEN

Erin's maternal instincts sent a flash of sorrow through her. She tucked the feeling away and focused on Judy Temple. "How far along?"

"From the size of the fetus, I'd say about ten weeks."

"Then she may not have known about the pregnancy," Erin said. "Especially if her cycle wasn't regular."

Temple waved her fingers at the assistant, who handed her what looked like a flattened Q-tip. "I'll do a buccal swab for fetal DNA, but the lab is backed up."

"Isn't this case pressing enough to rush?" Brooks sounded impatient for the first time.

Temple leveled another heated glare at him. "To you and this family, of course. But what about those other families who are desperately waiting for results? Who am I to tell them this case is more important than their loved ones?"

"Because this is the type of violent crime that sparks more killing," Brooks fired back. "Rushing the results would be a preventive measure."

Temple shrugged. "I'll put in a request." She jerked her mask-covered face at Erin. "I'll put her name as requesting investigator. It might make the lab move faster."

"Go ahead." Most of the time, the Prince name was a hindrance, but every once in a while it served a noble purpose.

Brooks leaned toward her. "Remember, Mary Kelly was pregnant."

His low whisper sent fresh fear over Erin.

They watched the rest of the autopsy in silence, the results mostly unsurprising. Temple confirmed the throat wound as the ultimate cause of death and believed the entire assault lasted less than thirty minutes.

Temple seemed to be in better humor once the procedure ended. "I'll tell the lab to rush the fetal DNA if at all possible. If we tell them it could help us stop a spree killing, they might be more inclined to listen."

"Thanks." Brooks left the suite.

Erin followed, desperate to shed her protective gear. She yanked it off and threw it into the bin marked toxic waste. "But Mary Kelly was the last Ripper victim." Erin addressed his earlier comment. "If this person's a fan of Jack's, he's picking and choosing."

Brooks folded his suit up before throwing it away. "Since Merritt works for your father, we shouldn't have any problem getting in to see him, right? If he knew about Bonnie's pregnancy and cared about his reputation as much as you think, he's got motive."

Erin scrubbed her hands with the antiseptic soap. "Definitely. I want to ask him about the girl, too."

"We need to prioritize, so while we're waiting for Sergeant Clark to get the warrant, I think we should start contacting the BDSM clubs. We might get a lead on the child there, too."

She hated to admit he was right. "It's barely eleven a.m. I doubt many will be open."

"Then we make phone calls. Email Bonnie's picture to them. Describe her; whatever it takes."

Brooks held the door open and they walked into the bright fall morning, the sun's glare reflecting off the buildings making Erin's eyes water. She fished for her sunglasses and noticed the message light blinking on her cell.

"Daniel's owner texted me back," she said, rolling her eyes. "Modern technology is eroding the human experience. But we've caught Will Merritt in a lie. Bonnie never worked there."

"She lied to her parents, too," Brooks reminded her. "So he might have been protecting her."

"Why not help us find her killer?"

"That, I don't have the answer to." Brooks donned his coat. "So let's find some BDSM clubs and then go talk to Merritt again. You drive. Traffic here is worse than Philadelphia."

"Blame the tourists," Erin said.

Only four of the ten known BDSM clubs answered their phones. Erin dutifully emailed the cell phone picture she'd taken from the printed one Carmen gave her, asking whether the owners knew Bonnie. None recognized her, but they all promised to pass the picture around.

Erin ended a call. "The guy from The Black Rose claims ninety-nine percent of the BDSM porn on the major sites is fake. They're put out by studios trying to cash in on its popularity."

"Surprise, surprise," Brooks said. "He give you anything else?"

"He thinks she probably did pay-per-view like I mentioned last night, which means we need to go deep into the web to find her, and it's still a long shot. But, get this." She turned to face Brooks reclining in her passenger seat. "He ran through a list of the standard BDSM equipment. We didn't see half of it in Bonnie's attic."

"Maybe she couldn't afford it," Brooks said.

"But it's the stuff people who watch that sort of porn expect to see. It's what they're paying for."

Brooks rubbed his temples. "Marie went through the entire house. We've got a list of everything she found." He opened his little notebook and started flipping through. "Handcuffs, rope, a whip, the nipple clamps. Condoms. The knife and gun."

"But no gag? No restraint? Any other BDSM stuff? Or a harness? Or a cock ring? What about any of the really painful stuff like spreaders?" Erin still shuddered at the idea.

"No," Brooks said. "Something's been bugging me about the attic scene. Maybe that's it. I assumed BDSM when I saw the items, but I could be wrong. Maybe she just filmed rough sex. Most people do what's familiar to them." He rubbed his temples. "I'm not making sense."

Erin's heart palpitated, a fine sheen of sweat misting over her lower lip. She turned the heat off and the air conditioner on full blast. "You're making perfect sense."

"What?" Brooks asked.

"You said most people do what's familiar." Erin's throat tasted like she'd inhaled a pound of sawdust. "Bonnie Archer was a victim of sexual assault. She kicked the drug habit, but we don't know whether she really made peace—if there is such a thing—with her attack. Rape porn is one of the web's dirty treasures. What if that's the kind of porn Bonnie filmed? Her healing bruises would make a lot more sense."

Dizziness swarmed over her. She didn't want to search through the dark web looking at rape porn even if it was fake.

Brooks considered this. "You could be right. I'm no profiler, but the BDSM culture isn't about control or pain in the sense that they want to hurt the other person. People enjoy the pain. The goal isn't to humiliate or degrade. But, rape porn?"

Erin's stomach lurched at the words. *Get a grip, Prince. Be cold and analytical.*

His thin upper lip disappeared into his mustache. "I've seen some, and it gets obscene. You're talking about an entirely different type of participant."

"Who might lose his shit if he found out he'd gotten Bonnie

pregnant."

"We need to talk to the Archers again. Find out if Bonnie sought any kind of therapy," Brooks said. "If she believed she wasn't good enough, she might have been talked into filming by someone she thought was better than her. Someone who promised to give her a cut and help her get out of her current situation. Someone who had everything she wanted in life."

Erin put the car into gear. "Someone like Will Merritt. Let's head back to the CID and see whether Clark's got the warrant."

CHAPTER FOURTEEN

E rin kicked her chair, sending it rolling across the squad room floor and straight into Sergeant Clark's bad knee.

"Goddamn, Prince! Watch it!"

Heat crept through her.

Fowler, who'd been immersed in paperwork, snickered. His riding partner Max Ramirez, a barrel-shaped firecracker of a man, burst out laughing. Ramirez ducked behind his files at Erin's glare.

"I'm sorry," she said. "I can't get that little girl's voice out of my head. She reached out to me, and there's nothing I can do. This sick bastard must have put her up to it. She's in danger."

"I'd like to know how she knew to call you Princess," Brooks said. "It's not that original of a nickname, but it's not known outside of work, right?"

"It's strictly a Metro P.D. thing," Erin said. "I can't stand it. But it's stuck with me since I was on patrol."

"So, how'd the little girl know your nickname and personal cell number?"

"Probably from the shitstain uniform who talked to Channel 4," Clark said. "So far, the media has only the basics, but an 'unnamed source' is quoted as saying the Metro's Princess is taking the lead. My guess is Brooks's right, and the same asshole told the little girl about Buck's Row. As for the cell, you're talking about cops with connections. Even if it's unlisted, it's not that hard for a cop to dig and find it. It's all a prank to get under your skin."

"Channel 4 referred to me as Princess?"

Fowler let a chuckle escape.

Erin wasn't sure whether crawling under a rock or beating the reporter's ass sounded like the better option.

Clark scowled. "We've got bigger issues. Have you heard back from Sarah Archer yet? If Merritt's telling the truth and she and Bonnie were close, we've got to assume Sarah may be at risk."

Erin already had Sarah on her list of people to worry about, for more reasons than one. "We've got two different stories on the cousins reconnecting. Sarah's lack of response might just mean Will Merritt's a liar. I left another message on the way here. Fowler, did you find out that information for me?"

Fowler stopped digging through the teetering mound of scattered notes on his desk. "Neil Archer works for one of the big insurance companies. Carmen's a teacher. Quiet lives, private people, according to their employers. Other than speeding tickets, both are clean."

As Erin expected, she had to cross her t's and dot her i's. "And Neil's brother?"

"You know how hard it was to find the guy's name?" Fowler asked. "I had to search the public records and birth records. Computers make it easier, but it still sucked. Screens give me a headache."

She made a rolling motion with her hand, signaling for him to get to the point.

"Simon Archer. He also happens to be the executive counsel for the National Governors Association."

Erin threw up her hands and sank onto her desk. "Well, isn't that wonderful? Neil Archer will never tell us what the family fought over."

Brooks gave a low whistle.

Erin drummed her fingers on the desk. "Their legal counsel is probably the mother of all watchdogs. Fowler, you get an address?"

"Yeah. Chevy Chase. Richie-ville, second only to your neck of the woods." He smirked at her.

"I don't live in McLean," she snapped, not in the mood. "I only grew up there." She pushed off the desk, back aching from the awkward position. "No wonder Sarah isn't calling back. She probably has to clear it all with her father first. We'll visit her parents first thing in the morning if we don't hear from Sarah."

"I bet that'll go over well," Brooks said dryly. He made a face at his Styrofoam cup of thick coffee. "Sergeant, did you get the warrants?"

Clark sank into Erin's chair, rubbing his knee.

She'd have to buy him a decent cup of coffee as an apology.

Clark handed her a wad of paperwork. "The warrants for Merritt's DNA and Baker-Allen's security footage. I already sent a uniform to the drug clinic with the warrant. Her phone company emailed the last three months' records. They're in that pile, too. Pretty regular stuff. Calls to her parents, Merritt, her cousin. Her school. So far, looks like she lived as privately, as everyone says. But," he pointed a long finger, "she's also got several incoming and outgoing calls to the same unknown number. Another drop phone, of course. Tech guys say they can't trace anything."

Erin's adrenaline rush watered down to a pathetic stream. "So we serve the warrant and get the DNA. Then what?" If Erin's next scene involved the body of a child destroyed like Bonnie Archer, how could she keep working? The kid's death would be on her hands.

"Merritt lied about meeting Bonnie at Daniel's," Brooks reminded him. "After the autopsy, we head to Baker-Allen and hit Merritt with that and the pregnancy. If he's innocent—and I think he is—he'll talk. He's hiding something."

"Go to the Adult Learning Center after you finish at Baker-Allen," Clark said. "Ferret out the administrator, teachers—anyone who knew her at all."

Erin compartmentalized the tasks, regrouping. "What about ViCAP? Did you get a hit?" The FBI's Violent Criminal Apprehension Program compiled information about major violent crimes across the country and helped connect similar crimes. But countless offenders still operated under the program's radar.

"Nothing that matched," Clark said. "Which is good, I guess. Nice to know there isn't someone else in another part of the country doing this shit."

"I'd rather he'd gone somewhere else." Erin slipped her loaded gun into the holster on her hip. She checked her Taser, making sure it had a full charge and could be easily accessed from the outside pocket of her bag.

The freak had her phone number. Could he get her address?

"How secure is your house?" Clark read her mind. "I still think we're dealing with a prank, but you need to stay alert just in case."

"My father had a security system installed. It's military-grade. A housewarming gift. I'm not on social media. But people can still find someone if they want to badly enough."

"Always be suspicious," Fowler said. "What about Abby?"

Erin's heart lurched at hearing her daughter's name, but she refused to consider the implication. "Brad is going to call her school and make it clear she's to be watched at all times, and a teacher has to hand her off to one of us and no one else."

"Good," Clark said. "You guys see anything that makes you nervous, or you get another call, I'll put a uniform on the house."

"Thank you." Erin put the warrant into her purse and motioned to Brooks. "Okay, Lurch. Let's go talk to Will Merritt. See whether he knows any kids."

"Merritt doesn't strike me as the type to involve a kid. Or to play mind games," Brooks said as they walked to the car. "It's calculating.

Devious. He looked wrecked. And why Lurch? I'm not freakishly tall."

"I'm five-five on a good day," Erin said. "To me, you're Lurch." She winked and then slid behind the wheel. "Merritt could be acting. Trying to throw us off."

Brooks considered it. "Maybe. The killer probably wore gloves. If Merritt's involved in the porn, though, his prints should be in the attic."

"Motive." Erin pulled into traffic. "Along with Bonnie being pregnant. Merritt said himself he's not attached." The idea sounded better the more she thought about it. "Maybe she did tell him, and that was the final straw. He has a kid call to fuck with me because I pissed him off and he wanted to send his own special little message." But another idea popped into her tired brain. "Then again, if some woman found out her man got Bonnie pregnant while he filmed with her, she might snap."

"And she's trying to tell us that by the Jane the Ripper passage?"

Erin shrugged. "Maybe a part of her wants credit for her work."

"There's no indication the killer knew about Bonnie's pregnancy," Brooks said. "Her uterus wasn't destroyed like Mary Kelly's. It may be a coincidence. Or a motive for murder. It's too soon to tell. The kind of killer you're talking about is usually disorganized. There aren't usually signed notes left for the cops. None of this adds up, including the idea the killer is a woman obsessed with Jack being female."

"It doesn't have to add up for someone to become obsessed with it." Erin kept hearing the little girl's voice and was interposing Abby's face into the nightmare.

Brooks sighed and stretched his long legs. "But nothing about this case makes sense."

"Murder is supposed to make sense?"

"No, but there are certain types of killers and certain types of kills. At first, I thought Bonnie's was about rage. Passion. Overkill."

"So?" She turned onto Prince Drive and hoped he didn't notice the namesake.

"So, that kind of killer doesn't usually taunt. He either feels remorse or justifies it and goes on. He doesn't settle in for the long haul."

Erin parked at the back of the enormous parking lot, unwilling to use the company spot she had clearance for.

"This guy doesn't make sense. He's not the remorseful or justified type of killer. That scares the hell out of me."

Erin ignored the rash of chills on her arms as they exited the car. She zipped up her coat—a black puffer style much less gaudy than the expensive Burberry from the night before—and they started the long walk across Baker-Allen's parking lot.

Clouds muted the sun completely, making the sky match the pavement and Erin's mood.

Baker-Allen's main office looked like something from the future, all sharp angles, and glass. It also boasted adjacent buildings with various testing areas, a fitness center, and a daycare. Her father was nothing if not cutting edge.

"How many locations are across the country?"

Erin gripped the signed warrant like a talisman. "Just this one, but they have offices in a dozen other countries."

"Do you and your father get along?"

The question surprised her, and she nearly tripped over her feet. "Yes. Why would you think we didn't?"

"He's obviously a powerful guy with a multimillion-dollar company. Instead of the family business, you're a cop. Don't get me wrong—I admire that. But since you didn't follow in his footsteps ..."

"Billion-dollar company." The *Washington Business Journal* had recently named her father as one of the most influential people in the District. "I had no interest. My father and I are fine. He's a bit old-school, but he's supported me."

He'd probably find out all about her half-sister before the day ended. Lisa knew everything that went on at Baker-Allen, and Erin had little chance of escaping without having to deal with her.

They walked into the Baker-Allen lobby. Everything about the space represented sleek, controlled technology. Too much steel and digital contraptions for Erin's taste. Some sort of sophisticated light display glowed on the wall instead of simple paint.

She stopped at the administration desk, which was larger than Abby's bedroom. "I need to speak with Will Merritt." With any luck, the lobbyist had gone to Capitol Hill. She'd rather wait outside the sessions to speak with him. The sooner she left Baker-Allen, the better.

"Do you have an appointment?" Margo Kepler stared at Erin with a blank expression.

Despite having worked the desk for over a decade, Margo hadn't recognized Erin. Or had simply forgotten her. It wouldn't be the first time. Maybe it would work in her favor this time, and Lisa wouldn't know of her arrival.

"We need to speak with him about an ongoing case." She showed her badge, followed by the warrant. "And we need your security footage from yesterday—one p.m. through ten p.m." The judge had played it surprisingly safe with their timeline, and Erin wasn't complaining.

Margo called upstairs to request Will Merritt to come to the lobby, and then called the head of security to deal with the warrant. Erin could throw out her last name and simply walk in, but then she'd have to deal with Lisa. Only special people had full access to the top-level offices. People who appreciated the business. People who came from her father's first marriage and therefore counted as his real child.

"Before we deal with this guy," Erin turned to look up at Brooks, "how do you want to handle the pregnancy? I'm all for asking him point blank. It's motive."

"Agreed." Brooks nodded, his eyes focused on something behind Erin.

A well-built man who would have been right at home in an Ultimate Fighting ring glided toward them. The badge on his navy suit read *Gomez—Head of Security.* "How can I help you?"

Erin gave him the warrant and explained what they wanted. "We need the raw footage. Time-stamped."

Gomez slowly perused the document. His gray hair shined like gossamer beneath the lobby's bright lights. "Seems everything's in order. Do you want to wait in your father's office while I get it for you, Investigator Prince?"

So much for no one putting it together. "No, we're interviewing Will Merritt."

"I'll make a copy and have it here at the front desk." Gomez smiled pleasantly, but Erin hedged. What if he screwed with the footage? She glanced at Brooks, debating on asking whether he'd like to accompany Gomez. Instead, she asked about Will Merritt's security clearance.

"Low-level," Gomez said smoothly. "His card only gets him in the main entrance."

Merritt trudged toward them, looking far worse for wear than last night.

Gomez excused himself, glancing sideways at Merritt on his way back to the security offices.

Will Merritt's puffy eyes and wrinkled clothes made Erin wonder whether he'd slept at all. He hadn't shaved, his jaw spotty with wiry peach fuzz.

He pulled on his already loose tie and unbuttoned his tailored suit jacket. "I'm not sure what else I can tell you."

"Hello to you, too," Erin said, feeling the receptionist's eyes on them. "Let's go into one of the downstairs conference rooms." She led the way down the east corridor and then waited for Will and Brooks to enter before closing the door.

Merritt pulled out a chair, its feet dragging across the sturdy Berber carpet, then fell into the chair with a dramatic sigh. "I didn't sleep. I keep seeing Bonnie lying there. All that blood."

"Now that some of the initial shock has worn off, I want to confirm you didn't go any farther than the top attic stair," Erin said.

Merritt shook his head.

"But we'll find your fingerprints in the house because you've been inside before. Including the bedroom. On say, the headboard."

"I already told you." Merritt crossed his arms and leaned back. "I'm sure you will."

"But you maintain you've never been in the attic?"

"I've never been in the attic." He spoke through gritted teeth. "Are we going to do this all over again?"

Erin sat down across from him while Brooks remained standing. "So you didn't know Bonnie liked to make sex videos?"

Merritt focused on his lap. "She wasn't into that sort of thing."

Erin rested her elbows on the table and clasped her hands. "But she was. We found evidence of recording equipment in the attic, plus some other fun sex stuff. Someone took the recording device and the videos. Probably her killer."

"So you think Bonnie filmed someone, and he got pissed off? He gutted her for that?" He directed his question to Brooks, either too irritated or too intimidated to speak directly to Erin.

He didn't strike her as the sexually dominant type. Then again, the man she had gone out with three times didn't strike her as a rapist, either.

"I think blackmail is a real possibility." Erin leaned across the table, closing in on Merritt's personal space. "There's no way Bonnie could afford the house on her own, waiting tables. I think her parents knew this, too. They didn't want to think about it. So she had an additional income."

Merritt continued to shake his head, rocking slightly. "I can't help you."

"Were you helping her out financially?" Brooks asked. "You cared for her. There's nothing wrong with someone in your financial position offering to help. If you did, you need to tell us. Because if her financial records show big deposits in your name, you'll be hearing from us again."

"My financial position?" Merritt laughed. "I'm a second-year lobbyist. I can barely afford a lifestyle, let alone help someone else out." His eyes slid to Erin. "My name isn't Prince."

She smiled, determined not to let his gibe get under her skin. "Let's just get down to it—I had it right last night, didn't I? You got sick of the blackmail and killed her. Then you felt guilty and called it in."

"Are you serious?" The veins in Merritt's neck bulged. "I would never … she didn't film me. Or blackmail me. Bonnie was a nice girl!"

She believed him, but Merritt wasn't telling them everything. "Fine, but you've been lying to us. Bonnie didn't work at Daniel's. You should've known we'd talk to the owner."

He glared at her with red eyes. His skin had a grayness usually reserved for someone on his deathbed. Sorrow, or guilt?

"We don't think you killed her." Brooks smoothly took on the role of friend again. "But Investigator Prince is right. You're hiding something. You lied about Daniel's, and you lied about her cousin Sarah. Her parents say the two of them haven't spoken in years."

Brooks could have won millions with that poker face.

Merritt's brow furrowed. "They're lying. They talked all the time."

Erin pushed him a little further. "Why would grieving parents lie about something like that?" Was Merritt aware of the family estrangement? He claimed he and Bonnie didn't share deep thoughts. "Were there family issues?"

"I have no clue." He spread his arms wide across the table. "She talked about Sarah a lot. 'Sarah's so busy with school, Sarah's stressed. I need to call Sarah and check in on her.'"

Erin leaned forward, focusing all her attention on his reaction. "Did you know Bonnie was pregnant?"

The remaining color drained from his face. "I didn't." He stared ahead, not looking at Erin or Brooks. His chest jerked. "How far along?"

Will Merritt was either innocent or one hell of an actor. "Ten weeks," she said. "We'll need a DNA swab for paternity."

Will stiffened and straightened his tie. "It's awful, but the baby can't be mine. We used protection every time."

"Condoms break," Erin said. "And frankly, a baby is another motive for murder. I can't see you being too thrilled about knocking up someone like Bonnie."

"Stop talking about her like that," Merritt snapped. "You might think you know me because you come from all of this," he swept his arms around, "but I grew up barely above the poverty line. Both my parents worked two jobs. My uncle died from alcohol. My not being serious with Bonnie had zero to do with where she lived or her past. It had to do with what both of us wanted."

Erin refused to back down. "So you're saying she cheated on you?"

His face heated, but his gaze dropped down. "I told you we weren't exclusive." His lower lip trembled, and wetness brimmed in his eyes.

Will Merritt wasn't the one who didn't want a serious relationship. Erin reached into her bag and retrieved a tissue from the wrinkled packet. "All right, you cared about her. More than you want to admit. Fine. Maybe you think not telling us everything you know is protecting Bonnie's memory, but you're hurting our chances of finding out who did this."

Merritt's throat tightened, the veins in his forehead bulging with the effort not to cry. "I promised her I wouldn't tell anyone. Her parents would be devastated."

"They already are," Erin said. "Not getting closure will only make their lives worse." She glanced at Brooks out of the corner of her eye.

He nodded, and a foolish swell of pride rushed over Erin. Maybe she could do this job after all.

Merritt sagged down in the chair. "Bonnie was a stripper. Her parents don't know. She didn't want them to."

"Did you meet her at a strip club? When?" Brooks asked.

"At Sid's Gentleman's Club. A lot of men from Capitol Hill go there."

"For their nighttime meetings, right?" Erin asked dryly. "What would you call that? A power hard-on?"

Merritt ignored her. "It's strictly dancing. There's no hooking going on. Men paid Bonnie good money to dance. She never drank, never did drugs. She wasn't breaking her probation."

Erin jotted the name down. "Thank you. Did Bonnie tell you about being raped when she was fifteen?"

Merritt's chin dropped to his chest. "Yeah."

"Is that why she made the videos?"

Merritt's head shot up. "I didn't know about any videos at first. When I found out, I couldn't believe … I told her she deserved better. The things she did … the way she saw herself. It broke my heart."

"How did Bonnie react when you tried to talk to her about it?" Brooks asked.

"She wouldn't listen," Merritt said. "She'd close up completely and then ask me to leave. So I kept my mouth shut." Regret colored his tone.

Erin wanted to say something encouraging, but she could think of

STACY GREEN

nothing to make the man feel better. "Is that why she had so many bruises on her arms and legs?"

Merritt nodded. "She told her parents she was taking a self-defense class. I asked to have sex with the lights off—every time I saw the bruises, all I could think about was her allowing someone to treat her that way."

"Did Bonnie's having sex with other men bother you?" Erin asked.

"She only did it for the money," he said. "The way she saw herself bothered me. I thought things might get better ... and maybe she'd eventually change her mind." His chin wobbled, the muscles in his neck straining.

Erin pressed on. "Do you think that's what she wanted to talk about when she called yesterday?"

"I have no idea," Merritt said. "I couldn't sleep last night, thinking about what she wanted to tell me. What if the killer was already there, and she needed my help?"

"I don't think so." The white lie wouldn't hurt. Erin had no idea whether Bonnie had called Will Merritt for help, but he needed to hear he couldn't have helped her. "Any idea who she made the videos with? Was Sarah involved?"

Merritt's lips curled, his cheeks reddening. "No, and she never said anything about Sarah being involved. You need to ask her yourself."

"We're working on it," Erin said. "Do you have any idea why Sarah wouldn't call us back?"

Merritt shook his head. "Bonnie mentioned Sarah being under a ton of stress with her thesis. Maybe she's not checking her voicemail."

Except the story broke on the news this morning, and most people stayed glued to their phones, these days. Erin kept the thought to herself and pulled the second warrant out of her bag. "I'm sorry to have to do this, but this is the warrant for us to take your DNA. You have twenty-four hours to go to the Criminal Investigations Division on M Street, and one of the forensics people will swab you." She'd debated bringing the kit here and doing it herself, but she didn't want any issue if things went to court.

Merritt's fair skin turned green, but he nodded.

What would he do if the baby was his? It certainly wouldn't help his case for innocence. "If the baby's yours—"

"I don't think it's mine, but I want to know."

His grief oozed out of every pore. Erin longed to give the young man his space, but she had one final question. "Were there any little girls

80

in Bonnie's life—or yours?"

His eyebrows drew together, exhaustion etched into his handsome face. "What? No. Only child."

"What about anyone named Jane?" A long shot Erin had to take, but Merritt again shook his head no.

"Last question, I promise. Did Bonnie have any interest in history? Maybe criminal history? A lot of people like to read about serial killers and that sort of thing."

Deep lines etched into Merritt's forehead. "Not that I ever heard."

"Thank you for being honest. Please call me if you remember anything else."

The door swung open, and Erin's heart dropped all the way to her toes, yanking her confidence with it. Lisa stood there, looking perfectly chic, as usual. The black business suit accentuated her runner's figure, cropped black hair framed her tanned face, and bleached white teeth gleamed through a fake smile.

The daughter from Calvin Prince's previous marriage represented everything Erin never managed to achieve. Slim and tall, with a dazzling smile and dark eyes, Lisa's Italian heritage blessed her with the ability to tan, while Erin kept the sunscreen companies in business. Lisa embraced Calvin's conservative values, while Erin and Brad constantly questioned them. Erin hadn't lied when she said she and her father got along. They did. But more like acquaintances. Lisa had taken everything else.

"I heard you were here interviewing one of my employees without my permission." Lisa glanced at Brooks. "Is this your new partner?"

"Yes." Erin refused to cower. "We're here on a case. Will Merritt is a witness to a murder. I don't need your permission to interview him."

"This is a private company," Lisa countered. "I have a right to know what's going on behind closed doors, especially when it could affect our reputation."

"There's no threat to anyone's reputation." Erin felt suddenly protective of Will Merritt, who had turned meek in Lisa's presence.

Lisa held up her smartphone. "He found his girlfriend gutted in Columbia Heights." She glanced at Merritt. "Interesting company you keep, Mr. Merritt. I'd say the association could affect us. Nice picture, by the way."

Lisa held the phone out to Erin, but she refused to take it.

The salacious headline of Channel 4's web article said enough. *Slaughter on 16th Street.* A bad picture of Dan Mitchell bringing Bonnie out in a black bag accompanied the headline, along with a shot of Erin and Brooks standing on the porch. At least she'd been dressed nicely. But the photographer had taken the shot of her looking up at Brooks, an almost green expression on her face. Brooks, in turn, appeared to be the picture of calm. A professor assuring his student.

"Detective Brooks," Lisa said. "Your résumé is quite impressive. I speak for the entire city when I say I hope your experience helps find this terrible person. Erin's still new at this, so she will certainly need your help."

Lisa's sweet smile made Erin want to punch her.

"It's Investigator," Brooks said. "And Erin's doing fine. I'm still learning the ropes here. I didn't get your name, however."

Lisa brushed by Erin. "Lisa Prince, Executive Vice President of Information Systems and Global Solutions."

She offered a beautifully manicured hand to Brooks. Lisa kept her fingernails impeccable. Erin didn't have the patience or the time to get hers done.

"I'm sorry your first case is such a nasty one." She gave Erin a derisive look. "Mr. Merritt, I trust you're not a suspect in this terrible tragedy?"

White-faced, Merritt's head whipped back and forth like his neck muscles had become elastic. If Lisa saw him as a liability to Baker-Allen, she'd fire him without remorse.

"He's a material witness, and he's not required to tell you anything," Erin said. "This is a sensitive investigation. If any of it gets out, it could damage the case." Erin looked pointedly at Merritt. "The interview is confidential. Lisa, I'm sure you and Dad will understand."

Lisa caught the underlying threat, her mouth ticking up in a sneer. "No need to worry."

"Good." Erin walked toward the door, thinking she'd love to find a way to charge Lisa with interfering in an investigation if she ran her mouth. "Mr. Merritt, we'll see you later."

"Around six," Merritt said. As he exited, he ducked his head and mouthed a silent *thank-you* to Erin.

Her heart grew a tiny bit fond of him.

Brooks waited until Lisa sauntered through the door. "It was nice meeting you, but Erin and I need to get moving."

"Of course," Lisa said. "Erin, next time, call ahead. I'd love to catch up."

Erin grumbled and marched through the lobby.

Gomez waited at the administration desk. "Here are your copies,

Ms. Prince. You'll see Will Merritt didn't leave the building until nearly eight thirty last night."

"Thank you." She shoved open the heavy glass door and breathed in the wet air. Rain fell in a delicate mist. Its coolness did nothing for the anger pulsing through her.

"Wow." Brooks turned up the collar of his coat. "You two really hate each other."

"Hate's a strong word." Erin stomped across the parking lot. "It was that obvious?"

"You seriously could have cut the tension with a knife." Brooks stood next to the passenger door of her car.

"I'm sorry," Erin said. "Lisa loves making everyone else feel uncomfortable."

"I noticed. I admire you standing up for Merritt."

"I know what it's like to be helpless in her line of fire." She spat out her next words. "Do you feel the same way as Lisa?"

"About what?"

"My inexperience." Exhaustion and stress made her blunt. "You're working with a handicap on this case."

"Of course not. That article was ridiculous. The media's looking for the juiciest angle." He braced against the chill. "I'm lucky you got stuck with me."

Erin cleared her throat. "All right, then. Let's go to the strip club."

CHAPTER FIFTEEN

"Y ou know, I've only been to a strip club once," Brooks said as they parked across from Sid's Gentleman's Club on K Street. "Back during my vice days."

Erin raised her eyebrow. "Isn't going to a strip club a rite of passage for men?"

He shrugged. "My dad never told me things like that."

Erin caught the disdainful tone but didn't push it.

"Strippers never interested me." He glanced around. "I can see the top of the White House from here."

"Because it's basically around the corner. Less than a ten-minute walk."

Sid's made no attempt to hide its identity. A large, burgundy umbrella guarded the entryway, the club's name in bold white script. A sandwich shop sat right next door.

"Nice," Erin said as she opened the door to Sid's. "Get your fill of the girls dancing, get drunk, and go have a sub. Perfect single guy's night out."

She blinked, her eyes adjusting to the dim light. She hadn't been in one of these places since college, and Sid's was certainly nicer. A full bar with a large mirror took up most of the back wall, with the stage to the right. Sultry jazz music played over the speakers, but the stage stood empty. "I guess two in the afternoon is a slow time."

Brooks murmured in agreement as a curvy young woman dressed in black dress pants, a white shirt, and a red tie approached them. Her silken black hair hung around her face in thick waves, and her full lips were every man's fantasy. Her olive skin gleamed with the perfection of youth. Erin felt pasty, old, and chubby next to the young hostess.

"Can I help you?" The woman's husky voice bore a hint of an alluring Middle-Eastern accent, the lilt perfectly matching the mysteriousness of her green eyes.

This girl looked barely legal enough to serve alcohol.

"I'd like to talk to the manager or owner. Both, if possible."

The brunette cocked her head. "They usually only talk to people by appointment."

Erin unzipped her windbreaker to show her badge. "It's urgent."

The girl's eyes widened.

Erin envied her ability to use eyeliner without making a mess of it. "I'll be right back with the owner."

Erin and Brooks stood awkwardly between the tables and the stage. Sid's appeared to be cleaner than any of the clubs she'd gone to, but she still didn't want to sit in one of the booths.

The waitress returned with a man Erin would have never imagined as a strip club owner. He wasn't much taller than Erin, but his presence demanded attention, his jet black hair cut in a trendy style made to look messy. Rich, olive-colored skin contrasted perfectly against his white Oxford shirt. He'd left the first three buttons undone, revealing a smattering of chest hair and what appeared to be a Sanskrit tattoo on his collarbone.

His eyes met hers and he smiled—the kind of smile that invited a woman to confess her darkest secrets.

"I'm Yari Malek, owner of Sid's. How can we help the police? And before you ask, I'm a United States citizen. I was born here. My accent is from growing up surrounded by my family."

Behind his smile, Erin recognized the edge to his tone. He'd probably had to defend his citizenship to countless people since the 9/11 terrorist attacks on Washington, D.C. and New York City. She didn't condone the hatred or the generalization of an entire religion, but she didn't have time to soothe any bitter feelings Yari Malek might hold.

"We're not here about your citizenship, Mr. Malek." She matched his edge. "I'm sure you're telling the truth." She made a point to take a long, lingering look around the club. "Since you're a reputable businessman."

He grinned, his dark eyes twinkling. "All right. Please, call me Yari. How may I help you?"

"We're here about Bonnie Archer. She's one of your employees."

Malek nodded. "Part-time, evenings. She's due in tonight, actually." His wonderfully shaped, dark eyebrows knitted together. "Is she in some kind of trouble?"

Evidently, Malek didn't watch any more than the first few minutes of the news. "I'm sorry to tell you someone murdered Bonnie in her home last night."

Malek's attractive face sank into an appropriate shocked expression. His glossy eyes darted between Erin and Brooks. "My God. Do you have any leads?"

"People of interest," Brooks said. "Did you know Bonnie well?"

"As well as anyone else here, I suppose," Malek said. "She was a private girl. Not rude or antisocial, understand. She came in, did her job, and went home."

Sid's might cater to a higher-end clientele, but human needs all came down to the same basic things. "Her job ended at dancing?"

Malek grinned, but his tone was humorless. "We don't charge for sex, here. Of course, I can't control what the girls do after hours, but that's their business."

Erin wanted to tell him she didn't care whether he had a side business as long as it didn't affect her case. Instead, she asked another question. "How many nights a week did Bonnie work?"

"Two to three," he said. "She went to school as well."

"About how much did she make?"

"Depends on the day," Malek said. "We cater to a high end clientele, so my best girls easily make a couple grand a night after they pay the house."

Only in the sex industry would someone have to pay to work there. "So Bonnie could have been bringing home five or six thousand a week in cash?"

"Sounds about right." Malek nodded. "Why do you ask how much money she made?" He looked at Brooks as though he expected Erin's male counterpart to jump in at any moment.

Brooks said nothing, and Erin decided to change tactics. "I'm trying to learn all I can about her. Did she have any specific admirers? Guys who bothered her?"

Malek walked to the bar and waved off the beautiful hostess, who'd been watching their exchange with wide-eyed interest.

She obediently nodded and hurried out of sight.

Malek reached over the shiny wood counter and retrieved a bottle of bourbon. "Since you're on duty, I won't offer you a drink."

His silky voice held a teasing tone, and his dark eyes shined with a look Erin imagined made most women melt.

He grabbed a glass, poured two shots, and then downed them one after the other. "First off, an admirer and a man who bothers the girls are two different things. Admirers come back during the same girl's shift and give great tips. The creeps try to follow them home."

"Did that ever happen to Bonnie?" Brooks asked.

"Not that she told me." Malek set the glass on the counter with a thud. "I have security to keep an eye on my ladies. I think if anyone had been a problem, I would have heard about it."

"Did you or the other dancers notice bruises on Bonnie?" Brooks asked.

Malek shrugged. "As long as the girls look good on the stage, I don't pay any attention. Several of the ladies are excellent with makeup. Bonnie likely covered any marks. You'd have to ask the other dancers."

"What about admirers?" Erin pressed.

"Bonnie didn't really have anyone specific." Malek looked down at his empty glass, his tone growing soft. "Certainly not because she wasn't beautiful. She had an ethereal quality that made men want to watch from a distance. Almost like she stood on a pedestal. She didn't have to fully disrobe to keep their interest."

"So she was a snob?"

"No!" Malek shook his head. "She just seemed kind of ... too sweet and delicate for this, which draws a certain man. Those men tip nicely but are looking for a different experience."

"They want to see a real dancer instead of bump and grinding?" Brooks asked.

"Yes, these men are looking for more mystery than flash. Bonnie showed less skin than the others, but she matched their earnings." His gold ring glinted beneath the yellow bar lights. "Wait, I almost forgot about Tori."

Erin's pen paused. "Tori?"

Malek's soft lips inched into a smile. "An older gentleman who prefers to dress like a woman. He used to come in every week, but there was an issue with Bonnie a couple of months ago."

"You're saying Tori is a cross-dresser?" Erin could hardly grasp the significance of Malek's information. *Jack might have dressed like a woman to avoid detection.*

"A very skilled one. Always elaborately made up, dressed impeccably, with a stylish black wig. A real gentleman. Or lady. I'm not sure of the politically correct term."

"And something happened with Bonnie and Tori?" Erin asked.

"She danced for him once—a lap dance. He must have said something she didn't like because she grew angry, yelling at him. My security asked him to leave. He never returned, and Bonnie never mentioned him."

"She didn't say what they argued about?"

Malek shrugged. "She only said she couldn't believe the balls on him." He smiled wryly. "Her phrasing, not mine."

"What about friends?" Erin asked. "Did Bonnie ever talk about anyone staying with her? Her boyfriend?"

A muscle in Yari Malek's jaw twitched. He reached again for the bottle of bourbon but didn't pour another glass. "Bonnie never talked about boyfriends, but we all had the impression school kept her too busy. As to your first question, no. She didn't have anyone staying with her that I'm aware of."

"Bonnie was pregnant," Brooks said.

Malek's face darkened. "I wondered."

"Why?" Erin asked. "I don't think she was showing yet."

"She stopped having drinks. She always needed a cocktail before her shift to loosen up. But a few weeks ago, she stopped. She quit smoking, too. She said she needed to get healthy, but I sensed she wasn't being honest."

"And you have no idea who the father might be?"

Malek's dark eyes flashed, his chin jutting out. Had she pushed him too far? "I didn't know she had a boyfriend."

Erin glanced at Brooks. The frustration on his face matched her own. Bonnie kept to herself, and no one knew a damned thing about her. The broken record grated, and it wasn't going to help them catch her killer.

"I'll need a list of your employees. Please tell them to call me, especially if they know about Tori." Erin handed him a card and watched him pocket it.

"Why do you need a list?"

"Background checks," Brooks said. "No offense to your establishment, but women in this line of work tend to have a different social circle. We need to make sure everyone checks out."

"I run background checks on all of my girls." His jaw muscles flexed, his tone hinging on unpleasant.

Brooks smiled. "I assure you the police department will be more thorough."

Malek nodded stiffly and then called for the girl who'd greeted them. He told her to make a list of employee names. "But I can't give out personal information."

"Of course not," Erin said. "Make sure you give them my number."

"I'll gather them all tonight and let them know. Most of them are working, since it's Thursday. That's when Sid's gets busy."

He sagged against the bar. "I don't understand why this sort of thing happens to good people like Bonnie."

Brooks stared at him for a long time without saying anything, but Erin sensed a question brewing. Brooks didn't disappoint her.

"What about her cousin, Sarah? Did Bonnie ever mention her? Or a friend named Jane?"

Malek smiled and poured another drink. "Jane? I don't know anyone by that name. But Sarah's the one person Bonnie talked about. They seemed close."

"I thought so," Brooks said. "What can you tell us about Sarah?"

"She's a student at American University, getting her master's, I believe," Malek said. "Surely, you've informed the family?"

"We have," Erin said, "but Sarah hasn't returned our calls."

"There is some family discord," Malek said.

Erin perked up. So had Bonnie confided in this man but not Will Merritt? "Bonnie told you about her family issues?"

"Only briefly," Malek said. "She and Sarah came in shortly after they reunited. Bonnie mentioned it when I gave them drinks on the house."

"Did Bonnie ever mention spending time with a friend who had a young daughter?" Erin asked.

"No," Malek said. "But I told you—"

"You weren't close," Erin finished.

The brunette returned with a list of about twenty people—all women, including the bartenders.

Brooks made a humming noise, looking at Erin. "I'm good here if you are."

"For now." She nodded to Malek. "Don't forget to get the message to the girls."

Erin's mouth watered at the scent of fresh bread coming from the sandwich shop. The dreary day had stretched into late afternoon, and they had skipped lunch.

She checked her watch. "The director at the Adult Learning Center leaves at five. If we want to talk to her about Bonnie's interaction with the staff and students, we need to hurry."

Brooks stopped near the sub shop's door. "Do we at least have time to grab a sandwich?"

Erin's stomach issued a growl worthy of a hungry grizzly. "Absolutely."

While their sandwiches were being prepared, Erin made a few phone calls and then joined Brooks at the table.

"So Sarah's at AU. I called in a favor and got her roommate's name from the registrar. Fowler found the address. It's about six blocks away from the university. He stopped by, and the roommate said Sarah's been staying at her parents' house the past few days."

"You've got a contact at American University?" Brooks asked.

"My alma mater and my parents still contribute to the alumni fund. Sometimes you have to wade into the muck to get results."

Brooks chewed slowly, clearly savoring his ham and cheese. "Sarah's lack of response bugs me."

"Yeah, but think about it," Erin said. "Bonnie's parents didn't know they reconciled, so it's safe to say Sarah's didn't, either. If she's hunkered down working on her thesis, maybe she didn't hear about it until this morning. And she's trying to find a way to talk to us without alerting her father. Trust me, I know the exact kind of cloth someone like Simon Archer is cut from. The National Governors Association would disapprove of his niece—and that's a high priority for someone like him."

She took a swig of Diet Coke. "You know what bugs me? Everyone talks about Bonnie being this nice, private girl. Her boss at the strip club says she wasn't the sexually promiscuous type, yet she's filming porn. No one really knew her at all. Now we've got a cross-dresser in the mix, who pissed Bonnie off."

"Jack the Ripper's alleged way of escaping," Brooks said. "But cross-dressing isn't that uncommon. Tori may be a coincidence."

Erin rubbed her aching head. "I feel like we've got a bunch of threads and no way to tie them together."

"Things aren't always so neat," Brooks said. "Sometimes you have to keep grabbing at the threads until the right one sticks out."

CHAPTER SIXTEEN

Charlie paced, no longer able to stay in his hiding spot. He pointed his finger at Mina. "You shouldn't have called her."

Mina's eyes turned liquid. "The princess can help us."

"No one can help us, Mina. It's just you and me together, like it's always been."

The little girl sniffled. "But I saw her on TV."

Charlie wanted to bang his head against the wall. Why did he get saddled with the kid again? He felt bad for thinking it. Mina didn't have anyone else. "Just because you saw her on TV doesn't mean she can help us."

Mina's cherub lips trembled. "Then what do we do? I don't want it to happen again!"

"Be quiet," he hissed. "There's nothing we can do but lay low and hope it's over soon." He didn't believe that, but he wouldn't scare Mina.

He mustered his silly smile, the one that always made her laugh. "Close your eyes and rest, now."

CHAPTER SEVENTEEN

The sky remained the color of steel, but the mist stopped by the time Erin and Brooks arrived in the Edgewood neighborhood of northeast D.C. Nestled between Rhode Island Avenue and Michigan Avenue, Edgewood was yet another area struck by gentrification. Many of the 1900s row houses had already been renovated, and young professionals gave the area an up-and-coming vibe. New shops and restaurants had popped up since the last time Erin came out here on one of her first sex crimes cases.

A woman had caught her live-in boyfriend molesting her six-year-old daughter. Erin sat with the woman while she described what she'd witnessed, allowing her then-partner to ask all the questions. After they'd left the woman's house, Erin had to pull over to throw up. Brad talked her out of transferring to another department.

"It's a stepping stone to homicide," he'd said. "The big leagues. Isn't that where you want to be?"

At the time, she'd said yes. Thinking about the slaughter of Bonnie Archer's body, Erin wasn't so sure.

Homicide meant the opportunity for big cases and making a real difference. And the chance to finally prove to her sister and father that becoming a cop meant something. She took pride in her job, and not making a lot of money didn't change that. As far as being in the headlines or on the nightly news, she'd had enough notoriety to last a lifetime.

She parked at the far end of the Adult Learning Center lot. The new car had been a present to herself for her birthday, and she didn't want door dings in the first six months of owning it.

Brooks stepped out and looked around. "Decent neighborhood," he said. "I like the old row houses in this city. So many different ones, like home. All with stories to tell."

"They are pretty cool." She and Brad considered buying in one of the older neighborhoods, but she wanted Abby to go to the safest and best schools without being completely sheltered. So they'd ended up in Arlington, investing in a duplex and enrolling Abby in private school.

"A lot of them have original fixtures like clawfoot tubs and crown molding. They also have the shitty wiring and bad heating." She turned her attention to the Academy of Hope's three-story brick building. Trees stood on either side. Their dying fall colors would soon give way to gray skies, ice, and snow. Joy.

"It looks like a community center," Brooks commented.

"It was," Erin said. The L-shaped structure had freshly cleaned bricks and a cheerful portico at the entrance. Welcoming and safe. "Two teachers started the academy in the eighties. They worked out of a church. This is their third location, thanks to a big grant." She led the way to the entrance.

Inside smelled clean and new, along with the distinct academia scent of printed papers, brewing coffee, and microwaved lunch. A reception desk sat in the middle of the wide hallway.

A woman with a bright smile and dangly skull earrings smiled at them. "Can I help you?"

Erin and Brooks showed their badges. "We're investigating the murder of Bonnie Archer. Is the director available?"

The receptionist's smile disappeared. "I saw it on the news this morning. Who would hurt her like that?" She tugged at a string on her orange sweater. The Halloween kitty's eye had started to unravel. "Bonnie was so nice."

"You knew her well?" Brooks slouched against the tall counter, unthreatening.

"Not well," she said. "Just in passing. But she stood out. Never in a bad mood, always said hello and goodbye. Always asked about my day. Just a happy person." She blinked, her heavy mascara ghosting against her skin. "I can't understand it."

"We can never truly understand these things," Brooks said. "All we can do is find justice for her." He offered a kind smile. "The director?"

"Yes, of course. Dr. Key's office is down the hall, the first room on the right. We've got an open-door policy."

"Thank you," Brooks said. "Are most of the classrooms upstairs, then?"

"Yes." The skull earrings danced. "We use the downstairs for social areas and meetings."

"Social areas?" Erin asked.

"We believe an informal environment with a solid academic structure makes adult students feel more at home. We encourage them to socialize and get to know one another. They're the only ones who can empathize with each other. A lot of students end up having study groups in the downstairs areas."

"Did you ever see Bonnie in any of these groups?" Erin asked.

"Yes," she said. "During the summer."

Erin leaned onto the counter, lowering her voice. "Any chance you could tell me the names of the students in her group?"

Wide eyes answered her. "I'm not allowed to for privacy reasons. You'd have to ask the director."

"Thank you," Erin said. "We'll see ourselves to her office."

Erin stopped at the first open office door.

A Black woman looked over her tortoiseshell reading glasses. "Hello. Can I help you?"

Erin and Brooks introduced themselves.

"We need to speak with you about Bonnie Archer," Erin said.

"I thought we'd be hearing from you." She took off her glasses and rubbed her eyes. "Stephanie Key."

She looked to be in her mid-forties, with a few wrinkles around her eyes. Her glowing ebony skin needed no makeup, and her gray suit made her appear professional yet stylish.

She motioned to the chairs in front of her desk. "Please, sit."

Erin sat and pulled out her notebook. She could barely decipher her earlier notes. "To confirm, you're the director of the Adult Learning Center, correct?"

Dr. Key nodded. "Yes, of both our GED program and our Pathways program, although each one has its own coordinator."

"Pathways is a different program?" Brooks questioned.

"It's for students with a diploma or GED who will enter the workforce or go on to college. We have readiness programs for each."

"Which Bonnie was interested in, right?" Erin asked.

"After she completed her GED." Dr. Key reached for the phone. "Why don't I invite the GED coordinator to talk, as well? He would know more about Bonnie than I do."

Erin and Brooks waited while she made the phone call, speaking quietly.

"Thank you." Dr. Key hung up the phone. "Brian is on his way down. He's in-between meetings."

"Do the coordinators also teach?" Erin asked.

"No," she said. "Our coordinators deal with the Department of Education and the local schools. They facilitate teacher training and student tracks. Brian makes it a point to connect with all his students. I knew Bonnie in passing and by reputation. He's spent time with her." She leaned back in her chair, rubbing the tender skin beneath her eyes.

"Please tell me you have an idea of who did this."

Brooks sidestepped the question. "We're working very hard. What can you tell us about your students?"

Dr. Key considered for a moment. "Our GED program is a mixed bag. We have young adults, like Bonnie, who made poor choices in their early lives but are getting back on track. We've also got older adults who want to get their GED, as well as foreign-born students."

"What about social class?" Erin asked. "Are most of these people from lower socio-economic backgrounds?"

Stephanie Key smiled. "You don't have to worry about political correctness, Investigator Prince. Yes, most of the students are poor. Many of them grew up on the streets or ended up there. Our minority segment is larger, but not by much. We have plenty of white students, too."

A knock on the door stopped Erin from asking her next question. She and Brooks turned to see a tall, sandy-haired man with wonderfully broad shoulders standing in the doorway. He smiled at them, revealing perfect teeth. An all-American poster boy, and the sort she'd never gone for, but looking at his blue eyes, she could see making an exception.

"Brian Reese." He extended his hand. "And this is Vanessa Carrington."

A short woman with spiky hair stood behind him.

"Vanessa is the language arts teacher. Bonnie needed to finish language arts for her GED, and spent a lot of time with her."

Brooks stood and motioned for the petite teacher to sit.

Red streaked her eyes, and her tawny skin appeared pale. "I keep thinking this isn't happening." Her voice trembled. "It's a nightmare."

Brian Reese wedged into the small space between Dr. Key's desk and her bookshelves. "How can we help you?"

Erin cleared her throat. "Tell us about Bonnie's time here. Was she a good student?"

"Oh yes," Vanessa said. "She flew through her math course, but had some issues with reading and writing. She worked hard, and she always had a good attitude. One of those people who brightened a room." Vanessa played with a loose button on her sleeve, twisting it until it popped off.

"She wanted to enter the Pathways program once she earned her GED," Brian said. "She was set to finish this spring and, assuming she passed the GED test, would enter Pathways in the fall."

"Did you spend much time with her?" Erin asked.

Brian crossed his arms, making his biceps bulge, and furrowed his brow. "Not a lot. When students enter the program, they work with me to figure out their course schedule. Then, if they have any issues, they can always come to me. Since Bonnie started, I only saw her in passing until she stopped in to talk about Pathways a few weeks ago. She was excited about it, and I was excited for her."

Beautiful and young, Bonnie clearly knew how to attract men, at least when being paid for it. Brian Reese was flat-out hot. He didn't look the sort who would need any help getting a girl, and Erin didn't know too many women who wouldn't have been attracted to him. "So your relationship with the students is from afar, essentially. Unless a question or problem arises."

"Exactly," Brian said.

"When did you last see Bonnie?"

"I've been away at a conference," he said. "I flew home late last night, so I haven't seen her—or any of the students—for nearly a week. But we hadn't spoken much since we discussed Pathways. Just exchanges in the hall."

Erin caught Brooks's eye. Nice of Reese to offer his alibi.

"We'll need to confirm you being out of town." Brooks said the words casually.

Brian cocked his head. "Really?"

"Anyone with any contact with Bonnie is a person of interest," Brooks said. "We've got to rule out everyone we possibly can."

"Of course." He crossed one ankle in front of the other, unfazed. "What do you need?"

"Do you still have your boarding pass?" Brooks asked.

"I probably do. I crashed as soon as I got home and then rushed to work. I might have the parking receipt, too."

Convenient. "Those would be great. We can send a uniform to pick them up later."

"Anything I can do to help." He caught Erin's gaze and smiled at her, his blue eyes bright.

Erin turned her attention to Vanessa. "You knew her best among the staff? What was she like? Did she have any issues with anyone?"

"Sweet. Smart. Caring." Vanessa wiped her constantly watering eyes. "I told you she brightened the room. We all liked her."

"Did you or anyone else ever notice her being bruised or injured in any way?" Brooks asked. "Anything that might have prompted you to ask her if she needed help?"

All three staff members shook their heads.

Erin suspected Bonnie kept her bruises hidden. "She participated in a study group this summer?"

"A math group," Vanessa said. "Math came easily to her, and she wanted to help other students. She spent a couple of hours tutoring a few times every week."

"So she interacted with a lot of students." Brooks looked at Dr. Key with the expression of a boy caught digging into the cookie jar. "I don't suppose we could have a list of your enrolled GED students?"

"Absolutely not without a warrant, as I'm sure you expected," the director said.

They had no probable cause for a warrant. Not yet, anyway. "Are there any students she spent more time with than others? Any she might have hung out with outside of class?"

Vanessa thought before answering. "I don't know for sure, but my gut says no."

"Why?" Erin leaned forward. "I thought she was a social butterfly."

Vanessa pulled a tissue out of the pocket of her baggy sweater. "I'm not using the right terminology. She came to learn, and while she was nice, she didn't spend her time talking and getting to know people." Vanessa shook her head. "I got the distinct impression she wanted to keep her private life private."

"How so?" Brooks pressed. "Can you give us an example?"

Vanessa thought about it for a moment. "Before class and during breaks, most students chatter about something other than school. Bonnie listened, but she wasn't very talkative."

"Did you ever ask her about friends and family?" Erin kept an eye on Brian Reese. He knew the students and likely counseled them on some level. He struck her as the kind of man who could easily convince a woman to confide in him. His expression gave nothing away, his gaze on the teacher, seemingly unaware of Erin's observation.

"I did ask whether she had people supporting her at home," Vanessa said. "She told me her parents were supportive and were helping her with her homework. Her cousin, as well."

And, right back to Sarah. They needed to find her soon. A troubling thought brewed in the back of Erin's mind. She stowed it and asked her next question. "What about a boyfriend? Did Bonnie have one?"

All three shook their heads.

"She stayed focused on school," Vanessa said. "She worked part-time, but she mentioned once she didn't have time for anything serious."

That at least backed up Will Merritt's side of the story.

"There was one student," Brian Reese said. "I never thought anything about it, but I saw her leave with him a few times. Walking in the direction of the Metro. I assume they both rode the same line, but they seemed friendly."

"What was his name?" Erin leaned forward, hoping for a response.

Brian glanced at Dr. Key and her face hardened, the fine lines around her mouth deepening.

"It's not a privacy violation," he argued. "You're not giving his information out."

She stared at him for several tense seconds before nodding.

"Ricky Stout," Brian said. "Brilliant kid, just twenty-one. He grew up in Anacostia, so you can imagine what he's seen. He's in the Pathways program."

"Another Black male who made it out and won't make it to the news," Stephanie Key said, a sharp edge creeping into her voice. "He's worked hard to get his life straightened out."

"Is Ricky in class today?" Erin asked.

Dr. Key shook her head. "Not until tomorrow night. I'm sorry, but you'll need a warrant if you want any other information on a student."

Brooks seemed satisfied, but after Dr. Key's last comment, Erin wanted to know why the woman remained so protective over one student's privacy when another had been brutally murdered.

CHAPTER EIGHTEEN

"Sarah's still not answering, so I called her dad. Simon Archer refused to take my call until I told him Calvin Prince was my father." Disgust colored Erin's tone. Simon Archer had kissed her ass when his assistant finally put the call through.

She reached for the half-full coffee pot and took a careful whiff. Semi-fresh. Good enough. "You should have heard the guy. 'Ms. Prince, the National Governors are so grateful for your father's monetary contributions. He's made a huge difference in our cause.'" She dumped two sugars into the coffee and stirred. "Then I asked him whether he knew his niece had been murdered last night. Tone completely changed."

"Why else did he think you were calling?" Brooks clutched two donuts wrapped in a flimsy napkin.

The corners of Erin's mouth crept up. "I may have forgotten to mention I was a cop."

Brooks's laugh was a lot heartier than she would have expected. "Well done. What did he say?"

They walked toward Sergeant Clark's office to debrief him. "He'd heard the news. Such a tragedy, but her lifestyle. Blah, blah, blah. I asked him about Sarah, and he got defensive."

"Did you tell him they were in contact?"

"No. I wanted to wait. I said her name came up as family, and we needed to talk to her. He said the same thing as his brother, 'the girls haven't spoken in years.' He said Sarah is staying at their house, hunkering down on her master's thesis." She gave her coffee another stir. "Just like I thought—Sarah's probably trying to find the chance to call without raising her parents' suspicion. Simon didn't try to hide his disapproval of his niece."

"Did he offer the information about Sarah willingly?"

Erin took a sip of coffee and scowled. Every time she drank the station coffee, she swore she'd buy a single-serve machine along with a huge supply of pods. "He told me his daughter's whereabouts were none of my business."

During their conversation, Simon Archer had dripped venom, but his constant references to Erin's father pissed her off.

"So I told him I knew what it was like to be close to your parents and that this whole thing reminded me I needed to catch up with my father today. He took the hint." She wished she could have been in Archer's office to see the look on his face. "Did you get anything back on Ricky Stout?"

"A sealed juvenile record. Not surprising. Last known address was a shelter two years ago. Still, it's worth swinging by."

Sergeant Clark's door stood open, and he motioned them inside. "Please tell me you've got something. Bonnie's parents have already called me twice today."

Brooks ran through what they had so far, which amounted to a pile of questions and no answers.

"I still think we could be looking for a female killer hung up on the idea of Jack the Ripper being a woman," Erin said.

Clark rubbed the muscles in his shoulder. "Brooks, what do you think?"

Nerves tightened Erin's stomach. Would Brooks make her look like a fool?

"I'm not completely against it," he finally said. "I think we've got to follow the leads we have, and other than the papers, we don't have anything leading to a woman—yet. We need to keep our eyes open, though."

Erin filled Clark in on the phone call with Simon Archer. "So, Sarah is safe, but if she knew about Bonnie's sex videos, she might be in danger. And she's our best link to Bonnie."

"Ricky Stout, too, who may only be an acquaintance," Brooks reminded her. "His is the only name we've got. Any chance we can get a warrant for his contact information?"

"Come on." Clark rocked back in his chair, and the headrest smacked the back wall. "How many years have you been a cop? We don't have probable cause, and no judge will be eager to issue a warrant to put another Black man in jail without something rock solid. Get a phone number and match it to Bonnie's records. Then, maybe."

"There's nothing in the system for him," Brooks said. "He hasn't filed taxes. Every online search came back with the wrong Ricky Stout. He's got class tomorrow night. We should pay the school another visit, hang around."

Erin winced. "You'll have to go without me," she said. "Abby's got a school thing I can't miss." She'd promised her daughter she would attend her concert.

"No problem," Brooks said. "I'll keep you updated."

"The drug clinic sent over the records," Clark continued. "Bonnie was clean. Merritt came in for his DNA swab, too."

Erin checked her watch. "He wasn't supposed to come until six."

Clark shrugged. "He got off early today. Our computer guys checked the security footage from Baker-Allen. Merritt did exactly what he said he did, and there's no evidence of tampering."

Erin hoped her sister hadn't fired Will Merritt. The guilt would eat at Erin until she had to do something, which would be calling their father. Cue a fresh battle between her and Lisa.

Clark's chair creaked as he reached for a note on his desk. "What about the strip club owner?"

"Sarah came into the club a few times to see Bonnie, and we have the list of employees. We'll run them through the system, see whether they've got anything interesting in their backgrounds and who their known associates are."

Clark nodded. "Yari Malek's number is listed in Bonnie's cell contacts, but there's only a couple of calls to him. He's her boss, so it's not unusual."

"What's the status on her full phone records?" Brooks asked. "We need more than the call log on her phone."

"At least another day. They have the warrant, but the fucking companies are more concerned about a lawsuit over privacy violations than helping out a murder investigation." Clark sat upright. "Temple hasn't released Bonnie Archer yet. She's waiting on some additional tests, and she's asked the forensic anthropologist to examine Bonnie, as well. Apparently, some of the cuts nicked the bones." He glowered. "Which means her parents are stuck in limbo and frustrated. With some of the shock worn off, they may be able to tell us more. I'd like to know what caused the family divide because it obviously affected Bonnie's life."

"I'll call Mrs. Archer," Brooks said. "Hopefully, I can talk with her before we speak with Sarah. Do we have anything on the fingerprints from Bonnie's apartment?"

Clark nodded. "Merritt's were found in the bedroom and living room, as we expected. Nowhere near the body. At least two other sets of prints don't match anyone in the system. The lab is still working on the rest of the trace evidence Marie's people collected. And I'm trying to get a rush on the fetal DNA." He glanced at Erin, suddenly looking far older than just a few days ago. "Any more strange calls?"

"Not yet." Erin hedged, unsure whether she wanted to know the answer to her next question. "Have you read the article on Channel 4's website?"

Clark curled his lips as though the air in the room had gone sour. "That reporter likes her tabloid shit," Clark said. "Nothing she said matters. What matters is what's going on right now. Make something happen."

Brooks's call to the Archers turned out to be a bust. They wanted answers the police couldn't give, and their limited knowledge of their daughter was increasingly apparent.

A chill raked up Erin's spine. How many years did she have before Abby stopped sharing every minute detail of her day and became a sullen teenager who thought the world—including her mother—was against her? Could Erin navigate those teenage years well enough to keep Abby out of trouble? Would she become a bigger hypocrite and use her family connections if Abby got in trouble?

Her father had done as much with Lisa, and she'd turned out to be a cold, successful bitch living a shallow existence, feeding off the misery she inflicted on others. Lisa had never been held accountable for any of her behaviors.

Thinking about her sister made Erin remember Lisa's smug words from earlier. Maybe if she sucked it up and read the damned article, she could put it out of her mind.

Bonnie's murder remained on Channel 4's home page. The "Princess" reference stood out in bold beneath the picture of herself, Brooks, and Clark talking on Bonnie's porch. Titles identified the men, Sergeant, and Investigator, respectively. Erin's caption read: *New homicide member Erin Prince—known as "the Princess" among the ranks—is the daughter of Washington power-elite Calvin Prince.*

Red danced in her vision. Forget about the princess dig. How about the misogyny? What century did they live in?

"It's bullshit." Fowler leaned against her desk, offering her Hershey's Miniatures, this time.

Erin took three and steamed. "Some asshole uniform who thinks he should be a homicide cop talked to that reporter who always wears a skirt barely covering her ass. It's the closest he'll get to the real investigation."

Erin couldn't defend herself or speak out against the reporter, and it burned the hell out of her. Freedom of speech didn't exist for everyone. "It's not just the nickname. Did you read the caption? They might as well have said I was a secretary! I didn't realize we'd jumped back in time."

Fowler shook more chocolate into her outstretched hand. "They're going with the angle that sells. It's just a way to get Calvin Prince's name in the article and get more hits. Don't you know anything about metadata?"

She chewed the last chocolate. "This is why women still fight to be equal, because of those who rely on their *ass*ets more than their brains. Like that reporter."

"Fuck her. Focus on the victim. This job isn't about accolades. It's about bringing in scum-sucking criminals before someone else gets hurt. So do your job, Princess." Fowler winked at her and sauntered off.

Her phone vibrated, and a blocked number flashed on the screen. Erin's insides twisted into a painful knot. "Erin Prince, Homicide."

Soft, rapid breathing filtered over the line. "Is this the Princess?"

Erin snapped her fingers, signaling to Brooks. He wheeled his chair over, and she moved the phone from her ear so he could hear. She didn't want the little girl to hear office sounds and hang up.

"Hi, sweetheart. I'm glad you called again. Will you tell me your name?"

A couple of seconds of silence and then, "Mina."

"Mina. That's so pretty. Do you need help, Mina?"

"It's going to happen again if you don't stop it." Mina's voice trembled with tears.

Erin's stomach bottomed out. She struggled to keep her tone even and not barrage the girl. Mina couldn't be more than five or six. She might clam up if Erin started badgering her. "What's going to happen again?"

Mina didn't answer right away, and Erin worried she'd hung up.

Then the child sniffled. "Me and Charlie are in trouble. That's why I called again, even though he said not to."

"Who's Charlie?"

"He's the boy who takes care of me, but that's not what I'm tryin' to tell you." Childlike impatience mixed in with Mina's fear.

"I'm sorry."

Brooks slid a note across her desk. *Give your desk number. Can trace call.*

"Mina, can you do me a favor?" Erin asked. "This is my cell phone, and it's about to die. I really want to hear what you have to say. Can you call this number?" She recited her direct line.

Mina spoke as though she didn't hear it. "We're so scared," the little girl whispered. "Poor Bonnie."

Erin's heart stopped. "Who are you scared of?"

"Bonnie was nice to us." Mina's words shook with the effort not to cry.

Her desperate voice made Erin think of her own little girl sitting safely at home with Brad. The sudden urge to take her daughter into her arms nearly overwhelmed her. "Mina, is the person you're afraid of named Jane?"

"I can't tell you. But it's going to happen again." Mina's bell-like voice made the words sound more ominous. "Bye."

The call ended. Erin threw the phone across her desk and knocked a plastic holder full of pens onto the floor. "Brooks, we've got to find Mina."

CHAPTER NINETEEN

Frantic calls were placed to child services. No Mina in the system. To NCMEC—no Mina listed as missing. No Mina associated with any active cases or known criminals. A search for Charlie came up with three kids in the system, with only one older than ten. They are the foster parents for all three, and they denied knowing anyone named Mina or Bonnie Archer. Juvenile arrest records pulled up half a dozen Charlies. Tomorrow, Erin and Brooks would start tracking them down.

Erin took two aspirin and turned toward Brooks. After talking to the Archers yet again, Brooks looked as sick as she felt. Bags bloomed beneath his eyes. His narrow face seemed longer, his cheeks hollowed out. His five o'clock shadow only made him look haggard. "You get anything from Bonnie's parents?"

He tossed back his umpteenth cup of coffee before answering. "They don't know anyone named Mina or Charlie—Bonnie never mentioned any children to them. And they stick to not knowing a Jane, for that matter."

Erin watched the digital clock switch to nine p.m. She didn't want to add up the hours she'd worked today. "Did you tell them about the pregnancy?"

He shook his head. "I'll leave that to the medical examiner. Coward's way out, but I didn't want to tell them over the phone."

"Can't blame you." The Archers' pain was about to multiply astronomically. Erin selfishly thanked God she didn't have to witness it, but she considered that a small respite compared to the heavy load on her conscience. Mina had called Erin for help twice. If she was the next victim, Erin was to blame.

Erin closed her eyes, replaying the words over. What had she missed?

Her desk phone rang.

She dived for it. "Erin Prince, Homicide."

Instead of Mina's little voice, the officer manning the front entrance coughed like he was trying to hack up a load of phlegm and then said, "Sarah Archer is here."

Sarah Archer waited in the same interview room Will Merritt had sat in last night, in the chair closest to the window. She hugged her knees tightly to her chest, her strawberry blonde hair trailing across her reed-thin legs. Her small feet rested in front of her on the chair, her lithe body drawn into an impossibly tight position. Erin hadn't been flexible before she had a child, let alone after. Sarah'd chewed her fingernails to the quick. Her pale, youthful skin radiated even with minimal makeup.

A small surge of jealousy nagged Erin. As a child, she was the chubby kid in the corner with the wavy brown hair who didn't quite fit in. Her last name was the only reason many kids socialized with her. Eventually, she'd grown out of her ugly duckling phase. Still, she'd never quite shed the mental state, especially when she perpetually carried an extra ten pounds no matter how much effort she put into losing them.

"Hi, Sarah," Erin said. "I'm Investigator Erin Prince, and this is my partner, Investigator Brooks."

"Hi." Sarah's soft voice shook as she rocked back and forth.

"I'm very sorry about your cousin," Erin said. "Thank you so much for coming in to talk with us."

Tears welled from Sarah's closed eyes and seeped onto her cheeks. "I can't believe it. Poor Bonnie."

Sarah's teary eyes focused on Erin. They were two different colors: one brown and one startlingly blue. Not exactly a rare phenomenon, but still unsettling.

Erin turned one of the free chairs around, so she faced Sarah. "Why didn't you return my calls?"

"I've been at my parents'." Sarah played with the gold watch on her left hand, turning it in fast circles. "Working on my thesis. I shut off my phone. I heard about Bonnie this morning. The horrible things they said about her ..."

"Because of Bonnie's drug history?" Brooks asked.

"Apparently, she must have been asking for it." She made a disgusted noise. "My parents are judgmental, and they don't forget." She wiped her eyes. "When I tracked her down a few months ago, I was amazed at how hard she had worked to stay sober and get on her feet. Anyway, I couldn't listen to them, so I left for the day. When I got home, my father told me you'd called him."

Erin kept her voice calm and soothing, hoping to get Sarah to relax. "Your parents aren't aware the two of you reconciled?"

"They are now." Her soft voice took on a hardened edge. "I'm not concerned about their feelings anymore. I only kept it from them for Bonnie's sake. Her parents would have been upset."

"Can you tell us about the family falling out?" Erin fought the tension rising in her. They might finally have someone willing to talk about the rift.

Sarah focused on her slender hands as if debating whether to betray her family's trust. When she looked up again, those strange eyes gleamed with determination.

"The summer she was eight, and I was six, a family friend sexually abused Bonnie. They didn't want to believe the truth, but Bonnie's parents did. They took her away and got her counseling, but I guess it didn't work. By the time she turned fourteen, she was having sex and doing drugs. She hated herself." Sarah wiped away new tears. "Then she got raped. It took her a long time to get straightened out, but she did. This is so unfair."

Erin handed the girl a tissue and gave her a moment. No wonder Bonnie's parents remained bitter. If Brad allowed something like that to happen and then didn't believe her daughter, she'd never forgive him.

Sarah's slender body curled tighter, her hands locked around her knees and her bleary eyes focused somewhere to the right of Erin. She loosened her grip to chew on a fingernail, still not making eye contact.

Erin's grip tightened on the box of tissues. "Sarah, were you abused by your parents' friend, too?"

Sarah's contrasting eyes locked with Erin's, her posture rigid. "No, of course not. Why would you ask that?" She perched on the chair, muscles tensed, ready to bolt.

Because I know how to spot a victim of sexual abuse.

Erin called on her expertise in working sex crimes. "It's a logical question. Your father's friend abused Bonnie, and the two of you spent a lot of time together. It makes sense he would move on to you once Bonnie was removed from the picture."

Sarah's hair whipped back and forth. "My parents didn't allow that to happen. I was never alone with him after that." A muscle in her cheek twitched. "Which tells me deep down they knew Bonnie was telling the truth. My father's reputation was just more important."

"Your parents are still friends with Bonnie's abuser?" Brooks flipped through his notes and jotted something down.

"He moved away long ago, but it didn't matter because they never believed her. It made them look bad, so they couldn't accept it. You know?"

Yes. Erin had witnessed it more times than she wanted to think about during her brief tenure as a sex crimes investigator. Many women didn't want to believe a husband or boyfriend could be capable of hurting their child. Some flat out refused. Add that to the high-profile life Simon Archer led, and everything made twisted sense.

"You have a name?"

She shook her head. "They never told me. Bonnie didn't like to talk about it."

"But you were six when all of this happened." Erin watched the girl's strange eyes. The different colors reflected light in subtly different ways, and the effect was fascinating. "So I assume you grew up hearing your parents' version?"

"They wouldn't talk about it, but Aunt Carmen told me the truth."

"So you had some contact with your aunt and uncle?" Erin asked.

"Just with Carmen, back in high school. I knew I wasn't getting the whole story, and I wanted to know why Bonnie had disappeared from my life. Carmen told me, and she told me all about Bonnie's problems. I felt terrible." She snatched another tissue out of the box on the table. "My parents and I had it out. I got grounded for speaking with her. I finally realized what sort of person my father is." Her delicate face took on the sharp expression of an eagle hunting for prey. "He doesn't care about anyone but himself and his reputation."

Erin had said the same thing to her own father, years ago. Their fight had been something of a wake-up call to him. "I'm sorry. I know this is tough for you. Did you ever notice Bonnie being bruised or injured?"

"A couple of times." Sarah touched her biceps. "Around here. She said she took self-defense classes. I thought that was a good thing. A way for her to feel like she had control over her life and safety." Her voice hitched, and she fidgeted with the tissue.

"Did she lie? Do you think someone else gave her those bruises?"

Sarah went rigid and didn't answer.

Erin studied the girl. She seemed so fragile, so desperate to believe she hadn't missed some crucial sign of her cousin's impending danger. But if they were so close, why wouldn't Bonnie have mentioned the sex videos? "We have reason to believe Bonnie sold amateur porn videos online, and her bruising came from those sessions."

Sarah flinched back against the chair. "Bonnie wouldn't have done that."

"Why?" Brooks pressed.

"She didn't like sex." Sarah's tone was adamant.

Brooks made another note. "Would you have tried to talk her out of it?"

Sarah pursed her lips and tilted her head. "I ... I don't know."

Brooks gave a short nod. "But you knew she worked as a stripper."

"She was still dealing with a lot of self-worth issues." Sarah looked out the window.

"The owner of Sid's mentioned you came in with Bonnie a few times," Brooks said.

Sarah twisted the tissue into a ropelike strand. "She liked working there. She said her boss treated her well. Better than the other girls. But Bonnie wasn't like them."

"How do you mean?" Erin asked.

"It's not what you're thinking," Sarah said. "I'm not saying those women are bad for stripping and Bonnie was good. I'm saying Bonnie was special. She had this sort of contagious lightness about her. I think people wanted to be around her because of it. Does that make sense?"

Erin nodded. "Did Bonnie have any issues with Sid's clientele?"

"The cross-dresser," Sarah said immediately. "I don't remember his name."

"Tori?" Erin supplied.

"Yes. He asked Bonnie to dance one night, and something happened. She wouldn't say what, but she told me she got him kicked out." Sarah's disconcerting eyes narrowed. "She got so upset about him. She wouldn't tell me what he said, just that he was a hypocrite."

"Did she ever mention him again?"

Sarah shook her head. "She said she wanted to forget about him."

Jack might have disguised himself as a woman. But that was only one line of inquiry. "Did you know about Will Merritt?" Erin asked.

Fresh moisture built in Sarah's eyes. "I think he's in love with her, but she didn't want to be tied down. He accepted it. But I think he would have waited for her."

At least Erin's female instincts weren't completely off. "I hate to ask this, but would you mind allowing us to fingerprint you? There are two sets of prints in Bonnie's house we can't identify. If one set is yours, ruling them out would be a huge help."

"Of course," Sarah said. "I've been at my parents' since Wednesday, so I'm not sure that will help."

"Fingerprints can stick around for a long time," Erin said. She offered a conspiratorial smile. "So you've been holed up at your parents' in Chevy Chase? No trips into the city?"

Sarah shook her head. "I wish. My thesis is killing me." She flinched. "Bad choice of words."

"It's all right," Erin said. "Can you give us the names of Bonnie's other friends or classmates?"

"She didn't mention any of them. I got the impression she kept to herself."

"What about Brian Reese, one of the school counselors?"

Sarah nodded. "She talked to him about their college program. She was excited about it." Her voice caught as she realized the sad finality of her cousin's dream.

"And nothing else about Brian, maybe about him being inappropriate?"

"No," Sarah said. "Why?"

"We need to get a clear picture of her life. Think back over the last few months. Did Bonnie mention having issues with anyone?"

"No ... well, no, not really."

"What is it?" Erin prodded. "Even if it seems trivial, it's important."

"She talked about a boy at school who asked her out." Sarah smiled. "She called him a boy because he was only twenty-one. She wasn't interested. I think it took him a while to get the hint."

Erin's pulse kicked into her throat. Out of the corner of her eye, she saw Brooks sit up straighter. "Did she tell you his name?"

"No. She said he was Black, though. I remember because we talked about how my dad still lives in the dark ages." She banded her arms over her narrow chest.

Ricky Stout? A possibility, but dozens of Black males attended the Adult Learning Center. "Anyone else? No other female friends?"

"She didn't have many friends. Bonnie had trust issues. The only women she talked about were the ones she worked with at Sid's." Her face twisted into sorrow. "I wish I hadn't waited so long to find her again. Now she's gone." Sarah turned away and cried.

Erin's throat swelled, and she reached for the girl's fragile hand while Brooks offered another tissue.

"When did you last see Bonnie?" Brooks asked.

"A week ago," Sarah said. "We'd planned to get together, but I canceled because of my stupid paper." Her head dropped against her thin knees. "Maybe I could have helped her."

"I'm sure that's not the case," Erin said gently. "How did Bonnie seem the last time you spoke?"

"Fine," Sarah said. "She understood why I couldn't make it because she was busy with school, too. Everything was going so well in her life. I just can't believe this happened." She drew in a long, shuddering breath, her striking eyes unsettling. "The news said she was cut up."

"I'm sorry." The words seemed so flat, so worthless. Erin debated about asking her next question. If Bonnie had told anyone about the pregnancy, it would have been Sarah. She hesitated because the parents hadn't been informed, but if Simon Archer used his political clout, he could build a fortress of red tape around his daughter, making it difficult for them to speak again. She decided to chance it. "Did you know Bonnie was pregnant?"

Brooks's head jerked toward Erin.

Sarah's hands went to her mouth. "Oh my God, no." Fresh tears rolled down her cheeks, and she rocked from side to side.

"I'm sorry to be the one to tell you." Erin felt like a broken record. "I thought maybe she confided in you."

Tears streamed down Sarah's cheeks as she shook her head. "She still had a hard time trusting people after what happened when she was a kid."

"I hate to ask this," Brooks said, giving Erin a dark look, "but her parents don't know. The medical examiner will inform them tomorrow."

She dabbed her face with the wadded tissue. "I won't say anything, I promise."

"Thank you." He looked at Erin like a father silently chastising a kid.

"By chance, did you ever go into Bonnie's attic?" Brooks asked abruptly.

"The attic?" Sarah's creamy skin turned ashen. "The news said that's where it happened."

Erin shot him a look, wishing he'd been more subtle with Sarah.

"I'm just asking because we'll need to eliminate fingerprints up there as well."

"I helped her put the air conditioner away a few weeks ago," Sarah said.

"Did you see anything strange up there?" he asked.

Her eyebrows came together, mouth bowed. "Like what? Junk?"

"Anything you thought looked odd?"

Another shake of the head. Exhaustion crept into Sarah's face, her skin more pallid than when they had started the interview.

"We just have a couple more questions," Erin said. "Have you heard of a little girl named Mina or a boy named Charlie?"

Sarah's feet came down off the chair, her boots clacking onto the floor. She cocked her head. "Mina? Charlie? I don't know any kids."

"What about Bonnie? Did she ever mention either one of them or mention a friend having a little girl?"

"Maybe one of the other dancers at the club? But Bonnie didn't socialize with those girls."

"What about Jane?" Erin asked. "Did Bonnie ever mention anyone by that name?"

Sarah rubbed her temples. "No, I don't think so."

"And Bonnie never mentioned the cross-dresser again?" Brooks asked, his eyes bright.

She frowned. "No, that I would remember."

"What about Jack the Ripper?" Brooks's blunt question surprised Erin. "Did Bonnie have any interest in him, maybe as a research topic for school?"

"Jack the Ripper?" Sarah repeated the words slowly as though she didn't understand. "I have no idea. She never mentioned anything like that, but I'm starting to think she didn't tell me many things."

Brooks nodded, his gaze never leaving Sarah's face. "Can you tell us where you were yesterday afternoon and evening?"

"My parents'," Sarah said. "I told you—working on my thesis."

"Right," he said. "Were you there by yourself?"

Creases lined Sarah's brow. "My mother stayed in all day, and the cleaning lady came during the evening. You'd have to ask Mother when. I was locked away in my room."

"We'll be sure to ask her." The undercurrent in Brooks's tone bordered on condescension.

Sarah's eyes grew large, and her mouth slack. "Surely, you're not asking me for an alibi?"

"It's procedure." Brooks tucked his notebook into the pocket of his slacks. "We need to cross you off the list."

"Thank you for coming in," Erin said. "If you remember anything else, call me." She handed Sarah a card. "We may need to talk again. I don't want to come between you and your parents, so will it be possible to arrange a meeting if we need to?"

"I think so," Sarah said. "As long as I have a little notice."

Erin and Brooks walked her to the main entrance and watched as the officer buzzed her out.

"You shouldn't have mentioned the pregnancy." Brooks didn't

waste any time.

"Why not? Sarah's the one Bonnie would have told." A weariness, unlike anything Erin had ever experienced, settled into her bones.

His lips pressed into a thin line. "Bonnie's parents haven't been told. And how do we know she won't run back and tell?"

"She said she wouldn't." Erin sighed. She'd made a gut call, and she stood by it.

"That doesn't mean she won't."

Too tired to argue and afraid she would pass out if she kept standing, Erin walked toward the squad room. "So, how does Sarah not see the bed and video equipment in the attic?"

"Bonnie probably piled junk on it. Or maybe she hadn't gotten into the porn yet. Sarah did say that was a few weeks ago. My guess is she knew about the amateur porn, though. She tried too hard to act like she didn't when you asked."

"We had a cool September," Erin said. "They could have put the air conditioner in the attic mid-month." She didn't say anything more, her thoughts cluttered.

"But," Brooks prompted, "you don't think Sarah's being entirely truthful either, do you?"

Erin's body suddenly ached as though she'd just finished a marathon. She'd never participated in one, but she imagined the level of fatigue surging through her had to be similar. "I think the chances of Sarah being sexually abused by the same man who hurt Bonnie are high, even if the parents put a stop to it once Bonnie came forward. Her body language is indicative of an abuse victim. She's extremely protective of herself. Not defensive, but ... guarded."

"Why didn't you push her on the issue?"

"Because you can't go at a sex victim like a bulldog," Erin said. "Being abused may not be pertinent to the case, especially since the guy's long gone. It's part of what shaped her life and personality—including her general distrust." She unlocked her bottom drawer and retrieved her purse. "If our juvie Charlies turn out to be a bust, then what?"

"We talk to every one of the dancers at Sid's about Mina and Charlie," Brooks said. "And we keep looking for Tori. Maybe one of them can tell us his real name. Then we go back to the school. Keep hammering. Those are the places Bonnie spent her life. We also check into Sarah's background. See if she's been in trouble or in treatment for anything. Simon Archer might have handled his daughter's abuse differently."

Erin sagged against the wall. "I need to sleep. Start over fresh in the morning if I can sleep. I doubt I will, between bad dreams and waiting for the next phone call."

Brooks retrieved his coat from his chair. "We should warn the dancers at Sid's. If the killer targeted Bonnie because she danced and then rejected him, one of them could be the next target."

The unspoken possibility hung between them. Erin crossed her arms over her waist against the sudden rush of chills. "I'll see you tomorrow. I'm going home to hug my daughter."

CHAPTER TWENTY

Abby slept like a log, completely oblivious when Erin squeezed in next to her. Her butt hung off the side of the twin bed, but she didn't care. She buried her face into Abby's tangled hair and wrapped her arm around her daughter's slim waist. She sensed Erin's presence, snuggling into her with a satisfied sigh that brought tears to Erin's eyes. How had Abby gotten this big so quickly? It seemed like just yesterday she'd brought her tiny baby girl home from the hospital to the first apartment she and Brad shared. He'd been Abby's father figure from the start. Her worthless sperm donor had disappeared soon after Erin told him about her pregnancy.

Erin didn't care as long as she had her daughter. She pulled Abby closer and tried not to think about the fear in Mina's voice or the agony in Carmen Archer's.

Brad peeked around the open door. "I thought I heard you come in."

She could have stayed with Abby all night, but also needed to sleep. The bed wasn't big enough for both of them. She kissed her daughter's soft cheek and carefully peeled herself away.

She met Brad in the hallway. "This has been a day from hell. The little girl called again. Her name is Mina, and so far, we can't find her anywhere."

Brad dragged his hands through his already messy blond hair. "Maybe it's a crank. Someone who saw the article is putting their kid up to it."

Erin couldn't remember all the uniforms on scene last night. "Maybe. Could be the asshole unnamed source who told the reporter my nickname was Princess. Just trying to mess with me. But why? I don't have a beef with any of them."

"They might have one with you, though," Brad said. "People are assholes in general. Speaking of, Dad called."

She rolled her eyes and shuffled toward her room. A hot shower sounded like heaven but so did passing out in her clothes. "Stop. He's not an asshole to you."

"He's not exactly a loving guy."

"He could be worse. What did he want?"

"You," he said. "He said you and Lisa had a spat at the office."

"That bitch." She shoved open the door to her room and flopped onto the bed. Decision made. "The guy who found Bonnie is a lobbyist for Baker-Allen. We needed his DNA and had follow-up questions. Lisa showed up and did her thing."

"She told Dad a different story," Brad said. "Boy, there's a shock."

Erin set the alarm on her phone and plugged it in. "Did he sound pissed?"

"No, he'd heard about the case and said if you need anything more, come straight to him. He'll get anything on Merritt you need."

"In other words," Erin spoke into the pillow, her eyelids already sagging, "don't make a scene. Keep things behind closed doors."

"Exactly." Brad didn't quite manage to hide his bitterness. "That's the same thing he said to me when I came out to him."

"I'm sorry," she said. "But he's better. You guys are better now."

"Thanks to you." Brad dragged the quilt out from underneath her and covered her with it. "Get some sleep."

"These next few days are going to be busy," she said. "You're able to help with Abby? Or do I need to ask Mrs. Bakas?"

Ellen Bakas, their next-door neighbor, was a widow whose grandchildren lived three hours away. She doted on Abby, and Abby adored her—along with the decadent Greek desserts she kept in stock. Erin usually didn't mind leaving her at Mrs. Bakas's house, but she didn't want to leave Abby with anyone outside of family right now.

"I've got it. Just solve your case."

She slurred something about how badly life would suck without him, but exhaustion prevented her from making any sense. She'd have to do something special for him as soon as she solved this case.

CHAPTER TWENTY-ONE

I no longer have control over my own mind. The demon has insinuated himself in every crevice, using my skill for his dark deeds. He laughs with glee at the letters in the newspaper, for we did not send them. Unless I have forgotten doing so, which may be the truth. Voices war inside my head, and I know I'm going mad. My memories fade in and out. The demon enjoys the blood. My only solace is ridding our city of another dirty slag.

—JTR
30 September 1888

I like their pain—an unexpected part of this little adventure. At first, killing them was a means to a necessary end. Still, every time I jam my knife into their flesh, through tissue and muscle and into precious organs and arteries, I feel a rush unlike anything I've ever experienced. Better than any anti-anxiety drug, recreational or off the street. Gloriously fucking addictive. I might keep doing this after I've taken care of the second traitorous bitch.

She let me in, of course. How could she refuse?

I watch her fat ass bounce as she walks ahead of me to the living room. Her robe doesn't flatter her plushy shape. Her thighs rub together when she walks, like two big marshmallows fused together. At this point in her life, with her pot belly and jug thighs, men don't notice her. At least, men who aren't just as fat and gross as she is. That's probably why she became a lesbian.

I let her talk for a minute, rattling on about something I don't give a shit about, and then I make my move. The fat woman's eyes bulge when I punch her in the stomach, like a fat-ass doughboy getting the stuffing knocked out of him and his eyes are the first orifice his innards can squeeze out of. Her eyes don't pop out, but I would have laughed if they did. Maybe I would've stuffed them into her big, fat mouth.

She doubles over, sausage fingers clutching her middle. I hit her again, this time in the left temple. She drops to her knees, squealing like a baby pig taken off its mama's teat.

"What are you doing?"

She doesn't sound so smart anymore. She sounds like a desperate woman who knows her time is up.

I kick her in the head, sending her overfed body flat to the floor. Her skull damn near smacks the fireplace.

I straddle her, my ass sinking into her thighs. "Tying up loose ends."

The knife takes a lot longer to sink through her extra layers of skin and into her stomach. I should have kept the cleaver. I shove as hard as I can, half-expecting to see yellow fat escaping from the wound. She screams something I can't understand. Or maybe I'm not listening to the words. I am caught up in the feeling of her body collapsing on itself, of the sight of the blood spurting, and of the guttural fear in her voice.

"What's it like to know you're about to die?" I ask. "Are you scared? Do you think you'll go to Hell?"

She screams loudly, and I hope the neighbors don't hear. I should be cautious and cut her throat completely, but that takes all the fun out of it. And that's not what Jack did, anyway.

She twists and jerks, trying to fight me off. I dig my knees into her sides, jam them up under her ribs, and hit her in the face again. Shock and being out of shape have fucked her chances of winning. I grip the knife with both hands and shove it deeper, jerking it toward her chest.

Her rolls bounce like a swollen Jell-O mold. This time, her eyes really do pop, at least to an extent. Red streaks burst across the left one as it hemorrhages from stress and pain. Glorious.

Blood gurgles from her wounds and then her mouth. I must have nicked something important. Anatomy isn't my strong suit.

She keeps bouncing, making me bounce. My work becomes uneven and not as accurate as I'd like. Her eyes roll back in her head. If I don't end it now, she'll pass out. I want to have the final decision.

I lean over and grab one of the decorative throw pillows off her ugly couch. Her rolling eyes refocus, and she raises her stumpy arms in a final attempt to fight me off. I smack them away and press the pillow over her face, putting all my upper body weight on it.

"This is what you get for being a tattle-tale."

CHAPTER TWENTY-TWO

Three damned days and nothing. No more calls from Mina and absolutely zero leads on anything. The paper found crumpled in Bonnie's attic didn't have a single print—bolstering Erin's belief that the killer deliberately left it behind. With help from Fowler—who quickly volunteered for the task—Erin and Brooks had talked to every stripper at Sid's. All liked Bonnie, and all expressed shock and grief.

The dancers described Tori as an older man with great makeup skills and nice clothes. He usually wore a dark, loose-fitting dress and a black wig cut in a stylish bob. He didn't keep an account or tab with the club and always paid with cash. Bonnie's disagreement with him surprised her coworkers, who considered Tori a perfect gentleman who happened to like wearing ladies' clothes. Bonnie refused to discuss Tori, and her coworkers dropped the subject. No one knew his real name or any Jane, Mina, or Charlie who might have been associated with Bonnie Archer.

Subsequent searches at neighboring bars and strip clubs came up empty except for The Point. The low-key gay bar on the waterfront was a known favorite of the LGBT community, and several bartenders remembered Tori frequenting the establishment within the last two months. However, he hadn't been seen in a couple of weeks. All cash transactions and no decent images on the security footage meant yet another dead end.

Bonnie's phone records proved useless. Calls to her work, her parents, Sarah, Will Merritt, and her school, as well as several calls to an unlisted number, probably a throwaway phone. Another dead end.

Brian Reese's alibi checked out as expected. Ricky Stout skipped his night class. A trip to the shelter listed as his last address yielded exactly nothing. No one knew where he'd gone. The director was on vacation and was the only person who had worked at the shelter when Ricky would have been living there. Erin left her card.

The Charlies with juvenile records went nowhere. The computer people had yet to hit on Bonnie's porn videos—another job Fowler volunteered to help with until he found out the search was for rape porn.

Well past midnight, she had holed up in her room, half under the covers, watching the stuff of nightmares. Women tied up and screaming, begging for mercy.

This world is full of sick fucks. Erin pulled up another site. The amount of pay-per-view porn sites on the dark web astounded her. New ones seemed to pop up overnight, and Erin couldn't get in without giving her credit card information.

The videos were fake and usually poorly acted, but cold sweat still soaked Erin's nightshirt, and the memories still rushed back.

She hadn't screamed. She let him do it because she thought fighting back would get her killed. Abby couldn't grow up without her mother.

Rape crisis counseling helped her move on, at least to an extent, but she struggled with trusting men, with trusting her own judgment.

Every second of every video she watched made Erin physically ill, and she wanted to shut it off. Still, she remembered the cleaver sticking out of the girl's destroyed body and pulled up another video. After a couple of hours, her ringing phone gave her a respite from the latest filth. Sergeant Clark flashed across the screen as she answered.

"Prince."

Erin froze at the grave tenor of his voice. "It's another body, right? It's not Mina, is it? Or a boy? Mina talked about Charlie taking care of her."

"Not a kid, thank God. It's a middle-aged female in Takoma Park." Worry colored Clark's baritone. "Mitchell says it's the same killer."

Clark rattled off an address as Erin fumbled for paper and pen.

"Get over there ASAP. Brooks will meet you."

Dawn hadn't yet reached the horizon when Erin parked her car in front of the restored craftsman home in Takoma Park. After waking her snoring brother and getting his assurance Abby would be taken care of for the day, she'd rushed to the car, still trying to wrap her mind around the sergeant's words.

Not Mina or Charlie. Not another struggling young woman in a challenging neighborhood, but nearly her polar opposite—a forty-something college professor in a middle-class suburb.

Takoma Park was trendy, fun, and loaded with security-cautious people who could afford to install alarm systems. People who noticed someone strange on their street and had no problem calling the police. So why would someone who so obviously planned his attacks risk coming to a place like Takoma Park? Did he need to up the thrill factor?

KILLING JANE

At least it's not a kid.

Erin shut her car door, and gooseflesh immediately covered her arms despite her fleece jacket. The last week had brought nothing but gray skies and a dampness intent on leaching warmth from the skin. Death lingered everywhere: prickly brown grass, often swampy with rainwater; the brilliant red and gold fall leaves turned putrid and crisp; perennials reduced to a tangle of stems. Erin would welcome an early snow just to cover the decay.

Headlights shone in her eyes. Erin shielded her face and then waited for Brooks to park behind her car. He unfolded his long form and emerged in khakis and a snug fleece jacket, looking fresher and more put together than Erin. She'd tugged on what she hoped were clean jeans and a long-sleeved shirt, and she was pretty sure her socks didn't match.

"I just got here," she said by way of greeting. "I suppose you've heard the basics. This victim has nothing in common with Bonnie."

"Sometimes the common denominator is the random selection." Brooks followed her up the walk. They stood side by side at the base of the wide steps.

Erin loved the house at first sight and took a moment to appreciate it. Like many of the revitalized homes in the area, it looked as though it had weathered the decades, soaked in the city's history, and came out stronger. She studied the rectangular porch. "No sign of breaking and entering. So our victim knew the guy, just like Bonnie?"

"My gut says a preliminary yes. Who called in the body at this hour?" Brooks glanced around. "This isn't exactly a night owl sort of neighborhood."

"That's one of the most interesting parts." Sergeant Clark emerged from the shadows of the porch.

Erin jumped at the sound of his voice and hoped the men didn't notice.

"The 911 call came from an untraceable number. Probably another damned pay-as-you-go. We're searching the property to see if the caller tossed it."

"So the murderer called it in?" Erin hoped her voice sounded steady.

"Possibly, but not until about forty-five minutes ago. Mitchell puts preliminary time of death at around eight hours ago. But the killer might have returned, admiring his work and all." Clark shuddered. "You need to talk to Mitchell. We've got another message, but there's more to this one."

Erin hesitated on the wide front porch. The blazing lights did nothing to shed the sensation of walking through the devil's doorway. Her knees weakened, and sweat beaded her hairline. Her chest tightened.

Brooks stood somewhere behind her, patiently waiting. Could he sense it? Did he feel the weird humidity crawling out of the house?

Terror washed over Erin, but she had to overcome it. Another butchered woman waited for them. She willed her feet to move forward.

The sharp, pungent odor of decay assaulted Erin and Brooks as they crossed through the welcoming entryway. She covered her nose and tried to breathe through her mouth. Dan Mitchell and his assistant knelt in the large living room, positioned on either side of the body. Wide columns separated the living room from the entryway, and Erin couldn't help but think she'd crossed the threshold of Hell when she saw the dead woman.

Virginia Walton lay in front of the fireplace, her pink robe and nightgown hiked up to her knees. Fuzzy slippers covered her feet.

Erin's gaze went to the mahogany fireplace mantle. Scrawled in dark blood were the words *snitch* and *1888 Hanbury Street*. Beneath the address, the initials *JTR*.

"The second Ripper victim." Erin forced the words out.

Copious amounts of blood saturated the carpet. Erin dug her toes into her shoes in an effort not to sway. Her breathing sounded ragged and fast. Beside her, Brooks sucked in a raspy breath. The noise somehow steadied Erin enough to take stock of what lay in front of her.

Virginia Walton's left arm lay across her left breast. Her legs were drawn up with her feet resting on the carpet, the knees turned outward. It made Erin think of being stuck in the stirrups in the gynecologist's office. Swollen and purple, the woman stared blankly at the fireplace.

Long, ropey strands extended from the vicious cuts to the abdomen.

He filleted her. Like the fish her father caught during one of the family vacations to the lake. Erin remembered standing at the doorway of the little building where the men went to cut the fish. The smell made her sick, but the way the helpless fish flopped while her father dragged the knife through it made her and Brad run screaming to their mother. Their older sister had laughed.

That hateful laughter echoed through Erin's head as she edged closer. "Those are her intestines." Erin sounded as though she spoke into a bell jar.

Dan Mitchell swiveled around on his toes and then pointed to Virginia's pelvic region. "He tried to cut her uterus out, too. And her bladder."

Erin shifted her gaze to the woman's face. Part of the right earlobe was missing, and blood crusted along the right side of her face and neck. "Did you find the earlobe?"

"Not yet," Mitchell said softly.

"Jack the Ripper cut off part of the right ear," Brooks said.

"Catherine Eddows," Erin said. "The fourth victim. Jack sliced her whole body up. Severe facial lacerations, and part of her ear was missing. He destroyed her labia. This," she pointed to Virginia Walton's body, "isn't as bad as that."

"He's inspired," Brooks said. "But he's trying to be original at the same time."

"The weapon is different from the cleaver that killed Bonnie Archer," Mitchell said. "These cuts were done by a long blade, at least six inches. Incredibly sharp, to do all of this. And he left something behind."

Sweat blistered on Erin's face as Mitchell handed her a clear evidence bag containing a piece of college-ruled notebook paper covered with blood and bodily fluid. She could only make out a few words, once again written in modern black ink.

I no longer have control
Voices war
The demon blood.

—JTR

Tendrils of the same evil energy from Bonnie's crime scene ghosted around Erin with the strength of an iron fist. If an act of cruelty left an imprint, surely this must be it. "I've spent the last few days digging into Ripper lore. I can't find any letters matching the passages we've seen so far—not even the ones known to be fake."

She handed the bag to Brooks with more force than intended, as though the crux of evil rested in the handwriting itself. Erin hated the way the fear seeped into her voice, but the world seemed to be spiraling out of control, and she had no clue how to stop the bleeding. Literally.

Brooks cleared his throat. "She appears to have been smothered. Do you agree?"

Mitchell glanced down at the woman's purple, swollen face. "Definitely. Some of the cuts are antemortem, but the worst of the damage was done postmortem."

Erin asked the question she wasn't sure she wanted an answer to. "How similar to the second Ripper victim is this?"

"Very close." Clark glared across the expanse, shaking his head. "The Ripper did worse things to Annie Chapman—the victim found at Hanbury Street—but we can't deny the similarities."

"I don't understand it," Erin said. "Our killer is inspired by the Ripper murders, but neither one has been exact. Especially with these notes. So what's the killer's obsession about?"

And what about Jane—or Jill, as the lore called her? Erin didn't say the name out loud, but it rested on the tip of her tongue, waiting for the right moment. What better role model for a killer than a woman who escaped justice—and history—for butchering at least five prostitutes?

"I don't think it's all about Jack." Clark motioned for them to follow him back to the entryway. He lowered his voice. "We have to keep this information contained. Aside from us, Mitchell's the only one who's seen the body and the message. And Marie is the only other person who knows about the first note. If the press gets wind we have two women killed by a nut job paying homage to Jack the Ripper, all hell will break loose. That doesn't help us catch him. The Ripper stuff is all window dressing. Same with the notes. Distractions."

Brooks clearly agreed, his head bobbing up and down, his face passive and thoughtful as usual. "So, we know why Bonnie is a whore. Why is the professor a snitch?"

"There's got to be a link between the two women. He chose them for specific reasons." Clark looked down at his phone, his crooked index finger scrolling over the screen. "I need to notify the next of kin."

He pointed to the fireplace where several pictures of a thirty-something woman and a gap-toothed little girl held court. "I'm assuming that's her daughter. We found her contact information in the professor's cell. It lay on the dining room table with her purse. Wallet and credit cards still there."

"Is the daughter local?" Erin's heart beat a little bit faster. "If she's got a child, maybe that's Mina. Maybe she was too scared."

Clark's brow furrowed, his graying eyebrows knitting together. "Not sure, but I'll find out. Although I can't imagine a daughter orchestrating something like this for her own mother."

"That doesn't have to be it," Erin said. "Maybe the daughter had a drug problem, and that's the connection to Bonnie. An old friend from the past asks for help, and Bonnie agrees. The dealer tracks her to

Bonnie's place, and then Bonnie gets it. Same thing happens here." Reaching, but they needed to put this gruesome picture together before another woman died.

Brooks crossed his arms, looking between Erin and the sergeant. "I wouldn't rule it out, but this seems way too bloody for something like that. You've worked a drug homicide," he said to Erin. "Doesn't this feel like the opposite end of the spectrum?"

He meant to be conversational, simply tossing a theory back and forth the way partners do, but Erin's skin heated with embarrassment. Why couldn't he back her up in front of Clark? "I guess."

"The number is a South Carolina area code," Clark said. "So if she is in town, she's visiting. I'm going outside to make the call." He shook his head, looking disgusted. "It's not right, but this murder will make the news. Possibly national. A prominent, white college professor literally slaughtered in her home. That'll be the sickeningly sweet icing on the press's shit cake. Her family can't find out that way." He took one last, long look toward the dead woman. "Figure this out before things get worse."

Brooks strode back over to Mitchell.

Erin took her time, trying to gather her emotions. She focused on the issue at hand. "We're sure she was killed at least eight hours ago?"

Mitchell nodded. "She's in pretty good rigor."

"So, somewhere around eight or nine p.m. last night." Erin spoke before her partner could. "That's when he attacked and smothered her. Let's work the scene. When's the crime scene crew due to arrive?"

"They're at least twenty minutes out," Mitchell said. "Some kid found a guy in a dumpster. The body's a few days old, and the scene is a mess. Marie's been there for several hours."

"You couldn't call another crew?" Erin asked.

"Marie worked Bonnie's murder," Brooks spoke up. "It's better if she works this one. She has an idea of what to look for. Using her will help keep the information contained." He knelt to look closer at the victim. "Is that bruising on her face from the suffocation?"

Mitchell took a closer look, slipping on a pair of glasses that made his eyes enormous. "He punched her in the face before she died. She's discolored from suffocation and the effects that followed."

He touched Virginia Walton's forehead, which had a strange blue circle of blood in the center. "But this almost looks like lividity. Just the initial stages."

Erin tried to figure out the size of the blood pool. "If the killer turned her over, wouldn't it be obvious?"

Dan pointed a gloved finger to the center of the enormous bloodstain. "At first, I thought the circumference was smaller than Bonnie Archer's because the carpet soaked up the blood, but Virginia died before the major cutting. And you can see she simply bled out." He touched the soft flesh of Virginia's outstretched arms. "This looks like possible lividity here, too." His eyes danced like he'd won the jackpot. "Can you help me turn her over?"

A body in rigor is literally dead weight, and Virginia Walton had ample flesh on her frame. Mitchell and Brooks carefully turned her over.

Time stilled. The whoosh of blood roared in Erin's ears to the point of being painful. Her lips moved, but no sound came out of her mouth.

Brooks appeared to be rendered mute as well. Huffing, he stared down at the dead woman's back as though he didn't quite believe what he was seeing.

"Holy hell," Mitchell said. "Does that mean what I think it means?"

The killer had signed Virginia's ample back, slicing into her flesh with the flourish of someone who clearly enjoyed the task.

Jane the Ripper.

CHAPTER TWENTY-THREE

"The killer *is* a woman," Erin whispered, unable to speak any louder.

Brooks stared back at her, white-faced. "If a woman did this ..."

"Look, women are vindictive, cruel creatures when they're scorned. Add a little insanity and obsession, and you've got the perfect recipe." Erin slapped the back of her hand against her palm. "Every instinct I have tells me we are dealing with a woman. She even signed her fucking name in the victim's skin."

"But why?" Brooks countered. "Common sense—not to mention crime statistics—indicates the killer is a man. Why wave the truth around like a red flag? The name could be a red herring."

Erin's patience thinned. "She wants credit. She's proud of what she's done. The media will love her."

Brooks rubbed his face until the skin turned red. "All right, fine." He ticked his points off on his fingers. "Virginia Walton is over fifty. She's not pregnant. She's not a prostitute or drug addict. You're quite a ways from the Ripper's preference."

"It's still possible," Erin said. "You've seen what a woman is capable of."

"Don't tell me what I know." Brooks's brow furrowed. "I know people are capable of terrible, terrible things. People can masquerade as anything. Women can be the most vicious creatures on earth, and the most resourceful." He closed his eyes. "But, this. Physically ... how?"

"She incapacitates first," Mitchell said. "Both Bonnie and Professor Walton were beaten first. If the killer planned and had the right tools, it's plausible."

"But why the name Jane?" Brooks asked. "The lore calls her Jill the Ripper—Jack and Jill. So why hasn't she used that name?"

"Maybe her real name is Jane." Erin arched an eyebrow. "Considering how she's cutting people up, it's not high on my list of things to ask her."

"Don't forget the cross-dresser at the strip club," Brooks said. "Jack supposedly dressed like a woman. It's just another piece of the lore this killer's choosing to emulate."

"A cross-dresser who seems to have disappeared. Bonnie's the only dancer at Sid's who reported any issues with him. I don't think he's the killer." Why the hell was Brooks so against the killer being a woman? The questions boiled inside her, but she fought them back. Erin took a deep breath. "We can't rule anything out at this point. What happened to keeping the idea as a possibility and continuing the investigation?" She gave him a sly smile. "Those were your words, weren't they?"

Brooks chuckled as he nodded.

Erin followed the trail of dark crimson dots on the hardwood floor leading to the dining room. "She wasn't as careful this time. Maybe Jane ran out of time."

The crime scene team carried their gear through the front door. Hopefully, they would pick up something useful to help identify the killer.

Erin crossed through the two mahogany pillars separating the living room and dining room, stopping at the pool of blood next to the antique dining room table. "She stood right here."

The mess on the table nearly gave Erin hives. Essays on dreams and their impact on everyday life had been stacked neatly next to several textbooks and an agenda. Professor Walton still operated in the old-school world. Most people used their phone or computer calendars to plan their lives. More red caught her eye. One of the folders had a series of drips on the inside panel, its contents scattered over the table.

"Damn," Brooks said. "I hoped we'd catch a bloody fingerprint."

He seemed resigned, but she noticed his trembling fingers.

Her blue latex gloves shone beneath the modern chandelier light. Erin carefully thumbed through the papers. "Oh, shit."

"What?" Brooks had started leafing through the planner.

"Virginia Walton is a counselor at the Adult Learning Center."

"So there's our connection to Bonnie Archer," Brooks said. "If Virginia knew Bonnie, why didn't she come forward after her murder?"

Frustration built into a scream from somewhere deep in Erin's gut. Every time she thought she'd found a crack in this case, another unanswered question snapped it shut. "So much for asking her now."

CHAPTER TWENTY-FOUR

The fetid air clawed at Erin's throat, and her stomach heaved. She stepped out on the porch to breathe in some fresh air.

"Investigator Prince." The redhead's shrill voice cut over the din of birds greeting the dismal morning.

Crap! The press vultures must have arrived shortly after the crime scene crew. Erin nearly flipped her off, but throwing fresh meat on the lawn would have caused less of a ruckus. The last thing she needed was the reporter who kept calling her "The Princess," asking questions while she felt sicker than a dog. She couldn't let the press know the crime scene had overwhelmed her, or Red would have a field day with it.

"I heard the victim has multiple stab wounds. Is this related to Bonnie Archer's murder?"

Erin stepped off the porch, wincing as the digital cameras clicked away. "No comment." She'd pretend she'd come out to check on the status of the search for the throwaway phone.

She dropped to a squat and twisted to look beneath the porch. A scrollwork border kept critters from burrowing underneath, and no way could someone squeeze the phone through one of the intricate loops.

Red wasn't ready to give up. "If it's not related to Bonnie, why are you here?"

"Because I happened to be on rotation." Erin pushed through the dead rhododendrons and scanned the foundation.

"Isn't that a lot of pressure for an inexperienced homicide investigator?"

Erin's gaze snapped toward the redhead. A lackey held an umbrella over the reporter to protect her perfect hair. "No comment." Erin strode toward one of the uniforms searching near the backyard.

"What does your father think of you going into homicide? Surely he would rather you do something safer."

Erin changed direction and closed the distance between her and Red. She lowered her voice. "Listen. These murders aren't about me or my family name. Do the victims some justice, will you?"

After checking with the uniform, she stalked back into the house. In the entryway, she placed a call to Metro. She needed the moment to settle down before facing the crime scene again.

Erin rejoined Brooks in the dining room. "I talked to Fowler. He cross-referenced the numbers on Bonnie's phone with the 911 caller's. Not a match. He lives near American University, so he's heading in to interview the staff."

Brooks watched Marie gather trace material from the dining room. "It was worth checking."

Erin scowled.

Brooks gave her a sharp glance. "Something wrong? Beyond the obvious nightmare of a morning?"

"Just that asshole reporter. Nothing major." She rolled her neck to relieve the tension.

"I think being an asshole is a requirement on a fledgling reporter's résumé," Brooks said without humor. "Mitchell's getting the victim ready for transport."

"Jane." Sickness built in Erin's throat. "How could one woman do this to another?"

"Let me ask you something," Brooks said. "Why are you so sure it's a woman? We could still be looking at a smoke screen, and a damned good one."

The lack of sleep and stress of the case made Erin want to snap back *Because I am.* But instead of losing her cool, she thought about the question for a moment. "It's Mina. I keep hearing the sheer terror in her voice and the way she said *her.* Like she was afraid of that person, not worried about her."

"Possibly," Brooks said. "Or maybe your memory is tricking you. It happens to all of us." Brooks raised his hands in either defeat or frustration. "For the record, I'm confused as hell, and you could well be right." He glanced at the blood on the hardwood floor. "Do you think we can grab a quick coffee while Marie's team does their thing? It's been a long day already, and the sun's barely up."

Erin nodded and strode out to the porch. "You don't want this to be a woman."

Brooks looked up at the somber sky. "Do you?"

Erin tilted her head as she thought. "I don't care what gender the killer is. I just want them stopped before they kill again."

The drizzle picked up as they walked to the car. The reporters—with Red front and center—called out more questions. Erin and Brooks ignored them.

Erin's phone pinged with a text. "Sergeant Clark says the daughter's still in South Carolina. She teaches and can be alibied. So that wipes the theory."

Brooks sighed. "At least we can throw it out quickly."

Across the street, a woman in a blue robe watched them and waved at Erin.

She glanced at Brooks. "Have we talked to any of the neighbors yet?"

"Not yet," he said. "Most are just waking up."

"Let's see what she wants." Erin crossed the street with Brooks on her heels.

The short, stocky woman met them at the bottom of the steps. Her hair was still stuck up from sleeping, and an intoxicating aroma of coffee wafted from her. "What's happened? Is Virginia okay?"

Erin guessed her to be about the professor's age, although Virginia Walton's swollen face made comparison impossible. She made the introductions before responding. "I'm afraid we can't give you details, but she's deceased."

The woman sagged as though she'd been hit.

Erin glanced at the darkening clouds overhead. "May we have your name?"

The woman stared across at the Walton house, dazed. "This is awful." After a few moments, her eyes focused. "Susan. Susan Novak." She ruffled her hair. "I had a feeling she was in trouble."

"How so?" Brooks held his arm in the direction of the front door. "Why don't we get out of the rain."

"I don't know her well." Susan climbed the steps. "But we talk, coming and going. Sometimes we have coffee together."

Erin and Brooks followed her to the shelter of the porch.

"What did Virginia tell you?" Erin asked.

"She's been through a lot the past couple of years." Susan played with the belt of her robe. "Finally coming out and then trying to navigate that lifestyle as a middle-aged woman."

"Virginia Walton was a lesbian?" Erin asked.

She nodded. "I didn't care, mind you. I'm not one to judge. Live and let live, I say. But the transition was hard. That's why she came here from South Carolina. She had taught at a small Christian college there. You can imagine their reaction."

"Right." Erin remembered the whisper-mongering among her parents' friends after Brad came out—though most of them already suspected. Apparently, in their conservative circle, daring to own one's sexuality was a greater crime than the actual preference. "Did she have issues with her colleagues at American University?"

"She never mentioned any. She's had a tough time of it. Maybe she latched on to someone she shouldn't have."

"Did you see anyone unusual around last night?" Brooks asked.

"No, but I went to bed early." Susan's voice shook. "I normally don't."

"Did she have a girlfriend?" Erin asked. "And have you noticed any visitors recently?"

Susan thought for a moment. "Virginia never mentioned a girlfriend, but she has had a visitor. A dark-haired girl. Small thing, and half Virginia's age."

Erin clung to a neutral expression. "How often did this girl come around?"

"I only saw her a few times a couple of weeks ago." She glanced around them to look at Virginia Walton's violated home. "But ever since she showed up, Virginia had become edgy. Nervous. She didn't like my noticing the girl, and I thought maybe she was a student at AU. That's probably some sort of violation."

"Quite possibly," Erin said. "Did Virginia mention the girl's name?"

Susan shook her head. "No, I'm sorry."

Erin chewed her bottom lip, hoping to figure out how to proceed. She pulled her phone out of her bag and brought up Bonnie's picture. "Is this her?"

Susan retrieved a pair of reading glasses from her robe pocket and pulled the phone closer to her face. "It could be. She looks small, like this girl. Same hair. I never saw her face clearly. I just can't be sure."

"Thank you." Erin stowed the phone. "You've been a huge help. Our sergeant will come by in a while and ask you more questions." She handed her a card. "Please call me if you think of anything else."

"Of course." Susan's face fell. "God, Virginia is dead. You don't think about something like that happening here."

"We believe it's an isolated incident," Brooks said. "But do take extra precautions."

Erin stopped at the bottom of the steps and glanced at the pack of reporters and their camera crew crowding the crime scene perimeter. "Let's get uniform started on talking to the rest of the neighbors before the reporters beat us to it."

Brooks nodded. "I'll go. You get the car started." He jogged through the drizzle and spoke to the point officer manning the perimeter.

Erin started the car and turned on the heater as she waited for Brooks. She'd spotted a coffee house a few blocks away on her way to the scene. It'd give them a chance to figure out how the pieces of the two murders fit together and what the next steps were.

Brooks didn't waste any time and was in the car before it had a chance to warm. Erin drove the short distance to the coffee house.

"We need to talk with the bartenders at The Point," Erin said as she parked the car. "It's a high-end private gay bar in a safe area of the city, which might be the perfect spot for someone relatively new to the local scene. Virginia might have checked it out."

"I want to get my hands on Bonnie's laptop. The killer stole it because he was on there."

"You mean Jane," Erin said.

"I mean the person who wants us to believe it's Jane."

Erin got out and closed the door. She glared at Brooks across the roof. "The killer has signed the name Jane to both murders, so as far as I'm concerned, the killer is Jane." She struggled to push down her building exasperation but failed. "Look. I'm trying to be polite, but I'm tired and cranky, so I'm probably going to sound like an asshole. Why are you so against this killer being a woman?"

Brooks's face smoothed into a plastic-looking, fake expression as they crossed the parking lot. "I'm not against it. I'm trying to look at the entire picture. Tunnel vision in an investigation causes major mistakes. I learned that the hard way. And we might be looking at a man in cross-dress. Don't forget Tori."

They reached the door, and Erin shivered as the warm, coffee-permeated air greeted them. Brooks hadn't shared the entire truth, but she doubted she'd get anything more from him. "Bonnie wasn't a student at AU, so if the professor got involved with her, she didn't break school rules." She strode to the counter and placed her order. The barista poured the brew and handed it to her.

After Brooks had his coffee in hand, they grabbed a table away from the pickup counter.

"What about societal rules?" Brooks asked. "We're in a liberal zone, but how would people react if she were dating a girl half her age?"

"No clue," Erin said. "The missing videos might answer a lot of questions. What if Bonnie and Virginia were seeing each other, and Bonnie told Virginia about making the porn? Jane finds out and gets pissed." She inhaled the rich aroma as the steam rose from her cup.

"If Tori's our killer, what's his motive? Although plenty of men who cross-dress still identify as straight males, so I suppose he might have had a thing for Bonnie and got jealous." She shook her head. "But why call the professor a snitch? Bonnie's videos aren't illegal. Unless Virginia planned to tell Bonnie's parents. Then again, if she cared for Bonnie, that doesn't make sense either."

Worry lines carved their way across Brooks's forehead. "To make someone suffer the way these two women did takes enormous anger, not to mention psychotic tendencies. Whoever did this enjoys inflicting pain on people he—or she—believes wronged them."

Erin remembered the malevolent atmosphere at both crime scenes and shivered. "Absolutely."

Brooks sipped his coffee, the stress of the morning evident in his eyes. "I don't think we have a clue what any of this is about. We've been on the wrong track the entire time, and I have no idea how to find the right one."

Erin gawked at him. In the few days they'd worked together, she'd quickly learned to count on Brooks's quiet confidence.

CHAPTER TWENTY-FIVE

Most of the neighbors had been interviewed by mid-morning. They claimed Virginia Walton had kept to herself, and none had more to contribute. No one else noticed any visitors, but the area struck Erin as sterile and segregated. Most of the neighbors knew little about each other and preferred it that way.

"Where are we at on trace material?" Erin stood near the heating vent in the dining room, willing to put up with the stench of the house in exchange for warmth. Her fingers throbbed from the cold.

Marie grumbled something unintelligible. She sat on the floor, surrounded by white boxes. "This woman did not like technology. Boxes and boxes of printed records. She's got papers from students going back to her college in South Carolina. She brought it all with her. It's going to take days to catalog. Beyond the mess of paper, we're finding the usual mishmash of hair and fiber. No fingerprints so far, and I'm not expecting to find any belonging to the killer. He's too smart. Wait, she." Marie peered over the stack she'd marked for evidence. "You think it's a woman?"

"Both crime scenes have been signed with a woman's name," Erin said. "We don't have hard proof yet, but it's a definite possibility."

Marie shuddered. "I can't imagine one woman doing this to another."

"Neither can I," Erin said. Her phone vibrated in her pocket, and Sarah Archer's number flashed on the screen. "Hello?"

"Investigator Prince."

Sarah's shrill voice made Erin's ear ring.

"I just saw the news. Is it true? Is Professor Walton dead?"

"I'm afraid so," Erin said. "How do you know her?"

"She's my thesis advisor." A choking sob came over the phone. "She knew Bonnie, too. My God, who's doing this?"

Erin headed outside to find Brooks, fresh chills rushing through her. "We're going to find out, Sarah." Rain fell as she waved to Brooks to get in the car. "Stay put. My partner and I are coming to talk to you."

The drive to Chevy Chase took nearly an hour. Erin drove with the radio turned off, still trying to come up with something to put Brooks's mind—and hers—at ease, but she had nothing. Brooks caught up on phone calls while Erin drove, giving her a chance to think.

The investigation had gone nowhere from the start, and they'd done nothing but spin in circles. Virginia Walton's murder might have widened the playing field, but it only multiplied the sense of confusion.

A woman both Bonnie and Virginia trusted executed those brutal killings. Intellectually, Erin accepted that women were capable of despicable things. Women killed lovers and children, and women abused and tortured. Women killed multiple people. Her emotional side couldn't make sense of any of it.

Sarah Archer had connections to both women. She'd likely been sexually abused around the same time as Bonnie. She might be hiding something, but Erin couldn't see meek Sarah as a killer, especially when Virginia Walton probably had at least fifty pounds on her.

Erin tried to navigate the giant jigsaw puzzle of evidence. The murders weren't about obsession or ritual, but were punishments inspired by the exploits of Jack the Ripper. Could the mutilation simply be a smoke screen or a taunt because the killer believed she couldn't be caught?

And was Sarah the next victim?

They were near their destination when Brooks clicked off the phone and put it away.

"Carmen Archer claims she had no idea Sarah and Bonnie reconnected. She didn't sound too happy about it, either."

"Did she talk to you about the sexual abuse?" Erin asked.

"No, but she backed up Sarah's timeframe on the family fallout and admitted she spoke to Sarah several years ago. Asked me not to mention it to her husband."

"Well, I can't blame the Archers if Sarah's version is true. Anyone who rapes a kid deserves to have his dick cut off, at the very least. As far as I'm concerned, their lives should be an automatic forfeit." Erin's words came out more vehement than she'd intended.

Brooks jerked back.

Erin worried she'd gone too far. "I'm speaking from a parent's perspective. We can't toss all the pedophiles into the abyss. But I'd like to."

"It would be wonderful if justice could be that black and white," Brooks said. "Speaking of pedophiles and all things scum of the earth, you need to let me ask Ellen for help. She might even be able to do it without her NCMEC resources. She's got a friend who can basically track anything online."

"Legally?" Erin asked.

Brooks shrugged. "I don't ask those questions. They've been able to help me catch some extremely bad people. I trust them."

Erin wanted nothing more than to cut corners. Their case was one of many, and the computer guys had to prioritize. "Sergeant Clark won't like it. I don't want to piss him off on my first major case. You shouldn't, either." She turned onto the approach to the Archer estate.

"Think about it. Ellen could give us the break we need." Brooks stared ahead at the house—a big Greek revival with cultivated flowerbeds already prepared for the oncoming winter. "Nice digs."

"Definitely," Erin said. "McLean, Virginia, is the top dog when it comes to money and snobbery, but Chevy Chase doesn't lag too far behind."

"Isn't McLean where you grew up?"

"Yep. As for the Archer family dispute, some grudges never go away, especially when a kid's involved. They just get stronger."

"Like you and your sister," Brooks said.

Erin shot him a look. "That's more than a grudge and it's not something I want to talk about."

"My bad. I'd like to ask Sarah about the messages left behind."

Erin parked the car. "You mean the killer calling Bonnie a whore and the professor a snitch?"

He nodded. "She's family, and it's going to be hard for her, but right now, she's the only person connected to both of them. We have to push her this time."

Erin chewed on her lip. "She has an alibi for Bonnie's murder. Her mother confirmed it, and the housekeeper remembered Sarah's car being in the driveway because she'd blocked the girl in." She turned and leaned against the door. "And you said you had a hard time seeing a woman kill Virginia because of her size. Do you believe Sarah is physically strong enough?"

"If she incapacitated her, then possibly." Brooks narrowed his eyes in thought. "But Sarah's afraid of her own shadow. I honestly can't see her having the presence of mind to commit either murder. She knows more than she's telling us, though, even if she doesn't realize it." He stroked his mustache. "As for the Ripper being a woman, we've got to consider it, although I think the cross-dresser is more likely."

He opened the car door and stepped out. "You think the medical examiner will have any luck expediting the DNA on Bonnie's baby? That could help narrow things down."

"I hope so," Erin said, and got out of the car. "Our killer may simply be a jealous ex, and Will Merritt lied to us about the nature of his and Bonnie's relationship. He may still be involved somehow, even if he's not a suspect."

She and Brooks hurried toward the door through mist-like sprinkles.

He nodded. "Definitely possible. In that scenario, Sarah's out of the equation, and there's no connection to Virginia Walton, which makes no sense."

Erin rang the doorbell. "Sometimes the connection is in the randomness of it." She smirked.

Brooks grinned down at her. "At least we're communicating."

Erin recognized the woman who answered the door. Not her face, but the sort of person she was. Her polished skin gleamed like heirloom china, and the woman's most-likely graying hair was dyed a shining blonde to match her daughter's. She dressed like Erin's mother and her conservative friends: expensive, tailored tweed slacks complemented by a cream cable-knit sweater. The only pieces of jewelry the woman displayed were pearl earrings and a beautiful diamond wedding set. Her stylish house slippers appeared made for snow, but would probably result in soaked feet. They looked great with her outfit.

Old wealth and proud of it, ready with a subtle insult, but unlikely to be outright rude.

"Can I help you?" Her soft voice seemed to match her outfit, and Erin became acutely aware of her own faded jeans and unruly hair.

"Investigators Erin Prince and Todd Brooks. We're here to talk to Sarah about Bonnie's murder."

"And a new development," Brooks added.

The woman's skillfully applied blush dimmed. Her careful smile diminished enough for her mouth to sag, and she aged at least a decade. "Professor Walton. Sarah is devastated."

"I'm sure," Erin said. "We do need to speak with her. Your name is Melinda, right?"

"Melinda Archer." The woman's dark eyes narrowed, and she leaned forward to get a better look at Erin. "You're Calvin Prince's daughter. You spoke with my husband yesterday."

"Yes."

Melinda's voice immediately warmed. "We attended his rallies for the last presidential election. He was a wonderful speaker. I told your father he should run for office. He got a kick out of it. Of course, your father has been a wonderful contributor to the National Governors."

Erin plastered a smile on her face. Her older sister had been telling her father to go into politics for years. Erin could only imagine how Lisa would worm her way into the White House.

"I'm sure he did get a kick out of it. May we come in?"

"Of course, dear." Melinda stepped aside, beckoning them into a large, tiled entryway. Her slippers slapped against the floor as she led them into a posh living room. "Please make yourselves comfortable. I'll make you some tea."

Erin and Brooks both refused the drink and asked again to see Sarah.

"You must have something to drink," Melinda insisted. "I'll be right back."

"Well," Brooks said as soon as the woman shuffled away, "the Prince name reigns again." He nudged her. "See what I did there?"

Erin shot him a dark look.

"What I find fascinating," Brooks said, "is how her attitude completely changed when she realized who you were."

"Welcome to my world," Erin said. "Here's where things get really smarmy—I'm going to try to use it to our advantage."

Melinda re-entered with a tea tray and set it on the coffee table. Her mouth dropped into a deep frown. "Sarah's a good girl. She's under a lot of stress."

Erin crossed her legs and then thought better of it when she realized her socks didn't match. She planted her feet on the floor. "Mrs. Archer, why do you say that? Sarah's not in any trouble."

"Of course not." Melinda's voice pitched high and then went back to conspiratorially low. "It's Bonnie, to be honest. Sarah reconnected with that girl out of guilt, and I don't want her dragged into whatever her cousin got into, especially while Sarah's trying to finish her thesis."

"Someone slaughtered your niece like an animal," Erin said. "Worse, actually. Hunters kill the animal first."

Melinda quivered, looking at Brooks as if he might intervene.

Erin didn't give him a chance. "Please get Sarah for us."

Manicured nails tugged at the expensive pearls, and Melinda's eyes narrowed as they searched Erin, traveling over her too-casual clothes, lingering over her slightly ragged fingernails and the extra roll of belly flesh that made itself known whenever Erin slouched.

She straightened and returned Melinda's appraisal.

"We have contributed heavily to your father's many fundraisers. You might treat me with respect."

The cool voice hit Erin's nerves with the force of a burning match. "I'm trying to solve two homicides." Her gut twisted, a hundred insults yearning to be released. "Please don't make me ask you again to get Sarah."

CHAPTER TWENTY-SIX

Wearing yoga pants and a loose-fitting man's shirt, Sarah sat with her legs crossed, elbows on her knees, chin in her hands. Her mismatched eyes stared at them in disbelief. "I don't understand what's happening." Her voice sounded rough and deeper from the hours of crying.

"I'm sorry to do this, but we need to ask you some questions." Erin tried to be gentle. Melinda had disappeared, probably to call her husband. "What do you know about Bonnie and Virginia Walton's relationship?"

"I didn't know they had one. I told Bonnie a long time ago my professor volunteered at her school and that she was a psychologist. She still had anger issues and needed to figure out her future, so I thought Bonnie should talk to her. Professor Walton is"—Sarah broke off and shifted uncomfortably—"was a great listener. Bonnie didn't like the idea. We never discussed it again." She stilled, and then her hands flew to her mouth. "Oh my God. I told Bonnie about Professor Walton. Is this my fault?"

"Of course, it's not your fault," Brooks said smoothly. "We're not sure why they were both chosen."

Erin gave her a moment to calm down before picking up the questioning again. "When did you give her Professor Walton's name?"

"A few months ago," Sarah said. "Bonnie mentioned calling her to learn more about the college program, but she never said anything more."

"Do you think she would have told you if they started spending time together?" Erin asked.

Sarah shook her head. "I thought Bonnie was open with me, but I guess not. And the professor wouldn't have said anything."

Erin watched Sarah closely. "We have questions involving information from the crime scene."

She blanched. "I don't want to look at pictures. I can't."

Brooks glanced at Erin. He wanted her to push. "You don't have to." Erin's voice took on a calming tone. "But the killer left a message."

Sarah stiffened. "All right. Go ahead."

"Please keep this between us." Erin leaned forward, keeping her voice as flat as possible. "The killer carved *whore* on a beam in Bonnie's attic and *snitch* on the professor's fireplace mantle. Does that mean anything at all to you?"

Sarah shrank inside the loose shirt until the collar reached her nose. "Bonnie wasn't a whore. She worked at the strip club, but never slept with any of those guys."

"The killer might have considered stripping just as damning as prostitution, but calling the professor a snitch doesn't make sense if she didn't know Bonnie well," Erin said. "I assume you knew Professor Walton was a lesbian?"

"She didn't keep it a secret."

"Did Bonnie date women?" Brooks asked.

Sarah's head emerged from her collar. "I—she never said anything about it. She didn't want to get serious with Will Merritt, but she never said anything about an interest in women. Is that what you think went on?"

Erin hated having to be evasive with her answers. The family deserved any details they wanted, but the investigation was too delicate, with too many gaping holes, and Sarah was a suspect.

"It's hard for me to imagine Bonnie letting someone else in. She didn't trust many people." Sarah looked over her shoulder toward the doorway. "You can thank my father for that."

"That's tough to forgive," Erin said.

"I haven't forgiven him." Sarah's tone flattened. "They're my parents, and I love them. They've given me every opportunity in the world, paying for school and my apartment and anything I need. All I have to worry about are my classes. But everything about my world has to be approved by them because Dad's an important man. It's exhausting. What happened to Bonnie—he played a part and never took responsibility. It's so typical of him and everyone I grew up with." She stopped, flustered. "Does that make sense?"

"Perfect sense." Sarah could have been describing Erin's upbringing. Money and privilege brought numerous opportunities, but came with different rules. Once she broke free and started living on her own, Erin managed to shed most of her bitterness toward her father.

Sarah had yet to forgive.

"I guess you would understand," Sarah said. "I've heard my father talking about your family. What do they think about you being a cop?"

Erin made an effort to keep her expression neutral. "It's complicated."

"I understand." Sarah twisted her watch around her slim wrist. "After all the things they said about Bonnie's murder being her fault because of her circumstances, I wonder what they'll say when I tell them the same person killed Professor Walton."

"Please keep that information to yourself," Erin said. "We have very little to go on, and if it gets out, people will panic."

"Okay," Sarah said. "I wish I had something more for you."

"Did you ever go to the professor's house?" Brooks asked.

"Once," Sarah said. "I was kind of a wreck about my thesis—I had to trash most of the first draft. She told me to stop by."

"What's your thesis on?" Erin asked.

"This is actually my second thesis. Professor Walton said the first one was too personal and not nearly analytical enough. It read like a memoir. So I had to start all over again." Sarah withdrew into her shirt collar. "It's a quantitative study and analysis on recovered memories of childhood sexual abuse and how victims individually react."

"You're a psychology major?" Erin remembered the ulcer-inducing months spent writing her own thesis.

"Yes. I've been working on it for so long, and I'm about ready to give Professor Walton the final draft." She wiped a tear off her cheek. "Of course, I can't do that now."

Erin leaned back in the chair. "I'm sure the university will assign you a new advisor. Did Bonnie's experiences give you the idea for the thesis?"

"In part," Sarah said. "I've known other people who have been sexually abused. No two of them react the same way. That's the heart of my research. Why some victims live relatively normal lives and heal while others derail like Bonnie." Sarah's voice grew louder as she spoke about a topic she clearly felt passionate about. She straightened and leaned forward, hands on her slim thighs.

"Why do some become perpetual victims? Do you know that 17.7 million American women have been victims of rape or attempted sexual assault? And then there are the unreported rapes. The Justice Department says over eighty percent of rapes on college campuses aren't reported. Women are too scared, and not coming forward allows another woman to be victimized." Spots of color appeared on Sarah's cheeks.

"We have to do something as a society to stop this. Instead of getting better, it's getting worse. The same with sexual abuse of children."

Erin's head buzzed as though she'd been dropped into a pressurized chamber. Tension pounded against her skull. Her brain seemed stuffy.

She wanted to run from the room and out into the fresh air, but she couldn't look away from Sarah's bright, contrasting eyes.

The girl stared back, face flushed. "I'm sorry. I got carried away."

Erin's lungs burned like she hadn't breathed in several minutes. "You're passionate about it. I'm sure your thesis is great."

"It seems so trivial now." She reclined against the chair back, emotions depleted. "Who would do this to them?"

"What can you tell us about Professor Walton's experience at the Adult Literacy Center?" Brooks asked. "Did she ever talk about anyone there? Maybe someone she had an issue with? One of her students?"

Sarah ran her fingers through her long ponytail, examining the strands she'd pulled out. "Well, she had an argument with one of the students at the Adult Learning Center. Professor Walton seemed upset by their altercation. She thought a lot of him. Anyway, he had an issue with a class. She tried to talk to him, and he got in her face. Called her a dyke and a bunch of other names."

"Do you remember his name?" Erin asked.

"Ricky," Sarah said. "I don't know the last name. But she didn't report it. By not reporting him, she thought it might help his attitude."

Erin shot Brooks a look of satisfaction, but he remained focused on Sarah.

"Why did the professor tell you about this?" His normally gentle voice held the ghost of an edge.

"Because I just happened to talk to her shortly after," Sarah said. "I called her with a question on my thesis, and I could tell she was upset."

"So you and Professor Walton were close enough for her to confide in you?"

"I think it was more of a timing thing," Sarah said. "She needed to talk to someone."

Erin glanced at her partner. He'd never looked so excited in the short time she'd known him.

He didn't take his eyes off Sarah and asked the next question. "Sarah, we're certain Bonnie made amateur porn—likely rape scenarios—as a way to earn extra cash. You're sure she didn't tell you?"

Sarah set her jaw and crossed her arms, her defiance betraying her. "She wouldn't have done that after what she went through." Her ponytail bounced as she shook her head. "No way."

"We have strong evidence she did," Brooks said. "She may have confided in Professor Walton."

"It's possible the videos led to her murder," Erin said. "Virginia's too. We're still putting things together, but Bonnie may have involved the wrong person. I'm not sure how Virginia fits in yet, but you visited Bonnie at home plenty of times. Even if you didn't know about the movies, you could have."

Sarah's mismatched eyes popped open, her pupils dilating. "You're saying I might be in danger?"

"We have to consider it a possibility," Erin said. "You need to be cautious while the investigation is ongoing. Stay here with your parents. Make sure the security system is on at all times. And if anything strange happens, call 911 immediately."

Sarah covered her mouth with her slender fingers. "I can't believe this is happening. You're wrong."

"I hope we are, for your sake." Erin stood to leave and asked the question she'd been dreading. "Sarah, we need to ask where you were last night."

"You're not serious." Sarah's hands slipped down to rest in her lap.

"I'm afraid so," Erin said. "You're the main connection between these two women. Eliminating you as a suspect is crucial."

Sarah blew out a shaky breath. "I was here. I never go anywhere anymore."

"And your mother can verify this?"

Sarah nodded.

"Any other staff?" Brooks asked.

"I honestly don't know," Sarah said. "But I park in the driveway because my father's cars take up all three stalls in the garage. So my car was here."

Heels clicked on the tile floors as Melinda Archer swept in, her arms going around her daughter's shoulders. "I can confirm my daughter remained home all evening, Investigator Prince. Considering her a suspect is insulting. Sarah's devastated, and she's exhausted from all of this."

Erin ignored the woman and gently touched Sarah's shoulder. "Please call me anytime, even if you just need to talk. We'll show ourselves out."

Brooks closed the front door behind them. "Why didn't Virginia Walton call us after Bonnie's murder? If Virginia's the snitch, then it's a safe bet Bonnie did talk to her. Or the killer thinks so, anyway."

"I'm more focused on Ricky Stout." Erin felt energized as they walked down the stone path. "He knew both of them. He's got a juvenile record. It's still not enough for a warrant, but maybe we can get the director at the ALC to talk."

Brooks's eyebrows raised. "Do you think that's likely?"

"The director's first priority is protecting her students and the program, which I get," Erin said. "But it's time for her to start talking." Though the rain had stopped, she zipped up her coat against the wind. "We need to swing by The Point. By the time we get there, it'll be late enough for a full staff to be on hand. Hopefully, someone recognizes Virginia Walton."

Brooks opened the passenger door. "Sarah's hiding something," Brooks said. "Don't tell me you didn't see how defensive she got about Bonnie's amateur porn. She knew. What's the point of lying about it?"

"I noticed." Erin slid behind the wheel. "On the other hand, I come from this type of environment. To someone like Simon Archer, those videos are scandalous. Sarah's got to protect his name, so the less she tells us, the better. She's grieving and torn between helping her cousin and dealing with her parents. I get it."

Brooks crossed his arms. "Sometimes people don't want to face the hard stuff, especially when they're younger. We want to believe what's easy and convenient."

Erin sighed. "Yeah, and a child becomes a victim over and over again."

"I'm not saying it's right," he said. "And you're missing the point."

She raised an eyebrow, waiting for him to continue.

"You aren't looking at Sarah objectively. Her mother pissed you off, and you feel more protective over Sarah because you recognize her mother as the sort of person you've grown up loathing and rebelling against. Yet, you think the killer is a woman. Now, tell me, who's the one person both Bonnie and Virginia have in common?"

Erin sighed. "Okay, we'll double-check with the neighbors, but Sarah's alibied for both. Not to mention, she's got a clean record. We have no physical evidence to tie her to either murder at this point. Marie's team is still looking for trace evidence, and Sarah's fingerprints and hair can probably be explained in both cases."

Brooks held up his hands. "All I'm saying is that her dishonesty is hurting the investigation, and we need to push her for the truth."

Erin started the car. Brooks had a point. "Let's check with the cab companies and private car services, as well, to see if we can't break her alibis."

CHAPTER TWENTY-SEVEN

Erin dropped Brooks off at the Walton house to pick up his car and hadn't gone two miles from the crime scene when Clark called for them to get back to the CID. Virginia Walton's daughter had apparently left home at the crack of dawn as soon as she was informed of her mother's murder and would be arriving at the station shortly.

Erin told Clark what Sarah had said about Ricky Stout. "You think it's enough for the judge to issue a warrant for his personal information?"

"We can sure as hell try." Clark cleared his throat. "Two vicious murders in three days. All depends on the judge. I'll do everything I can."

Erin threaded through traffic, working the case over in her mind. Maybe, if they were lucky, they'd catch a break. "Damn." Brooks's little wind-up car wasn't in the CID's lot. Hopefully, he wasn't lost. GPS had its merits, but in an old city like DC, it tended to muck people up, especially with the construction.

"Princess!" Fowler called out as soon as she entered the squad room. "Lovely morning, wasn't it?"

She growled a response.

Fowler grunted in return. "Yeah, well, I don't have much to give you. Professor Walton's colleagues at American University had little to offer other than the professor kept to herself, and she certainly wasn't discriminated against for her sexuality." Fowler made a face. "The dean wanted to clarify that his former employee's civil rights weren't violated. As a fairly new hire and an adjunct professor, Walton wasn't around long enough to form any bonds with her AU peers."

"Great. Yet another victim no one really knew. Today keeps getting better."

"It's about to get worse," Fowler said. "The victim's daughter is waiting for you in Interview Room A."

"My mom was a good lady." Rylan Walton clutched a nearly empty packet of tissues. Her bronze skin was raw beneath her eyes. A lock of her thick, curly brown hair escaped the messy knot on the top of her head, and she tucked it behind her ear. "She didn't deserve this." Her breath hitched in an asthmatic wheeze.

"Of course, she didn't." Erin spoke softly. "Thank you for coming in so quickly." She checked her watch. Brooks still hadn't arrived.

Rylan wadded up several tissues in a white-knuckle grip. She stared across the table at Erin, the pain in her eyes searing. "What are we waiting for?"

"My partner."

Rylan rubbed one of the tissues across her eyes, further irritating her already raw-looking eyelids. "I did an internet search on you."

"Excuse me?"

"When Sergeant Clark called and told me what happened, he said to ask for you if he wasn't here when I arrived. I wanted to know who I would be talking to. Your dad is a big-time defense contractor, right? He contributes to a lot of conservative causes. Another article mentioned you being a cop."

"Oh, I see." Erin struggled for a better response. Sometimes she hated the internet.

"So, you grew up rich, white, and conservative." Rylan's tone wasn't accusatory, but matter-of-fact.

"I suppose that's a good way to summarize it," Erin said. Where the hell was Brooks?

"Normally, I try not to judge because I know what it's like when people have pre-conceived notions about you," Rylan said. "I grew up half Black in the South, and my momma is gay. So I've spent plenty of my life dealing with prejudice from people with your kind of background."

Erin sympathized. People could be ugly to those outside their circle. "I'm sorry."

"Don't be. And don't let it affect how you help my mother."

"Your mother's life choices aren't my business and have no bearing on how I work the case." Erin put her hand on her chest. "My goal is to catch the person who did this."

"That's all I wanted to hear." Rylan's watery eyes drifted toward the clock. Erin wasn't going to make the woman wait any longer.

"Let's get started without my partner," Erin said. "Tell me about your mother's decision to move here from South Carolina. Why did she leave?"

"She needed a change after she and my dad split," Rylan said. "Then Mom got the courage to come out as a lesbian. I always found it funny it took her so long because she married my Black father in a state where it wasn't accepted at the time." Pride filled her voice. "My mother went through a lot and never gave up."

"How did people in her life take her coming out?" Erin asked.

"Some were surprised. My father had known for a long time. Instinct, I guess. Some of her friends and family shunned her, though, but some were okay about it."

"Your parents had an amicable split?"

The lock of hair came loose again. Rylan twisted it around her index finger. "Yes. No attorneys. Just a mediator."

"What about after your mother arrived here? Was she happy? Did she have friends? Anyone special?"

"At first, it was tough," Rylan said. "She basically started from scratch, and she was lonely, but everyone accepted her. She never talked about any issues like that. She kept herself really busy."

"Did she date anyone?"

Rylan shook her head. "I don't think so. No one she mentioned, anyway." She pressed her hands against her mouth. Her eyelids fluttered to stave off fresh tears. "I just can't believe she's gone. It's not real."

Helplessness descended over Erin. She had no words of comfort to offer that didn't sound trite. How could she pretend to understand what Rylan felt? "Can you tell me about her work with the Adult Learning Center? Her colleagues at the university didn't seem to know much about her outside of their work environment."

"She loved working at the ALC." Rylan gave a brief smile. "She said it was more fulfilling because those students were so desperate to better their lives. A lot of the students at the ALC are at-risk." Her features softened as she continued. "They didn't finish high school or are being forced to go because of a court mandate or pressure from their parents. Others are adults trying to get on their feet, but they've got a lot of baggage keeping them down. My mom loved being able to help them."

Virginia Walton had touched a lot of lives in her short time in the city. "Did your mom ever mention anyone specific at the Adult Learning Center? Anyone she had an issue with?"

"She talked about a lot of different students." Rylan hiccupped as she sobbed and pulled a fresh tissue out of her crushed packet. "Please tell me how this happened. Was she targeted because she was gay? Is that why he ... cut her up?"

"We don't think so," Erin said. "But we're still gathering evidence. Did your mother talk about a woman named Bonnie Archer?"

Rylan frowned in concentration. "The name rings a bell. She may have mentioned a Bonnie once or twice. I think she went to the ALC."

"Did your mother ever mention Bonnie coming over to her house?"

Rylan gave a slight shake of the head. "Why would she? Students didn't come to the house."

Erin mentally sighed. She'd hoped for a stronger connection between Bonnie Archer and Virginia Walton. "Did she ever mention a Black student from the ALC named Ricky?"

Rylan pursed her lips while she thought. "Not that I can remember. Why?"

"One of her thesis students said your mom told her about an argument she'd had with Ricky a couple of weeks ago. It was fairly heated and apparently frightened your mother."

"Oh, Christ." Rylan threw her hands up. "So because a Black man from the streets confronts a white professor, he might have killed her? And you're basing that on ... let me guess ... a rich white girl's interpretation of what my mother said?"

No." Erin gazed steadily at Rylan. "I'm trying to get some more information before we go to the ALC."

"Well, let me give it to you," Rylan said. "My mom liked working there better than she did American University. She took the job at AU because of the pay."

"I understand," Erin said.

Rylan barked out a hoarse laugh. "But you don't. My mom grew up in the South married to a poor Black man who worked his ass off to put food on the table. She knew how easily underprivileged kids could fall between the cracks and have zero opportunities in life, whatever their color. Those are the kids she wanted to help. Most of the students at American University are rich white kids who don't have a clue about the real world. So excuse me if I don't put much faith in some thesis student's recollection of what my mother said. I guarantee you Mom wasn't worried about how to handle that boy." She sneered at Erin. "You don't understand shit."

Erin inhaled deeply. She couldn't allow a grieving relative to get under her skin.

"Wait a minute." Rylan leaned back in the chair and narrowed her eyes. "Bonnie Archer. I just remembered why the name sounded familiar. Someone stabbed the poor girl to death." Her nostrils flared. "That happened three days ago. You think the same person killed my mother?"

Fury darkened Rylan's bloodshot eyes and reddened her cheeks. She smacked the table as she stood and leaned closer to Erin. "My mother is dead because you can't do your job?"

"We're working on it." Erin remained calm. "It's a complicated case, and we don't have much to go on."

The anger rolling off Rylan filled the small room. She had a few inches on Erin and several pounds of lean muscle. "Three days." She glowered at Erin. "And *you* didn't protect my mother."

"Your mother wasn't on our radar as a possible target." Erin adopted a soft tone, imbuing it with as much empathy as she could. "A killer like this usually targets similar victims, but we believe Bonnie and your mother were targeted for a specific reason."

"What reason?"

Rylan deserved answers, but Erin didn't have any ... at that point, they only had tenuous theories. "I'm not at liberty to say. It's an active investigation."

"And it's my mother at the morgue!" Rylan pounded the table. More hair escaped the knot as she shouted. "Not at liberty, my ass. You don't have a clue who's doing this. You're just giving me face-time and hoping I'll tell you something that will help because you don't know your ass from a hole in the ground."

"I'm sorry." Erin fought to keep her composure. "We're doing our best, I promise."

"Your best isn't good enough. You have no idea what I'm going through. Have you ever had a call telling you the most important person in your life was dead? Have you ever had to go into a fucking morgue and identify their body?" Tears streamed down Rylan's face.

"No, but—"

"But nothing," she spat. "You don't know anything about me. Or my mother. Or Bonnie Archer, evidently." Rylan crossed her highly toned arms and stared back, daring Erin to argue.

Erin's skin heated, and her stomach roiled. How had she gotten so off track with the woman?

Rylan gripped the back of the chair with both hands, leaning against it, looking down at Erin as if she'd just scraped her off her shoe. "Are you the best we've got? My mother *deserves* the best." Her face crumpled. "And you're not it."

Erin bit the inside of her lip to keep from reacting. "My job is to go over every piece of information we have and decide what's relevant and what's not."

Rylan's head jerked back. "Oh, you're going to decide? Like you decided after that girl got cut up? Like you decided while someone slaughtered my mom?" She slammed the chair against the table.

Erin slid back from the table and stood.

The door swung open, revealing a flustered-looking Brooks. "I'm so sorry." Brooks offered his hand to Rylan Walton. "I got delayed, and my partner's still new to working homicide. Let's you and I start over. How about that?"

Erin's mouth fell open.

Brooks shot her a look. "Sergeant Clark wants to see you." He stood there in pressed pants and an ironed shirt, his dumbass mustache twitching. "I'll take it from here."

Erin never wanted to scream at someone so badly in her professional life. The vitriol bubbled on her tongue, but she saw Rylan from the corner of her eye. Making a scene would accomplish nothing. "Fine. I'll speak to you after you two are finished." She turned her attention back to Rylan, who looked both smug and distraught. "Again, I'm sorry for your loss. We'll find whoever did this."

She shut the door and marched out of the room. Bright spots danced in her vision. What the hell had just happened? Weren't partners supposed to present a united front? Brooks had strode in and treated Erin like a kid caught joyriding with her older brother's car.

Anger rolled through her. She stalked around the corner, intent on going straight to Clark's office, but her superior waited in the hallway.

Clark crossed his arms over his big chest. "What the hell, Prince? What happened in there?"

He'd been watching on the live feed. Had Brooks been as well?

"We never had a chance to establish any kind of confidence," she said.

"You alienated her."

"She alienated herself. She already knew my family background and made a judgment before she even met me."

"Which you then fulfilled." Sergeant Clark shook his head. "You had the right idea but the wrong words. She's grieving. She's probably got a chip on her shoulder about race, and God knows what else."

He took off his glasses, cleaned the lenses, and then put them back on. "And the truth is, you come from a different world than most people. You've rubbed elbows with the President of the United States more than once, and other bigwigs. You went to an expensive private school, where you were protected and sheltered from real life."

"Not by choice," Erin said. "I got out of it as soon as I realized how little I knew about the rest of the world."

"You did," Clark said. "You don't judge by skin, class, sexual preference, or anything else. You're fair. And fierce. I know." He pointed in the direction of the interview room. "That woman doesn't. All she knows is her mother is dead, and you're a Prince. She found some basic shit about your family on the internet, and she needs someone to lash out at. You gave her the perfect opportunity."

Erin's hands fisted against her hips. Frustration tickled the back of her eyes. She would not allow angry tears. "I tried."

"I saw. It's not your fault. It's an experience thing. Think back to when you first started working in sex crimes and talked to a victim's mother for the first time. You didn't know what to say, did you?"

"Somewhat," Erin admitted. "But I'm a mom, too. Common ground came easily."

"Exactly. Not so easy in homicide—which is a good thing. That's where years on the job come in. The more you do it, the better you get. You learn to read people."

Erin frowned. "Like Wonder Boy in there."

"He's good, and you know it."

Heat crept up her neck. "He embarrassed the hell out of me. And where'd he disappear to? Didn't you call him back?"

"He was near The Point, so I told him to follow up. Turns out one of the bartenders remembered Virginia Walton coming in more than once over the past couple of months. She had a heated conversation with another customer who matches Tori's description two weeks ago—the last night Tori was seen at The Point."

"But the bartender can't definitively ID Tori?"

Clark shook his head. "He never got that close to him, but he's positive the person was either a masculine-looking woman or a man in drag. I'd say that's pretty good odds. Talk to Brooks for the details. As for him embarrassing you, that's your fault. He had to play off what you started with Rylan Walton. It's not personal."

Erin threw up her hands. "So you're saying life and death is a game?"

"Dealing with people is a game," Clark corrected. "The sooner you learn to play, the better off you'll be."

Just like everything else in life. Do the dance, pull the right strings, and learn to work the system. God forbid anything ever be as simple as right and wrong. "Tell Brooks I'll meet him at the Adult Literacy Center in Columbia Heights in an hour. I'm going to grab something to eat."

"Before you leave ..." Clark handed her a signed warrant. "We lucked out. The judge is an LGBT supporter. I might have hinted this could be a hate crime. Made me feel a bit scummy, but we got our warrant for Ricky Stout's contact information."

Erin tucked the warrant into her bag. "First good news I've had all day."

CHAPTER TWENTY-EIGHT

C harlie didn't know what to do anymore. Mina wouldn't stay quiet. She'd always listened to him in the past, but she fixated on that homicide cop as if she could somehow magically save them.

Anxiety rippled through him in shockwaves. He wished the end was in sight. He was tired of being the voice of reason for the others. They never wanted to listen and didn't give a damn about anyone else.

He thought about running away, escaping into the dark with Mina, but he'd tried that before. They always got caught.

He had no choice. He couldn't go to the police because he shouldn't know the things he did. He couldn't fight because he always lost. And he worried about not being able to protect Mina for much longer.

Charlie sank into his secret hiding spot and cried silent tears.

CHAPTER TWENTY-NINE

Erin didn't eat. Instead, she drove to Columbia Heights and used her Bluetooth audio system to call her brother. The irony of driving a nearly new car with all the bells and whistles wasn't lost on her. She only used her trust fund for important things like a down payment on a house and a reliable vehicle. She justified the Bluetooth as a safety measure.

"Maybe he's right," she told Brad as she navigated the traffic around the National Mall. Tourist season slowed in November, but the traffic never seemed to change. "We grew up with everything, and even though we left the nest and the lifestyle, we still enjoy a few perks, like the cars we drive. We can't imagine what it's like to be poor or a minority."

"Speak for yourself," Brad said. "I'll give you the poor. But I'm a minority."

"Fine, but skin color is something a person can't hide. You lived in the closet for a long time. Yeah, it sucked, but you could walk into a store and buy whatever you wanted without the clerk expecting you to rob the place."

"Walton's daughter is our age. She didn't have to fight for a right to sit at the counter."

"No," Erin said. "But she's got a valid point about racism and how I can't relate."

"Who can?" Brad asked. "So Brooks knows how to talk to her. That means he's good enough to fake it, not that he can actually commiserate with her. He's just better at pretending he doesn't have an opinion." Brad snickered. "That's never been your strong suit, anyway."

Erin rolled her eyes. "Whatever. The entire thing made me feel like an asshole."

"'Cause you are," Brad said. "Two women are dead, and you're gettin' all butthurt because your partner taught you a lesson. Quit being a whiner and learn from it."

"Thanks a lot."

His laugh filled the car. "You called me to lift your spirits. That's what I'm doing. Stop feeling sorry for yourself. You get to bust your ass and stop a sicko and learn some things in the process. So what if you were humiliated? Welcome to life."

Brad always knew exactly what to say to make her see things clearly. He also excelled in pushing every damn button in the process.

"You're a self-righteous asshole."

"But am I right?"

Erin jabbed her finger against the car's touch screen and ended the call. "You won't get me to say the words."

CHAPTER THIRTY

Erin waited for Brooks beneath the portico entrance of the Adult Literacy Center. She chose a heavier coat this morning, but the damp chill still seemed to permeate the fabric and leach warmth from her bones. She always hated this time of year for its drab coloring, but this stretch of gray days felt like some kind of record. She needed to see the sun again.

"I'm sorry," Brooks said as soon as he walked up. "I made you feel terrible, and I didn't intend to. I needed to make Rylan feel like the police were on her side because we are."

"And because I mucked the interview up so badly."

"You two just didn't gel. It happens."

Erin sighed. "I don't have enough experience to keep it from happening again."

Brooks thought for a moment. "Experience is honed by repeatedly being in the situation, which also takes a toll on you. So it's a double-edged sword."

Some of Erin's anger ebbed, but the humiliation clung to her system. "Couldn't you have handled it differently? She won't want to talk to me now."

"Don't worry about it. The best thing we can do for her is to find her mother's killer." Brooks brushed past her and took the steps two at a time.

Erin bit her tongue and followed him. "I'm afraid Rylan and the reporter are both right. I'm a liability. I'm sorry."

He slowed down. "We're a team. Don't let one interview mess with your head. Did Sergeant Clark tell you I went to The Point?"

Cold wind gusted from the north. Erin zipped her coat up to her chin. "Sounds like Tori, but we've already checked the paper trail from The Point. Nothing."

"I want to review the security footage again, this time looking for Virginia Walton. She might be easier to spot than someone wearing all black. At least we've got a face to look for." Brooks stopped walking and turned toward her. "For what it's worth, I get the insecurity. Every good cop has it."

"Yeah?"

He nodded. "Erin, ego is the worst thing to have when you're a cop. It keeps you from seeing what's right in front of you. You're doing fine. Stop second-guessing yourself and trust your instincts. You're going to make mistakes. So will I. But we have to keep trying, because these families and the victims deserve justice."

Resolve surged through her. She straightened her shoulders and braced herself for the task ahead. "Then let's go."

The Adult Learning Center seemed like a vastly different place than last week. No smell of lunch, no sounds of brisk work or joking students. Only the cars in the parking lot hinted at life going on as usual.

"Rylan said her mother knew Bonnie in passing," Erin said quietly. "So maybe they didn't talk."

"Or Virginia didn't tell her daughter. If she knew something, she might have been afraid to share it after Bonnie's murder."

Wearing jeans and a button-down shirt and looking like she needed another cup of coffee, the director, Stephanie Key, waited for them at the desk. "We canceled classes today. Everyone is shocked and heartbroken. We saw Virginia nearly every day."

"If Virginia is one of the counselors, why didn't she talk with us about Bonnie?" Brooks asked.

"You'll have to ask Brian," Dr. Key said. "I'm not sure the two of them knew each other. We have more than one counselor."

"How many of the staff are here?" Erin asked.

"Quite a few. I wanted everyone to have the chance to speak with you."

She led them down the hall, past her office, and into a large social area filled with big couches, well-loved, comfy-looking chairs, a couple of end tables, and a snack machine. Erin counted seven women and two men, including Brian Reese.

"Small staff."

"Only our two front desk assistants aren't here," Dr. Key said. "We have to run a lean operation despite the grant." She walked over and took the empty chair next to Reese. "As I said, we are all just devastated. The news said the same person who killed Bonnie killed Virginia. Is that possible?"

Erin never understood how the news media managed to weasel into crime scenes and thread information together when every single official had been told to close ranks. Then Erin pictured the beautiful redhead and her sly smile—no prizes for guessing how she got the information.

"It looks like it," Brooks said. "Bonnie's cousin, Sarah, suggested the two of them discussed some of Bonnie's personal issues."

Reese snapped his fingers. "That's right. I remember Bonnie mentioning that when she came to talk to me about Pathways. She'd already spoken with Virginia."

"Any idea what they discussed?" Brooks raised an eyebrow.

Reese shrugged. "The program, Bonnie's options."

Erin studied him. "Why didn't we hear from Virginia the other day?"

"She had classes at AU the day you spoke with us," Brian said. "She only met with Bonnie a couple of times about classes. She didn't really have anything to contribute. I told her not to worry about it."

Erin inwardly bristled. "Don't you think we should have made that decision? Virginia may have known something about Bonnie Archer that got her killed."

"Then why didn't she come to you anyway?" Brian seemed unfazed. "She didn't have to do what I told her to."

His smooth delivery reminded Erin of all the preppy boys she'd endured growing up. Hounding him in front of the group wouldn't get them anywhere, so she changed tactics. "How many of you knew both Bonnie and Virginia?"

Vanessa, the language arts instructor, raised her hand. "I didn't know Virginia as well as the others. We had different schedules."

"Did Bonnie ever mention her?"

"No. We told you Bonnie never shared anything personal."

"What about Virginia?" Erin asked. "I assume you were aware she was gay?"

Everyone nodded.

"No one cared," said a thin woman whose black boots looked heavier than her.

"Did she mention dating anyone?"

The woman bit back a sob. "Virginia didn't want to get into a relationship. She didn't have the time for it, so she spent her social life here, helping us."

"You two were close?" Brooks asked.

"I teach the computer courses, which means I work a lot of nights," she said. "Virginia worked nights, so we chatted."

Brooks looked at Dr. Key. "What did Virginia do here?"

"We were blessed to have Virginia as a volunteer. She was a skilled psychologist with a lot of experience. In addition to tutoring some students in math, she provided counseling in all areas. Emotional, mental, career."

"And only volunteered?" Erin asked.

"We didn't have the money to pay her when she first came on. She'd just come from South Carolina and wanted to be involved. She didn't care about the money and wouldn't take it when we freed up funds."

"This is going to sound strange," Brooks said. "Did Virginia ever mention counseling an older male student who cross-dressed?"

The entire group stared at him. Dr. Key finally spoke up. "No. If she did, that's confidential. We stay out of our students' personal lives."

So, not out of the realm of possibility, but Erin didn't think Bonnie's cross-dressing customer had anything to do with either murder. "Were you aware Virginia had an issue with Ricky Stout?"

Dr. Key's eyes snapped to hers. "We resolved that."

"So, she did report it." Erin made a note.

"She came to me the next morning." Dr. Key leaned forward in her seat, tapping her finger on the armrest. "Let me clarify. She wasn't concerned for her safety but for Ricky's."

"How so?" Erin asked.

Dr. Key hedged.

Erin considered the warrant she had in her bag. She didn't want to bring it out yet. She wanted to get everything she could before she pissed off the director. "I'm not asking you to divulge anything Ricky Stout may have told you, but Virginia Walton is dead, and we're trying to solve her murder."

Dr. Key sighed. "Ricky frequented her office. He comes from a terrible home environment—drugs and abuse—and he had no one. I think he became attached to Virginia. She was sort of like a mother figure. He came to her about advice in all sorts of areas, not just school and career."

"Did he ask her about Bonnie Archer?"

"She never mentioned it." Dr. Key's jaw set.

If Ricky Stout had ever mentioned Bonnie, Stephanie Key wasn't going to say a damned word. Erin understood the need to protect her student body, but two people had been murdered.

The thought popped out before she could stop it. "Is it because Ricky is Black?"

A couple of people sucked in shocked gasps as though Erin had spoken a forbidden language.

"Excuse me?" the professor said.

"You're protective of Ricky Stout," Erin said. "I realize you have rules to play by, but I think there's more to it. Are you afraid he'll be railroaded because he's a Black male with a sealed juvenile record, and the dead women are white? I can't blame you if that's the way you feel. A certain precedent's been set, and race relations are a serious issue in this country. I'm sorry to be blunt, but I'm trying to solve two brutal homicides, and I'd rather deal with the elephant in the room now before we go any further."

Erin glanced at Brooks, expecting him to shut her down, but he watched the director with interest, the vein in his neck pulsing.

Dr. Key crossed her legs, her movements lethargic and her face drawn. "Did you have any Blacks at Sidwell Friends School, Investigator Prince? The Obamas' daughters attended, but you were there before that, right? Things have come a long way."

Erin didn't react as Brooks's attention switched to her. She answered his unasked question. "Sidwell Friends School is the Harvard of Washington's private schools. A lot of politicians and people with political influence send their kids there. Chelsea Clinton attended at the same time as me." Erin had met the First Daughter a few times, but she hadn't socialized with her. "To answer your question, yes, there were. But a minority."

"So it's fair to say it's hard for someone like you to grasp the economic divide in this country—race excluded?" Dr. Key asked. "Not just in social class and wealth but in education."

"I've been a cop long enough to be well aware of it," Erin said. "I also don't deny every one of those things exists, but I'm not here to debate them. I wouldn't be asking about a Black male if he hadn't already been mentioned as knowing both dead women and having an issue with one of them. Race and social class aren't affecting my judgment. Is it affecting yours?"

Dr. Key appeared to weigh her options.

She wasn't the only one who had done her research. Stephanie Key came from a broken family, grew up poor, and earned scholarships to college. Her mission to help other young adults stemmed from her own experience, and the instinct to protect them came naturally.

"You need to tell her," Brian Reese said. "If they don't have a warrant, they'll be back with one."

Dr. Key glanced at him and then around at the rest of the group. Vanessa nodded.

Dr. Key folded her hands on her lap. "Ricky is my nephew."

Erin watched Brooks out of the corner of her eye. He nodded along with the director's words. He already knew Ricky was her nephew.

"All right then," Erin said. "So you have a personal interest."

"He's a good kid who saw his mother murdered. My sister."

"I'm sorry."

"Ricky was only seven. I'd gone off to college, and his daddy was in prison. My parents couldn't take him because of their health. He went into foster care, and I was never able to get him out."

Dr. Key likely hadn't wanted him to get out of juvie. A problem kid would have made her career a hell of a lot more difficult. "We'll have a warrant to unseal his juvenile records by tomorrow."

Dr. Key's lips thinned. "He was angry. Lashed out at anyone with authority, including teachers. He got physical with more than one, and he dropped out at sixteen. Two years ago, I hired someone to track him down on the streets, and I went about setting him straight. He's been doing well, keeps a job, and he has a place to live."

Erin moved to show her the warrant and ask for Ricky's address, but Brooks spoke up. "How was his mother killed?"

Dr. Key looked at Brooks for a long time. "Her boyfriend stabbed her twenty-two times in front of Ricky. He watched her bleed to death while he waited on the police to get there."

A perfect recipe for violence. Erin produced the warrant. "Where does Ricky live?"

Contact information in hand, Erin marched outside, searching for a way to diplomatically handle the tension eating at her.

Brooks easily caught up. "Nice work on the race call. You handled that well."

She tried hard to sound rational. "You knew Ricky Stout was her nephew and didn't tell me?"

"I wasn't sure," he said. "I did some digging and found out Dr. Key's maiden name was Stout. I didn't tell you because I wanted to let the whole thing play out organically. I had no idea about him seeing his mother murdered, but if he saw her stabbed as a kid, this makes a lot more sense."

Erin stopped in the middle of the sidewalk. "How are we supposed to work together if we don't communicate? We're like two roommates who have no interest in getting to know each other."

"You're wrong," Brooks said. "I want to get to know you, and I like working with you. We've just got to fine-tune our routine. Figure out how to share the bathroom." He smiled at his bad joke.

Erin rolled her eyes, snatching her ringing phone out of her pocket. "Hey, Sergeant. What do you have?"

She listened as Clark rattled off numbers. Her heart raced. "Sounds good. We're going to talk to Ricky Stout, and then we'll be in."

"What is it?" Brooks asked as soon as she ended the call.

"We finally got financials back on Bonnie Archer. She'd paid two months ahead on her mortgage, and she had over a hundred thousand in a savings account. Her parents are coming into the station to discuss the new developments, but I bet they're totally unaware."

Brooks let out a low whistle, staring into the darkening horizon. "Well, that's one hell of a stripper."

"Or an online porn star. Clark's trying to get the overtime approved for the forensic examiners to find her on the web, but we don't have time."

She'd end up regretting it, but every instinct told her there would be more dead women soon. "Get Ellen and her friend on it. Find Bonnie Archer's sex videos. If we get lucky, Ricky Stout will be a star."

CHAPTER THIRTY-ONE

Ricky Stout lived in a one-bedroom, second-floor apartment in a crummy building on 12th and U Street, right above the Walgreens. A patrol cop stationed on the corner served as a wary deterrent for neighborhood thugs. The uniform hadn't seen Ricky in a couple of days. He'd also called in sick to the tire shop where he worked part-time.

"I think she warned him." Erin and Brooks stopped by Clark's office to give him an update. "Now he's on the run. I put out a BOLO, but I wouldn't be surprised if he's holed up at Dr. Key's place. I'd like to get into his apartment, but we'll never get the warrant."

"Put more pressure on the DNA lab again," Brooks suggested. "If Bonnie's baby is Black, we might have enough probable cause."

Erin didn't think so, considering the current environment. Everyone worried about further pushing the racial issue, especially judges and law enforcement. Unless a case came wrapped in a red bow, a judge likely wouldn't issue a warrant for Ricky's DNA.

Sergeant Clark handed Erin the printout containing the information the warrant dredged up about Bonnie's financial information. "Here's what's interesting. She made a hundred grand in less than six months and all of it appears to be monthly transfers from an offshore account."

"Six months? Holy shit," Erin said. "I'm in the wrong line of work."

"No way did she make that from selling porn, even if she had a pay-per-view site," Brooks said. "Without the backing of one of the frequented sites, it's word of mouth."

"What if she didn't set up a pay-per-view site?" Erin asked. "What if it's buried deeper? One of those things where the user has to give their life away for access."

"Like the child porn creeps," Clark said. "Rape porn isn't that taboo, though." He held up his hands at Erin's look. "I'm not saying it's right, but you can find it on any internet search, half of it by simply searching for rough sex. The buried stuff on the deep web is usually the freak show. Animals, real violence, snuff films. Dark and twisted."

"Which means she could have charged a mint for it," Erin said.

"It makes more sense, given this amount of money." Brooks leaned against the wall, ankles crossed, looking completely unconvinced.

"Unless you have more specific search information and people with the access to the right things," he cut a look at Erin, "we aren't going to find it."

"Maybe there's another source of income," Erin said. "Will Merritt lives nicely, but he doesn't come from money. I can't see him being her sugar daddy, but Sid's is frequented by all sorts of Capitol Hill types. Who's to say she didn't have someone else on the side? Someone who fell in love with her and wanted to help her."

"But why the offshore deposits?" Brooks asked. "Why not cash?"

"Because he's married and influential," Clark suggested. "Big cash withdrawals raise questions with the wife. He keeps money in an offshore account because if the wife finds out about his philandering, she'll take everything. This way, he's got a safety net. Then Bonnie comes along, and it's the perfect way to help her."

"Or pay her blackmail," Erin said. "We keep talking about her blackmailing one of her sex partners, but what if it's Simon Archer? Her uncle's likely got the means to pay her, and if it ever got out that he covered for a child molester, he'd be ruined."

"Where does Virginia come in?" Brooks asked. "She and Bonnie are loosely connected by the school and Sarah, but her murder doesn't make sense in either of those scenarios."

"The killer called Virginia Walton a snitch and herself—or himself—the name Jane. Maybe Jane's the jilted wife. Bonnie confides in the professor. Jane takes them both out. Or Simon paid someone to take care of the situation, and you're right about Jane being a smokescreen."

Clark played with a yellow stress ball, squeezing it until his knuckles nearly popped out of their sockets. "Where are you with Sarah Archer's alibi for both murders?"

"Two neighbors remember Sarah's car being there the night of Bonnie's murder and last night," Erin said. "Out of twelve local cab companies, no one has picked anyone up from her parents' home in the last ten days. So far, none of the places providing personal drivers have any record of picking Sarah up, either. One company has picked up Simon at his home multiple times, but not within the last week and never Sarah."

"So, other than her personal connection with both women, we've got nothing else on Sarah Archer?" Clark asked.

"No," Erin said. "Brooks doesn't think she's telling us everything."

Clark mushed the ball between this thumb and index finger. "What about you?"

Erin shrugged. "I think she's got her head buried in her thesis and doesn't see anything she doesn't want to. We've still got to go back over the security footage from The Point, and I think our time is better spent trying to find Tori and talking to Ricky Stout."

"Probably so," Clark said. "Let her stew unless we get something on the trace evidence side."

The same desperation from this morning flashed across Brooks's face. "Tori might be a legitimate suspect, but he's a ghost, at this point. Where does Ricky Stout fit into all of this? And don't forget Mina and Charlie. Who are they to our victims? I still feel like we're chasing our tails, and we've fallen off the map."

Erin didn't want to admit she felt the same way—flailing in the dark searching for something living only in her imagination.

Clark rolled his neck from side to side, wincing as it cracked. "The assistant chief's on his way down to bitch at Fowler and me for the lack of progress in the Ted Moore case. No one wants to talk about which gangbanger killed the guy. Imagine." His deep voice dripped with sarcasm. "And this double homicide. With the goddamned media in tow."

He turned his angry eyes on Erin. "Speaking of which, you want to tell me why you told that redheaded reporter the same person killed Bonnie and Virginia?"

"What?" Erin's guts lurched. "I didn't say anything to her but 'no comment.'"

Clark pointed at his computer. "The article says you confirmed."

Erin shook her head, but then the moment came back to her. The reporter goading her about her family, angling to use her involvement as the main story. "I said victims. Plural. Oh God, I'm sorry."

"Don't worry about it. I'm sure her panty-chasing source would have told her anyway, but you need to be careful what you say, Prince. These people will twist your words to the very limit of the First Amendment."

The mistake didn't hinder the investigation, but Erin's pride wanted to run away in shame. Stupid rookie mistake.

"The Archers are going to come at you hard," Clark said. "They called me this morning as soon as Channel 4 broke the story, asking why we suddenly have more manpower with a prominent professor as a victim."

"We have more manpower?" Brooks looked around Clark's crowded office. "Is there a turd in your pocket?"

Clark snickered. "Not until the assistant chief's done with me, but apparently that's the line of bullshit the media is peddling."

Erin couldn't join in the humor. She kept picturing the redhead's smug face. She'd played Erin exactly as she wanted to.

Clark waved his hand in the direction of the door. "So you two better get out of here unless you're interested in bending over for an epic ass douching."

Erin hurried out the door.

Brooks caught up with her in the hallway. "Erin, wait a minute."

She stopped but didn't turn around.

"You didn't jeopardize the case."

She rubbed her eyes until stars danced in front of them. At least she hadn't had time to put mascara on this morning. "I played right into her hands."

"You did."

"Thanks."

"I'm not going to say it doesn't matter because it bugs you," Brooks said. "So it matters to you. But you live and learn for next time. That's all you can do."

"You're right." At least she could still fake confidence. "How do we handle the Archers?"

"We go in soft, understanding. Expect to be yelled at. They're hurting, want answers, and see us as the reason they aren't getting any information."

"How do we softly ask them whether they knew Bonnie made amateur porn?"

"We don't unless we absolutely have to. Kid gloves, right?"

This had all the makings of a grand clusterfuck. Erin kept silent as she led the way down the hall to the open interview room.

Carmen Archer sat at the table, staring blankly at the wall, looking drastically different than she had a few nights ago. Locks of her hair clung to her tired face, and gray bags hung under her eyes. Her cheeks drooped, and her mouth sagged. She'd aged a decade in days. Her husband paced the small area in front of the window. He stopped short at Erin's knock, his bright, angry eyes homing in on her.

"We're sorry to keep you waiting," Erin said, taking the seat across from Carmen. "How are you holding up?"

Carmen shook her head.

Neil immediately turned on them. "How are we holding up? You couldn't make any headway on our daughter's murder, but you're adding additional investigators because the bastard killed a more prominent woman? Or is it because some crazy person is copying Jack the Ripper?"

Erin froze, trying to think of the right response. Red must have talked to the right people this time.

"I'm not sure where you heard that, Mr. Archer." Brooks kept his voice soothing and patient. He sat down next to Carmen. "Our unit is stretched thin. We've had some help from our sergeant, but everyone's overloaded. Investigator Prince and I are the only two working the case. As for a Jack the Ripper copycat, we have no such thing."

"That's not what the reporter told me," Neil Archer said.

"What reporter?" Erin asked.

"The one from Channel 4 who called an hour ago. She said both women were gutted like the Ripper victims, and the killer left messages referring to the Jack the Ripper murders."

Erin tried to keep her face neutral, but inside, her heart galloped. A lot of people had access to Bonnie's crime scene, but Clark managed to keep the professor's on lockdown thanks to the quick thinking of the responding patrol officer. Only a handful of people knew about the messages.

Jane must still be a secret, or the press would have run with the information.

"We can't comment on details." Brooks deflected again. "But I can tell you this isn't a Ripper copycat."

"I think you're lying," Neil said. "At this point, I trust the media more than you."

"Mr. Archer, we've told you everything we can. That's why we wanted to talk to you today. We have more information to share, which means more questions to ask."

Nothing shook Brooks, Erin grudgingly admitted. Either that, or he managed to hide it well.

"Why haven't you formed a task force, then?" Neil demanded. "Two women are dead. What's it going to take?"

More murders. Erin didn't dare voice the idea, and no answer would satisfy Neil. "Would you like to sit down? The things we're about to ask you aren't going to be easy to talk about."

"I prefer to stand," Neil snapped. "And before you say a word, we know Bonnie and Sarah had started talking. She called us and apologized. Carmen talked to her."

"What did she say?" Erin rested her hands on the table, giving Carmen what she hoped looked like a kind smile, but felt more like an exhausted grimace.

"She said she found Bonnie because she missed her." Carmen sounded hoarse. "They kept it from her parents. She knew we would have understood as long as Bonnie stayed away from Simon."

Neil grunted, eyebrows slashing into one solid line at the mention of his brother's name.

"You wouldn't have approved?" Brooks remained standing as well, leaning against the wall, hands in his pockets. "Even though Sarah wasn't the reason for your family falling out?"

"She's a reminder," Neil said. "She told you about Bonnie's sexual abuse. My brother accusing her of lying really screwed her up. She believed she had done something wrong. Therapy helped for a while—until puberty turned everything upside down. She started hanging around the wrong people. She was raped. Then she got addicted to painkillers. All to deal with the self-loathing my brother caused."

"Did Simon molest Bonnie?" Erin asked quietly. The vast majority of children were molested by family members or close family friends. Sarah had said a family friend, but she might not have been told the entire truth. Little kids lied to protect their parents all the time, no matter how horrifically the adults made them suffer.

"No." Neil clenched his hands like he wanted to throttle her. "I'm not giving you a name. It's in the past, and Bonnie's dead. The bastard got away with it because my stupid brother, the big-shot attorney, is an asshole. Bonnie had obvious physical signs of being molested, but we had no DNA, no hair, nothing. Just an eight-year-old's word against a powerful man."

Erin didn't comment on the slip. "If you didn't report it, then how do you know DNA evidence couldn't be recovered?"

"He made sure it didn't exist."

Erin wanted to argue that a search warrant would have garnered an extensive search of wherever Bonnie said the abuse took place and that DNA could hide in places people never think of. Instead, she said, "Bonnie was old enough to understand what happened and who did it. Why didn't you allow her to tell the police?"

Neil's mouth puckered, the bags beneath his eyes making his face appear swollen. "Because my brother said he would act as defense attorney and make our lives—including Bonnie's—hell. She'd always had an active imagination. She entertained everyone with wild stories. He even had home movies of her and Sarah doing plays. These weren't typical kid plays. They always had bad things happening, always had conflict. Bonnie didn't want to have to talk about it. She didn't want to have to fight her uncle. She wanted it to go away." His voice cracked. "Simon coached Sarah. She stood in their living room and primly told us Bonnie told her I had done it, and she'd made up the story so the abuse would stop."

"Sarah was six years old. They taught her how to lie," Carmen said. "She told us she needed years of therapy to deal with it all. Sarah became nearly as much of a victim as Bonnie."

Erin worked to keep the harsh accusation out of her voice. This was her specialty, the experience she could bring to the table to match Brooks's homicide knowledge. "Do you seriously believe Sarah needed years of therapy just for being coached to lie as a six-year-old?"

Carmen's pale face turned a blotchy red. "I don't know."

"You realize this same person likely abused Sarah as well, either during the time of Bonnie's abuse or after? Especially since the abuser had access to her."

Tears trailed down Carmen's cheeks. "We tried to talk to Simon and Melinda, but they were so livid and made so many threats. We had to put Bonnie first."

"So you decided Bonnie would be better off by cutting ties with the family and going to therapy?" Erin held no judgment. She'd like to think she would have made the man pay if Abby had been a victim, but she'd seen too many families go through absolute hell during the trial phase. She also knew full well how powerful money and influence could be.

Neil jerked his head up and down. Tears welled in his eyes. "When she started doing drugs, I blamed myself. I never could stand up to Simon."

"Sarah believes the man who abused Bonnie left town sometime after you found out."

"Yes." Carmen rubbed her already bloodshot eyes. "I don't understand why we're going over this. It has nothing to do with Bonnie's death."

"We're trying to gather as much information about Bonnie as we can," Erin said. "You're sure he's no longer living in the area?"

"Positive." Neil Archer spoke with finality.

Erin's nerves rippled with desperation. "I promise you the information will stay with us," she tried again. "We need to know Bonnie's state of mind in the last few months, and with Sarah back in her life, it's possible they discussed the abuse. Don't you think finding out Sarah had taken her place would have devastated Bonnie? She may have tried to contact him, looking for closure."

"She didn't." Neil's stern gaze landed on Brooks. "I'm not answering any more questions about it. You said you had a suspect?"

How could he be so sure? He'd said the man was an important figure—did he remain in the public eye? Or had Neil Archer made it his life's mission to keep tabs on the man he more than likely allowed to continue molesting other little girls? In Erin's mind, that sad truth hurt the most. Neil should have stood up to his brother to prevent future victims.

Brooks took over. "Did Bonnie ever mention a man named Ricky?"

Both parents shook their heads. "I don't remember a Ricky."

"You knew about her study group at the ALC this past summer, right?"

A tiny glow of pride in Carmen's eyes. "I did. She loved helping others. Was Ricky in her group?"

Shaking his head, Brooks directed his question to Carmen. "We'd hoped you might be able to tell us more about him."

"She never mentioned him," Carmen said. "And she told us everything as part of her therapy."

Erin glanced at Brooks. He scratched his chin and then the back of his neck. Letting them wait for a minute. Or working up to the anger he expected to receive?

"What is it?" Neil demanded. "We have a right to know about our daughter's case."

"Mr. Archer," Brooks started. "Please understand we have to keep some details private because the investigation is still open. We can, however, tell you your daughter had over a hundred thousand in a savings account. Is that something you set up for her?"

Neil Archer blinked. "That's not possible," Neil said. "We helped her out occasionally, but we couldn't do much. She had a grant for school, but there's no way. You must be mistaken."

"I'm afraid we're not," Brooks said. "Which means Bonnie did something you didn't know about to earn quite a bit of money, and it likely got her killed."

"Not drugs," Carmen said as if drugs were the only real evil Bonnie could have wandered into. "She was clean."

"Yes," Erin said. "But she could have been dealing. Bonnie never worked at Daniel's. She worked as an exotic dancer at Sid's Gentleman's Club, near the Capitol." Erin couldn't bring herself to say stripper. It seemed like a cruel taunt to the already shocked couple.

"No." Neil's fist shook the table. "You're lying."

Carmen's eyes darted to her husband's and then to the table, her hands clasped as though in prayer.

"I'm afraid we're not," Brooks said. "We've confirmed it with both establishments as well as her boyfriend. We also found evidence she made films in the attic." He cleared his throat. "Of a sexual nature. Our crime scene experts believe a wireless transmitter was taken along with her laptop."

Neil's face bloomed red. "Are you saying our daughter made porn?"

"We don't know anything for sure," Brooks said. "We're telling you the facts as we know them."

"I don't understand." Carmen Archer appeared unfazed by the attic revelation. "Sarah told us she introduced Bonnie to Virginia Walton. We already knew Bonnie had spoken with her about Pathways. If Bonnie was killed because of this money or something bad she got herself into, then why would the same person kill the psychologist?"

"We think Bonnie may have confided in Professor Walton." Erin wasn't at all sure of this, but she had to give them something. "Carmen, how long have you known that Bonnie worked at the gentleman's club?"

Carmen paled further. "I didn't."

"I watched your reaction," Erin said gently. "You weren't surprised."

Carmen said nothing, not quite looking at her husband, who stared at her as if he'd never seen her before.

"I'm not trying to cause friction," Erin said. "And I don't judge Bonnie. But she told you about Sid's. What else did she tell you?"

"Nothing," Carmen said.

"You knew she took her clothes off?" Neil turned on his wife.

"I heard her on the phone a few weeks ago." Carmen looked her husband straight in the eye, her body braced for an argument. "I confronted her, and she explained she made more money there. She said the men never touched her. Her drug tests always came back clean. She begged me not to tell you. She knew you'd be angry and would want to give her money." She turned back to Erin. "In 2008, when the market crashed, we lost a good chunk of Neil's retirement. Things are tight. Bonnie didn't want us helping her."

Neil shook his head, eyes wet. "You should have told me."

"I promised her I wouldn't. She didn't want you to be disappointed. She wanted to make it on her own."

"Did she tell you anything else?" Erin asked. "Did she say anything about filming or selling videos online? Or mention anyone she might have been working with?"

"No," Carmen said firmly. "She didn't."

Erin sighed.

"I would tell you," Carmen insisted. "I want her killer found!"

"Of course," Brooks said. "What about a Jane?"

Another no. "We told you she didn't have many friends."

Neil Archer paced again. "So you still don't know anything beyond accusing my daughter of using her body to make money?"

The break in his tone told Erin he knew his wife spoke the truth.

"We have one strong lead we are following up on and a couple of other possibilities," Erin said. "This case will be solved."

"We need the name of Bonnie's abuser." Brooks swung the conversation back to where they'd started. "I'm not convinced she earned $100,000 making amateur movies of any sort. She may have been blackmailing him, and he decided to take care of her."

"It wasn't him. He's in California," Neil said flatly.

Erin didn't believe him, and Brooks's skeptical expression said he didn't either. Bonnie's pig of an abuser probably had nothing to do with her death. She had eyes on a bigger prize. If Sarah had been abused and told Bonnie, the older cousin might have decided to target the man responsible for their abuser going free, especially if the abuser couldn't be located.

"What about your brother, Simon?" Erin watched Neil's slouched form turn rigid at the mention of his brother's name. "Do you think he'd have the financial means to pay Bonnie that kind of money?"

Neil's teeth clicked together. "You'd have to ask him."

She and Brooks promised to keep the Archers updated, but neither parent looked confident.

As soon as the couple left, Erin asked, "What if all three blackmailed Simon, or Bonnie's abuser, or both? I don't think they had anything to do with Bonnie's murder, but they lied when they said Bonnie's abuser lives in California."

"I thought the same thing," Brooks said. "Let's see if Clark can get a warrant for their financial information."

"No chance in hell," Erin said. "They're the grieving parents, and we've got nothing on them but gut instinct. The judge will rage on about invasion of privacy."

Sergeant Clark stormed out of his office. "I called Channel 4, and they confirmed they have a story. Of course, the vultures won't reveal their sources." His stern gaze traveled around the sea of cubicles and straining ears. "I *will* find out who did it, and their ass will be on a silver platter on my fucking desk."

"Can you get them to sit on the story for a day or so?" Brooks asked. "Promise them an exclusive, maybe an interview with one of us."

Clark shook his head. "I tried. They're running it on the nine o'clock news."

CHAPTER THIRTY-TWO

They watched the news from the small break room at the CID. The three of them, plus Fowler and the assistant chief, a surly woman who always looked as though she'd been sucking on sour lemons, surrounded the television. Clark passed the time answering his phone and fielding mini-crises while Brooks made guy-centric small talk with Fowler. Who the hell cared about the Wizard's chances for a good season?

Erin's stomach soured. She wished she'd grabbed the Tums out of the medicine cabinet this morning. Someone here likely had a pack, but she'd have to leave her post, and as soon as she did, the news would go from a top story about a skirmish in Afghanistan to the D.C. murders.

The silver-haired lead anchor, his pancake makeup as firm as his voice, announced the top local story: "The Princess and the Ripper."

Erin froze. The men's eyes shifted to her, but she didn't acknowledge them. Her forehead throbbed as blood pulsed through her.

Red—real name Camille Torrence—stood somberly in front of the yellow tape at Virginia Walton's home. Savvy camerawork framed the scene perfectly, capturing just the outer edge of the lot, where the naked trees and morose sky provided an appropriate backdrop. Torrence's bright blue coat stood out as the only splash of color, sucking in the viewer's focus.

"Is a modern-day Jack the Ripper terrorizing Washington, D.C.?" Torrence spoke with importance but also with the gossipy air of a friend desperate to deliver the juicy goods. "And is a rookie homicide investigator, known as The Princess, capable of catching him before he kills again?"

Erin's grip on her plastic water bottle tightened until water spouted out.

Torrence blew through the description of both murders, barely acknowledging the women's names, and then moved on to the messages, describing those in detail. She didn't mention the killer being a woman, so Jane remained secure—but for how long?

The rest of Torrence's four-minute story focused on Erin, detailing her time as a sex crimes investigator and her move to homicide while

176

subtly hinting her family name played into her promotion.

"Prior to the Ripper case, Prince worked just two homicides. Concerned citizens are demanding to know why she's the lead investigator on such a volatile case."

Cut to a shot of Brooks and Erin standing by their cars, Brooks confessing his fear and confusion about the case. The shot and seeds of doubt already planted by Torrence made it look like he'd chastised Erin.

"We can only hope the police are able to work together to find this killer before yet another innocent woman is brutally murdered."

Back to the lead anchor, who lamented the tragic killing and the politics of police work, indicating Calvin Prince must have lined someone's pockets for Erin to have such a major role.

She'd heard enough. She hit the OFF button and slammed down the remote before turning to face the gathering peanut gallery—other investigators, two of the uniforms at the scene that night, and more who had no reason to be there. Shift change, she realized. Nice excuse. Her eyes met those of J. Acosta's, and the empathy coming from them nearly broke her.

"Who leaked the information about the murders?" Her hoarse voice cracked in the effort to hold back tears. She would not cry in front of these people.

"They don't have all the information." Clark looked sideways at the uniforms. "You people are supposed to be out on the street, not here. Beat it."

He waited until the crowd cleared, leaving only Brooks, Fowler, himself, the glowering assistant chief, and Erin. "It could be any number of people," Clark said. "Only those in this room, plus Mitchell and Marie, know about the name. But the crime scene people, the uniforms, and someone from the M.E.'s office have access to the other information. Trying to find out who leaked it is a waste of time and resources."

"Neither of which you have, Investigator Prince." Assistant Chief O'Rourke's husky voice came down like a gavel. "With this information out, your reputation is at stake."

"I earned my promotion." Erin kept her voice even.

"Right now, that doesn't matter," O'Rourke said. "Perception is what matters to the people who decide whether or not you have a job. After this, if another woman dies, you'll be first in line for the fallout. The chief and the mayor will see you as a public relations threat to the department."

"Are you kidding me?" Erin said. "No offense, ma'am, but you of all people know how difficult it still is for a woman in this job."

"That's why I'm giving you this warning. The whispers about your family connections, however unfounded they may be, are now public. Am I to understand you've postulated this killer may be a woman inspired by the theory that Jack the Ripper was a female?"

Erin's jaw throbbed from clenching. "I think it's a possibility we have to consider. The name 'Jane the Ripper' has been signed at both scenes."

"Which could all be a distraction," O'Rourke said. "Do you have any women on the suspect list? A female who had issues with both Bonnie Archer and Virginia Walton?"

"The only woman connected to both of them is Sarah Archer, Bonnie's cousin," Erin said. "She's devastated, and she has alibis for both murders."

"She's also the daughter of a prominent member of the National Governors Association," O'Rourke said. "But we do have another suspect—a male suspect, correct?"

"Ricky Stout, a student at the literacy school, as well as a cross-dressing male at the strip club where Bonnie worked." Erin struggled to remain respectful of the assistant chief. Politics played front and center in nearly every homicide investigation in D.C., and Erin didn't envy her superior's job, but tiptoeing around Simon as a suspect infuriated her. "We also believe he may have had contact with Virginia Walton at another club, but we don't have any tangible proof. Simon Archer is a potential suspect. Bonnie may have been blackmailing him." She set her jaw and waited for the backlash.

"About that," Fowler cut in. "I've been going over the Moore case, looking for something I missed, and I found it—the National Governors Association. Moore's been donating to them for the past five years. I talked to their media liaison this afternoon, and she told me Simon Archer procured the donations." He glanced at Erin and raised a graying eyebrow. "Guess the two of them go all the way back to their days as undergrads, but I can't find any correspondence between Simon and Ted Moore—no emails, no paper trail other than the donations to the association. Simon hasn't returned my call."

"Are you finished?" O'Rourke's lips barely moved.

"Nope." Fowler popped a Hershey into his mouth, clearly enjoying making the assistant chief wait. "Ted Moore moved to California the same year Bonnie Archer was molested, and he returned six months ago, around the same time she started receiving big deposits into her account.

And get this—his documentary on the local gangs aired three weeks before Bonnie received her first big deposit."

Erin's pulse hammered against her chest. "Neil claimed Bonnie's abuser moved to California, and he seemed confident he couldn't have killed her. Being dead's a pretty good alibi."

Fowler grunted. "Moore donated to the Governors Association because Simon had something on him."

"We need to take a closer look at Simon Archer." Adrenaline pumped through Erin. "If Bonnie blackmailed Moore, she likely blackmailed her uncle as well. Especially if she reconnected with Sarah and found out she'd been abused, too. Simon decided he needed to wipe his entire past clean. You think he had Moore killed?"

"Nah," Fowler said. "Moore's murder reeks of a gang hit. One of the big gangs in Anacostia is known to castrate, and he mentioned them several times in his documentary. With him dead, though, Bonnie loses her blackmail income. That could be the catalyst for going after Simon— or she upped his dues."

"Did Sarah Archer admit to sexual abuse?" O'Rourke's sharp voice interrupted their exchange.

Erin braced for the argument. "No, but it makes sense, and my gut tells me—"

"Your gut isn't good enough." O'Rourke's nostrils flared. "What about Ricky Stout? Is there a possibility he's the cross-dresser?"

"The cross-dresser's a middle-aged white male," Erin said. "Ricky is a twenty-one-year-old Black."

"Then see if he knows anything about the cross-dresser," O'Rourke said. "Don't do a damn thing with Simon Archer unless you get tangible proof Bonnie blackmailed him. I'm not getting into a political mess unless I absolutely have to. And drop this Jane the Ripper business unless we have something absolutely concrete. If the name breaks to the press, we will never get a handle on it. Do you understand?"

"Yes, ma'am." Erin willed her tears to hold off a few minutes longer.

O'Rourke pressed her lips into a thin line. "Life's not fair, Prince. This sucks for you, and it sucks for the department. But it sucks for those women more. Find this guy, and prove that reporter wrong."

She nodded at Clark and shot a nasty look at Fowler. "If you talk to Simon Archer about this, don't treat him like a person of interest. Be subtle. If the press hears we're looking into him, I'll shove that entire bag of chocolates up your skinny ass." Her heels clacked down the hall.

"Erin, I'm sorry," Brooks said. "This whole thing is bullshit. But you have to try to put it behind you and keep your head in the game."

"Hey." Fowler awkwardly patted her shoulder. "Everyone's stressed about this case, but we all have a common goal. Forget about the rest of the bullshit, and do the job. If things get tough, I've got a full bag of chocolate with your name on it." He headed for the break room door. "I'll be wasting my time trying to get people to turn on a gangbanger if you need me."

Erin stood silently and stared straight ahead.

"Fowler's right," Clark said. "For what it's worth, I've got faith in you. But if you don't have any in yourself, you'll never survive in this job."

Erin waited until his footsteps faded away and then rushed to the ladies' room. Tears came fast and furiously, her throat raw from trying to be quiet. Embarrassment washed over her in hot waves. What used to manifest as self-consciousness about her weight and looks and the ability to appeal to the opposite sex had matured into an adult complex about whether or not everyone she cared about saw her as a failure.

Crying jag over, she ventured to the mirror to see how bad she looked. Her thick waves hung limply from running in and out of the rain all day. She should let her hair grow long enough for a real ponytail instead of a stubby turd-tail attached to the back of her neck. She didn't have the patience, though.

At least her complexion, however pale, remained acceptable. A few wrinkles around her eyes to match the sandbags from lack of sleep. "Ugh. Pull up your panties, and go catch a killer."

Only Brooks remained in the squad room. He stood when she entered.

She held up her hand and forced a tired smile. "My brother likes to tell me my brain is my own worst enemy. I'm working on that. Anyway, I'm sorry for all of this."

He stuck his hands in his pockets, the corners of his mustache twitching. "Thank you, but it's not your fault someone leaked the info."

Erin breathed a sigh of relief.

Brooks tried to smile, but he didn't quite manage it. "Anyway, Ellen's friend found one of Bonnie's videos."

"How?" Erin perked up, but the gray pallor of Brooks's face didn't offer much hope.

"Sheer luck. Most of these sites are paid via Bitcoin, and getting a subpoena for any of their financial records is nearly impossible since the vast majority of the transactions are overseas. Ellen and her team have been after a specific child porn site they think is using a server in Ukraine. It's a miserable endeavor without much hope of success, but she's bullheaded. Anyway, a video with Bonnie showed up."

"On a child porn site?"

He nodded. "Remember, she looked younger than her actual age, but the oldest comment on this video is four years old."

"She would have been twenty-two. Still, that's a stretch."

"Not for the guys who only want teenagers," he said with disgust. "This site caters to a variety of scumbag preferences. Grouped by age and sex of the kid. Bonnie's video was in a special section: girls who enjoyed being molested as a child and want to be further dominated."

Erin wasn't quite sure she understood what he said. "Is that what the site says?"

"Oh no, they don't consider themselves molesters," Brooks said. "The specific wording is 'Peter and Patty: children who were loved by adults and never want to grow up.'"

"I think I'm going to be sick."

Brooks pointed to the bottle of antacid on his desk. "I was."

"How bad is the video?"

"As bad as you'd expect from something like that."

"So, not fake?" Anxiety exploded like a bomb in her chest. Her abdominal muscles tightened, her legs flexing with the reflex to run. She would have to watch the video.

"It's possible." Brooks reached for the antacid and took another swig. "Most of the rape porn videos are people living out extremely sick fantasies, but some are questionable. Bonnie was a drug addict during this time. She likely got involved with all sorts of people willing to use her."

"Can Ellen's people get anything from the video, like an ID on the prick?"

"He's covered up. All black, right down to his mask and gloves. The only piece of anatomy we see is his penis. It's not white. Could be Black, could be any other ethnicity. Impossible to tell."

Erin still tried to wrap her mind around Bonnie's torment. "So whether the video is real or not, she's been doing this for a while. Her self-worth was all sorts of fucked up."

"It's one of the saddest things I've seen," he said. "But apparently not all that shocking to Ellen's people. Kids who are sexually abused and don't have any real support system have a hell of a hard time getting healthy. That's how so many kids end up running away and being taken into sex trafficking. Deep down, a lot of them believe they deserve it."

"But Bonnie did get help." Erin's voice bordered on desperation. "Her parents got her therapy."

"So they say." Brooks put the cap back on the antacid, his face twisted like he could throw up at any second. "A therapist is required to report sexual abuse of a minor. I went back to the year Bonnie was eight and all the way up to her turning eighteen. No reports."

Tension clotted in Erin's neck and shoulders. Why the hell couldn't they get one solid answer to some part of this mess? "Neil Archer is so angry at himself and his brother, and it's obvious he loved his daughter. I can't believe he didn't get her therapy."

"Maybe he did, but whoever did it chose not to report it. Maybe Simon Archer paid the therapist to be quiet."

Erin rubbed her temples, wishing away the dull ache. "If Simon's not involved in the murders, he still deserves to be trussed up and hung out. On the other hand, if Bonnie's been doing amateur videos that long, maybe she really did make $100,000, and we're off on the blackmail angle."

"No," Brooks said. "I dug into her financials. Most of these amateur porn sites are paid via Bitcoin. Bonnie's went into the same account as the offshore deposits, but the Bitcoins are infrequent and amount to a few hundred bucks a month."

"Simon Archer has an alibi for the night of Bonnie's murder. Fowler confirmed Simon Archer attended a fundraiser. He still could have paid someone to kill her, figuring that would still be cheaper than Bonnie continuing to blackmail him."

Brooks balanced his hip on the corner of his desk. "Bonnie and Virginia's murders are about more than money."

"Maybe that's what the killer wants us to think," Erin said. "He throws in the Ripper stuff to keep us confused."

"I suppose."

Erin motioned for the bottle of antacid. "I don't believe it either, but I'm too tired to come up with anything else right now."

CHAPTER THIRTY-THREE

E rin crawled out of bed before the sun came up. Brooks had emailed her the video of Bonnie last night, but she put off watching it, hoping for one night without nightmares. Her mind barely gave her the opportunity. Scenario after scenario went through her head in a vain attempt to try to piece things together. Everything leading to Bonnie's murderer fell apart when she tried to tie the professor to it. Some crucial piece eluded her.

When the sky turned silver, she threw off the covers and cued up the video.

Brooks's description hadn't done it justice. Either Bonnie Archer possessed exceptional acting skills, or she was raped again as an adult. Or—and this option broke Erin's heart—Bonnie agreed to make the video. But her physical and emotional pain resonated throughout the entire video.

Simon Archer needed to take responsibility for Bonnie's miserable life. What would Erin's father say if he knew the truth?

He would cut off any funding for anything associated with Simon Archer, even if it meant no longer supporting an association he believed in. He wouldn't want the Prince named tied to a scandal, and he possessed a moral compass—he just didn't always apply it to business.

Five-thirty. Her father would be awake, probably finishing his morning treadmill routine. The truth would stop at her father. Necessary steps would be taken. An excuse would be made to cut the funding. Bonnie's name would never be mentioned. And Simon Archer would feel the sting.

Erin's stomach bottomed out when she drove into the CID's small parking lot. News vans from every local outlet, including CNN, had staked out a spot in the minuscule space. As rabid as the hungry gulls flying over the Potomac, searching for any morsel they could find, the pack of reporters descended, moving as a single unit toward Erin's car. Anxiety plugged her throat and sweat dampened the roots of her hair.

The taste in her mouth reminded her of when she'd taken Lisa up on her dare to eat dirty sand.

Torrence appeared at her car window, shouting questions. Erin's panic flashed to anger. She shoved her door open and stepped out, badge and bag clutched in her opposite hand. She and Torrence locked eyes. The redhead's expression was far too smug.

Their voices blended, and camera flashes made Erin's eyes burn as the media surrounded her. Her breathing quickened and became shallow. *Back the hell up.* One voice stood out from the rest.

"Investigator Prince," Torrence shouted. "What can you tell us about the new Jack the Ripper?"

"No comment." Erin squared her shoulders and stalked through the throng, which parted just enough to keep her from completely losing her mind.

By the time she buzzed into the building, her damp curls stuck to her face and she was sweating all over. She dragged a hand through her messy hair as the back of her neck grew hot, and a tingling sensation slid down her spine. Erin spun around, expecting to see Torrence bulldozing her way into the lobby.

"Sarah, what are you doing here?"

The tall blonde uncurled her long legs and stood. Her fair skin had gone stark white, and purple circles beneath her eyes highlighted their contrasting colors. "I saw the news. I wanted to talk to you."

"The news doesn't have accurate information," Erin said. "Whoever's feeding them tidbits isn't privy to the real details." *And God help the bastard if I find out who he is.*

"So Bonnie and Professor Walton weren't killed by a Jack the Ripper freak?"

Her hopeful expression reminded Erin of a small child's who still believed sweet talk could earn a treat. "I'm not at liberty to discuss those details."

"You told me they were cut up." Sarah wrung her hands. "Before that, you asked me about Jack the Ripper and told me about the messages left. Jack the Ripper killed whores. This killer called Bonnie a whore—"

Erin put a hand on the girl's trembling arm. Sarah towered over her—she had to have at least six inches on Erin's short frame. "This Ripper stuff is probably all bunk. The press bought into it, but we haven't. We're not going to panic and start making mistakes. We have several suspects. I promise you we'll find the person who killed Bonnie and Virginia."

"Please find out who killed my cousin and Professor Walton," Sarah said. "And don't let them kill me."

"I don't think that will happen," Erin said. "But it's a good idea to be vigilant for a while. You're still staying at your parents'?"

"My father insists." Sarah scowled. "He claims it's for my safety, but it's all about control, with him. He's made me completely dependent—he'll only pay for school and allow access to my trust fund if I behave the way he thinks I should." Her strange eyes flashed. "I envied Bonnie's freedom. We were polar opposites, but she leveled me out. She understood my life better than anyone. I don't know how I'm going to go on without her. I tried so hard to understand, but I finally accepted you can't always understand a broken mind." Sarah's chest heaved, her eyes watering. She reached into her leather bag and retrieved a delicate handkerchief with three intricate monogrammed letters.

Erin gently touched the lacey hem. "Ah, the hanky with your initials. My grandma used to make those. She believed they helped separate us from the lower-income groups."

Sarah dabbed her eyes with the white cloth. "Sounds like she and my father would get along."

"She was something else," Erin said. "Thankfully, my dad's ego isn't nearly as large. His snobbery is a lot more subtle." She tried to smile but faltered when she saw a fresh wave of tears in Sarah's eyes.

"You're lucky," Sarah said. "My father still believes status is everything and that it's our duty to maintain the gap between social and economic classes. I think that's why he hated Bonnie so much. She threatened his perfectly controlled family picture."

Erin hated to push when Sarah barely held herself together, but getting Sarah to give them Ted Moore's name might break the investigation wide open. "Sarah, I need to ask you something."

"Okay." Sarah wiped her eyes.

"Child molesters aren't capable of stopping." Erin spoke as gently as she could, making sure to give Sarah personal space. "Whoever did this to Bonnie would have needed a replacement. Are you sure there's nothing else you want to tell me?"

Sarah's eyes briefly closed, and then the mismatched pupils stared daggers at Erin. "I wasn't molested. I told you that already." Her tone hardened, clipped, and bordered on arrogance. "Why can't you let it go?"

"Because I've worked with many victims of sexual abuse." Erin lowered her voice to a whisper. "And the person who hurt Bonnie is still out there. Do you think he could be the one who killed her?"

"I've got no idea." Sarah narrowed her eyes, arms tight around her waist, hands in her armpits, her narrow hip cocked.

Her sudden aggression seemed like a major twist, but many abuse victims used anger as a defense mechanism.

Erin stepped back, hoping the additional space would help Sarah relax. "Do you happen to remember Ted Moore? Your father's old friend?"

Sarah's aggressive stance stiffened. The vein in her neck pulsed. She shook her head. "Is there a back exit to this place? The reporters weren't here before."

Erin motioned for the desk sergeant. "Let me have a uniform escort you. Is your car out front?"

"Took the metro," Sarah said. "I had some stuff to do on campus, so I left my car there. The station is a couple of blocks away from here. Easy walk."

Erin reached a hand out, but Sarah pulled away. "I promise you I'll find the person responsible for killing your cousin and Virginia." Failure swarmed over Erin as she watched the girl shuffle behind the uniformed officer to the back exit. So much for a good start to the day.

The morning briefing had already started when Erin slipped into the room. "Sorry I'm late. Sarah Archer was waiting in the lobby. She didn't admit to being molested, but I think we're on the right track with Ted Moore." She took a chocolate donut from the box on Fowler's desk and filled the group in on her conversation.

"I got nothing from Moore's financials." Fowler licked pink frosting off his fingers. "And we haven't found anything to link him to an offshore account yet. We need a warrant for Simon Archer's financials."

Clark barked a laugh. "On circumstantial evidence? I'm not shaking that tree. Not without something in black and white."

"Everything points to Simon having Bonnie and Virginia taken out," Erin said. "Sarah and Bonnie's reconciliation is a threat to him. Simon learns all he can about Bonnie from his daughter. Then he sets things up like dominoes and hires someone to make them fall. Meanwhile, he's got Sarah sequestered at his place to make sure she keeps quiet. Virginia is collateral damage because Bonnie confided in her."

"What happened to your Jane theory?" Brooks asked. "If you're suspecting Simon Archer, where does Jane come in?"

The one snag she couldn't eliminate. The idea of Jane the Ripper, combined with the messages, had seemed gruesomely romantic and completely random. "Maybe Simon hired a woman to kill Bonnie and Virginia because he thought they'd trust her? Or Jane's a ruse, like you've said from the start."

"I'll also have Marie check to see if Simon Archer's prints are in any system," Clark said. "He's a public official, so it's possible, but a long shot. If we get a hit, we'll compare them to the ones at both crime scenes. Prince, we can't go after a man like Simon Archer without a mountain of evidence to back us up. We've got to have something more tangible than his relationship with Ted Moore—and there's no proof beyond Moore's donation."

The chocolatey-goodness of her cake donut suddenly tasted like sawdust. Erin knew the game, and Clark had a point, but she hated it. "What about Virginia Walton?"

"Her autopsy was unremarkable. She suffered, as Mitchell theorized, but the killer carved the name on her back after she died." He used a black marker to scribble on the whiteboard hanging in the middle of the squad room and slashed a black line to create a column for Bonnie and a column for Virginia. Beneath, he listed the known elements of each woman's life, underlining the overlap.

"We're getting the security video from The Point today. We'll start with the night the bartender mentioned, but we might have to expand the date range. We'll all have to take turns going cross-eyed looking for Virginia Walton on bad security video. And thanks to Brooks's breakthrough"—Clark's derisive tone made it clear he knew damn well how Brooks had ascertained the sex video of Bonnie—"we know Bonnie Archer made the amateur stuff for a long time. Our forensic guys have already combed through Virginia's computer and found nothing that suggests a connection to the online sex world. Her files consisted mostly of school-related information. Prince, what about that box you guys found in Virginia's bedroom?"

"We skimmed through it at the scene," Erin said. "More school stuff, dating back several months. Nothing we can use. Temple didn't find any trace material during the autopsy?"

"Temple recovered a few hairs and fibers we're going to test, but that's going to be like pissing in the wind," Clark said. "Brooks, you said you had something good for us."

Brooks nodded, looking slightly more rested than he had last night.

He still hadn't shaved, and the scruff didn't make him look anything but unkempt. "Guess who called me this morning?"

Erin reached for a Styrofoam cup for coffee. "Who?"

"Stephanie Key. She's on her way, with Ricky Stout and their lawyer. Apparently, Ricky has something to tell us."

Ricky Stout's lawyer was a thin, bald man with a groomed beard. His trench coat hung loosely on his small frame, and his briefcase looked heavier than he did. While an officer led the group back to the interview room, he made an announcement in a voice loud enough for the entire department to hear.

"I'd like to make it clear I'm a member of the NAACP. I won't stand for this police department railroading another innocent Black male for the murders of two white women." His orator's voice and sharp eyes begged for a pulpit to use for his own agenda, and he had sauntered into the offices with the explicit instruction he and his client would only speak to Calvin Prince's daughter.

In the past few years, Attorney James R. Thomas had made a name for himself, taking on mostly Black clients and structuring many of their defenses around racial bias. Only two had made it to trial. He walked away with a victory and a hunger for more. Ricky Stout represented more headlines for the attorney, especially with a Prince painted as the villain.

"You should go in with me."

Erin, Brooks, and Clark stood on the other side of the two-way window, watching the trio wait impatiently.

"I mucked up the interview with Rylan Walton, and I didn't consider race as an issue."

Thomas paced in the room, glaring at the window, hands on his narrow hips. "He's looking for a fight."

"He wants to talk to you," Brooks said. "Ricky came on his own. We have nothing to hold him on. If I go in, I'll piss off the attorney, and things will go downhill from there."

"Go in there with confidence and compassion," Clark said. "Be his friend, and follow your instincts."

"If it goes south, I'll come in," Brooks said. "But it won't."

Erin wished she hadn't chosen to wear a threadbare tank top underneath her sweater. She wasn't about to show off her damp and doughy body. "All right. Let's see what Ricky Stout has to say."

KILLING JANE

"It's about time." Thomas had shed his overcoat to reveal a silk shirt and sleek trousers. Soft in all the wrong places, his body resembled a pre-pubescent girl's. "We're here voluntarily, and the first thing you do is keep us waiting."

Erin took her seat across from Stephanie Key and Ricky Stout. "Thank you for coming in."

"My client," Thomas sat down, tiny bits of white froth at the corners of his mouth, "is a young Black male working to better his life. I won't have him being treated like a street thug because he's poor."

Ricky Stout groaned.

While Thomas could only be called homely, Ricky existed at the opposite end of the spectrum. The man was beautiful. His fitted blue shirt accentuated the width of his shoulders and was lovely against his glossy skin. High cheekbones, brooding eyes, and sculpted lips completed the picture. He smiled shyly at Erin.

She smiled back. "We have absolutely no reason to do that." She offered her hand. "I'm Investigator Erin Prince."

Ricky took her hand in a gentle, firm grip, his warm hand much larger than her own. "Nice to meet you."

His politeness changed her tactics. "Ricky, your lawyer said you wanted to tell us something. Do you mind if I ask a few questions first?"

"No, ma'am."

"Erin, please. Ma'am makes me feel as old as I am." She winked at him.

He tried to smile back, but the worry lines dug into his dark skin. "I can't believe this happened to Bonnie and Ms. Walton."

"It's awful." Erin matched his quiet tone. "Can you tell me how you knew them?"

"I met Bonnie at the ALC. We had a reading class together. She struggled with that. I suck at math. We helped each other out."

"That's nice. I suck at math, too. So, you two spent a lot of time together outside of school?"

"Why is that relevant?" Thomas piped up.

Erin raised an eyebrow at him. Surely he wasn't that stupid.

"James, it's fine," Dr. Key said. "I don't think Investigator Prince is out to get Ricky."

"Thank you. Ricky?"

"Some, I guess. We walked to the Metro together. She took a different train than me, but sometimes we got coffee and worked on homework."

"You're graduating this year, as well?" Erin asked.

"As long as I pass the test." He tapped his fingers on the table. "I don't take tests too well."

"He's working really hard," Dr. Key said. "He can do it."

"Of course, he can," Erin said. "Hard work always pays off. And good for you. I can't imagine going back to school as an adult." Although, with Abby in fourth grade, Erin had begun to realize that being a parent essentially meant going through school all over again.

Thomas made a sharp sound. "I'm sure there are many things about Ricky's life you can't imagine, Investigator *Prince.*"

Heat rose in her cheeks, but she kept everything else where it belonged. She kept her attention on Ricky. "And what about Virginia Walton? I'm sure your aunt told you we heard about the disagreement you had with her."

"Aww." Ricky dragged his hands over his face. "I'm a dumbass. I got pissed off and ran my mouth like a fool."

"Did she think you threatened her?"

"No! I called her nasty names. I didn't mean it. I just took it out on her."

"What did you take out on her?"

"My grade. I didn't want to take responsibility for it, and she called me on my attitude. But I apologized."

"Good for you." Erin continued to play the friend, although it wasn't hard with Ricky. "Back to Bonnie for a minute. Her cousin said you asked Bonnie out, and she turned you down."

He drew his shoulders in. "Yeah."

"Did that upset you?"

"Prince," Thomas warned.

"I'm not asking anything out of context," Erin snapped. "Ricky isn't a child, he's a smart adult. Why don't you let him use his common sense?"

Thomas tensed like he wanted to come over the table at Erin while Dr. Key stewed.

Ricky grinned. "At first. I liked her a lot, but she had issues." His smile faded, sadness in his eyes.

"Bonnie had a hard life," Erin said. "Things that happen to us when we're kids can really mess us up. Some people rebound better than others."

Ricky picked at an imaginary thread on his shirt, eyes everywhere but Erin's. His nerves rolled off him like sound waves.

"Ricky," Erin asked softly. "What did you come here to tell me?"

Ricky didn't respond right away. Erin waited. He trusted her. He liked her. She sensed that as much as she sensed his tension, but his eyes shone with fear.

"Ricky, go ahead." Dr. Key placed a hand on his arm. "You didn't do anything wrong, and they're going to find your fingerprints."

"Stephanie!" Thomas rose from his chair.

Dr. Key clamped her other hand on his wrist. "Sit. I brought you here in case something happened. This is what he came to say. He's going to explain the situation and be done with this."

Erin had to remember to breathe. "How many times were you in Bonnie's house?"

"Once." Ricky studied his nails, sucking in his right cheek to the point it looked painful. "I didn't want to do it."

Erin's eyes flickered to the camera mounted in the corner, making sure the red light blinked. "What didn't you want to do?"

"Did you find the camera and all the other stuff?" Ricky said the words in a fast breath as though he'd decided to get it over with.

"We did," Erin said. *Conversational. Don't get excited. Don't scare him off.* "But we haven't been able to find any videos. Would you happen to know where they are?"

"Online."

Erin laughed, trying to break the tension. "Can you narrow it down just a bit, Ricky?"

"I don't know the names of the sites." His face twisted as though he'd eaten a bad apple. "That shit is disgusting. They're like one giant machine. Click on one, and you're in the matrix."

"You mean you click on a video and go to something different? Like they're layered on top of each other?"

Ricky nodded.

"I know exactly what you mean." Erin made a face to match Ricky's. "In the past few days, I've watched so much offensive porn. I don't mean rough sex or fetishes. I mean extremely violent. And you described them perfectly. Layers and layers. We can't hope to get through them all."

"Yeah," Ricky whispered. "Violent."

"Ricky, did Bonnie tell you she made rape porn?"

A single tear ran down his cheek. "I told her she was better than that. The porn's one thing, but she didn't need the money. She did it for kicks. She called it her therapy."

Erin's eyes watered. "Did you ever watch one of the videos?"

"Only part of one she showed me." He looked at his aunt, who nodded and took his hand. "I *do* need the money. So when Bonnie told me she sold amateur porn online and she wanted to do it with a Black man, I thought about it. I liked her, and maybe doing it would make her like me. She offered me a grand."

"For one video?"

"I need to get my car fixed," Ricky said defensively. "And it's not illegal."

"Of course not," Erin said. "But you didn't do it?"

"Not after I realized what she wanted me to do. I've seen rough sex ones and the ones that are supposed to be rape but are obviously fake. This stuff was on a whole other level. Violent. Degrading. She did it willingly." He shook his head, trying to get the image to go away, more tears falling. "She wanted me to do that stuff to her, and I couldn't. Not for any amount of money."

"You're a good guy." Erin wished she could take Ricky's pain away. She said a silent thank you for her decision to call her father. Someone needed to be held accountable. "So we'll find your fingerprints in the attic?"

"Just one time. She had the laptop up there. She wanted me to see the setup and watch the video."

"I'm sure you're trying to get his juvenile records unsealed," Thomas said. "If you succeed, you'll match the prints. We're getting ahead of you."

"I tried to help her," Ricky said, his throat sounding tight with emotion. "She was nice. Smart. Bonnie got off the streets and got clean, just like me. But she said she needed to do it. It made her feel."

"Made her feel what?" Erin asked.

"Feel," Ricky said. "She said doing those videos made her feel."

"Clearly, Bonnie had issues no one knew about," Dr. Key said. "Ricky has been struggling with whether or not to come forward. He didn't want to become involved, and we didn't know whether what he knew had any merit. After Virginia's murder, we knew he had to come in."

My ass. You wanted to keep him quiet and out of it. From the looks of it, keeping quiet was killing Ricky.

"Thank you, Ricky," she said. "You mentioned Bonnie not needing the money from the videos."

Ricky wiped his eyes with the back of his hand. "She had settlement money from something that happened a long time ago."

Erin glanced at the two-way mirror, half expecting Brooks to meet her gaze. "Did she say what?"

"No, just that she was set up because the settlement obligations hadn't been met yet. He still owed her another $150,000."

"He who?"

Ricky shrugged. "She didn't tell me anything else."

"Do you have any idea who else was involved in her side business?"

Thomas glared at her, motioning for Ricky to stay silent. "He told you what he came to say."

"Two women are dead." Erin looked the attorney in the eyes for the first time. "And this man you're so afraid we're going to railroad is obviously grieving for his friend. He wants to help. Don't you want justice for these women? Or does it not matter?"

"Of course, it matters."

"Then stop interrupting me. I'm not asking anything your client shouldn't answer. Am I, Ricky? Because if you want to invoke counsel, you have the right. But you're not here as a suspect."

"I don't need him." Ricky rolled his eyes at Thomas. "My aunt wanted him here, but he doesn't care about me as a person. He's got his own agenda."

"Ricky." The lawyer adjusted his silk tie. "That's simply not true."

"Then let me answer the questions. I want this to be over with. Just Bonnie and another man, Ms. Prince. And it wasn't even her side business, it was his. Plus he had sex with her."

"Did she tell you anything about him? The smallest thing might help us."

"She knew him from her time on the streets. He wore a mask in the video."

"What color was his ..." Erin's cheeks burned, "skin?"

"Brown. Didn't look like a brother to me, though. Maybe an Arab."

Dr. Key elbowed him. "Middle Easterner is the correct term."

"Sorry, but that's what he looked like and sounded like. So did the woman behind the camera, although her accent wasn't as noticeable. Her voice sounded real husky—not like a smoker's but throaty. Sexy—until I saw the rest of the video. She seemed to be the one giving the orders." Ricky shivered, sinking lower in his seat. "She got off on Bonnie's pain. I thought I might get sick listening to it. I couldn't finish watching."

Adrenaline raced through Erin with such force she nearly jumped out of the chair. "Did the man have any tattoos?"

"Here." Ricky's long fingers traced his collarbone. "Fancy lettering in a different language."

Sanskrit.

CHAPTER THIRTY-FOUR

"**Y**ari fucking Malek." Erin burst into the room, slamming the door into the wall. "That dirty sonofabitch. Ten to one, the DNA test says he's the father of Bonnie's baby."

Brooks dropped his phone into his breast pocket. "I just got off the phone with the manager at Sid's. Malek left work the night before last and told the manager he'd see him in the morning, but he hasn't returned to work, and he's not answering his phone."

"How much you want to bet he plucked Bonnie off the street when she was strung out and desperate for a fix? He feeds her habit. They get close. He figures out she's been abused and sees his opportunity. I wouldn't be surprised if he passed her around."

"What about the woman behind the camera?" Clark asked. "You have any idea who that might be?"

"His hostess," Brooks said. "Remember her?"

The beautiful, raven-haired woman who greeted Erin and Brooks at Sid's had left her radar as soon as they walked out of the club. But she remembered the young woman's voice. Ricky described it perfectly. "Shit. She's in on this with him. You think she could be Jane?"

"I've got no idea." Brooks held up a list of names Erin recognized as the employees from the strip club. "Aleta Gilani. Nothing came up on her initial background check, and she cooperated when we questioned the employees."

"Do we have a home address?" Erin asked.

"No, but she might have been living with Malek. Or using a different name or staying with a relative." Brooks leaned against the wall. "What's the motive for murder, though? Filming the porn isn't illegal unless they used underage girls."

"I wouldn't doubt it," Erin said. "If Bonnie talks, she opens up the door for their entire operation to be discovered. It could be a lot bigger than we realize. Don't forget about Simon. He could have found out about Bonnie's extracurriculars and orchestrated the entire thing. We need to question Malek and Aleta." Erin turned to Clark. "Can we get a warrant for Malek's house?"

"Not a chance," Clark said. "We don't have proof he's on video.

We can't corroborate Ricky's story."

"Brooks and I both saw the tattoo," Erin said. "It's not enough probable cause?"

"With nothing to link him to the professor. No way." Clark crossed his arms. "You need something more. Go back to Sid's and see if you can get any of the girls to tell you anything. Bonnie's probably not the only one he did this to."

"What about Malek? He could be planning to skip town if he hasn't already."

"I'll send a uniform to check his house. You guys see if you can get something more to back Ricky up, and then we'll bring him in."

Erin dug her keys out of her pocket. "I'll drive."

Men liked to watch strippers over their lunch break, so Sid's was busy when Erin and Brooks arrived. A pulsating bass blared as three blonde women in pink thongs danced for an appreciative group of men dressed in business attire.

With the exception of his slicked-back hair, the manager resembled a watered-down version of Malek. "As I told your boss, I haven't heard from Yari since he left, night before last." He glanced around the crowded room. "I don't see why you have to question the girls."

"Because one of their colleagues was murdered." Brooks's surly tone carried over the music. "We have more questions."

The manager led them to the dressing rooms, where several dancers milled about in various stages of undress and makeup. None seemed particularly happy to see the cops, and no one had any information.

"Where's Aleta Gilani?" Erin asked. "The hostess with the black hair and green eyes?"

The manager's square face went carefully blank. "Vacation."

"Until when?"

"Two weeks."

"Nice vacation," Erin said. "Could I get her home address? We need to clear up a couple of things with her."

His cold, dark gaze bore into Erin, a muscle in his cheek flexing. "Ask Yari."

Erin smiled. "Thank you so much for your help." She handed him her card.

He threw it in the trash behind the bar.

She and Brooks reconvened in the sub shop next door—a good dose of salt and carbs to help clear her head. "We need to bring Malek in. That guy's going to call him."

"You think he's lying about not knowing where he's at?" Brooks took a large bite out of his flatbread sandwich.

"Do we have a reason to think he's not?"

"No, but the cruiser is sitting on the house. Malek's car is still in the driveway. If he takes off, we'll know."

Erin let out a huff of air. Brooks was right, except they could be watching an empty house. Malek already had plenty of time to escape.

"We need to keep following the money," Brooks continued. "Simon Archer's the most likely candidate. If Malek is Bonnie's business partner and pimp, then he's probably getting a cut. Same goes for Aleta, although she might be higher up in the stable."

The stable. Erin still hated the term. Most sex traffickers had one and used a seasoned girl, already broken down and completely dependent, to control the newer ones.

"So, if Bonnie decides she's had enough and wants to get away from Yari, he loses his cut of the blackmail money. Bonnie talks to Virginia Walton about what she should do. Yari and Aleta take them out and concoct this Jane the Ripper thing to confuse us."

Erin had been so sure the killer was a woman obsessed with Jane the Ripper. Her lack of homicide experience had diluted her ability to be objective. She slumped in the seat. "Well, shit. I guess I had that one wrong, didn't I?"

"Don't be so sure," Brooks said. "You've got good instincts, and I've learned not to discount those. What did Sarah have to say when you spoke with her?"

Erin picked at her bread and mulled over the earlier conversation. "At first, it bugged me that Bonnie likely started blackmailing her uncle around the same time her cousin came back into her life. After talking to Sarah, I don't think she knew about the money."

"Why?" Brooks said. "Sarah hates her dad for what he did to Bonnie. She might have encouraged the blackmail. Watching him twist would be wonderful revenge."

"Yeah, but ..." Erin wished her partner had seen the frightened young woman in the lobby this morning. "Sarah's very fragile. She's been sheltered in the arms of money and wealth, and if she was sexually abused, she had to keep quiet about it, even if she got help. She's the family embarrassment for someone like Simon Archer. He's kept her dependent on him to control her and protect his reputation. Bonnie probably already felt partially responsible for Sarah's abuse, and she may have felt like Sarah knowing about the blackmail would have caused Sarah more stress. So she kept some things to herself. Wealth and status in a city like D.C. can be all-powerful."

Brooks wadded up his sandwich wrapper, his eyes boring into her.

The scrutiny made Erin uncomfortable. "You were right about my empathizing with her because I come from a similar world. That's also why I understand her. She's not experienced like Bonnie. Bonnie knew people like Simon play by a different set of rules, and she knew where to attack—his wallet."

Erin's phone vibrated in her pocket. She read the text and almost knocked her soda off the table. Another blocked number, but the message sounded anything but childlike.

> I know what Yari Malek did. Meet me at Sal's on the Waterfront in thirty minutes.

Brooks tossed his napkin into the trash. "You know where that is?"

Erin choked down the rest of her sandwich. "No, but my car will."

CHAPTER THIRTY-FIVE

Washington, D.C.'s historic Southwest Waterfront ran the gamut in demographics. Many of the renovated buildings dated back to the city's first years, while others were trendy and new, seizing on the prime real estate offered by the Potomac. Unfortunately, Sal's belonged under the former.

The dive bar wasn't actually on the waterfront but a block off of it, in an alley that had probably once had a great view of the river before the expensive restaurant on the corner broke ground.

The stench of old leather, decades of smoke, and greasy food nearly overwhelmed Erin. She blinked, trying to adjust to the light and figure out who she'd come to meet.

"There." Brooks pointed to the beautiful, dark-haired woman waving at them from a corner booth.

Brooks slid into the booth first, and Erin sat across from Aleta Gilani, wincing as a crack in the leather cut into her thigh. "Why did you text from a blocked number?"

Aleta smoothed her luxurious hair, her gaze unwavering. "You can't be too careful these days."

"Thanks for saving us the headache of finding you. We've got a lot of things to discuss."

"I thought so. You've discovered what Yari and I did with Bonnie?"

"Sounds like you were in control and had a grudge against Bonnie," Erin said. "But why kill Virginia Walton?"

Aleta shook her head. "I didn't kill anyone. Yari might have, but I'm as much of a victim as Bonnie."

"Except you're alive," Brooks said.

Erin leaned forward. She could be on Aleta's side. "Tell us what you know."

"Bonnie was all sorts of screwed up," Aleta said. "She was molested as a little girl and then date raped as a teenager. Drugs put her on the street, and Yari found her. He convinced her he could give her a better life if she worked with him. A bed, three meals a day. No more tricks. All under her control. She fell for it."

Like so many other discarded girls before her.

KILLING JANE

Aleta's ruby lips twisted into a bitter smile. "Yari is a master manipulator. He knew how to play Bonnie. He became her friend, her only ally. He kept her loaded on pills. By the time I came into the picture, she'd gotten clean, but making those videos had become her newest addiction."

"Yari asked you to join?"

"He wanted someone else behind the camera, and he wanted another female. He offered me a lot of money." She shrugged. "I like sex, and I like pain. As long as Bonnie consented—which she did—I had no issues."

"How did Bonnie get into making the videos?" Brooks asked.

This time, malice darkened her grin. "I told you, Yari's a manipulative prick. And he likes to brag. One night we both got high, and he told me Bonnie had made movies long before she realized it. In those days, he tricked her out to a higher class of perv, all in the guise of helping him out for the money he spent on her. She left him and got clean when she found out about the videos."

"Then why did she go back to him?"

"Because he made her believe he was the only one who really knew her. By then, he had other girls, but convinced her she was still his favorite."

"That's when she became a willing participant?" Erin asked.

"I think she hated herself so much, she did it as a punishment." Aleta took a sip of the dark liquid sitting in front of her. "She never talked much to me about it, but she wanted to quit. The last time I saw her at the club, she told me she planned to tell Yari she was done with him.

"Why?"

"I figured it had to do with her rich boyfriend. She liked him."

Erin slowly digested the information. The case began to piece together like a patchwork quilt. "How is Virginia Walton involved in all of this? And what about Tori?"

"I have no idea about the teacher. Tori, the cross-dresser? You think he had something to do with this? He barely knew Bonnie."

"They had an issue one night," Erin said. "He never returned to Sid's."

Aleta waved her hand as though swatting a fly. "She gave him a lap dance, and he invited her to his place. He's a pervert who wanted to do a film and told her he'd wear a special black cape, like an executioner. She told him to fuck off and made security run him off."

"How do you know this?" Brooks asked.

199

"Yari told me." She laughed. "So I guess I should take it with a grain of salt, right?"

"What about the blackmail?" Erin asked. "Were you and Malek in on it?"

Aleta's dark eyes narrowed. "I wasn't. My family takes care of me. You'd have to ask Yari, but it wouldn't surprise me. The only thing he likes more than sex is money."

"Who's Jane? And Mina and Charlie?" Erin asked.

Aleta took another long sip of her drink, her eyes not meeting Erin's. "I don't know those names."

"Where's Malek?" Brooks asked.

"No idea. I haven't seen him since my last shift four days ago. I'm returning to my family and working in the family business." Aleta's hand trembled. "I don't want to end up like Bonnie."

Erin tried one last question. "Did you ever meet Simon Archer?"

"Bonnie's uncle?" Aleta cocked her head. "She mentioned him once. She called him a hypocritical bastard. But no, I never met him." Her eyes darkened, devoid of emotion.

"I'm going to call a uniform to take you to the office for an official statement," Erin said. "While you're there, consider telling the entire truth. Otherwise, you will spend the next twenty-four hours in a holding cell."

Erin jumped onto 695, bypassing the traffic choking up the roads around the National Mall.

Brooks hissed as she cut in front of a box truck, its horn blaring. "That was a ballsy bluff. We don't have enough to hold her. She came forward willingly."

"I can't tell if she's keeping information back or not. Let Clark have a go at her. He can spot a liar unlike anyone else I know."

"I wish Bonnie's phone records showed direct calls to Virginia Walton. That's the kind of evidence prosecutors like." Brooks's fingers dug into the leather.

"The records show quite a few calls to the school, most of them at night," Erin said. "There's no way to track where the call ended up. And the neighbor saw someone at Virginia's house who matched Bonnie's description shortly before her murder. But why the hell didn't Virginia call us after Bonnie's murder?"

Brooks straightened out in the seat, his right leg jerking like he might have been slamming his foot on an imaginary brake. "If Malek did this, he did it to punish Bonnie. Virginia is collateral damage. He might have scared her into silence and then decided leaving her alive was too risky. Same goes for Simon Archer pulling the strings. Fear trumps loyalty most of the time."

Erin's fingers ached from her tight grip on the wheel, but she couldn't relax. "You don't sound too convinced."

"It makes sense except for the Ripper and Jane angles. And who are Mina and Charlie to him?"

"Aleta's daughter and another family member who helps take care of Mina." The answer hit Erin like a metal fist. "That's why she didn't want to tell us she knew the names. She said she's going back to work with her family. Aleta's young, but old enough to have a small child. Either the rest of the girls at Sid's weren't aware of her, or were too scared to tell us."

Erin wrenched the wheel through traffic, her foot feeling like lead. "You were right all along."

Brooks huffed and clung to his seatbelt. "What about Tori?"

"Hell if I know." Erin honked her horn at a Porsche that cut her off. "Wild card, I guess."

"Coincidence." Brooks sounded unconvinced.

Erin gunned it and took the exit onto 16th Street. "I thought there were no coincidences?"

Brooks offered her a wry smile. "I guess there's a first time for everything."

CHAPTER THIRTY-SIX

While Columbia Heights' gentrification centered on bringing in bars and new condos, 16th Street Heights' residents enjoyed grand homes in a peaceful environment. Some had decent-sized backyards—a rare commodity in D.C.

"There's a bit of everything in this area," Erin explained. "It's pretty diverse, with a lot of younger families starting to move in. You'll see more affluent houses on one street and standard, low-middle-class on the next." She put Malek in the upper-middle-class section, since his house sat in the corner lot on Georgia Avenue. While many of the homes boasted bright, cheerful colors, Malek's was a simple white with green shutters. Nice, but not remarkable. She made an illegal U-turn and pulled up behind the unmarked car stationed a few houses down from Malek's.

"What are we talking about in terms of housing, here?" Brooks asked as he shut the door.

"Probably close to five hundred thousand for a single-family home," Erin said. "But I'm sure Malek brings that in from the strip club alone."

Armed with coffee and energy bars and listening to droning talk radio, the officers in the unmarked car greeted Erin with jovial smiles. The driver could have doubled as a bodybuilder. He had no neck to speak of, and his hands could have crushed melons.

He gave her a gap-toothed grin. "Hey, it's the Princess. You find the Ripper yet?"

His patrol partner, a man half his size with bat ears, chortled with glee.

Erin twisted up inside, wishing she could jam her Taser into the idiot's neck. He probably wouldn't feel it. "Yeah," she shot back. "He's in that house you're supposed to be watching. So you better not have screwed up."

Simmons curled his thick upper lip. "We're not the ones screwing up. No one's come out since we got here this morning. No one's gone into it. Place is a dead end, Princess."

She smiled sweetly. "Kind of like your job, huh?" Erin sauntered away before he could think fast enough to retort. "Sit tight," she called over her shoulder. "We're going to check things out."

Swollen clouds moved in from the east, ready to eclipse the already weak sun. The air smelled like rain, the wind bitingly damp again. She and Brooks casually walked toward Malek's house.

He grinned. "Jesus, Princess. You're not going to make any allies with that attitude."

Erin glanced over her shoulder. Simmons watched with a scowl. "A guy like that will never be my ally, no matter what I do."

"You should have asked him where he bought his steroids," Brooks said. "Or offered him the name of a good dermatologist."

She laughed. "I'll remember that for next time."

They jogged across the street, Brooks's strides almost twice as long as hers. "Looks like a quiet neighborhood."

"Most people are probably at work." Erin pointed to the older model black Jaguar sitting in Malek's driveway. "Except our guy. This is his only registered vehicle?"

"According to the DMV. I doubt he's got something unregistered. No reason to draw any unnecessary attention." Brooks strolled around the Jaguar, shielding his eyes to peer in the windows. The big muscle in his neck flexed. "Describe Bonnie's laptop again."

"Black, eleven-inch." Gooseflesh rose on Erin's skin. "She had a sticker of Wonder Woman on the logo."

"I think I found it."

Erin mirrored his stance, peering into the car. The tan interior appeared impeccable. No straw wrappers or crayons stuck in the cup holders. A few items littered the back seat: an umbrella, an ice scraper, flashy red gym shoes, and a black laptop with a Wonder Woman sticker over the logo.

"Shit." Adrenaline coursed through Erin and her mouth dried to parchment. She took the safety off her gun as they crossed the front of the house to the porch steps. No curtains moved in the window. No sudden shouts or slamming of doors. The street seemed eerily silent.

She eased up to the porch, waiting until Brooks took a defensive position to her left before ringing the doorbell. No answer came.

"He might have rented a car," Brooks said. "We can check with the rental car companies."

"We don't have a warrant."

"You couldn't make a case to persuade them?"

She didn't bother to hide her surprise. Maybe Brooks wasn't so strait-laced after all. "I don't know how your department in Philadelphia handled things, but Metro P.D. is all about procedure. You cover your ass because the next person up the food chain will leave you out to dry. And then your case is screwed."

"Good to know," he said. "We'll get a warrant for his credit card information, too."

"We don't have time." Erin's pulse beat at her temple. "If he's running, then his manager probably told him we came around again. Who knows whether Aleta's trustworthy. She might have found a way to warn Malek."

Brooks walked around the side of the house, his open coat billowing in his wake like a 1920s gangster. Erin followed, grimacing against the gusting, cold wind and trying to watch the windows for any glimpse of their quarry. Malek was one of the lucky people in the city with a backyard larger than a postage stamp. His outdoor patio looked closed up for winter, the chairs neatly stacked and the grill covered.

A bang made both of them nearly jump out of their shoes. Erin raised her gun and her ankle popped when she whipped around. Instead of Malek bearing down on them, a utility door swung open in the wind.

Erin breathed fast, trying to catch her breath. "It must not have been latched."

Brooks moved forward first.

Erin's blood pressure spiked, her hands numb with excitement. She gripped her gun tighter.

"Yari Malek," Brooks called. "Investigators Prince and Brooks. We need to talk to you."

A horn blared a few streets over. Mist fell. No sound came from the shed.

"Either it's empty, or he's getting ready to ambush us." Erin stood on tiptoes to whisper to Brooks. The sight of his artery pulsing only made her tension ratchet up a level.

The shed was made of cheap pressed wood and had no windows. They'd have to use the front door to find out the shed's contents.

"Stay back," Brooks whispered. "Let me go first."

She opened her mouth to argue, and he cut her off.

"You've got a child. I don't."

He edged forward, his hand closing around the latch of the door swinging steadily in the wind. Brooks eased the door in front of him, using it as a shield until he stepped to the other side of the door frame and could peek inside. "He's not in here."

Erin couldn't relax yet, but she moved to stand with Brooks as he pushed the door open.

Home maintenance necessities filled the shed. Various tools, a push mower, weed eater, weed killer, grass seed, and a nasty smell reminiscent of the bags of rotting leaves Brad left in the yard for a week before finally taking them out to the curb.

Brooks pulled a pair of wool gloves out of his pocket. "Do you have any?"

She shook her head, and he handed her one of his.

"Try to use one hand."

They stepped inside, careful to make sure the door remained open. The shed wasn't much bigger than Abby's bedroom, and Malek kept it neat and orderly, organized to the point of compulsion. The sight of the two discarded black yard bags made Erin's skin crawl.

"Might be rotting yard clippings," she said. "That stuff gets putrid, especially if it's wet."

Brooks opened the first bag.

The smell hit Erin and made her gag.

Brooks held the bag open. "That doesn't look like yard clippings to me."

He hooked the finger of his gloved hand around the collar of the men's dark blue dress shirt and carefully pulled it out of the bag. Dried blood covered nearly the entire front of the shirt, patches of it so thick they still appeared to be congealing.

The awful smell stole Erin's breath.

"Call Clark," Brooks said. "I think we've got enough for a warrant."

"And probable cause to go into the house right now," Erin said. "You up for it?"

She let Brooks do the honors of breaking a windowpane in the back door. He fished his hand inside, and the door unlocked with a click. Brooks slowly pushed it open, once again announcing their entry.

They stepped into a small but immaculate kitchen. Erin sniffed. "Bleach. Faint, but it's there."

"Why would he wear the bloody clothes into his house?" Brooks asked. "He's got the means to clean off outside." He eased through the door into the next room. Like most older houses, this one didn't have an open floor plan. Moving from room to room meant checking doorways, their weapons ready. First the dining room, then the living room.

"Nothing personal," Brooks whispered as they slipped through the house. "No family photos, nothing that ties him here. He doesn't want to implicate anyone else or leave a trail."

They reached a home office that appeared to have been ransacked. "Jesus Christ."

Erin halted next to Brooks and stared at the dried blood coating the hardwood floor. A torn piece of college-ruled notebook paper had been placed in the middle of the pool, presumably after the blood started to dry, because the words scrawled below the picture were still legible.

> The female wasps crawl through the streets like rats, strewing their filth behind them! No remorse for the lives they ruin. Only the drink appeals to them. I will take as many as I can before the demon eats me whole. He kept a kidney tonight. I do not know what will become of it, only that I am descending further into hell for which there is no escape.
>
> —JTR
> 30 September 1888

"Is that a kidney?" Erin stared at the shriveled human organ acting as a paperweight.

"Looks like it."

Streaked through the blood was the familiar signature: *Jane the Ripper*.

CHAPTER THIRTY-SEVEN

Within an hour, cops and crime scene technicians descended like locusts onto Yari Malek's property. Though they had a kidney, there was no body. The malodorous yard bag contained Yari Malek's dress shirt and pants, a pair of shoes and socks, and blood in various stages of drying, which coated nearly everything.

"Egotistical fucker embroidered his initials on his shirt." Erin huddled in the front yard with Brooks and Clark to bring him up to speed. "And then he didn't make sure he'd locked the shed door. It's like he wanted to get caught."

She shivered. "We found the rest of the missing equipment from Bonnie's attic in the trunk of his car. Including the digital camera, but the memory's been cleared."

"That bugs me." Brooks's rounded shoulders, drawn up to his ears to stave off some of the rain, made him resemble a hunchback. "Malek's careless with everything else, but he erases the memory?"

"Maybe he figured having a recording of him killing her would make his sentence worse," Erin said. "D.C. doesn't have the death penalty. Double homicide means life without parole."

"Again, it makes no sense." The more bits and pieces they uncovered, the worse the situation smelled—literally.

"So, whose kidney is that?" Brooks's chin disappeared into the turned-up collar of his jacket. Windburn stained his cheeks. "Did you get anything out of Aleta?"

Clark shook his head. "Not much more than what she told you. Insists she doesn't know Jane, Mina, or Charlie, and she has no clue where Malek would run. She maintains she's never had contact with Simon Archer. But guess what? Gilani's not her real name. She doesn't come up in the system."

Erin rubbed her temples. "It's possible she did this and then called to throw us off her trail. At this point, I feel like we're getting further from the answer instead of closer."

Clark stared into the gathering crowd of media. "I want to believe this is a man we're dealing with because then we've got a real suspect in Yari Malek. We're going to get into his computer. Maybe we'll get a break and see he liked the Ripper, and this is all an elaborate distraction. In the meantime, Aleta's cooling her heels in a cell. But she called a lawyer. Unless we get her real name and find something to hold her on, she'll be out by tonight."

The fine mist had turned into heavier drips. The flimsy hood on Erin's jacket barely covered the top of her head, leaving her forehead and face exposed. Her hair stuck to her cheeks, her lips were frozen, and her canvas tennis shoes had soaked through the toes. She cast a bitter glance at the media already preening across the street. Torrence and her crew showed up minutes after the crime scene crew. Her lackey held a different umbrella this time, a giant yellow one matching Torrence's coat. Erin wanted to run across the street and smack her upside the head with the yellow monstrosity. Instead, she huddled closer to Brooks, whose umbrella barely covered one person. She had to crane her neck to make eye contact with Clark, resulting in cold rain dribbling down her neck.

Brooks bit his lower lip. "Malek runs, but he leaves everything behind, including the computers that probably have evidence on them. All his expensive, monogrammed clothes, jewelry. His car, I can see, but he just left with the shirt on his back. The damn case has practically been handed to us, which is exactly why this all smells like bullshit."

Erin's phone vibrated, and the caller ID read *Brad*. She sent it to voicemail. "Simmons and his sidekick showed up around seven a.m. this morning, and Malek had already gone. That's a minimum eight hours' head start for Malek—or his killer."

"So we'll track Malek's credit cards," Brooks said. "Put out a BOLO. Go back to Sid's and hammer at his manager. I bet he's got an entire stable of girls on the side who have nothing to do with the strip club and everything to do with the sex trade. We need a list of those. We also need to find a way to get Simon Archer's financial records."

Clark blew on his hands, flexing his wet fingers. "Keep dreaming. Unless everything leads to him and is gift wrapped with a big, fat bow, it's not happening. We've got two options: Malek's the killer, and he used Jane as a distraction so he could skip town, or he's dead, and the killer planted all this stuff. Number one suspect is Aleta Gilani, who apparently goes by a fake name 'cause she doesn't exist in any system. Her sending us here is just another mind game."

Erin's phone rang again with Brad's number. She stepped away from the two men and punched the green button. "I sent you to voicemail because I'm busy, so this better be an emergency."

"Mommy!"

Her daughter's terrified cries sliced through Erin like shrapnel. "Mommy!"

Erin's throat swelled at the sound of her daughter's distress. "Abby, what's wrong?" Erin dug her keys out of her pocket, vaguely aware of Brooks and Clark's worried stares.

"S-s-s-something's wrong with Uncle Brad. He's lying in the hallway, and he won't get up. Mommy, he's so cold!"

Time stopped. Her surroundings faded into a gray mist. The cold rain pricked her face like glass shards and mingled with her tears.

From far away, as if he were talking through a tunnel full of cotton candy, Brooks asked whether she was okay. Her chest felt like someone had forced her into a corset and had cinched it tight. She couldn't catch her breath.

Her eyes stung as bursts of light hit her from all sides, and she screamed her throat raw, telling Abby to call 911 before her life went black.

CHAPTER THIRTY-EIGHT

The next hours came in flashes. A mad rush to her home where the ambulance sat, its emergency lights off. Abby in Mrs. Bakas's arms, sobbing uncontrollably. Mrs. Bakas gripping Erin's arm and telling her not to go inside.

Then Erin saw her brother—her anchor in this world—crumpled in a heap, his hands already going stiff in the beginning of rigor. A woman's ear-splitting keening drilled into Erin's eardrums and pierced whatever sense of control she had left.

She was the one screaming.

An undiagnosed brain aneurysm had ruptured—a tragic and fairly common occurrence, according to Judy Temple. Dan Mitchell took Brad to the Consolidated Forensics Laboratory, and Judy Temple came in on her day off to rush the autopsy.

With Abby at a friend's, Brad had been completely alone.

"Did he know what happened?" Erin sat in Judy's office that night. "Did he know he was alone and dying? If I had been there, could I have called the paramedics in time?"

Temple handed Erin a tissue. The normally harsh lines of her face smoothed into an almost motherly expression. "He might have had a terrible headache, some severe neck pain, but it was a very large rupture. Once it happened, it was all over quickly. You couldn't have saved him."

"But he wouldn't have died alone." Erin had gone numb.

Temple's cool hand folded over Erin's. "You should go home and be with your daughter and the rest of your family. You can make the arrangements together in the morning. There's no rush."

A bitter laugh scraped through her raw throat. "God, the arrangements. I can't wait to sit down as a family and do that."

Her parents had arrived at the forensics lab while Temple conducted the autopsy. Both of them appeared as numb as Erin felt. When Temple entered the small room designated for family counseling, she quietly told them the cause of death. Calvin and Helen Prince cried in each other's arms, asking God for guidance. They left together, and Erin promised to handle things that night. Except she had no idea what those things were.

"Who's driving you home?"

She blinked, looking at Temple but not actually seeing her.

"Erin." Temple rarely used her first name. She spoke slowly, enunciating each syllable. "Your car isn't here. You rode in with Dan, and your parents have left. Do I need to call someone?"

"I'll take her home." Brooks's voice snapped Erin out of her trance. He stood in the doorway of Temple's office, his coat soaked and his hair plastered to his head. "I'm sorry it took so long to get here. Clark wanted me to stay at Malek's house until the crime scene crew finished." Brooks took a hesitant step forward to touch her shoulder. "Erin, I am so sorry."

Her legs were as wobbly as a newborn calf's. Nausea burned the base of her throat, but she had emptied her stomach hours ago. She licked her chapped lips and rubbed her throbbing head so hard the skin on her temples burned.

Temple stood and narrowed her eyes. "Do you have a headache?"

"I'm fine. Dehydrated." Was that stone-cold voice hers?

"Do you frequently get headaches?"

"I'm working the most stressful case of my career," Erin said. "I get headaches."

Temple pursed her lips, her hands going to her broad hips. "I'm not one to tap dance around things. Headaches are one of the few ways aneurysms can be caught. A person's been suffering, she goes in for a checkup, and hopefully, the doctor sees it. Or she's there for something else going on, and it's a lucky catch." She paused and peered at Erin. "Sometimes these things can be hereditary."

Erin swayed, grabbing onto the back of the chair. "What are you saying?"

"It's probably nothing, but you should look into your family history. Most physicians believe two deaths from aneurysms in a family warrants a closer look. If someone within a few generations has the diagnosis, then you and anyone else in that direct bloodline should be checked out."

Erin simply couldn't take another shred of life-changing news. She wasn't sure she could put one foot in front of the other long enough to make it to Brooks's car. She pulled on her still-damp coat and zipped it up, turning her attention to her partner. "Let's go, please. Thank you for everything, Dr. Temple."

Brooks eased to a stop in front of Mrs. Bakas's house. The neighbor insisted she and Abby stay with her for at least the night. Erin hadn't put up a fight. She stared down the block at her own dark home. How could she live there without him?

She hadn't been able to find the energy to speak since leaving the forensics laboratory. The lights of Washington flew by like a dream, the monument shining above all the rest. She watched the blinking light at the top until Brooks's monotone GPS told him to turn, putting the city in the rearview mirror. Her brain slogged, unable to form a clear thought beyond the paralyzing sorrow leaking into every part of her body. Memories of Carmen and Neil Archer flashed, and then Rylan Walton. Only days ago, Erin had wondered how she would cope if she were in their positions.

"Erin?"

She continued to watch the house she shared with her twin. Had shared, she corrected herself. Only the night itself seemed darker than the empty house. Brad always left the porch light on for her.

Brad was dead.

The pain came in a jolt, crushing her lungs. She pressed her hands against her mouth to hide the sobs, but they persevered. Tears soaked her cheeks and fingers. Her airway ceased to work, the pressure on her chest so strong she could have been drowning. She could only manage nonsensical sounds. A coherent thought refused to come. She smacked against the back of the seat, her body rocking in time to the anguish.

"Erin!" A warm hand gripped her shoulder, holding her in place. "Breathe."

She clawed at her throat.

Brooks grabbed her wrists in his other hand. "Listen to my voice. Erin, you need to calm down. Your daughter needs you. Abby needs you."

Slowly, the debilitating panic subsided enough for Erin to see Abby in her mind's eye. Her sweet, broken little girl who'd walked in and found her beloved uncle dead.

"Abby."

"Yes, Abby." Brooks let go of her wrists but kept his hand on her shoulder.

"What is she going to do?" Erin's throat stung with the effort of speaking. "How can I help her through this?"

"Kids are resilient," Brooks said. "More than most adults. You'll help her because you love her. All you can do is be there for her and allow her to grieve."

"But I don't know how to be me without Brad." That was the heartbreaking truth. From birth, their lives were intertwined; one could not *be* without the other. She trusted Brad more than anyone. He and Abby were the center of her world, and now half of it had vanished. How was she supposed to be strong enough to handle losing Brad, much less strong enough to help her daughter?

"You'll figure it out because you have to," Brooks said.

She faced him for the first time since leaving the forensics lab. "Thank you."

Brooks drew a long breath. "I'm sorry, there's nothing I can do or say to make it any better. There's no making a person feel better in this situation. I'm here if you need me. And Ellen, too. She's still a licensed social worker. If Abby needs to talk to someone, call me. Ellen has plenty of connections."

Erin nodded. "The case—"

"Forget about it," he said. "If you want updates in the next few days, text me. But focus on your daughter."

She didn't know what to say, and she couldn't have spoken over the lump in her throat. So she squeezed his arm and exited the little car.

CHAPTER THIRTY-NINE

Hundreds of people attended the funeral. Erin recognized less than half of them, and most didn't know Brad. Mostly they were her father's colleagues and friends who'd come to pay their respects. Lisa had enough heart to keep her usual insults to herself. She used the wake as an opportunity to mingle and schmooze, but Erin didn't care as long as she wasn't talking trash about Brad. Brooks came, along with Fowler and Clark.

True to his word, Brooks kept her updated, but things had stalled. In addition to Virginia Walton's blood, the medical examiner found traces of Bonnie's blood on the clothes Yari Malek stashed in his shed. Erin couldn't imagine Virginia allowing him into the house if he wore the same clothes he'd killed Bonnie in. Still, the medical examiner was confident the clothing contained both victims' blood.

Malek had vanished and hadn't used his credit cards. Aleta's lawyer sprung her, and she'd gone off the grid. Brooks and Fowler convinced one of the older girls to give up Aleta's real name. "Aleta Gionese. Charged with prostitution, drug trafficking, and possession five years ago. Couldn't get the drug trafficking to stick, but she served a few months for possession," Brooks confided. "Not a single blip on the radar after her release. No credit cards, no driver's license, no utility bills."

"Gionese." Something in Erin's exhausted brain sparked. "Why does that name sound familiar?"

"Because it's been tossed around in the investigation of the drug cartels," Brooks said. "The FBI believes someone named Gionese is a major carrier for the Mexican cartel working its way up here. We don't know if Aleta is affiliated in any way, but since she managed to get one of the best defense attorneys in town within a couple of hours after we detained her, I'm thinking there's a good chance."

"If she's from that world, she's been exposed to killing," Erin said. "The cartels don't leave witnesses, and they always leave a message."

The good news kept coming. Bonnie's computer contained over fifty amateur sex videos starring herself, Aleta, and Malek in violent rape fantasies that turned Brooks green when he described them. In one particular video, Aleta beat the hell out of Bonnie, calling her a whore in both English and Arabic, threatening to kill her if she didn't behave. Brooks believed the video wasn't scripted. But Malek and Aleta weren't the only movie stars in Bonnie's world. Reese, from the Adult Literacy Center, took his turn at violence as well. His financials showed Yari Malek extorted Reese for more than twenty-five thousand—a damned good motive in any cop's book. So Reese, and his intact kidney, had been left to sweat it out in a holding cell while the forensics crew combed his apartment. Brooks seemed particularly excited about the scratches on Reese's arms, claiming they could be defense wounds, but Erin felt only numbness.

"We found Virginia on the security footage from The Point," Brooks whispered as Erin tried to eat something. "There's about ten blurry seconds of her talking to a tall person in black who may or may not be Tori, but there's nothing to trace. And he didn't leave any sort of paper trail from The Point, either."

Judy Temple came to pay her respects and quietly reminded Erin to look into her family history. Erin didn't tell her she didn't need to. In a crying jag the day after Brad's death, her mother talked about an aunt who'd died from an aneurysm around the same age as Brad. Erin stowed the information away to deal with later. All of her energy went into caring for her daughter.

Abby kept asking why this had happened. In her young mind, life was still supposed to be black and white. There should have been a logical explanation for everything; telling her bad things happened didn't cut it. Trying to explain how something went wrong in Brad's brain only scared her.

"Could that happen to you or me?" Her big blue eyes were loaded with tears. "I don't want you to die."

Thinking about Judy Temple's warning turned Erin cold inside, but she lied to her child and promised her she wouldn't die.

"Mother of the Year," Erin whispered as she poured another shot of tequila. When the wake at her parents' house finally ended, she crossed the acre yard to the Princes' posh guesthouse. Abby wanted to sleep with her grandmother, and Helen had been such a wreck, it would be good for both of them.

So Erin had the night to herself. She celebrated by doing shots of tequila, the first drink she and Brad ever got drunk on. Brad threw up, and Erin teased him for being a lightweight. He didn't touch the stuff for two years.

The guesthouse sat tucked away on the eastern end of the Princes' property, bordered by a thatch of evergreen woods thick with wildlife. The builders had the foresight to put in a large bay window on the eastern wall, complete with a cushy window seat. Erin curled up on the seat, a new tequila shot in one hand and a lime in the other. She leaned her head against the cool glass. Over the past few days, some of the heavy cloud cover dissipated, allowing a few stars and the quarter moon to be visible. In the meager moonlight, the woods seemed dark and much deeper than they actually were. Erin wished a deer or maybe a raccoon would come out. Anything to draw her attention away from the parasitic sense of loss.

Brad wouldn't want her to be like this. In fact, he would be ragging on her day and night. But this was a contingency no one prepared for, and she had yet to figure out how to navigate life with such a gaping wound.

The doorbell chimed, and she nearly dropped the shot. Midnight had come and gone. Her parents had gone to bed and hopefully fallen asleep. Maybe Abby had a nightmare, and someone had come to fetch Erin.

Erin left the shot and the sticky lime on the kitchen counter and hurried to the door, not bothering to check before she opened it. The last person she expected to see stared back at her.

"Lisa." Erin didn't have the energy for this. Her half-sister had gone home two hours ago, citing an early morning.

Lisa played with the collar of her designer coat. The stress of the day had melted off most of her makeup, and the circles under her eyes betrayed the truth: an overworked woman in her mid-forties. "I wanted to talk to you."

She couldn't handle a fight with Lisa. Not tonight. But she saw no sign of animosity in her sister's liquid brown eyes.

"I won't stay long," Lisa said. "Not even long enough to take off my coat. Dad's going to be out of the office for the next few days, so I've got to pick up the slack."

Calvin Prince had taken his son's death extremely hard. Although he'd grudgingly accepted Brad's sexuality, they were never close. Calvin now wore the regret like a crushing suit of armor.

"Is this about the company?" In their wills, Erin and Brad had left their trusts to each other, with stipulations made for Abby. Neither of them had shares in the company, so she didn't see what Lisa would need to talk to her about.

"No, it's about you. About us. Brad." Lisa bit her lip, her mouth twisting in a way that told Erin she didn't want to say whatever she stewed over. "About fixing things between us."

Erin's knees weakened. Her stomach growled. Was she about to pass out? "Listen, I really appreciate you coming to make amends. And that's something we can discuss, but not tonight. I'm just beat."

Lisa's cheeks flushed, the vein in her forehead pulsing the way it always did when she got angry. She took a deep breath and nodded. "Fair enough. Can we talk in a few days?"

"I'll call you, I promise." Erin intended to fulfill her promise. After all, Lisa had swallowed a lot of pride tonight. Erin headed back to take her last shot before passing out.

Her phone flashed with a text from Brooks. Her stomach dropped as she read.

Found Yari Malek.

CHAPTER FORTY

"You didn't have to come." Brooks stood at the edge of the Potomac, watching Dan Mitchell and his assistant negotiate a bloated corpse into a body bag.

Erin waved him off. She never welcomed death, but she welcomed the distraction. Her stomach, however, didn't appreciate the gas station coffee she'd sucked down to thwart the effects of the tequila. She popped in a breath mint. "Hell of a place for a body dump. If we're sure that's what this is."

Yari Malek floated to the surface underneath Arlington Memorial Bridge, mere feet from the backside of the Lincoln Memorial. Erin gazed up the hill at the monument. From this angle, it could have been a beautiful stone building surrounded by ornate pillars. Lincoln's impressive statue sat on the other side of the wall, overlooking the Reflecting Pool, meaning the backside of the monument wasn't a spot most tourists ventured. But it could be seen from Ohio Drive, which ran between the grounds and the river. At three a.m., moderate traffic still lumbered across the bridge overhead, and a car came by the scene every few minutes, the driver's mouth gaping.

"We're sure it's a body dump," Mitchell said. "I can't tell how long he's been in the water exactly, but my best guess is a few days. She slashed his throat and then went for his abdomen. She probably stabbed him a couple of times and then forced him outside. It's hard to tell, thanks to decomposition, but I'm betting his kidney is missing. Oh, and she carved her initial on his forehead too—after his heart stopped."

"Jesus Christ." Erin halted a few feet from the unzipped bag. The smell hit her in the face like a hammer. Her stomach roiled against it and she gagged, the liquor and crappy coffee threatening to make a second appearance. Mitchell tossed her a tube of Vicks. She swiped a generous amount beneath her nose and edged forward.

With skin blue and swollen to the point of bursting in places, Malek was virtually unrecognizable. Fish had chewed out his eyes and part of his nose. But the crimson *J* in his forehead couldn't be missed.

"Why not the whole name?" Erin asked.

"No time, is my guess." Brooks walked beneath the bridge, the structure partially hidden by the tall, reedy weeds browned from the cold weather. "I'm assuming it happened at night, so traffic was slow, but her time was still limited, so she stopped with the J. Then she shoved him in the water."

"Did she weigh him down with something?"

"Looks like it," Brooks said. "There's a rope tied to one of his ankles. It came loose from whatever she used, and he floated up."

"Pure luck, at least for us." Mitchell arranged the corpse's swollen hands over its chest. "Otherwise, she would be off the hook for this murder. We would have never found him."

Erin turned away from the putrid face of what had once been Yari Malek and tried not to think about Brad in his casket. He might have been peacefully asleep, except he was still, silent, and horrifically stiff. She cleared her throat and ignored her stinging eyes. "Where are we with Brian Reese?"

"Fowler broke him down an hour ago," Brooks said. "He claims that after Bonnie's murder, he and Malek had words."

"Reese thought Malek killed her?"

"Malek thought Reese killed her," Brooks corrected. "Reese just wanted to get out of paying Malek any more money because Bonnie was dead. Malek said that didn't matter; he still had the proof to ruin Reese's career. They apparently fought—a convenient excuse for the scratches on his arm. He swears that happened two days before Malek disappeared, and he left him alive."

"Of course, he does."

The Potomac's current rippled, and small waves quietly broke on the shore.

"What about Aleta?"

"Says he doesn't know her. We can't prove he's lying; she wasn't in the video he made, nor can we pick up her voice behind the camera. And we still haven't found her. The Gionese family lawyer claims she's no relation. No one believes him."

"So did Reese pay Bonnie, too?"

"He says no. We can't find any record of it so far."

"Virginia Walton found out about them, right? He threatened her into silence."

Brooks shrugged. "Reese says no. We're searching Virginia's computers at school and work for any correspondence about it. I'd feel better about him as the killer if Sarah hadn't come by the station earlier. Someone left this in her mailbox." He handed Erin a piece of white notebook paper carefully stored in a clear plastic bag. "She found it after we brought Reese in. He probably had it delivered, but the timing bothers me."

A lump grew in Erin's throat as she read the letter, all the noise from the road sounding as though it were coming through a vacuum.

Dear Princess,

I keep on hearing you might be the one to catch me, but you won't manage it. I don't like whores and tattletales, and I won't quit until things are right again.

Great fun, the last job was. I gave the lady time to fight, and she flopped like a dying pig. How can you catch me now when you don't even know where to look? I saved some things from the last job, and now they're so crusty I can't hope to use them. Too much red, but I like it so much. Maybe next time I'll cut the lady's eyes out. Good luck with your nightmares.

Jane the Ripper

P.S. Mina thinks you're a real princess. I know it's all a lie.

Erin thrust the letter back at Brooks. She didn't have the strength to be upset about being made a fool of again. The killer's brazenness terrified her.

"So, she didn't care if someone found Malek's body," Erin said. "She wanted me to know she's still out there. This was delivered to Sarah's parents' house?"

"No," Brooks said, his eyes roaming the letter again. "Her rental. Her roommate came home and found it stuck in the door, addressed to you in care of Sarah Archer. Her roommate told her she saw a dark-haired woman walking about a block away from their rental before she got home and discovered the letter, but they live in an area heavily populated with college students. It could have been anyone walking. Sarah and the roommate are terrified."

"Of course, their rental doesn't have any security cameras." Erin stared at the black water, half-wishing the river would rise up and swallow her. "If Reese isn't our guy, then it's got to be Aleta. She's a Gionese and knows what she's doing. She told us she liked pain. Where are Sarah and her roommate?"

"Roommate's staying with her boyfriend. Sarah's safe at her parents'. I told her to stay there and make sure the doors were locked and all the security armed."

Brooks looked up at the murky sky. "I think we can take Tori off our list. He's a coincidence. My gut tells me Simon Archer discovered Aleta's involvement with Bonnie and hired her to do his dirty work. Jane the Ripper is a ploy."

Erin didn't respond. Some twisted part of her felt disappointed at Jane for not being real. What a story to tell. *Christ, I'm losing it.*

"Aleta's probably not a legal citizen, but her daughter is, assuming she was born here—and if we're right about Mina being Aleta's daughter, Simon Archer could have threatened to have Aleta deported," Brooks said. "Mina would stay here. She did whatever she had to do to save her daughter, including killing three people. You're a mother. How far would you go?"

"I'd kill for Abby," Erin said without hesitation. "But I have options. There are people I could go to for help. My father ..."

"If Aleta is really another one of Malek's victims, she's been brainwashed and broken down," Brooks said. "She didn't have someone like your father to go to. Simon Archer might have seemed like the devil to her. Then again, if she is related to the Gionese affiliated with the cartel, Simon Archer might have signed his own death warrant."

Erin's stomach growled, the tequila reminding her that her last meal had been this morning. "She lied and managed to disappear as soon as her lawyer got her cut loose. How brainwashed can she be? How do we know she's not the master manipulator she made Yari out to be? She completely played us."

Mitchell zipped up the body bag, and Brooks turned to Erin. "To be honest, I feel like I'm drowning in a big pool of shitty theories that don't quite add up."

Her phone vibrated in her pocket. She answered without bothering to look at the ID, hoping Abby hadn't awoken to a nightmare and found out her mother wasn't there. "Prince."

"Princess!"

The high-pitched, childish cry paralyzed Erin. "Mina, what's wrong?"

"Jane's going to hurt us!"

"Mina, where are you?" Erin waved frantically at Brooks.

The little girl answered with a scream. Then silence.

CHAPTER FORTY-ONE

For the second time in two weeks, Erin knocked on Neil and Carmen Archer's door. After Mina's frantic call, she and Brooks decided to split up. Fowler joined Brooks at the strip club to try and force something out of the dancers and manager while Erin talked to the Archers.

Her patience long gone, she steeled herself against the confrontation. Neil Archer wouldn't like what she had to say, but a child's life was at stake. She no longer had any empathy for Bonnie's parents. They'd failed the girl time and again in her life, and they continued to fail her in death.

Neil wrenched the door open and glared at her with hollowed eyes reminiscent of a war veteran unable to speak of the things he witnessed. "What do you want at this hour?"

"The truth." She shouldered her way past him and into the foyer. "Get Carmen, because you're both going to tell me everything I need to know."

"Investigator Prince." Neil Archer's voice thinned to the consistency of a razor blade. "I don't know what kind of show you're trying to run, but we aren't the bad guys. Our daughter is a victim, and you've done nothing to find out who killed her."

"Listen to me." She slammed the front door and then stood on tiptoes to get in his face. He probably caught a whiff of the tequila from hours ago, but she'd gone past the point of caring. "Your daughter is dead, and you're not helping us find out who killed her. I buried my twin brother less than twenty-four hours ago, and all I want to do is crawl into bed and stay there. But I'm trying to find a killer before someone else dies. So let's start with Ted Moore."

Neil Archer jerked, stepping back as if she'd planted her fist in his chest—a scenario that wasn't out of the question, at this point. "Ted Moore is dead."

"No shit," Erin snapped. "I've got a little girl calling me claiming someone is going to get hurt again, and we just dredged our only suspect out of the Potomac. So it's time for you to come clean about who abused Bonnie."

"Investigator." Carmen Archer descended the stairs like a withered ghost, tightening her fuzzy robe. "I'm sorry to hear about your brother, but there's simply no way Bonnie's abuse has anything to do with this."

"I think Neil's brother is the key to this whole thing, and it all goes back to Bonnie being molested."

"Simon?" Neil Archer stood motionless as an old tree stump and just as oblivious. "I don't understand."

"Bonnie blackmailed someone in the last six months for a lot of money, and she told Sarah more cash would be coming." Erin didn't have time to worry about the Archers' feelings. "The most logical person is the man who molested her—or the uncle who helped cover it up. Ted Moore's return to the area and the timing of his documentary gels with the deposit. But Ted Moore's dead, and the only other person with something major to lose is your brother. Bonnie likely blackmailed them both."

"What does Professor Walton's murder have to do with it?" Neil asked.

"Bonnie confided in her." Presenting the theory as fact was the only chance she had of getting Neil to talk. "Virginia was killed because of what she knew."

Neil tugged at his graying hair. "My brother's a bastard, but he wouldn't kill anyone."

"We think he hired a woman Bonnie knew to kill her. And anyone who can lead us to Simon is in danger." Erin turned her attention to Carmen, who stood on the bottom step, wringing her hands. "This killer is vicious and is signing her name as Jane the Ripper, and a little girl named Mina is calling me, begging for help. She says Jane will do it again, and you people are all I've got. Give me something to throw at Simon Archer other than accusing him of covering up the molestation. Give me more details. Help me find your daughter's killer."

"Ted Moore molested Bonnie." Carmen hushed her husband when he rounded on her. "Enough, Neil. You think it's not going to come out? They're saying Bonnie made violent sex videos. That will become public knowledge. The least we can do for her memory is to help people understand why she had such low self-esteem."

Neil emitted a string of unintelligible pleas.

Erin stepped between the couple, focusing all of her attention on Carmen. "Keep talking."

"Ted and Simon went to college together. When the girls were little, Ted hadn't made a name for himself yet. Simon let him stay with them when Ted ran out of money. Simon and Melinda had a function, and Ted volunteered to watch the girls. Bonnie said Sarah was already asleep when he came into the bed." She clawed at her head, tangling her already unkempt hair. "He raped my eight-year-old daughter and then told her she would ruin her uncle's life if she told. He did it again a few days later. I noticed something changed in Bonnie, and she finally told me. We confronted Ted and Simon. Ted Moore is a great actor, and Simon wanted to believe him. He said Bonnie was a manipulative child who just wanted attention."

Carmen's broken tone turned bitter. "Sarah was so delicate, and people were drawn to her, especially with those beautiful, strange eyes. Bonnie got jealous sometimes. But for Simon to say Bonnie made something like this up? The doctor confirmed she'd been molested. She was … injured."

"But Ted Moore's semen was already gone." As a mother, Erin couldn't imagine any set of circumstances or any threat big enough to keep her from cutting off Moore's balls. No way in hell would she have kept silent.

Carmen nodded. "Simon said Neil must have abused our daughter, and we coached Bonnie to say otherwise. He threatened to call the police and have Neil investigated, and he assured us he would make our lives— Bonnie's life—miserable. We were too scared to do the right thing."

Judging them accomplished nothing, and the little voice in her head debated whether or not the security of her family name would have played a part in her decision. Brooks and Clark were right. No matter how far she ran from the Prince legacy, she would always view life through that veil of experience.

"How long did Ted Moore stay in town?"

"At least a couple of months," Neil said. "I saw him once, in the grocery store. Shopping with Sarah like nothing had ever happened." He slammed his right fist into the opposite palm. "I will never forget the look on his face. He grinned like a sly fox, patting the top of Sarah's head. His way of letting me know he'd gotten away with it."

The sick feeling swept over Erin with the force of a hurricane. How could these two not have considered the obvious? "What did Sarah do, that day?"

"She wouldn't look at me," Neil said. "Stared at the floor the entire time. And yes, we knew Moore had likely abused Sarah, too, but we had to take care of Bonnie first."

"How did you find out Moore went to California?"

Neil's chin jutted out, his narrowed eyes glossed over from the memory. "I got drunk and showed up at Simon's a couple of days later. He told me he'd banished Moore the day before. That Moore moved to California. I hired someone to find out whether it was true. Once he confirmed it, we tried to go on with our lives."

"He used the word *banished*?" The truth hit Erin like hives festering just beneath her skin.

"Yeah. They'd had an argument, I guess."

"You said you got Bonnie therapy, but therapists are required to report sexual abuse. There is none on record for Bonnie."

Neil shuffled his feet. "All I ever wanted to do was protect my daughter. I failed her by leaving her at my brother's. Risking her going into the foster system because my brother made my wife and me look like the ones who did something wrong terrified me."

"So you didn't get her therapy?" This family created their own brand of cancer by allowing their daughter to be victimized long after the sexual abuse stopped.

"We did," Carmen said. "Someone Melinda recommended. A friend of Simon's. He agreed to keep things quiet and focus on Bonnie's mental health."

"Jesus Christ," Erin hissed through her teeth.

"We tried to talk to Melinda and Simon, and they wouldn't hear of it. I begged Melinda to keep Sarah away from Ted Moore." Carmen's voice broke. "I don't know if she did. When I saw Sarah years later, and she talked about therapy, I worried Melinda didn't listen."

"Did you ask who her therapist was?"

Carmen's eyes closed. "The same one Bonnie went to."

A parent's job was to protect the child, even if the price required self-sacrifice. If she stayed one more minute, Erin would end up saying something guaranteed to earn a suspension. And Mina still needed her. Erin turned to leave, but Neil Archer seized her elbow.

Spit bubbled in the corners of his mouth. His hair jacked up in all directions. "I've lived with the guilt for years. I watched Bonnie go through hell time and again, and I couldn't do anything because she didn't trust me. She didn't think I would fix it because I never made things right with Ted Moore. He never had to answer for what he did." Something feral flashed in his eyes. A satisfied smile tugged at his frothing mouth. "But I guess he finally did, didn't he?"

Erin took a deep breath of the cold, stinging air. She yanked free of Neil's bony grasp and moved toward the door, never taking her eyes off him. "I'm going to ask you two one more time—do the names Jane, Charlie, or Mina mean anything to you? Do any of those names have a connection with Sarah?"

Still breathing hard and looking like something straight off the crazy train, Neil shook his head.

Carmen made a sound of recognition as something clicked into place. "Sarah's middle name is Jane. Her maternal grandmother's name."

Erin left them standing in the doorway, crying and holding each other. Her call to Sarah Archer's cell went unanswered, as expected. No one picked up at the Archers' Chevy Chase home. Brooks's phone went to voicemail. Erin left a message with the new information and told Brooks where to meet her.

"I'm stopping at Virginia's first. I need to check something."

Chapter Forty-Two

Virginia Walton's home in Takoma Park had been cleaned by a crime scene crew, but the aura of violent death still hung in the air like a cloying perfume. Violence like that left a black mark, a dark energy felt by all who crossed its path.

The dark energy clung to Erin as she eased through the house. She had no reason to be quiet, but silence seemed like the right thing. A jagged circle had been cut out of the carpet where Virginia's blood had soaked through to the subfloor. The wood had been cleaned, but the stain gleamed in Erin's flashlight beam.

She wished Rylan hadn't canceled the power and prayed she hadn't taken the box from her mother's bedroom. The night of the murder, she and Brooks didn't think much of it. Just a regular cardboard storage box marked as *old thesis drafts and works in progress*—Marie called the woman a "paper pack rat." The dates marked with a sharpie on the box were several months old. Likely not pertinent to the investigation. Had that decision changed everything?

Sarah Archer's words played on repeat in Erin's mind as she moved with quiet reverence down the hall. *My second thesis ... the first one was too emotional and personal ... like a memoir.*

Questions raced through Erin's mind. What about the Dear Princess letter? What about the letter Sarah received earlier?

Had Sarah really been ballsy—or disturbed—enough to hand deliver a letter she'd written? And why?

Because she could. You didn't see what was right in front of you.

Sarah had practically waved it in Erin's face the other day at the CID. The two of them had even discussed her embroidered initials on the handkerchief: *SJA*.

Sarah knew Erin would empathize with her upbringing and the terror of being cut off from the money.

The bedroom still held a faint whiff of Virginia's flowery perfume, and it looked exactly the same. Rylan must not have been able to bring herself to go through her mother's things yet. Erin didn't blame her. She hadn't been inside Brad's room yet. Mrs. Bakas had brought out his clothes for Erin to choose from for the burial. She blinked against the sting in her eyes and called up the memory of Mina's terrified voice to stave off the threat of crushing despair. She shined her beam into the corner and exhaled hard when she saw the box was still there.

Heart racing, she knelt and balanced the flashlight between her ear and shoulder. Dust rose from the papers, making Erin sneeze. She sliced her fingers on the paper's edges three times before reaching the middle of the pile and catching the name Sarah Jane Archer.

Her original thesis discussed unreported sexual abuse in children and their longstanding ramifications. Erin licked her thumb and tried not to let her disgust mess up her focus. She could easily see why the paper had been rejected. The tone was more conversational than academic, and instead of any real evidence, many of Sarah's theories were only conjecture.

It did read like a memoir, with names omitted, but the text made it clear that Ted Moore had molested Sarah, possibly before he touched Bonnie.

Things picked up on page five. Sarah theorized that violence in women throughout history could have resulted from sexual abuse and rejection from loved ones. *Women had been forced to live lies,* Sarah wrote, *and in some of them rose a violent need to lash out.* This time, she cited evidence.

The next four pages laid out the theory that Jack the Ripper was a woman. A woman Sarah referred to as *Jane.*

Brooks answered his phone this time. He swore when Erin told him what she'd read.

"She took the metro to the station the other day, which means if she walked to the metro, then she could have done it the night of Bonnie and Virginia's murders. Her mother and the housekeeper wouldn't have noticed, especially if Sarah was supposed to be locked in her room and working on her thesis. I missed it." Erin clenched the wheel until her hands throbbed. Sarah had practically given her the truth gift wrapped with a big, red bow.

"Don't beat yourself up," Brooks said. "You'd been dealing with the press, and we'd already eliminated her as a suspect."

"I'm on my way to Chevy Chase." The faintest tinge of pink decorated the eastern horizon. "I should be there before six, but traffic's picking up. Let's hope Simon Archer is still alive. And Aleta and Mina and Charlie."

"We just walked out of Sid's." Brooks's rapid breaths sounded like he might have been running.

"Please tell me you're in Fowler's car. He always uses the department ones. You need a siren."

"I can do that. Fowler!"

"You're still at least twenty minutes out." Erin jammed her foot on the accelerator and ran a yellow light. "I'll be there in five."

"Don't go in by yourself," Brooks said. "If Sarah's the one behind this, she's extremely dangerous."

How had Erin missed all of the signs? Sarah might be an incredible actress, but she thought back to Brooks's words. Had she ignored the obvious because she'd allowed her and Sarah's similar backgrounds to influence her?

A terrible thought skidded through Erin's racing mind. What if Mina was actually Sarah's child? What if she'd been kept hidden for some strange reason? But why? Unless Ted Moore had fathered the child, which made no sense. Simon's? A product of incest? Simon might have kicked Ted Moore out of their lives, but how long had he looked the other way? Or did he have a twisted thing for his adult daughter, and that's why she kept Mina hidden?

Then there's the question of Charlie, the boy who took care of Mina. An older brother? No, too dark. If Sarah had children, she kept them hidden. Those kids wouldn't look good for Simon's conservative agenda.

"Erin? Do you hear me?"

She took a sharp left into the Archers' stately neighborhood. "Hurry."

The Archers' small mansion seemed as lifeless as Virginia's modest home. A red convertible sat in the driveway. Sarah's car? Headlights off, Erin blocked it in and tried to summon patience.

She had to be wrong. But it all made sense.

Sarah and Bonnie had reconnected after Ted Moore came back into town. That had to be the catalyst. Sarah probably apologized and told her cousin what she'd gone through. They'd bonded again and hatched the blackmail scheme.

Why would Sarah snap on her cousin?

The answer came to Erin like a zing from a live wire. The amateur rape videos. Had Sarah snapped over the violence Bonnie perpetrated?

Virginia Walton was the snitch because she could have pulled out the original thesis and started talking.

Yari Malek was the filth responsible for turning Bonnie into a whore. Aleta—if she hadn't been killed—was another enabler.

Erin watched the house, bouncing in her seat and tapping her uneven fingernails against the steering wheel. Where the hell were Brooks and Fowler?

A call came through her Bluetooth, flashing onto the car's touchscreen as *unknown*. Erin's eyes never left the Archers' home. "Mina?"

The dark drapes in the house's front bay window parted. "I see you, Princess. Do you want to come play?"

Adrenaline flushed through her system until Erin's throat nearly closed. She should stall the girl and wait for Brooks, but the child could be attacked at any moment. Erin took the safety off her gun and exited the car.

"Of course, I want to play. I've been trying to find you for weeks."

The little girl giggled. "I know. I like games."

"Me too." Erin moved slowly up the walk, trying to see inside the small opening in the drapes. They fell closed, and Erin dropped to a crouch. Jane's weapon of choice appeared to be a knife, but Erin didn't know whether there was a gun in the house.

The click of a lock escaped into the stillness.

Erin's gaze shot to the front door, slowly opening into a mouth of darkness. "Mina? Is that you? Come out to me, sweetheart."

Pale feet appeared first. Erin tried to draw a breath, but her lungs fought against her. Never moving from her crouch, she slipped the gun out of its holster at her waist, keeping the weapon low. "Mina, are you coming out to play with me?"

Sarah Archer moved into the open doorway. Shadows obscured her face as she stepped onto the granite entry clutching a large knife dripping with blood. Her blonde hair stuck up in the back and tangled around her face. Dark streaks marred her ghostly white nightshirt.

"Princess." The excited, childlike voice of Mina singsonged from Sarah's lips.

Erin went cold and still inside, but her entire body convulsed.

"I told Jane not to do it, but she never listens to me."

CHAPTER FORTY-THREE

"**M**ina, sweetheart, can you come closer? I can't see you very well." The pieces clicked together. *I called Sarah from my personal cell. That's how Mina got the number.*

Sarah cocked her head, revealing clumps of blood on her neck. "Okay."

Slowly, she padded forward on tiptoes, the unmistakable gait of a whimsical child. The movement triggered a motion sensor, and artificial light suddenly bathed the front of the house. Sarah froze. Her eyes popped wide, and her mouth curled up like a toddler getting ready to wail. She jerked the knife into a defensive stance. In her other hand, she held an old, beat-up, leather-bound book.

"Mina, shut up." Her new voice was a tenor and decidedly masculine. Her expression shifted from a scared little girl to a surly teenager. "You're going to get us all in trouble."

Erin's knees throbbed, but she didn't dare stand up. "Charlie?"

Sarah's narrowed eyes met Erin's. Her lips curled in cocky, adolescent defiance. "Go away. I've got the situation under control." Her—*his*—voice cracked at the last word.

Her brain screamed this could not be real, but it very much was.

Charlie edged closer, knife still hiked up, face twisted.

Erin noticed more blood—Simon's or Melinda's? Or both? "Charlie, I don't want to piss you off, but I'm too old to kneel like this."

Charlie curled up his nose like he'd just noticed a steaming pile of dog shit. "You are old. You're what, like thirty-four?"

Erin mustered a smile. "Nice compliment. Thirty-eight and feeling every minute. Is it cool if I stand?"

He waved the knife, making blood fly. "Throw that gun behind you, and it's cool."

Erin obeyed, tossing the Sig Saur behind her into the yard. Hopefully, she hadn't thrown it so far she couldn't get to it if she dove fast enough. And the Taser rested inside her jacket, heavy and secure against her ribs. Her knees throbbed, and she made a show of shaking her legs out.

"Thanks. So, what's going on here?"

"I told you I got it under control." He cocked his hip, and his face twisted into a boyish, arrogant grin that turned Erin's stomach.

"That was you at the CID the other day," she said. "After I asked Sarah about being molested, she changed. I thought Sarah had just reverted to a self-defense mechanism, but you took over to protect her, didn't you?"

"No shit, Sherlock." Charlie rolled his eyes. "I am the self-defense mechanism. That's my job." He tapped his chest with his fist.

Erin held up her hands and tried to believe she really faced an angry teenage boy. "Dude, okay, but you've got blood all over you. Are you hurt?"

"Not me." He noticed the nightgown and made a face. "She keeps fucking everything up. We just want to live our lives."

"Jane?"

Charlie's eyes narrowed. "What do you know about Jane?"

"She's signing her name at the crime scenes," Erin said. "She's doing some bad shit, Charlie."

"I know." The voice cracked again.

Ridiculously, Erin pictured Brad at that age. Every week, he seemed taller and his voice different. Erin got stuck with the acne, and Brad had taken her to a makeup artist to learn how to cover it up without caking on the concealer.

"We had her under control for a long time, and then Sarah went looking for Bonnie. Brought all that shit back up again."

Erin didn't know much about multiple personalities, but its proponents believed horrific childhood sexual abuse was the root cause. A child's fragile mind split into various parts to cope with the abuse.

"At least Ted Moore is dead."

Charlie's cheeks flamed. "How did you know about him?"

"I figured it out." Erin lowered her voice, trying to sound friendly. No big deal. Two friends talking. "Did Jane kill him, too?"

"Bonnie thought money would hurt him more."

"Bonnie knew about Jane and you and Mina?" Erin hoped no more people lived in Sarah's head.

"She didn't believe we were real." Charlie gazed at the knife handle. "When Sarah first told Bonnie, she still had control. That's what therapy was about—integrating us. We all worked together. Sarah didn't have blackouts. Most of the time, we stayed quiet. Then Bonnie happened, and she didn't believe us."

"That made you all mad?"

Charlie watched the blood dripping off the knife. "It made Sarah mad—and Jane, but Jane's always mad. Jane started being louder, and Sarah couldn't stay in one piece. I tried to speak up, but no one listens to me. Mina's the only one I can help."

The protector. Charlie cared about Sarah and Mina. Maybe Erin could use that to her advantage. "So what happened?"

"Sarah decided to prove it to Bonnie. She let Jane come out, and Bonnie recorded it on her stupid computer. She freaked out, but I don't think she believed it. Then everything went wrong. Jane kept coming out more and more. Sarah broke down. Me and Mina tried to hide." Charlie suddenly glared at the knife. "Fuck!" The voice cracked again, going from a burgeoning baritone to a high tenor.

The sun continued to creep up in the east. Neighbors had to be starting their day. One of them would look outside and call the police.

Brooks would be here any minute.

Erin edged back a step. How far had she thrown the gun? "So why did she kill Bonnie?"

Charlie's heels rocked back, legs taut as if prepared to charge. "Sarah told Bonnie she was thinking about going back to therapy. Sarah knew Jane had taken over more and more because she lost big chunks of time. Then she caught that man raping Bonnie. Except, Bonnie liked it! She wanted him to do it. And then she told Bonnie about Simon, about what she saw him do ..."

"What did Bonnie see Simon do?" At least Erin had been right about the trigger to Bonnie's murder. The rest of the stuff she had yet to truly process.

"I tried to keep Mina from seeing it, but Sarah walked in and heard Bonnie screaming from upstairs." Charlie's head whipped back and forth, his free hand smacking against his temple. "We thought she was dying. That man had her pinned down, and she was bleeding. We screamed at him to stop hurting her, but Bonnie said she needed him to do it. What the hell?"

"Bonnie was all kinds of messed up," Erin said. "Because of what happened to her and Sarah when they were kids. Sarah split apart, and she had you to help her. Bonnie didn't have anyone. What did Simon do? Did he abuse the girls, too?"

Charlie's head dropped, and his shoulders shook. But Erin quickly recognized the laughter. She took another step back, edging closer to the gun. Sarah's head shot up. Charlie had vanished, and in his place a feral cat appeared, her contrasting eyes gleaming with hate.

She pointed the dripping knife at Erin and spoke in a raw voice. "You shouldn't have come."

The British accent sent chills down Erin's spine. "Hello, Jane."

CHAPTER FORTY-FOUR

J ane taunted Erin, slicing the knife through the air. "Erin Prince. I'm so glad to get the chance to meet you."

"You're quite a difficult person to track down."

Jane gave her a deadpan stare. "That's how I like it."

Erin scrambled to keep the conversation going. "I love your accent. It's British, right?" *Good grief. Is that the best I can come up with?*

Another chilling smile. "Right."

"So." Erin's trembling voice betrayed her fear. "Are you going to tell me what Simon did?"

Jane's lips twisted until her delicate-looking face seemed savage. "He's a hypocritical bastard. He let a child rapist go free, even though he knew his own daughter had been a victim."

"He wanted to protect his reputation." Erin tried to slow her breathing, preserve her energy.

"And his hobby," Jane snapped. "Daddy dearest always played dress-up with Sarah and Bonnie when they were little. No big deal—good fathers do that sort of thing, right?"

Mouth tasting like she'd eaten wet sand, Erin nodded.

"But I guess he liked it, because he kept doing it after Sarah grew up. And then he started going out and pretending to be a woman. Mister high and mighty morals was a cross-dresser who liked to go to strip clubs."

Nervous sweat stung Erin's eyes. "That's why Bonnie got so upset with Tori when she gave him a lap dance. She recognized her uncle."

"Aren't you clever?" Jane's accent dripped with sarcasm. "Bonnie didn't tell Sarah at first. Not until we realized Bonnie was a whore who needed to be punished. Then she told us about Simon, like that would somehow make me not want to tear out her guts!" Jane held up the knife. "I made Simon put on his favorite dress before I killed him."

Fear made Erin's throat swell nearly shut. She had to keep talking. "Are you Jack the Ripper?"

Jane threw back her head and laughed. "You dumb bitch. Do you think I'm reincarnated or I time traveled?" She held up the book. "Abberline was right about the Ripper. Let me tell you my favorite passage. I know it by heart." Jane tilted her head back, the words coming out as melodic as a lullaby.

> *"A child saw me this morning on my way to the post and hid in the safety of her mother's skirts. Lesions eat the flesh on my face now. My limbs work slower. Soon I will no longer be able to wield the blade. But a wasp has asked for my assistance in ridding her putrid body of the child she created in sin. She may be my last. I will make her my greatest.*
> *—9 November 1888"*

"What is that book?" Erin asked, hoping to buy time.

"My ancestor's diary," Jane said. "Two greats down the line. A midwife. A noblewoman trying to rid the world of the filth around her. Lost to history—until now." She examined the knife, delicately tracing the blade with her finger and pressing her lips to the blood-covered skin. "I can't believe you're so surprised. Women kill all the time."

Erin's knees knocked together. She had no idea if Jane had told the truth about the book or made up her own history. Both options made her bladder weak. "You decided to emulate her?"

Jane shrugged. "I took her name because she's a hero. And Bonnie deserved to pay." Her face twisted, her focus still on the knife. "The things she did ..."

"What about Virginia Walton?" Erin prayed she could continue to buy time.

Jane sneered. "She called Sarah after the murder. She said Bonnie told her about us, but the professor didn't believe it. She didn't want to go to the police without talking to Sarah first." She held the knife up again, gazing at it as though she'd found a talisman. "I had to take care of her, but I couldn't take all the credit. The real Jane inspired me."

"The letters were a nice touch." Erin tasted blood and tried not to allow her fear to overwhelm her. "If I hadn't remembered Sarah's initials, I wouldn't have suspected her. Did she call the police when she realized what you did to Virginia?"

"Charlie's dumb ass did that." Jane's mouth curled up. "Always meddling." The glare of the security lights cast her in shadows. "And Sarah is weak. She's always been weak. I'm strong and I take my strength from the heroine who scared the hell out of London in 1888. Gutting all those whores with such skill. No fear of anything. That's the way I want to live."

Erin didn't dare take her eyes off Jane. She visualized the yard behind her. The gun had to be close. "I think we'd all like to live that way. Most of us don't have the guts to try."

"I'm not a fool." Jane's accent thickened, the menace still coloring her tone. "There are things I would have done differently."

"You killed Yari Malek. Where's Aleta Gilani?" The alcohol she'd consumed earlier might come up, but she had to act. "Nice of you to make sure you got both Bonnie's and Virginia's blood on his clothes."

"Wasn't it? I stole the same shirt he wore the night I caught him fucking Bonnie." Jane spit out the words, her pretty face twisted into pure evil. "That little Arab bitch got away. I'll find her." Jane's head was down, her eyes on the bloody knife, her hand white from her tight grip. "Ted Moore didn't. He came first. When I realized he was back in town, I had to act. He was alive when I cut off his dick and stuffed it into his mouth."

Erin gathered all her courage and took a quick step back.

Jane's gaze shifted, a predator suddenly aware its prey was trying to escape. She slashed the knife upward, her long legs closing the distance between them before Erin could do anything more than raise her arms as a shield.

She screamed as the blade sliced through the tender flesh on the backside of her forearm.

Jane's fist slammed into Erin's stomach. She staggered back, feeling her insides knot into one painful mass. Jane screamed a war cry, raising the knife again. Erin dropped to her knees, the concrete tearing her jeans and her skin, and rolled for her gun. Her fingers raked through the muddy grass for the weapon, her knees and feet slipping in the struggle. Blood from her arm streaked over the dead lawn.

"Bitch!" Jane jammed the knife into Erin's calf.

She bit her tongue as the pain shot through her leg, every nerve ending on fire, but she kept digging forward.

Jane yanked the knife out, the burning sensation far worse than the attack. Then a strong foot slammed into the back of Erin's knee, snapping the joint in the wrong direction. Pain worse than childbirth tore through Erin, and she screamed into the wet earth, tasting the days of rain and lawn chemicals. Jane kept the pressure on her knee, but Erin squirmed around until she got her hand beneath her and inside her jacket. The gun was still too far away.

Erin's fingers closed around the Taser. She sucked in raw gasps of air, nauseated from the pain and the chemical taste on her tongue. Jane's athletic legs and youth kept Erin pinned in place.

Jane liked to see her victims suffer, so she wanted to see Erin's face when she died. Going silent and forcing Jane to turn her over was her only chance. She forced her body to go limp.

A hand clawed at her shoulders. Erin allowed Jane to flip her over onto her back. She blinked against the bright yard lights, staring up at the twisted, bloody visage of the devil.

Her nightgown more blood red than white, Sarah-as-Jane planted her feet on either side of Erin's hips. She spit on Erin's cheek.

A siren wailed. Nearby, maybe down the street, tires squealed. Erin blocked out the pain and made a final appeal. "Jane, let me talk to Sarah. We can help all of you to heal."

Jane laughed again, a hoarse, nightmarish sound certain to haunt Erin's dreams.

"You can't heal a broken mind, Investigator." She kicked Erin hard in the stomach and then squatted over her as though about to take a piss. "I heard about your brother. Such a tragedy for your family." She grazed the knife down Erin's cheek, leaving a trail of Erin's own blood, and then down to her neck, where her life force raced. "At least you'll get to join him sooner than expected."

Jane adjusted her grip on the knife, the blue eye cold as glacier ice and the brown gleaming like a cat ready to pounce.

"Stop!" Brooks shouted from somewhere behind them.

Jane's angry eyes shot up, and Erin pulled the Taser out of her coat and shot it straight into the girl's chest.

Jane wiggled like a beached seal. The knife fell. Erin grabbed it and threw it as hard as she could. She managed to roll onto her side as the other woman fell face first into the grass, her lean body still flopping.

Erin tried to get to her feet, but her injured leg lacked strength. Brooks's cold hands closed around her wrist, and he hauled her up.

His voice trembling, Fowler recited the Miranda rights as he cuffed a now-still Sarah.

Erin dug her fingers into Brooks's shoulder in an effort to stand on her own.

"Ouch," he said.

"Don't tell me about ouch!" She shot back. "That crazy woman stabbed me twice."

Brooks leaned down to look at her leg.

Her soaked jeans and the hot pain told Erin the wound cut deep.

"The paramedics are on their way, but you need to sit down so we can wrap that thing. You don't mess around with leg wounds."

She didn't argue, allowing him to help her over to the driveway. He took off his sweatshirt and used the arms to tie off her leg. "Why didn't you wait for me?"

"I intended to, but Mina called me."

Brooks's head swiveled from side to side. "Where is she?"

Erin stared at the young woman sitting up in the grass. Covered in blood, Sarah cried in pain, completely in a daze. Then, they locked eyes.

"Investigator Prince?" Sarah's normal voice broke through her sobs. "What's happened to me?"

Numb and cold to her core, Erin turned back to Brooks. "Right there, Todd. She's right there."

CHAPTER FORTY-FIVE

"You're not serious." Brooks's legs jumped like he wanted to come out of his chair.

Erin sat beside him in the U.S. Attorney's office, but she stayed quiet. Jack Marsh, the U.S. attorney assigned to Sarah Archer's case, liked to have the spotlight and didn't appreciate being questioned. Brooks would learn, in time.

Marsh folded his hands over his immaculate cherry desk. His thick black hair was slicked back with a product that made him look more stylish than smarmy. In his mid-forties, the guy had a face for the cameras and the personality of a fetid asshole. He also had a reputation for never prosecuting a case he couldn't win.

"Investigator Brooks." Marsh spoke in a disinterested tone. "In the last six weeks, two different psychiatrists from leading mental health programs—including a psychiatrist from Johns Hopkins who's been extremely vocal about the legitimacy of DID over the last decade—have interviewed Sarah Archer and her various personalities."

DID—dissociative identity disorder—was the updated terminology for multiple personality disorder. The semantics didn't matter to Erin. She'd witnessed multiple personas sharing a body. Most nights, she relived it in her nightmares.

"And the psychiatrists agree that Sarah Archer is very likely the real deal." Marsh finished with the same firm tone he used at the end of his closing arguments.

Erin rolled her eyes and resisted the urge to remind him there were no cameras in the room. "Each personality is strikingly different, right down to body language, accent, and inflection. Sarah's original psychiatrist, who diagnosed her with DID, provided recordings of their early sessions. Every personality acted the same as they do now, down to the smallest details. If Sarah faked all of this, she would have slipped up somewhere."

Brooks rocked back in his chair. "You do realize this diagnosis is so overused by defense attorneys that it's a cliché?"

Marsh's face reddened, and a thick strand of his carefully styled hair curled onto his glistening forehead. "I have some experience in the courtroom, Brooks. But I have to make my decision based on the evidence presented and the diagnosis of people a lot smarter than I am."

"And they're absolutely certain she didn't fake the entire thing?"

Marsh took off his designer glasses and made a show of cleaning them with a green cloth from his top desk drawer. "Nothing is certain in this world, Brooks. After listening to the experts and watching the video recovered from Yari Malek's safe deposit box, Sarah is a very sick girl. She believes she has multiple personalities, and there's nothing to indicate she had any awareness of what went on—including the moment she sliced her father's throat."

Bonnie must have realized the danger from her cousin. A few days before her death, she mailed Yari Malek a flash drive containing the video of Sarah's personalities. He'd put the drive in a safe deposit box and kept his mouth shut. For the past six weeks, Brooks and Erin had kept an eye on the unidentified females coming into the morgue, but so far, it appeared Jane had been telling the truth. Malek likely sent Aleta away to safety—but she hadn't been sure she could trust him, so she'd provided Erin and Brooks with her side of the story before slipping away with her family. The FBI believed Aleta's uncle to be one of the top men in the D.C. mob. Erin wished them luck proving it.

Simon Archer's corpse had been found wearing a black dress and wig, his throat sliced so deeply, his neck had been nearly severed. Melinda admitted he'd been cross-dressing for years. She had no idea he'd accidentally propositioned his estranged niece at Sid's.

From her hospital bed, her scarred face far from healed, Melinda Archer told how she and Simon quietly enrolled a teenage Sarah in the care of a therapist after weeks of bizarre episodes. The therapist treated her for DID and, by the time Sarah started her freshman year of college, pronounced her personalities integrated—meaning they were aware of each other and could function with Sarah in complete control. In the weeks leading up to Bonnie's murder, however, Melinda noticed her daughter slipping into old patterns. She lost hours of time. She talked in strange voices and became more and more withdrawn. The video Bonnie recorded of her cousin a few days before her murder also worked in Sarah's favor. At the time, Sarah claimed she still had control and allowed the personalities to speak, but in the video, she appeared to fight for control, and Jane screamed that Sarah would destroy them all. In short, the girl appeared to be coming unhinged.

The night of Bonnie's murder, Sarah broke the lock on her bedroom window and snuck out. She walked the half-mile to the nearest

Metro station and rode it to Columbia Heights. Melinda didn't want to believe it could be true, but after Virginia Walton's murder, she had her home security footage pulled. She saw Sarah both nights, sneaking out. Melinda had the video destroyed. She told Erin this in a deadpan tone, likely well beyond guilt. Melinda Archer's desperation to protect her child cost lives—and Melinda's spirit.

"Don't forget the diary," Marsh said.

The diary, in Erin's opinion, had to be the grand jewel of the evidence. Melinda Archer confirmed the story Jane had told Erin that night. The diary was a family heirloom and a semi-dirty secret. An antiquities expert declared the diary to be at least one hundred years old. Erin didn't know if its authenticity as the Ripper's journal would ever be proven, but the aged letter tucked into the back of the diary proved that in December 1888, from her presumed death bed, Jane Blackwood took responsibility for the Ripper killings. The midwife had contracted what sounded like syphilis and blamed her husband for sleeping with the London prostitutes. She'd shipped her young son to America to live with his uncle and sent the diary, along with the letter. Historical records in London's old Whitechapel area did confirm a Jane Blackwood's birth in 1864, but death records had yet to be found.

Every one of the passages found at the crime scenes were diary entries from Jane Blackwood's leather journal—entries which also described the Ripper killings in great detail.

Her mother claimed Sarah had been fascinated with the family history from a young age and copied the letters as a way of coping with her psychological issues. If experts declared the diary to be a legitimate record of the Ripper murders, the historical significance would be staggering.

"Investigator Prince's testimony helped me make my final decision." He looked pointedly at Erin, expecting her endorsement.

Erin didn't want to argue with Brooks. "You don't understand. I don't, either. I just know what I saw, and there's no way it wasn't real."

Brooks shook his head and held up his hands. "This is the wrong decision."

"What if she did fake it?" Erin asked. "Then she faked it as a teenager, faked it through treatment. Faked it with everyone for years. Even if that's true, wouldn't she have to be extremely mentally disturbed?"

"Plenty of people on death row are mentally disturbed," Brooks said. "But they can still stand trial. You don't think Sarah was in her right mind when she handed me the letter she wrote and told me the killer sent it?"

Marsh's mouth tightened. "The psychiatrist believes that is another symptom of her illness. We've all agreed Sarah Archer is unable to stand trial." Marsh spoke with finality. "There's no reason to put Melinda through anything more than what she's already experienced."

"And Simon looking the other way about his niece and daughter being molested remains a secret," Brooks snapped.

Marsh's eyes glittered. "That has nothing to do with the decision."

A lie. Melinda still had connections. Marsh had political aspirations. The combinations led to a decision to commit Sarah to the continuing care program at McLean Hospital in Massachusetts. A team of psychiatrists would grill and evaluate her progress. If at any time they believed the decision to be false, charges could still be brought. Erin expected as much, but she and Brooks weren't aware of the official decision until today. Bonnie's parents and Rylan Walton had filed suit against the District this morning, naming both Erin and Brooks as potential witnesses.

"Let me tell you what would happen if we decided to take her to trial," Marsh said. "After graphically detailing her sexual abuse, a defense attorney would put Sarah on the stand, and those personalities would emerge. The jury would see what Investigator Prince saw that night. More than likely, she'd be found not guilty by reason of insanity. Then where do you think she'd go? A psychiatric hospital. The decision we've made skips the waste of tax dollars and my time."

"What if she's found guilty?" Brooks demanded.

Marsh waved him off. "Wouldn't happen."

Brooks stood and started for the door. "You're making a mistake that will come back to haunt you. Someday, she'll be out."

"I realize you've worked some extremely unusual cases, Investigator," Marsh said. "Perhaps your experience is diluting your judgment."

"And Melinda Archer's deep pockets are affecting yours." Brooks stalked out.

Erin moved to follow, her knee burning. Her stab wounds had mostly healed, although she still endured the sting of healing nerves in her calf, and the knee Sarah knocked out of place throbbed for no reason, at times. One day soon, she'd start the physical therapy the doctor recommended.

"Investigator Prince."

She turned and regarded Marsh in silence, waiting for him to finish so she could catch up with Brooks.

Marsh sat in his big leather chair the way a king might preside over his court. "You agree Sarah belongs in a psychiatric facility?"

Erin hated going against her partner. He was a good man, a good cop, and a good friend. But he hadn't witnessed it. "Yes."

Brooks waited for her in the expansive lobby. He jammed his hands in his pockets and said nothing as they walked into the winter cold. January had arrived with a vengeance, dropping nearly a foot of snow over the city.

"You didn't see her." Erin spoke once they'd escaped to the relative warmth of the car. "You didn't see the way these people crawled out of her. Like she was possessed. A mental institution is her only chance to get normal again. It's likely she'll never be released. You know that, right?"

Erin shouldn't care about Sarah, but every time she thought about the way Sarah cried when she realized her father had died at her own hands, Erin agonized over not figuring it all out sooner. If she and Brooks had gone through Virginia's papers earlier instead of shunting them aside, then maybe Sarah wouldn't have had to live with having killed her father.

"Tell that to her aunt and uncle and to Rylan Walton."

In addition to the suit against the city, Neil and Carmen, along with Rylan, filed a wrongful death suit against Sarah and Melinda Archer. It likely wouldn't make it to court, but their tell-all book would make more money than Simon's estate could ever pay them.

"At least the Malek family won't be joining the suit," Brooks said. "Since the bastard tricked out little girls for years."

Additional investigation into Malek's computer and financial records showed Bonnie Archer wasn't the first child he'd plucked off the streets. DNA results showed Yari Malek to be the father of Bonnie's baby. Erin delivered the news to Will Merritt, and she couldn't tell whether sorrow or relief fueled his tears.

"You were right all along," Brooks said. "I didn't want to believe the killer was a woman—I didn't want to fight that sort of evil again."

Erin took little solace from his compliment. "You were right, too. I couldn't be objective with Sarah because I saw myself in her life. If I had, maybe Malek and Simon could have been saved. Even if they were scum."

A wry smile crept over Brooks's face. "Fair enough, but you had no clue how many people called Sarah's head home."

"So you do believe she's a true case of dissociative identity?"

"I don't know," Brooks said. "But a mental institution doesn't seem like justice for all the people she killed. She'll never have to answer for those murders."

"What about Melinda? She should be charged with obstruction of justice, at the least, and she's partially responsible for Virginia, Yari, and Simon's deaths. Everything she did to protect her child was wrong. If she'd done the right thing as soon as she suspected Sarah had come apart again, they might still be alive."

Brooks's dark eyes shot to hers. "For some people, right and wrong are both shades of gray."

Erin laughed and started the car. "I'm pretty sure that's a line from a movie."

"No, it isn't." Brooks turned up the heat on his side and held his hand over the vent.

"Pretty sure it is."

"You should come to dinner tonight. Ellen would love to see Abby."

In the weeks since Brad's death, Erin and Abby had taken Ellen Davis's advice and had started seeing a grief counselor. And Ellen and Brooks had slowly become a part of their lives. Abby thought Ellen was the most beautiful, fascinating creature on earth. Ellen seemed to love her as well. Erin just liked seeing her daughter smile again.

"We will, but it will be closer to six," Erin said. "I've got a stop to make."

CHAPTER FORTY-SIX

Erin hadn't been to her brother's grave since his headstone had been placed. Her mother wanted an ornate huge granite stone with Brad's face carved in it. Erin argued against it, knowing Brad would want something so ostentatious. To her shock, Lisa took Erin's side, and Calvin followed. So Brad's black granite stone was simple and beautiful, with a short epitaph: *Beloved son, brother, and uncle.*

Erin used her gloved hand to clean off the freezing snow and then stood with her shoulders rounded against the north wind.

"I finally went to the doctor." Her voice sounded small against the cold gusts. "I guess we're still two peas out of the same pod. The neurologist found a tiny aneurysm. She compared it to the scans Judy Temple took of yours and said mine is a lot smaller. It's not ready to be operated on yet, but she thinks it will be in a few months. I've got to go back for checkups, and when it's ready, I guess I'm getting some of my head shaved."

Erin still couldn't grasp that she had a ticking bomb in her brain, ready to explode without warning. The diagnosis was still too fresh, too close to the loss of Brad—too unreal. And she didn't feel any different.

Erin laughed, the cold air making her breathless. "Guess who went with me to both appointments? Lisa. She even held my hand when the doctor told me." Getting to know her sister wasn't as comforting as the companionship of her twin, but Erin appreciated their time together. "I haven't told Mom and Dad, but I will."

She banded her arms across her bulky down-filled winter coat. "I miss you every fucking day, Brad. But you wouldn't want me to sit around feeling sorry for myself, so I'm trying to move on. For Abby. That's why I'm having the surgery. I've got to be there for my daughter." Her voice cracked like a teenager's. "And I miss the shit out of you, but I don't want to die. Not yet."

The wind gusted again, dusk rolled in from the west, and Erin decided to call it a day. Besides, her friends expected her for supper.

As she trudged through the foot of snow on the way back to the car, she thought about the different ways the mind could break and how people dealt with it. Bonnie Archer's broke, and she punished the body she hated. Sarah's broke, and she split into parts to cope. Brad didn't have the chance to fix his.

"But I do," Erin whispered. "I guess you can heal a broken mind after all."

She stopped in the middle of a snowdrift. The cold cascaded into her boots, and the ice shot up her spine like nails. She heard Sarah Archer's soft voice in her head from the day they met at the station—*I finally accepted that you can't always understand a broken mind.* Erin's memory then flashed to Jane sneering down at her, ready to plunge the knife into her stomach, and replayed the feral woman's words—*You can't heal a broken mind, Investigator.*

Erin stood still until the cold pierced her heavy coat and her legs felt like blocks of ice.

What if Sarah Archer had known what she was doing all along?

CHAPTER FORTY-SEVEN

My Dear Brother,

The end comes for me. My waking hours are fewer and fewer, and much of my time is spent in a state of madness. Visions of things which are not present, a rage I have no hope of stowing, and such pain I am ready for death.

Before I depart this world and answer for my sins, I must leave the truth for the child I sent with you to America. I know you care for him as your own, and I pray he brings you peace over the death of your precious son. With God's grace, this diary will find you in the capital of America. Many of the accounts are of the mundane sort, the daily activities I now long for. But within the pages is a truth I must pass on to my son.

Dearest child, know that I sent you away for your own safety. The despicable French disease given to me by your wayward father progressed far more rapidly than I expected. Lesions, fever, loss of body weight, and fatigue, I accepted. But the mental decline placed you in mortal danger. That I could not allow. And so I gave you to your uncle. I pray someday you will understand my choice.

Know this, my son. The Great Evil is a scourge on good society. It will destroy your life and the lives of everyone around you. Beware the female wasps offering their bodies for a pittance. They spread disease and death and despair. Is it any wonder I tried to cleanse the city?

Mary Ann Nicols. Annie Chapman. Elizabeth

Stride. Catharine Eddowes. And lovely Mary Kelly, blessed with a child she happily discarded. By the blade of my father's surgical knives, those five will spread their filth to no other man.

I am weak, and the demon in my brain is stronger. It will not be long.

Remember always, your mother loved you enough to give you a new life.

After I am gone, do what you will with this truth. My only concern is that you know what I tried to do for your well-being.

All my love,
Your mother,

Jane Blackwood
—JTR

Mina liked the hospital because their private room looked out over a great big snow-covered yard with lots of bird feeders and colorful winter birds making tracks over the snow.

Charlie liked the hospital in Massachusetts because their mother said it was affiliated with Harvard, and that's where he dreamed of going to school. Maybe if Sarah had gone to college out of state, like he wanted, they wouldn't be here watching a bunch of birds fight for food in the snow.

Jane hated being in the hospital. She hated the view, she hated the staff, and she hated all of them. But she always had, ever since Sarah split apart. Because they were weak and stupid and couldn't take care of themselves. Jane spent their childhood fighting for them, only to have Sarah go to that fat, big-haired doctor and learn how to "integrate." If the bitch hadn't taught Sarah control, they wouldn't be in this mess. Jane would have been in charge a long time ago. But she'd been labeled the fucking bad girl, the psychopath who wanted to be like Jack the Ripper. Like Jack the Ripper was a woman. That had to be the dumbest theory of all the dumb theories about the madman.

Sitting quietly in the cozy chair overlooking the picturesque winter scene, Sarah Archer commanded the voices in her head to be silent.

Then she smiled.

ACKNOWLEDGEMENTS

Killing Jane was an idea that's brewed for nearly six years, one that required an enormous amount of research and many sleepless nights.

Without Detective Robert Freeman of the United States Park Police, this book wouldn't have been written. In the spring of 2015, I traveled to D.C. to start researching *Killing Jane*, and Detective Freeman graciously met with me at Dunkin Donuts (yes, seriously, and his suggestion) for two hours and discussed police procedures and politics in the district, and in the coming months, he answered numerous emails on specific crime scene details and procedures. Detective Freeman's patience and candor enabled me to get the cop stuff right, but also much of the descriptive imagery, including the Consolidated Forensics Building and several D.C. neighborhoods. He was my eyes and ears for this book, and I am forever grateful to him and his superior, Sergeant Lelani Woods, for allowing me to interview him.

Special thank you to Washington, D.C., Deputy Chief Medical Examiner Jan Gorniak for taking the time out of her day to tell me how their office worked and answering some pretty specific grisly questions.

Thank you to D.P. Lyle for his information on aneurysms as well as various post-mortem questions. Thank you to Dr. Stephen Anderson, a neurologist at the University of Iowa Hospitals and Clinics, for working me through diagnosing a brain aneurysm and the subsequent long-term treatment. To Detective Jennifer Roberts of the Cedar Rapids Police for her candor on what it's like to be a woman in the field. Thank you to Staca Sheehan of NCMEC for her willingness to answer so many questions and for the tour of the D.C. offices.

To Dr. Katherine Ramsland, thank you for your honesty and never-ending supply of resources.

To my family, words can't express how grateful I am. My husband Rob has never wavered in his support, pushing me to stay home and write even when he had to make sacrifices. I love you, and I couldn't have done this without you. To my daughter, Grace, thank you for being you and being so proud of your mom, no matter how dark and twisty she gets. To Mom and Dad, for everything. For always being there and believing in me even when I had no clue what to do.

Annetta Ribken for talking me off the ledge numerous times; Catie Rhodes for being a sounding board.

Kristine Kelly, for believing in me enough to push me down this path and for always being honest.

Rick Miles at RedCoat PR for working with me and pushing me to the next level. My agent, Italia Gandolfo, who believes in me enough for the both of us and never fails to kick me off the pity train and get me moving forward, and to my editor Liana Gardner, who pushed me way out of my comfort zone for *Killing Jane* and helped me make it the book I always wanted it to be.

Finally, to all of the readers who've supported me from day one: thank you, and I hope you continue to enjoy my writing.

Until next time,

Stacy Green

ABOUT THE AUTHOR

Stacy Green is the *USA Today* bestselling author of the Nikki Hunt series and other psychological thrillers and mysteries. Known for her love of serial killer lore and twisted crime stories, she is always looking for the next dark novel to enjoy. She started her career in journalism before becoming a stay-at-home mother and rediscovering her love of writing.

She lives in Iowa with her husband and daughter and their three spoiled fur babies.

www.StacyGreenAuthor.com